over
there

over there

by KYLE JARRARD

BASKERVILLE
PUBLISHERS, INC.

Baskerville Publishers, Inc.
7616 LBJ Freeway, Suite 510
Dallas, TX 75251-1008

Library of Congress Cataloging-in-Publication Data

Jarrard, Kyle, 1955-
        Over there / Kyle Jarrard.
            p.   cm.
        ISBN 1-880909-53-7
        I. Title.
        PS3560.A546O94   1996
        813'.54—dc21   96-46642

Manufactured in the United States of America
First printing, 1996

For Nathalie

Reality was born of dream-shreds
Far off, among the hired boats.
Like a Venetian woman, Venice
Dived from the bank to glide afloat.

–From "Venice," by BORIS PASTERNAK

Allons! to that which is endless as it was beginningless.

–From "Song of the Open Road" by WALT WHITMAN

*I*T STARTED TO BEGIN, as these things can, unexpectedly. Marc was simply walking down a street in Paris on his day off, a few days before the summer vacation was to begin, a month in the country. He was going along the sidewalk when across the way he saw a shirtless man taking a drink from a hose running into a steel drum, a worker stopping to look up at the white May sky, to wipe his red face and torso. He might have been seventy.

As Marc passed, a young man carrying blueprints stepped out of a bright yellow shed and shouted some orders. They were setting up a series of sidewalk tourist toilets. The old man nodded and bent to mix an enormous pile of black cement.

Grandfather Ansel?

That was where it started to begin.

But it wasn't Grandfather Ansel. Just someone who looked like him. A little. Not much, really. In fact, the whole thing might have been forgotten in the seconds that followed the sighting. But somehow, amid many distractions, it survived.

Meanwhile, Marc has been thinking: Now that another war has been called off, the TV game shows are proliferating. Which is good for the TV game show business. Which is good for Marc, who earns his living writing questions for the most popular quiz

1

show in the country. Question: Who was Grandfather Ansel? You have five seconds!

But who can think? No one can think these days. It's this unseasonable heat. It pickles you. All through the afternoon helicopters come from the south toward the north and the north toward the south in the steamy air. All the helicopters are white, a dozen now in ten minutes, nearing and fading, pesky as flies. Dignitaries here for a meeting? Businessmen and businesswomen evading their families, making millions, making love high over the Paris rooftops?

No matter, really. Another war has been called off, so why worry about what's ado in the sky? There is a semblance of peace here in the beginning, along with the man who didn't really look that much like his American Grandfather who disappeared in Mexico all those years ago. A shaky peace, with everyone remaining armed to the teeth, and an imperfect old man he hadn't thought about in years.

A mystery strains to unfold. It can turn out a number of ways. For invention's sake, for the unpredictable and the unknown. For no other reason than a sudden fear of your own demise and of the weightlessness of ashes.

It is the first day, and Marc is thinking it through. One bit of the story after another, and so on, letting it happen by itself, letting it come.

It's this heat.

❦

What does anyone really know about the man who claims to be this week's Man of Peace? The would-be messiah preaching an end to war, an end to fear, an end to all other saviours? Just who is he this time? For that matter, just who was he last time? Can any one of these peace men ever be trusted? You have two seconds! Bonus question: Why?

This is the currently popular subject, part of the quiz show to keep everyone busy, placated, blind. So we won't shoot our neighbors or our loved ones, perhaps. So we will pay our taxes, consume, pay our debts, dream of just-in-time solutions to everything besotting humanity and poisoning its abode, so we'll relax and go to museums. To the Dead Art, say.

Through another turnstile, to your left please, now right, watch your step. Guards in the darkened corners wait with their baby machine-guns. Packs of gawkers from around the world surge this way and that, hands flying, mouths snapping, barking a dozen languages. A skinny, underpaid guide tries in vain to shout them down, then gives up and bends like a reed, the flow spilling over her.

Marc comes and asks, Are you all right?

Weak, emaciated, like the mother of the Holy One, she raises her eyes to him and, in a faraway voice, replies, Of course.

But you look faint. Are you sure . . .

The voice turns to a witch's hiss. Don't touch me or I'll —

I wasn't going to touch you.

Yes you were! Those guards are my friends. Richard . . .

Abandoning her, Marc hurries into another chamber.

This one is darker, empty save a display in a corner lighted by two dim red bulbs. A dogshit smell fills the air. He draws near.

The old man with the bare torso and his shovel stares out from a work entitled: Another Man of Peace. Someone has stuck on a little heart sticker next to the sign that reads: Know Him. Across which someone has scrawled: Flash in the pan!

It is one of those new, real works of art. With a real, old man standing inside a window frame balanced atop a rusted oil drum. Water gurgles over the side of the barrel, dark and rank, into a foul, scum-filled trough where a pump slowly sends it off through black tubes and aloft again into the drum. One thinks of trapeze artists and cheap shopping center fountains. A few coins and wrappers have been tossed into the works.

The sharp odor drives Marc back a step or two. He bumps someone.

Wonderful, isn't he?

It's the guide girl again.

I know this man, Marc says. I saw him just —

You know, she says dreamily, it seems like everyone says that. They've all seen him, sometime or another. It's like he's our . . .

Grandfather?

3

Grandfather? She laughs. Of course not. Who needs grandfathers? No, it's not that at all. It's more like he's our . . .

Christ?

Are you kidding? Be quiet. Don't you let people think for themselves?

Water starts to spill out of the trough, thick with rust, fouling the floor.

Something's wrong with it, Marc says.

Damn! I mop all day. I mop all night. Do you know how much they pay me? God I wish someone would just take me away from here!

Hands over her eyes, she backs away into the gloom with a low moan.

What an actress! someone says.

It is the old man in the artwork.

Marc, annoyed, says, Perhaps you'd like to do her job?

And be a functionary? the old man bellows. Are you kidding? Me, I prefer the free-lance life. And stewed fruit and water.

Pardon?

Stewed fruit and water. That's the secret. Now shh —

Japanese tourists fly into the room, each in a yellow slicker and crotch-high boots, all flicking small plastic flashlights this way and that in the oily mist.

The guide girl, lost among them, sings, May I have your attention, please? Yes? Now, here in the beginning, we have — Excuse me, sir, could you please move aside?

Marc looks around, perplexed.

Excuse me? Could you please step out of the way?

It's him she's talking about. He hops aside, nearly tripping over the sludge tray.

The old man snickers.

The crowd turns, all eyes fixed on the work.

Someone says, He looks so real.

Real? As in Reality? Yes, that is the Big Question, cries the guide. Now, here we have Another Man of Peace. Note the absence of turmoil, per se, in the work. And note the sarcasm of his stare. The name of the artist? Anyone?

No one says a thing.

Right! No artist, no art, no nothing. Meaning?

No one speaks.

Right! No meaning, no nothing. Real?

Weakly, a man says yes.

How do you know? the guide asks.

The man says nothing, stumped. His companions pat him on the shoulder.

All right, she says, let's move along, please. There's a whole museum of this stuff to visit.

A few laugh, and then the mass flows out of the room with a low, sucking sound.

A guard steps out of a dark corner and says to Marc in a machine-like voice, Move along. You've had your view.

Oh, leave him alone, Richard, says the old man.

You shut up, the guard shouts. Now, out. Out!

                        *

A military band plays in the museum courtyard.

Yes, it has to be done. It will all depend on hard work, digging into the pile, shoveling it into the mixer. Maybe no one will believe it in the end. But there will be no turning back.

Grandfather Ansel had done such a thing once long ago. Then made a fire and burned it by the river.

A woman next to Marc, thrilled by the power of the march, says loudly, Spontaneous combustion, wouldn't you say?

He looks closely at her. But it is not the guide girl. It is some retiree from the wealthy suburbs, in the city on a jaunt.

No, I wouldn't say, he says.

Oh, go burn yourself, she spits, and walks off.

Then he remembers. It is Jeanne d'Arc Day.

The air is smoky and the brass instruments flash like flames. There can be no doubt now that he's on his way.

                        *

Everything comes out like a television program, like a bad movie script, says Marc's father, the civil engineer, one night long ago.

5

The day the world plugged in, it disconnected from itself, that's what I say. Don't you agree?

The doctor on the sofa breaks in to say that lifting weights is the best thing that ever happened to him, then throws back some more beer.

Excuse me, doctor, but did you hear what I said?

I heard you perfectly well.

Then what was I saying?

The demise of thought, I believe.

You believe? See? You weren't listening. Why is it when I say things that are true, no one listens? Why is it that no one listens to each other about the true things? Does anybody know the answer to that? Television will kill us all.

The doctor holds his hand to his own throat and nervously wiggles his eyebrows.

He ventures, It's just that we've known this for years, Henri. I mean, there is nothing . . . new in what you are saying. But weights! Now, there's a subject I can get into with you.

For years? What are you talking about? I don't have old thoughts!

The doctor shrugs. Then says, Lifting weights can help. I'm a doctor. I know.

The other guests chew peanuts and nod.

The two-hour cut flowers open wide, shrivel and collapse over the neck of the vase.

A fine party, thank you all very much, now all go home, says the wife. Good night, good night.

When they are all gone, the husband says, Nice party.

Oh, very nice.

I do like the doctor.

Yes, he's very nice.

A good man.

Apparently.

She cleans up the mess.

He opens a third pack of cigarettes and sits thinking of the demise of thought until he tires of thinking and goes into the bedroom where his wife is reading a fat novel.

Do you think I should lift weights?

No.

Good.

In no time, he is asleep.

His wife sits up, frowns at his exhausted body and begins to talk about their boy Marc, to wonder what he will grow up to be.

Personally, I think he'd make a wonderful lawyer. You know, like that big-time lawyer on TV. What's his name? Oh, no matter. He'd be a great lawyer. Daddy wanted me to be lawyer, you know. But then, girls didn't get to grow up to be lawyers in my time. Now they can, I hear. But not me. You know?

The log sleeps.

If only he doesn't end up a fool like you, all will be well. If he'll study hard and not be selfish . . .

She turns off the light.

Good night.

Marc's little-boy knees pop as he gets up from his crouch at the bedroom door and steals back down the hall to his room.

She always hears him go.

𝅥

Late the next afternoon, still long ago, a coal-fired locomotive squeals past the apartment building pulling a half-dozen cars full of sightseers. On the balcony, Marc picks up his baby brother so he can see the balls of black smoke rolling up. The crying stops. The tourists wave, as to the pacified, and furiously work the buttons on their automatic cameras. See the choo-choo, see the old train? The baby wriggles to be let go, let go.

Socked by the heat, Henri shouts for a beer — and a cold one this time, damn it!

Frances jams last night's dead party flowers into the trash can and calls out, We'll have to go to the store before dark!

What did you say? he cries back. I can't hear a damn thing with that stupid train!

Quiet! You'll wake Daddy!

As if cued, Grandfather Ansel sits up on the couch, scratches the mat of white hair on his bare torso and announces, I have had a dream.

His son-in-law and daughter look at him. Well?

I can't remember.

What do you mean you can't remember?

It was so powerful.

What about?

Something very . . .

What?

I'm trying to think.

Thought is dead, says the son-in-law.

Well, I'm going to the store, says Frances. Marc, bring the baby. Hurry up.

Marc the son, the baby-holder, the story-teller, the one who will someday look back on this picture. The remembering beyond his control. The images like scenes from a bad movie you can't get out of your mind.

Get more beer! the husband insists.

I'm going to the flower store!

More flowers, bah! Get beer!

I remember now, the old man says.

They turn to him. His torso seems to glow there on the couch. The grandson will think this years later and remember how the yellow glow of his body was surrounded by a wreath of bright blue.

I am a young man, he tells them. Visiting Europe and riding a night train from Paris to Venice. We stop in Milan about four in the morning and I can see the full moon through the window. Then a lot of people get on, dark, olive-colored people, and settle in for the ride to the coast and the dawn. One of them, a young woman of impossible beauty and grace, appears across from me. I cannot take my eyes off her face. I can no longer breathe and sit there, sure that I will die as she looks back. Am I dreaming? I ask myself. She shakes her gorgeous head no, no you are not dreaming. The violet moonlight bathes her face as she smiles — and then I go ahead and die. But it is not the death you expect. It is, rather, a slow falling through space, through warm violet light. It lasts only a moment, and then she catches me, or rather I catch her, it doesn't matter, and we carry each other away through the violet light until we are in Venice in the foggy dawn waiting on a landing for a hired boat. Another moment passes and a little boat with a green light appears. We dive into it and glide off through the water-city, through the last of the violet light scattering in the gray unknown. A dead man who'd never felt more alive in his life, and a goddess. Loose in their own miracle play. Loose in the wonderful fog.

He stops, then stretches out again on the couch.

They peer at him.

Is that all? the engineer demands.

Was that Mama? the daughter demands.

A goddess, he answers, closing his eyes. She was a goddess.

They peer.

As the train's whistle dies in the distance. As the baby crawls away. As the boy, getting to be a big boy, longs to go and put his hands, and then his arms, into the yellow glow around the old man, to be in his fire, to lie there with him in the heat dreaming of the goddess.

Blue irises! That's what we need! Hurry along, Marc, or the store will close! Frances cries.

Don't forget the beer! Henri shouts.

The boy balks, Do I have to carry the baby again? The hill is so steep!

The father barks, You will help your mother and be polite, do you hear me? Please, Frances, the beer!

A moon goddess.

⁌

Years later, Marc drags it all up from the bottom, trash and everything. For no reason, or for a reason that comes and goes as though someone were turning on and off a light.

In the living room, the black television beckons in a soft female voice, Turn me on.

In a few minutes he will go to the studio in the tower by the river to work. To dream up the latest quiz show questions. There are only four days of this left before the vacation. An entire month in the country.

Not soon enough to suit him, but very soon.

9

The rest of the staff will write the questions while he is gone. He will try to forget it all, especially the answers. Try to begin again, clearly.

There will be no television for thirty-one days. Just the wife and the boy already there waiting for him to arrive. And the baby that will be born. Space and blue air and beets in white bowls for lunch under the acacias.

※

All through that afternoon long ago Henri drinks and the old man-buddha watches, eyes half-shut, dreaming his dreams over and over again in his head. Nothing is said.

There'd been no blue irises. There would never be blue irises again, they'd shouted at Frances at the store. All through the afternoon and into the evening she stays out of sight.

Come nightfall they'll all have to listen to Father play the trumpet again, his sad trumpet.

※

A terrible way to begin. Who exactly is this old man? Why doesn't he stand up and be somebody? Why does he lie there glowing and dreaming like that?

There are many questions, here in the beginning. The beginning that seems ready to go wildly off track if something is not done.

So give the old man a crabstick, Marc decides, thinking it all over at his desk at the studio. Have someone give the bastard a crabstick so he can be mobile again if he wants to be. And say he is seventy-one and still recovering from a brain aneurysm at breakfast all those years ago. Now living with his daughter and son-in-law and their two children in Paris.

Grandfather Ansel of South Texas.

Long gone Grandfather Ansel back in a grandson's mind, for no real reason. By chance. But taking him over as if trying to be reborn in him, as if to emerge again alive.

There from the mind of the man in an office with a view into

10

an air chimney for the underground rail line. Into the black. Where the air reeks of smoldering butts and urine.

Into which the secretary ventures again and again to offer private services. Which he takes like candy between the quiz show questions. Between the answers, on the hard floor.

The drone beyond the window like Hell's foul breath.

Who was Grandfather Ansel?

The guests on the show scratch their heads. Which Grandfather Ansel exactly?

Wrong. Wrong. All leave. Thanks for playing.

New batch of guests. Who was Grandfather Ansel?

All scratch their heads.

Then one, the secretary dressed up like a boy, slams her fist onto the button and shouts, Your grandfather!

Right you are, son! But so what?

Pardon?

So what if he was my grandfather. Who *was* he?

No answer.

All leave. Thanks for playing.

The show's host picks up the answer card and reads to himself. Of course . . .

Ansel and Violetta would eat beets from white bowls in the yard while swallows spiraled against the tall lavender Texas sky. Violetta the moon goddess he'd met on the train to Venice. His Violetta, whose red mouth smiled at him always. His Violetta who ran with him down through the pecan trees to the muddy river to swim before dark, together through the brown-green water. He would tell her again how once he'd been on a slow, hot night train to Venice and had seen the moon through the window, had dreamed of her and awakened to find her there sitting across from him. That at that moment he was sure he had died and been reborn. She listened on the damp bank as the moon began to glow behind the trees, her black eyes flashing. The woman who had become his wife, who honored him — an understatement! — and changed his hospital diaper when he became a baby again.

11

Who was he? A man who never stopped becoming someone else.

❧

Haven't you got something to say? shouts the drunken trumpet. You haven't said anything in days!

Henri is on the bourbon today. Ansel pretends to be sleeping, to be dead to the world. He had never wanted to come to France in the first place, but dear daughter Frances had insisted that his staying in the old house in George West, Texas, after Violetta died was very much out of the question.

That battle long lost, why pay attention to anything anybody said anymore? Better to appear to be gone to this world. Never let them think they were in control.

Hey, I am talking to you!

A jab. Another.

Hey!

Ansel smiles, having a special thought of dear Violetta.

You're awake, you're smiling! Stop faking!

Ansel puts his hand to the crotch of his old man's trousers, gently.

Henri stares.

Henri, he says, I have had another dream. Would you like to hear it?

No, I would not like to hear it.

I dreamed that you were about to die, but didn't.

What is that supposed to mean?

How would I know? It was just a dream.

Daddy, don't quarrel, the daughter says. Henri, leave him alone. Enough of this childishness.

The men look at her, her arms filled with . . . blue irises! Frances is smiling wider than her face can stand.

See what I found? You'll never believe how far I had to walk! Isn't that right, son?

Little Marc lies crumpled by the door, exhausted, the sleeping baby in his arms.

So, shouts the husband, how much money did *those* cost me?

It was my money, she answers.

Your money is my money!

Not all the time.

The hell it isn't!

He takes a swipe at the bouquet, missing.

Violetta, Violetta, Ansel thinks, save me now again, just once again. Save me with a dream of you.

And for you, Daddy, here's a crabstick.

She sets it across his old man's knees.

He looks down at it, then up at her.

If you need it, that is, she assures him. As you wish.

How much was *that*? Henri cries.

The boy leaves the baby and edges near to touch the polished staff.

Yes, thinks Grandfather, something of my moon goddess does live on in Frances. An invisible fire reaching across time.

Get away from there! the ugly one shouts. Don't be touching that!

The boy withdraws.

Grandfather Ansel smiles like a lunatic, stands the stick before him, firmly places both hands atop it, and pushes himself up. The yellow glow with the blue border turns to a white sun as he lets out his first laughter in years. Teeters forward and turns and looks at them until they shade their eyes.

Darkness brings the golden trumpet out of its case lined with red felt and to the thin white lips of the man who believes he rules his kingdom still.

But how little time there will be! Only thirty-one days to tell the entire tale. Only thirty-one days to rush through the story, in pieces, as best he can. The thirty-one-day drama. Then all expires.

Mind you, such a thing wasn't Marc's idea. It was his grandfather who'd actually done such a thing, that summer after Violetta died. Taken the old typewriter and shut himself up for thirty-one days. No more, no less. Written a whole book.

Up there in the bedroom with the air conditioner buzzing full-blast. While the rest of the world went about its business in the white Texas heat, while the earth turned hard as concrete.

No one ever read a word of it, though. Because as soon as he finished it, he'd gone down to the river and made a fire there on the sandy bank and burned it.

That's what he told Marc's mama one time and that's what she told him.

No one knew what it had said. It remained a thing unknown, a hard dark seed.

Daddy, do you remember how you shut yourself up and wrote that book? Frances asks. What was it about? Mama? Was it a book about Mama?

But he is asleep. Clutching his crabstick.

Thereafter he was always asleep when that question came up.

2

MARC DRIVES OUT of the city at noon in a dark downpour. The radio beckons, Spin my dial. But the Quiz Show King knows better. It would only be his old shows. Not a measure of music. Not a note. All that's buried now.

Once again he thinks how the river of cars is like lava. Slowing, backing up, caking. Millions fleeing to the country. Each time he thinks how Armageddon will look like this and wonders if he is the only one to ponder such a thing there, jammed in, suffocating, head strapped in an invisible harness. Hour after hour, until the jaw locks firm and the spine seizes up, a bar of iron.

It is night again before he arrives at the country house. A giant moon emerges as he pulls onto the lawn. Leaning over the wheel and staring out, he feels the weight leave his body and waits there, in no hurry to go in and join the family dance.

All the flowers have their heavy silver heads turned to the moonlight.

The next morning they find him there asleep. The new father.

It is their second child, a girl, born the day before in the little country hospital down the road.

Why, Mr. TV's finally arrived! Now we can celebrate!

What took him so long, anyway? Leaving his wife and new baby in the hospital down here a whole day before bothering to show up. Who does he think he is, acting like this? You know, they say he's sleeping with his secretary. An Arab. What do you think, was he banging her right when his wife was giving birth? Wouldn't surprise me. The bastard. The lucky bastard. Them Arab girls know their stuff, seems. Ah!

Glass after glass of white wine, the clear milk of the land, pours into him in celebration. Leaving him dizzy and giddy, unable to have a complete thought before another takes over.

Another toast! boom old red-faced relatives and friends from all over whom Mother, dear aging Mother, has invited over for the occasion, tears in their tired little eyes over the moment, over the chance to relive the dream, the country dream when all was at peace, before divorce, before hatred, before the end. Of the days of the six-hour lunches, no less, and all those pretty maids in black skirts running about, and sweet cigars! Those were the days!

So what if he's banging an Arab! I say, Bang them all. Bang as many as you can. Are we men — or are we not? Ah!

Everyone is emptying bottles and cooking and eating and yelling, making wishes by the dozen. Another toast! This time to Summer! This time to Ourselves. Yes, Us! Ah!

Marc's second child is born and growing in the fertile shadows, its head heavy and red, its womb eyes turning, trying to see . . .

He drinks and waits for the party to end (it will take days) and everyone to scatter. Then he will go and bring the mother (Jeanne, another Violetta) and child home from the hospital. To the peace of the house by the river. To the peace of a month in the green, far off the lava flow, down in the river bottom where the air stays cool under the poplars.

Where the dream eases into you at last.

〰

It is late afternoon when Marc hits glass number such and such and the story gets rolling again. Jamming him deep in his deck chair under the blue cedar as if some high-speed chase had begun without warning.

For out of the mist of the green dream comes the old man and his stubby crabstick. Working their way like a pair of scissors across the lawn.

There is no one else around. All the drunk houseguests are napping on big iron beds in the white stone manse. Besides, whatever would they say? Seeing things, are you? Had enough to drink? Grandfather Ansel d'Amérique? Why, he's been dead since . . . when was it exactly . . . oh, yes, he disappeared . . . a long long time ago. Besides, Marc's mother would insist, why *aren't* you visiting your wife and baby at the hospital? Aren't you ashamed of yourself? Well? Grandfather Ansel, back from the dead? The very idea!

How many years had it been since Grandfather Ansel last crossed that yard? Twenty-five? And yet it really is like old times, back when they all took summer vacations together in the old house Henri and Frances had bought deep in the French countryside. A house a lot like Frances's family home in George West, Texas. A house by a river with a long sloping yard and thick trees and flowers.

Seeing him pivoting along, his nose puffed up like a plum from too much wine, the straw hat tipped far back, you would swear he is alive.

His voice, his ancient voice, opens with a growl: Don't expect me to help you with this thing. Is that clear? Because I won't. You're on your own. Be a man.

Then, pursing his lips and blasting air, as from a bottle of gas, he angles off back where he came from, into the mist, into the green shadows.

〰

They say the old man, then a young man, was sitting at the breakfast table with Violetta, as they had so many mornings, content not to talk or to plan or to hurry, but to listen to the dawn slowly filling the room with a rose light. In the low sash window the air conditioner clicked on and began to exhale a steady coolness that flowed down over the floor, bathing their legs. On the pale blue wall, above the calendar from the lumber yard, the long red second hand swam the face of the clock. It was not yet seven.

Ansel reached around to the shelf behind him and took down the razor. Violetta pushed her coffee mug to one side, watching as he eased the black plug into the wall, the signal that the night was fully over, that they could begin again.

They say that she was just then thinking that there would be no end to such mornings, such moments, that these would always be theirs, and only theirs, to share until death. And they say that later he said he'd been thinking the same, so that right then their souls, or the thing we think of as within, were aligned, as along a wire that when plucked makes a single tone only they could hear, can still hear, echoing.

His hard red thumb moved the button. He put the heads to his white cheek, moving over the stubble in a slow circle, lifting his chin and working the blades along his throat, a hint of burning rising to his nose. Cut whiskers sprinkled onto the white table.

Toast? she said, glancing at the sack of bread.

He clicked off the razor, set it back on the shelf, moved his hand over his face. I don't think so, no. Then he checked the time, ten after seven, plenty of time to sit some more, to be with her, watch her beautiful mouth when she ate a slice of golden toast and honey. Plenty of time before he would shower and put on his soft overalls, all very slowly, there was no rush.

Then, just before eight, they would again begin the long, stumbling embrace. Until he had to go, lift the garage door, start the red Ford, back it out to the street and drive away from her to the cotton gin. As she waved from the porch, clutching her nightgown collar to her throat. The wisteria and honeysuckle hanging heavy from the iron railings all around, and the spitting cooler making a lake of red mud in the hedge.

A half-hour — more! — before all that, still all the time in the world, an eternity. Even now she was only reaching out for the bread on the counter, her arm moving slowly through the rose light.

☙

For the first time in a year, the Quiz Show King goes down to the river below the garden wall and sits on the bank, the long dusk

18

finally ended. The water is strewn with stars.

Time is already slipping away, he thinks. There will be only a month to tell the story before time will run out, before he will have to step back inside his office as into a prison.

He breathes deeply, listening to the sound of sound, hearing the bitter trumpet of so many evenings ago. Somehow, it begins to play the words.

Where were we? Yes, the crabstick had arrived. Now the old man would be getting about, going freely in and out of the rooms of the Paris apartment as though reborn, looking, staring, touching their lives, things, secrets. The jealous husband would not like it, would count his poker chips, his cigars, hide his alcohol and men's magazines. The distracted wife would cradle her irises, unsure which vase to use for a whole hour, then another, until they went ahead and burst open anyway, peeled back, curled like burning paper and died over her gentle elbow. As her father watched, a hand in his old man's pocket, the other atop his crabstick, looking exactly the fool with his unnerving stare.

That stare! Those cold black eyes. The eyes of the ill, the mad. No, of a man whose brain had almost melted away, leaving just enough that he only stared, long and hard, at the simplest act or non-act, scene or memory, that he only spoke of dreams no one cared to hear.

A TV mummy, yes, a TV mummy with the crabstick and a will to live on and on.

Something moves on the river. A muskrat swimming for the other bank, its wake washing stars away. It has been a long, long year since Marc sat there in the dark, awake to everything around him and to everything in the dusty past, now shaking loose and rising as from the grave.

For no other reason than chance, perhaps. But it was well begun now, wasn't it? Weren't these words spilling forth like the water from the drum? Like this river running black to the sea?

There would be no stopping it. If you believed such things, that is. And Marc believed them. He believed them because the old man had believed, or so it seemed, and the old man had lived like no one else he had ever known. Without a moment's hesitation or regret. As one would swim an ocean were one's mind made up.

❦

They say that just when Ansel was thinking of touching Violetta's arm that morning at the breakfast table his face grew purple, then black, before he began to collapse. That she began her long journey to the body even before it hit the floor and the cry sounded, his and hers, together. That in that instant, she knew she would never again not be bending, stooping to help him, until she, too, would fall. They say she knew this.

❦

Hold it one damn second.

What does Marc really know, anyway? At best, only the outlines of the drama, as told him by others, or as imagined. And I question his motives, the why of it all. Does it give him pleasure to recreate me? What could I possibly exorcise in him?

No, I suspect he is afraid, and that it is the idea of his own death that is shaking him, unexpectedly, like an earthquake.

We remember our ancestors at such times, eh?

The dear, long-lost ancestors. Family.

Bah.

Let me be clear: This morbid trampling across my private life, my very existence, this retracing of my slow decline and disappearance, is dubious and unwholesome — pointless.

Marc is killing time, afraid to face time, his own decline, his own exaggerated march into the muddy stinking trench into which we all finally leap. Yes, leap. Often gladly, too.

Do not listen to him, he is saying nothing. And never forget that he knows I know this, can see right through his petty game, and will say it again and again.

I will be an echo, and infuriate him with questions, struggle with him. For I will not be used.

I will not be the stick that holds him up.

Period.

❦

Marc sits in the shade of the umbrella, squinting at the lawn gone white under the high sun, at the low limestone walls and the green of the trees against the sky. It is true, he admits, I never loved the old man. He remembers how he'd always wanted to yell at him for not understanding the simplest thing, for answering questions with questions, for his horrid flatulence and runny eyes. How he'd been forced to spend a thousand hot afternoons with him playing cards and dominoes, drinking gallons of iced tea and watching the old fart smoke low-tar cigarettes and pee on himself.

Be nice, be nice, your grandfather can't help it that he is ill. Be very quiet. And don't argue, never argue.

He'd spend a million afternoons alone with him while everyone else gadded about the countryside. He'd lived the life of a hostage to a sick and canny TV mummy who could count cards, remember so-and-so's batting average forty-five years ago, or sit saying nothing for days. The TV mummy they all insisted had lost its mind.

Be polite, smile, love someone for once. He needs all our love, do you understand that? Imagine if you were him, how would you feel?

Marc had tried, but it had not come.

And they would look at him and say, You should be ashamed! Telling your own grandfather to shut his mouth! Saying curse words to him!

He had never done that, but the old geezer said he had. Therefore it was true.

Marc had tried hard to care, but it had not come. Until now. Yes, maybe now it is different. Maybe now he can manage to care. If only for the disappeared and long presumed dead.

Is that how life works? An old dry seed suddenly opening? You never imagined it, but then there it is, pushing up out of the ashes on the riverbank. There, where nothing had grown for years.

Marc thinks in the night: The words have already taken over the meaning, gained independence, set up as a separate entity in a wide open land where no one will ever sit and simply wonder,

21

there being no time, where everything is a rush to fill space, quickly, without reflection.

Here and there on sandy plains a cardboard town is thrown up and cardboard people propped in position. TV mummies fan out to conquer a new world, plant signs that point nowhere, all mumbling nonsensically under the starless night sky, retreating into cold holes at moonrise to squat and tighten their wraps as the quiz shows begin and the audience screams the questions: Why does Marc do this? Why does he bother? Is he mentally ill? What is the song that burst from the drunk trumpet? Will we know it when we hear it? Will he tell us what he is talking about here, if anything? Who is he, exactly? Where do we go from here? And why? On and on until again they have filled the central computer to capacity and set it crackling and sparking and heaving on the stage, struggling to find the answers, as the announcer sits by on a high white stool applauding, waving to the crowd to join him, calling on the whole nation to stand and give an ear-splitting ovation as the machine finally freezes into silence — defeated yet again!

Prizes for each and all. Thanks for playing. Thank you, thank you.

And . . . cut! We're off the air now. Good show, everyone. Good show.

The world falls into sleep.

ⓔ

It will be only a day or two more before Marc can bring the mother and newborn home from the hospital. Most of the guests have faded away, gone back to their houses, and it is almost calm again.

He counts the minutes, while the older boy, all of four, bless his heart, whines and fusses, not wanting to be fed.

Each forced spoonful comes back out instantly, plopping onto the table. The tiny hands dive in.

Stop that, will you? Marc shouts.

Are you kidding? he imagines the child smarting back. I'm going to sit here and chuck this food around any way I please.

I'm going to lose my temper!

Well, it won't be the first time, will it now? Go for it! Show your stuff, old man!

Marc stands, looks for something to throw, glares at the child, then seizes the full jar of mayonnaise off the table and chucks it across the garden. An odd bomb that seems to hang in the green air, neither here nor there, not quite part of this world, an object from the beyond, suspended, its message, its meaning unclear, unresolved. Hanging there on the edge of irreversibility.

It strikes a limestone bench and explodes.

Damn it to hell! comes the shout.

Marc squints at the shadows of the nut tree.

Then he sees him.

The old man, roused from his afternoon read of the newspaper, flicking splats of mayonnaise and glass off his jacket. Staring at Marc as through a block of ice. As he had all those years ago. The stare cutting straight through your throbbing conscience, baring it. Take a look-see at yourself, son. See yourself for who you are. There's no changing it, either. Not a bit of it. You are what you are, forever.

Grandfather, help me be someone different!

Nope. Can't do. Impossible.

Grandfather!

Nope. Them there's the facts, son. Have to learn to live with yourself. With all the stupid, idiotic, insane things you're destined to do. And, boy, if anybody was ever destined to do a lot of them kind of things, it's you.

Grandfather!

I'll tell you this, though: You didn't get that black temper of yours from me. And you certainly didn't get it from your grandmother. Neither of us ever lost our temper. You hear me, boy? Not once!

Nothing can be done?

Nothing. Doomed. That's you. And you can thank your daddy for it.

Daddy?

A rotten dog. Now you know. Or maybe you already knew. Of course you did. A rotten, dirty dog. That's him. It ain't your fault. But you'll live with it the rest of your life. And there won't be a moment's rest, believe me. Now pick up this mess and get on with being a man. Do you hear?

It has been only seconds since the jar left the angry hand.

The child bursts into tears, another mouthful of instant whatever-it-is falling out.

Marc jumps up to clear away the evidence, the shards of glass, the white gunk strewn on the bench and gravel path. He scrapes at it, then charges off for the hose to wash it away.

Only a minute has passed before he stops and says, Why did I throw a jar of mayonnaise across the dream garden?

Yes, calls the old man. Why? Ask yourself that!

Marc looks around for him. But he is gone.

Your son is still crying, don't you hear?

Ⓔ

North of the garden, across the little country road, they have beagles that bay at dusk when the farmer drives back to the house with a pine box full of shiny white and red cow bones from the butcher's. An essence driving them to madness.

Ⓔ

By now I suspect you know why I have my doubts about this project.

I see him by the lamp in the open room, at the dining table, moving pen across paper. Thoughtlessly.

Distracted by the night outside, by the fading sound of blood-mad beagles, by the night wind, by a black moth that keeps circling, now left, now right, now gone.

I see him lift a cigarette, take a hit, try to think back. To when he'd read how some Indians in Mexico believe death is a big moth that lives in the desert. For a long time this had been his picture of death. Then, for years, there had been no picture. Now it is me. His new old man death.

He stops and stares out toward where he thinks of me sitting out here in the dark on the bench.

Waiting for more words. Our words.

Indeed, what of the general wish to fail? That all the bombs would be dropped on all nations, ending all this, once and forever. The wish for the advent of the time of the insects and grasses, all human life gone into the sour earth like wasted water. A tiring species' death wishes, the only words of any substance now that all the souls have been drained.

And yet . . . the wish of the last-minute rescue, of the saviour, the benevolent stroke that sets everything afloat again. The wish for the master, the guide, the announcer with all the right answers. So we won't have to think, to suffer the pain of thought, so we can relax and dream without guilt.

The wish to sustain purity, to make what is rare less so.

For all farms to survive and have baying dogs.

For the river to run, deep and green, along the black banks, carrying away the bitter brine.

For the eyes to see all this.

As midnight prepares to strike and Marc finds he cannot write any more than this. Words that are not the story. Words about words that will not come.

Go back to the old man, collapsed on the floor that morning in his kitchen in George West, Texas. How could you leave him there like that? Get him to a hospital. He needs urgent help.

Violetta's nightgown is soaked with sweat as she reaches for the black telephone.

There is thunder and then rain starts to fall on the yellow yard as she watches for the ambulance. If it lasts long enough, by tomorrow the whole lawn will be green again. If it lasts long enough . . .

Ansel lies there. Maybe dead. She cannot find the courage to kneel again and put her finger to his neck.

His face is so black it seems almost white. But she cannot understand why. Only stare and listen to the hot rain landing like missiles.

25

There is no whining siren.

❦

The heat saps.

Beyond the garden wall a machine grinds and clangs, laying open a trench for a new sewer pipe. The boy is napping in the manse, his mother and newborn sister still recovering in the hospital. There is nothing to do, nothing to think. The weather will simply not allow it.

Marc's eyelids droop as birds bat about in the dark trees and a bumblebee buzzes by the water spout. Everything that was so important waits for some other hour.

Later, he gets up to go stir a pot on the stove. As the light leans over into the afternoon. Thoughts of failure rising again.

A sudden pulse of insects' singing makes him turn his head and look back out the door at the garden in the hot light.

He listens a long time. It is ocean waves. Breaking invisibly over the dry stone wall.

❦

Again and again, Ansel and his new crabstick disappear from under their noses that Paris summer all those years ago.

Surely there is the heat to blame, but no one notices his absence for hours, no more than you remark a temporarily missing pet. It only dawns on them when the telephone rings with a sound like an animal dying and his voice bellows through the line.

Once, a little drunk, he calls from La Rochelle to proudly announce that he has just finished two dozen delicious oysters, *des fines de claire* of the gentlest gray-green, and that he would like to come home to Paris now but has no money left for a return train ticket. Would someone mind coming to get him?

Driven by Frances's icy stares, the son-in-law goes to retrieve him, wherever he is. These trips are made in silence. Which, of course, is a miracle, since the two men have plenty to argue about. About, for instance, whether it is or is not important in this life to always keep enough cash on oneself for the return trip. Or whether, perhaps, it might be the case that Ansel purposefully neglected to carry enough cash, the better to irritate his hosts, the better to annoy them and try their patience, was that it? But there is none of that on these little trips. Caught in the miracle, they remain civilized, like priests performing a quiet rite.

No matter what time they come in, Frances soothes the tired old man with warm milk and croissants and helps him to his bed. Then hands a cold beer to her husband and thanks him for having been so kind as to drive halfway across the nation to bring back her dear father.

Fury, then, breaks in the living room as the master of the house lets go. While the woman, who wonders why it is fury always breaks at the least sign of her kinder side, stands nearby and stares. While the older child watches his mother's face starting to change in a funny way that doesn't ever change back. While the old man, perched on his bed in his room, peers through the glistening yellow varnish at the swirls of the wood, hearing nothing around him now but the voice of the crab apple branch, remembering, yes, its hard slender thorns and taking a boy's baseball bat to its fruit all those years ago, hard and warted green apples that sprayed a milky white mess over the opposing team as he ran headlong for first base, for the rusted hubcap by the pear tree, a hundred kids screaming as one.

Everything says it is getting close to the time to be gone for good. Very far away.

The operation to save Ansel's life that day so many mornings ago in George West left him a baby again.

They say that his head swelled big as a watermelon, that his eyes and mouth disappeared. That when it was over, only part of his brain still worked, no one was sure just how much. Anyway, the surgeon who had had to remove part of the skull to get to the ballooned blood vessel and snip it out before it ruptured said, He will be a vegetable.

At the bed, Violetta sat hanging over the steel bars that penned him, saying in a level, confident voice again and again, We will make it back. And they say he heard her and squeezed her hand.

For months everyone prayed, and when the seasons had almost come full circle again, she walked the body on the gurney out to the ambulance for the ride home. A few of the nurses cried when Violetta smiled at the sight of the spring sun. It was the first step back.

≈

As you could have guessed, my grandson will leave no private memory untold. He will tell all, leave nothing unbared. Even my brain, with all the tiny clips left in it to stanch the hemorrhaging, with all its flaws. And he won't stop there, I assure you. Sooner or later, he will go after my heart, cut it open, too, show it to you.

But all in a young man's mind, no? No great harm done, right? Perhaps. Only there is the fact that he declines to step out of the womb of the past and live in the present. For the life of me, I cannot understand such sluggishness. When there is all the world to see and touch. When there are so many chance moments out there waiting to be lived. Why wade in the gutter with me?

I suppose it is his nature. I suppose, too, that romantic notions get the better of him, stop him in his tracks like that day he was reminded of me and my story when he saw that old man drinking from a hose at a construction site. Perhaps, yes, in some odd way, he misses me now that I am gone. That is the way it usually is.

Longs to be with me now that he realizes he's lost his gold-glowing granddaddy. Who wasn't so stupid after all. Why is it that people are condemned to realizing truth only when it is too late?

But does he actually think that he can bring me back and hold me up and learn from me? Whatever for?

Now, as for that surgery all those mornings ago, as for that massive stroke, a few facts are in order, the principal one being that, despite my state, I knew exactly what they had done to me. Even now, the memory of the pain lives in me like a bed of hot coals under cool ashes. But it is nothing.

Nothing compares to the time they came to my house one evening all those years later and told me out loud what I'd already guessed, what I'd already heard in the stone silence of hours —

Violetta was dead. I was as good as cured, I was back, and we had been ready to take a new hold on life together when she suddenly broke for the other side of the black river.

Everything else is maudlin gibberish.

◖

Mexico. Iguanas as long as park benches, heads raised, eyes fixed on the beyond, living statuary under an old yellow Mexican moon. The touch of bare feet at night on a cold stone floor. An old man alone at a cedar table on the tiny balcony overlooking the white-washed cobbles of the *zocalo*, deep in the bare mountains, up near the belly of the night, thinking of all the souls rising to take residence in the hollow peaks, where they say you go when you go.

Mexico. That's where Grandfather Ansel finally went that autumn. Far from the acid sickness of Europe. Into a place of yellow dreams, where they say life can begin again in old bodies. Depending on your will, your vision.

Mexico. The yellow land from which the old man never returned. The yellow land now pulling on the grandson, as into a pool of dust.

◖

The winter sky lies on the city like old carpet.

Correo aéreo, says the father.

It means air mail, says the son.

How do you know?

I learned it at school. Besides, what else could it mean?

Are you being insolent?

What?

Did you say *monsieur*? says the mother.

I did! Weren't you listening, Mother?

Don't you yell at your mother.

You do.

Do you want a beating? Right here? Right now?

No.

No what?

29

No *monsieur*.

Go to your room.

Yes *monsieur*.

The son trudges out, slams the door to his room and sticks his head under his pillow.

You are too harsh with him, Henri.

I won't have the boy yelling at his own mother! Or am I to suppose that you approve of such a thing?

Don't yell.

Don't start, woman.

Who's starting?

I'm getting myself another drink! God.

Go ahead.

I will. A nice strong one!

Be my guest.

And I'm going to sit and hold that luscious drink between these two hands and enjoy every drop of it no matter what you say.

Frances shuts the living room door, quietly, without drama.

To hell with the children! It won't be the first time!

Well, are you going to read the letter from Father?

Read it? Who cares what he has to say?

He is my father. Give me the letter.

Here!

She opens it. Then begins to cry. The last time an envelope arrived from Mexico with an illegible postmark it, too, was empty.

As if he were sending only a breath of air to say he was alive. Nothing more. Just an empty breath of air.

It tears her to pieces inside. It makes him laugh. And the laughter bangs around the thin walls of the apartment as inside a drum.

Once again, Marc comes to squat in the hall to listen. He used to do that with Grandfather, but the old man is gone to Mexico now. So he pretends he is still there beside him, being strong.

I give it a year, Ansel says.

More like a month, Grandfather.

You may be right. Does it bother you?

No.

You can talk to me anytime you want to about this. I might be able to help.

30

I'm fine. Thanks, though.

You're very strong, little Marc.

Almost every time it ends with the smashing rhythm of the bed springs. The boy retreats to his room.

Later, much later, the trumpet sounds again and Marc goes and looks from a distance at his dad in boxer shorts out on the icy balcony playing the damn thing, as to the whole city, the whole world. It is awful.

❧

Marc sits studying the stout wooden pillars holding up the porch, the uneven planks overhead, the ancient strength of structure. There is a pop of lightning to the east. His mind waits for thunder, and after a long while, it comes. Perhaps the storm will roll over in the late part of the night.

Soon the wife and newborn will return from the hospital and all will change again.

Inside, a raindrop falls through the chimney, hits a dried leaf.

❧

I can hardly believe how he mismanages the four-year-old. What happened today? He opened the door to end the boy's nap, found the lights on. The sight so disturbed him that he didn't even think to yell.

There was a pile of yellow excrement on the floor, here and there smeared by tiny feet. There was his billfold, rummaged, its contents strewn across the white bedcover, which also boasted a few smears of the yellow unspeakable stuff. And there, in the middle of the picture, sat the radiant tyke, shorts discarded, triumphantly announcing, Me sick.

My grandson looked to the nearby dresser for his toothache medicine, capsules of antibiotics. Several had been opened, powdery contents scattered.

Now he yelled, What have you done!

Me sick.

Did you take Daddy's medicine?

31

Yes?

Did you swallow it, did you put it in your belly?

No?

Are you sure you didn't put it in your belly?

No?

There are some capsules on the bed. Do we go to the hospital then? Have his stomach pumped?

Here, though, I give Marc an inch of credit. He thought, The child would never have swallowed such bitter powder. No cause for alarm. Remain calm. And he sincerely tried to do so, but in the end it proved too much to ask of himself.

What have you done, son!

The boy smiled. Mad?

In his tiny hands was the very expensive family camera.

Yes, Daddy is very mad.

O.K., the boy said cheerfully, as if all was settled.

Then he lifted the camera, peered through the viewfinder and snapped a picture of his dad.

Peekcha!

Oh, Miserable Fatherhood. And to think I was going to unleash a few pointed remarks about how no right-thinking reader would be silly enough to presume that, at some future moment, this narrative will explode forward with such force that one cannot help but be swept along, as by a tremendous wind.

No, I wouldn't bet on that. He has only the rest of a month, after all, to be done with the whole thing. That is, if he wants to try to match my feat of yore. The thirty-one-day novel. Like the two-hour flowers. A short life, followed by a lightning demise.

For it was also my choice at the end of that summer fling with words to take a bundle of branches and make a robust fire down by the river and toss the month's entire work within. For no other reason than the thrill of squatting and watching it burn and collapse into black ash.

Now comes my grandson to nag me. Trying to rewrite my words? Struggling to make me real again? Running to catch the old kite before it blows away over the trees and is lost forever?

The poor father. Tonight, I'll leave him be, his child's mess having wrecked his day. And to think he wanted time to dream of

Mexico! To dream the dream of Mexico, the dream I finally went and lived. To hear a thousand and one trumpets play La Cucaracha, driving a dusty old revolution?

Bah. Not so fast. I never even liked that tune.

Moon River? Now *there's* a song.

There were countless theories: He had died there, peaceably. He was still living there, peaceably. He was elsewhere, either dead or alive, peaceable or not. No one knew, and after a while no one had cared.

It had been easy for the son-in-law, who, when everything was said and done, when the Great Chase through the tropics was concluded, got over it all in no time. Resumed his selfish pursuits as if nothing had happened and nothing would ever happen again. The name Ansel and their exploits together in Mexico reserved for cocktail party chitchat and such, memories that burned a little less hot each year.

It had been hell for the daughter, who took much longer to get over Ansel's final fugue. It helped that, in the middle of the story, she had had enough sense to leave the bastard she'd married. It had helped greatly, but, in the end, not enough. Daddy had run away to stinking Mexico and got lost and probably died, and it was her fault, all her fault, starting with the day she'd tried to be the good daughter and insisted he move to Paris after Mother died, to be with her, her and Henri and the kids.

Marc had put it all away, buried it deep and left it unmarked. Or so he thought until the day the shirtless old man took a drink from a hose running into a barrel, a plain workingman stopping to look up at the white May sky, to wipe his red face and torso.

He might have been Ansel Gifford of George West, Texas. And so he was not to be forgotten, not to be wiped away like dust.

3

AND THEN THEY WERE FOUR. The young father, the young mother, the boy, the newborn. All together again. The rest of the month left to play model family. All the time in the world.

Champagne!

As if there hadn't been enough already.

A toast!

Deep down in the country Marc whiles his afternoons away wading through tall grass by the green river where fat white carp seem to follow as he walks in the gold light whistling some miserable old tune to keep the thoughts rolling.

Of Grandfather deep in Mexico, as good as lost. Perhaps combing the ruins of a brilliant civilization. Or pacing the coast down south, tasting the spray of giant blue waves, his crabstick stuck in the sand like the mast of a ship that foundered there centuries ago on the quest for El Dorado.

Then again, he could be far to the east on the limestone table of the Yucatán, just now hiring a poor old man, older than time would ever have allowed, to take him out on a jungle lake. Under the moon, parting the black water, the hiccuping outboard trailing white foam. Surely they will soon pull up on the mud bank of a little island, get out and sit a while. Alien to each other, not exchanging a word. Silently until the memory of countless human sacrifices sings from the deep at a low pitch only they can hear. Maybe this is not even the first time they have done this, taken the night ride together. Perhaps they are even old friends, or the proverbial opposites that they say come face to face once in a lifetime.

Suddenly Ansel turns to his companion, and seeing his dear Violetta, seizes the face and kisses the mouth. When it is done, the other stares blankly at him, then smiles, the rows of gold teeth glowing dully in the moonlight. No, *señor*, I am not what you are looking for. I am not that kind of man.

Ansel laughs and then the old man joins him. It is just some silly mistake, some unknown something perhaps born in the jungle, or in the depths of the lake, that possessed him, if only for the length of a kiss.

How many women were thrown alive into the ancient sinkholes? A thousand frogs are singing.

Ansel settles in the front of the boat and the other pulls the cord. They putter off toward the yellow lights of the little town.

It took Ansel almost ten years to make it back: After being a baby again, to learn to be a child, then to be a good boy, and later, much later, to grow into a young man in an aging body. All the while guided by Violetta's steady hand at the tiller. There was to be no miracle, but for the fact of a decade of patience. Day after day, for ten years of impossible nights and days. Long months together sunk deep in privacy as the indifferent seasons changed and television told time through changes in the sports programming. Air-conditioned nights of baby food and tears, nights waiting in the pale blue glow of the space heater, praying each in their own way for full recovery, nights under the floor lamp sorting out any bills that could be paid, stacking the others in the order of the coming months, years. Days of sitting until the buttocks were numb, slow days in July that never seemed to end before they began again, quick November days when night falls after lunch. The dusty plastic plants in the hall. Handfuls of purple and red tranquilizers set out in the white bowl at the breakfast table where it had all begun. The dead time when God ignored them forever.

Listen to him blabber.

To him, you see, the idea of death is a sweet candy, an idée fixe more serious, more real than life itself. Tonight I stand in the garden and stare in through the window, see the lamp by his table, watch him chain-smoke, bending forward, now raising his head, now leaning back down into the words again, fishing, thinking he is thinking.

Look, he jumps slightly. Across the room the elm flooring has popped by itself. What is making him so nervous? Fear of failure?

And to think this night he keeps repeating: It is advancing, taking on a life of its own, becoming more real every day.

Perhaps, but to whom?

Besides, he has only just begun, and poorly at that, his unsteady boat only now losing hold of the sand, setting out.

And to think he thinks it will be going somewhere new! Perhaps he will someday understand how impossible that is. But likely he cannot bear to admit such a thing and wants to stay drunk with the clouded certainty that each and every life is destined to discover new territory, to push the borders out. Bah. That payout is a relic in an attic full of black spiders and red centipedes and gray beards of dust.

This humid river bottom! I hate it. But I only have to think of my bones on a Mexican beach half a world from here to warm myself tonight.

Look, the chair's tall back holds his head like a vise now. The proud father of two, looking at the window pane, seeing my eyes in the glass, vainly taking them for a reflection of his own.

Why doesn't he halt this game and take care of his new family? Jeanne, his Jeanne, is near again, and yet somehow as far away as the moon. He could have gone to her and been with her on nights like these, in the quiet warmth when you hear only slowness — the flow of the river through the old mill, the clack of trains in the damp black distance, the breath of lovers face to face. He could go to her but it might not be that way anymore with the fire of birth dying in her, leaving her shrunken and pale with the dark newborn alive in her arms. Maybe he is afraid of her now. Or is it that, through some ill-considered half-thoughts, he has given up on her? So easily, as men will do?

I stroke my imperial beard and worry about him a little.

🍃

It is late one afternoon near Christmas and Henri has gotten a good start on holiday drinking and the two-hour flowers are dead.

Frances says, It is time for you to go and get Father. We cannot simply abandon him in Mexico. I fear for his life.

She speaks from her flowery armchair where she has been sitting for some time gazing at the irises draped over the side of the vase on the spindly table. Thinking of the latest letter, or rather envelope, from her father, the one with a golden pyramid stamp, this time postmarked Patzquaro. Wishing she could imagine the words he might have written to her, to carry her away, as on the arm of a new *beau* through the gathering night and across the ocean to Mexico and into the jungle full of night flowers exploding open, red and green and yellow, like silent fireworks. Walking with him again. As years ago in Texas when he could still easily outwalk her on the paths by the Nueces River, always staying just ahead, turning now and then to point out slick stones or those that might crumble, loose earth or hidden holes so she wouldn't break her ankle way out there, so she wouldn't slip and tumble into the river. Staring down the bulls in pastures full of heavy grass as they passed through half-running and laughing as she had with packs of children more years ago, when they would taunt the beasts for hours and be charged and all come home soaking wet and shaking with fright. To be scolded and stripped by an angry mother and shoved to bed early in summer when the sun stayed high in the trees until it was so exhausting that even the big people undressed and lay down to sleep before sunset. Who knows, Frances wonders, perhaps those sunsets never even happened. Perhaps the sun had simply sat there, frozen in its own red pool . . .

Go and get your father in Mexico? No more! I'm finished fetching him! *C'est fini*! Are you out of your tiny mind?

Oh yes, Frances wants to answer, I am splendidly out of my mind. Yes.

Now and forever, in fact. Or definitely since that morning in the ice storm all those many years ago. When her fate became sealed in a sudden banging together of metal parts, two cars sliding into each other on a bridge outside George West as slate flew like nails. The crash leaving them stranded in the storm miles from town with no heat.

His vehicle was less damaged and maybe a little warmer, so Frances had climbed out of her coupe and into his. Without the slightest reluctance, almost without a thought. To sit and wait for help. Out there in the middle of nowhere.

Just her and a stranger, an odd-looking man, a foreigner who talked funny and talked a lot. About how things happened like that when you least expected them, changing the rest of your life. Then, too, about how silly these run-ins are, and about how, no, they weren't going to freeze to death out there on the farm-to-market, how someone, surely, would soon be along. Not to worry.

Good thing nobody was hurt, she said to him.

He thought a while and then answered, quietly, I wouldn't be so sure about that.

Are you hurt?

I hurt all over. Every part of me. But it is not a pain.

What do you mean?

It is something else. Something more powerful.

You talk funny. Where are you from?

Anywhere you'd like, anywhere you'd like me to be from.

And what if I didn't want you to be from anywhere at all?

I could be that, too.

Why are you being so nice to me?

It can happen, they say. Just like this.

You're very strange.

Not really.

And, no, he wasn't strange at all. Hardly singular at all. In the end. Which is somewhere nearer now, but not quite here yet, as Frances, trying a very new thing called being Frances again, sheds her fear.

Go find my father and bring him home! Or is it that you'd like

38

to kiss sex goodbye for the rest of your miserable Frog life?

Her words are a knife in his soft white gut, pulling up hard.

Leaving him, a mere Frenchman, no choice, really.

❦

Tonight the barometer is rising so quickly Marc taps the glass to jiggle the needle to be sure it's not some aberration. It flicks even higher but drops back in place. Still impossibly high. As if everything were being crushed in an invisible ocean.

Nearby hangs the Mayan mask, the clay face. Will it burst, too? Break into a hundred pieces after all these years? Dear aging Mother's precious mask? That would certainly kill her. Be the final straw.

The sound of it hitting the floor would be no sound at all. It was too old and soft for that. Another sad accident. Marc could see her rising from her bed deep in the far back bedroom, shuffling through the damp halls on the thin, gray rugs, emerging in the *grande salle*, her new crabstick, the one he'd finally bought her the other day, raised menacingly, like a stinger, then striking the floor with a frightening boom.

Who has broken my mask!

Mother, it simply fell from the wall. Please, come and sit. Don't excite yourself.

I do not want to sit!

Mother!

Again the crabstick rises, again it pounds the floor. Shaking the house. More things tumble from the walls, which seem to move in and out as if the heat had left them short of breath. Windows shake, panes crash. Doors slam, shutters knock, soot and leaves blow out of the fireplace.

Mother!

Who has broken my mask! One of your rotten children? They were playing with it, weren't they? They were playing with my mask!

No, Mother. In this heat it simply —

Silence!

He obeys. It will only be a few seconds longer and then it will be over again. It is the second time in a week.

She begins to cough and choke. The tip of the crabstick slips wide and she starts to fall. But Marc runs and catches her just in time, carries her, light as a baby, back down the long halls, along the mildewed walls that narrow to a single black door. To her room.

Try to rest, Mother. I can fix the mask.

Fix the mask? So you're God?

Rest, Mother.

If you're God, then where is my father? Do you want to tell me?

Rest, Mother.

You know, your daddy almost brought him back that last time, but then he failed. Then everything else failed.

Rest.

That's all I do now. And wait.

Rest.

He closes the heavy door and wonders how long she will last. It can't be long.

Something the matter?

It is the mother with the newborn asleep in her arms.

Mother had a bad dream is all. She'll be all right.

If only we could all sleep like this baby all our lives.

Yes, Violetta, if only we could.

Violetta? My name is Jeanne.

She darts into a room, slams the door.

He hears the baby begin to wail. And then the four-year-old joining in. More doors slamming and adult voices trying to outshout little ones.

Then, all at once, it is quiet again. As if a huge blanket had been thrown over the house, leaving only the thick, hot air.

Marc cannot understand it. Had he called his wife Violetta? How would he ever explain it? Why, that was my grandmother's name and I've always honored my grandmother and, well, you see I'm writing this story and she and Grandfather are in it . . .

He picks up the pieces of the mask and assembles them on the tabletop. It can be done. Glued and fixed. Rehung, new scars and all. But rehung. To cover the shadow it has left on the wall.

As if nothing at all had happened.
As if everything were intact.

⟨

As intact as that afternoon only last summer when Father, dear
hacking Father, stopped by the country house on his way somewhere. Walked in and sat down as if he still had a right to do so
despite the now-distant divorce. For old time's sake.

Marc had managed to keep up appearances, taken the bottle
of *pineau* out of the icebox and poured the sweet elixir for them.
Hoping that one drink and a couple of cigarettes would do him
and he'd be gone. Back into the dark.

It wouldn't be that easy.

It was the fault of the mask on the whitewashed wall, which
Henri, excited by his *apéritif,* spied and leapt at like a jungle cat.

The mask! That damn old mask!

Grandfather sent it to Mother, didn't he?

Your Grandfather? Hardly. *I* was the one who sent it to her.
From down in Mexico that year I went looking for him. You remember the story. Where your mother made me go and try to find
him? What a horrible mess that was! I don't know why I ever
agreed —

I remember.

Do you? Anyway, that damn thing came from Patzquaro. I
won't ever forget that name. It was there I sighted him standing in
a line outside a crappy little bank. I'd recognized the crabstick as
you would the North Pole and yelled out the window of the bus
I'd rode in on. But in a blink we were gone around a corner and
off through the dirty guts of the town to the station. By the time I
got back to the spot where I'd seen him, it was dark, the bank was
closed and the dirt street deserted. I stood there a long time wondering if I hadn't imagined the whole thing. No one, after all, was
that lucky. Spotted him the second I rolled into town? Who was I
kidding?

So what did you do?

I sought a comfortable hotel.

Did Grandfather really die down there?

41

Nobody knows.

You said that when we were children. You told me and Jean-Jean that again and again, that nobody ever really knew.

Poor Jean-Jean. Why'd you have to bring up Jean-Jean?

I'm sorry, Father.

Jean-Jean was a nice boy. A very nice boy. Why did he have to go and do that?

Father, I don't think we'll ever know.

You know, it's the same with your grandfather. We'll never know. But poor Jean-Jean. I read somebody else jumped off Notre-Dame a few weeks ago.

Marc poured them fresh ones.

A gulp later and the pains of that old nightmare swept away. May I continue?

By all means, Father.

So . . . acceding to a mild depression, later that evening I had a few tequilas, alone, and was generally enjoying the silence of the hotel bar. As I was belting back perhaps my fifth round, a couple of sunburned Americans (you know them immediately) stumbled in, saw how dead the place was, said, Shit, double-shit, very loudly and left. I soon left also, mildly content with myself and the world at large. As if all had reached some cosmic settlement that would be revealed to me in the coming hours. The bartender's knowing nod as I departed seemed to confirm it. Whatever it was.

But, as nature would have it, I couldn't sleep. Being no fool, I'd seen to it beforehand that my room had a balcony, with scrolled ironwork, a chair, a table for a glass and view of the main plaza. Anything less as regards accommodations can crush the heart and mind, especially during those waning hours when you feel utterly abandoned in an abandoned land. Disrobing to my boxer shorts to fight the heat, I went outside with my bottle of bourbon and a cola and poured myself the standard. That first sip was delicious, and I immediately thought of women, any woman.

Patzquaro was dead and it wasn't even midnight, at least by my watch, which may or may not have been working. No people, no vehicles, no birds, nothing. Only a low breathing, but not of the wind. The breath of an old tired country.

In such moments, one assesses progress, if any.

And?

I drank another drink. Thought it over again. Came to the conclusion that Ansel was Ansel and that if I knew Ansel he'd stick out like a sore thumb again. When had I ever been one to call it quits?

Never, Father.

Besides, being unemployed (again) at the time, I had months to spare, all my credit cards and a mind to find him for the sake of proving to myself I could do it. Not for Frances, but for the sport. As men will do with guns or fishing rods or race cars. For the thrill of action and the surge of feeling alive after all these years pinned like a dry insect to a board and covered with glass. Which was our life in Paris. Our apartment life, our box life. Our very ordinary mess.

Mulling this, I stopped after the two nightcaps, for there was work to do the next day. I stepped back through the blue curtains and lay on the white sheets and pondered the ceiling beams, the small black scorpions darting back and forth. Yes, he was near.

Someone, somewhere was plucking Moon River.

ɪɕ

From the shelf, my grandson, desperate for inspiration, opens an old notebook and finds a youth he dreamed of years ago:

The Mason jar a quiet American boy
filled with thick pesos — silver!
a wad of their soft paper money — millions!
and buried out under the hackberry tree
by the dachsund's pen while everyone
was gone to the shopping center.

The shovel sticking in the gray clay.
The note to the future that read
Today is May 5, 1960 A.D.

By Christmas the earth was level again.
He dug down — nothing. Dug some more,

43

to the left, to the right. Nothing.
What are you doing! shouted his father.
Who in the hell gave you permission
to dig up the whole damn yard like this?

And the shovel got locked in the trunk
of the solid gold Cadillac at the curb —
the one that ended up on the bottom
of the sea in the boy's fondest dream
with Pancho Villa himself flipping a centavo
into the milky green water, teeth flashing.
Adios, Padre. Adios.

And to think he thinks this is poetry. He is only playing with words, with pictures. Pictures that don't necessarily add up to anything. Don't you understand this haphazard, scrapbook style yet? There is nothing here but the parts. Add as you will, but the sum could be zero.

Or, worse, a web of lies. A network of deception.

No, nobody so obsessed with the past will ever get any pity from me. All Marc's digging in the gray clay is desperation. And where does desperation get you? Nowhere, except maybe to this point in the story without his having told you the bare facts: Since no one knows what really happened to me (and this much you already knew), then everything you read here is Marc making it up. It may sound good, it may all seem to fit, but it is made up. Invented. Period.

Perhaps he should even be chided. To what end does a man explore the past, or reinvent it? Can he imagine while in its seizing web that he can ward off death?

There must be a reason. A reason other than pure romance, simple nostalgia.

🌿

It is the first Wednesday of the month and the sirens all across the country scream at noon. Dogs wail, fish dive. But the creatures for whom the scream screams give it no more than a flicker of thought, and then the screaming ends. As if the Man of Peace has passed his gentle hand o'er the citizens' heads, cleared their brows, smoothed their messy hair, and sent them down the winding lane with their tunes to picnic on the rocky ground where war is buried without a marker.

◖

Into the evening Marc's father rattled on, so intent on telling the story that, once the pineau bottle had been drained, he went straight to the old cabinet and retrieved the whisky. Marc got new glasses and ice.

The next morning, Henri continued, in that awful hour when you're not sure whether you're sane or not, there I was, wandering through Patzquaro, still a little drunk, gadding about, staring, smelling wood smoke and sizzling meat.

Sure enough, though, luck struck hard again. For there he was, Ansel, buying a Mayan mask off a peasant in the market.

Contrary to what you'd expect, I didn't rush up to him, but held back, observed. I could take my time, do as I pleased. The little chase was already over.

I was amused to see that he'd knocked the price of the thing way down, to something near zero. Still, he did not appear to be entirely satisfied and seemed ready to further humble the vendor with his banter about inflation and the elderly and such.

I simply said, Ansel.

And he simply turned, looked me up and down and said in a dry whisper, Oh, hell. Leave the dead alone.

Then he handed me that mask.

It's paid for, Henri. Take it home to Frances and the children. Tell them you never found me. Do you understand? I am dead.

I stared down at the mask, a hideous face baked into some jungle-inspired fright, and it was as if it seized my face and held it locked in place, a minute, two, three. When I looked up again, he was gone.

Sixty, spits the peasant. *Nada más, nada más, très bon marché, see vous play?* Hey, you buy or not, mister?

I quickly paid the price, had it shipped home.

45

I was only a few steps from the market when I realized that Ansel was as good as a hundred miles away.

It was really him?

Yes. It was your grandfather all right. Now gone, already.

So what did you do?

I settled on a bench by the plaza and sounded my needs. My deeper needs, I mean. This took maybe an hour, maybe half the day. I don't recall. But when I was done, I rushed through the back streets in search of what a man needs most when he needs everything satisfied all at once. I paid the price, and by evening, newly enlivened by my rediscovery of the wonders of the opposite sex, I took a wild guess that Ansel was heading for Mazatlán and the Pacific Ocean.

Knowing full well that it was a wild guess, that luck is an erratic bitch. Knowing full well that this whole thing could well get out of control. But to tell you the truth, I hoped so. I hoped so a lot.

4

ANSEL HAD MADE IT BACK toward his old self only so far after the surgery. Any further advances would be infinitely long, imperceptible. All became suspended, stagnant. As if he were stuck on some back road for the rest of his life, staring out across endless bare fields. Why, what happened to everybody? Where'd everybody run off to? Wasn't there civilization around here in George West just a damn minute ago?

Hell, we're right here, Ansel. What is your problem? You getting another headache, son? Maybe you ought to have a cold one.

Maybe I ought to is right, he heard himself say.

I'll get you one, somebody said.

Then there he'd be, not out in the middle of nowhere wondering what the hell had happened to time and all, but playing dominoes in the back room down at the fire station with the boys. Just like always. Just like forever, as if nothing had ever interrupted the flow of such things.

There were a half-dozen men slumped over rickety card tables. The air smelled of Florida Water and cherry tobacco and sweat. In a corner stood a big black fan, the head rusted at a tilt toward the ceiling. Against a wall sat the cold-drinks box on top of which so-and-so's dog was stretching out to sleep.

Get off there, Jane! yelled Randy Graves.

The dog got down with a bark. Randy reached into the box, swished his hand in the ice and seized a soda pop for Ansel.

Here you go, ugly.

47

Ugly yourself, said Ansel.

Just like always, like one field following another forever and ever, the horizon refusing to be caught up with.

The cold drink went down like likker. Like back when they all drank themselves crazy and tried to beat back the brush fires of youth. Until there was nothing left but hard shells, the stuff you find on the blackened ground that resisted to the very end.

They played with real ivory dominoes, slapped them down with tremendous force, opening their mouths only once in a while, to dispute the weather, the look of this year's sorghum, the car that went off the road and rolled by the Huxley farm with all those little children in it, or the Russians and that son of a bitch cigar-chomping bastard in Cuba.

As for Ansel and his physical problems, well, everyone knew he'd been real sick, but it didn't get talked about: What was there to say? They dealt him in and kept quiet about it. Did their thinking about it, for sure, but kept it to themselves.

Besides, they were too busy watching that they didn't get skinned every afternoon. For Ansel was still the best domino player around. Even though that blood vessel in the front of his brain had kinked up like a garden hose right in the middle of his prime.

They say that his head ballooned, almost burst, that he almost checked out. Might've been just as well if he had, some said, instead of going back to being a baby like that for all those months, hell, years, wearing diapers, hitting the bottom of existence. You had to be real special, something else again, supernatural even, to come back after all that and be halfway normal.

(Some of them still secretly listened to him sit down and stand up and stuff to see if they could hear the crinkling sound of a diaper. Men down there couldn't help but try to know crap about other people even though they'd never ever admit it. So far, though, nobody'd heard any crinkling sound, so maybe Ansel wasn't wearing one anymore. And that was good. Hell, one of these days he'd be normal again. All the way back from wherever the hell trouble takes you when it takes you away like a tornado in the night.)

So it was no surprise to anyone that afternoon, with the dust coming in off the street when a car passed and the locusts droning like a hundred airplanes and the trees drooping in the heat, that

Ansel was quietly whipping the tar out of them once again.

Sam Adair finally said, You sure they didn't stick a computer up there in your brain when they had your head opened up? I mean I heard the U.S. government does that to people. Sticks little computers in them. Jesus, man, I ain't never seen nobody play dominoes like you play dominoes. It ought to be illegal.

Ansel smiled but kept concentrating. Maybe he'd been listening to that crap or maybe he hadn't, you could never tell with him anymore.

Everybody else was embarrassed, though, and held their tongues. So Adair just swallowed his medicine and kept his mouth shut. Hell, Ansel was probably the best damn domino player in the world.

ℓ

Frances waits by the telephone in Paris with the children for news from Mexico. A month has passed with only a single call from Henri to say he'd sighted her father in a market but then lost him again, to say take care and he'd call when he knew anything more.

His tone had been civil. As if something fundamental had changed in him. Was he perhaps having a pleasant time of it? Was that it?

Frances could not decide and began to regret the whole mission. Suddenly, it all seemed a ridiculous fuss. Why not let the old man be? Why not call off this absurd manhunt? Who was Daddy hurting doing as he pleased?

It was all silly. Like always running to the store for irises and sitting with the boys on the couch and watching them open, close and die. Had she lost herself somewhere?

More than anything she wanted the phone to ring once more, for Henri to say: Look, Frances, love, I give up. I am coming home to you on the next flight. Meet me at the airport at 8:30 tomorrow morning. Bring the boys. I've quit drinking. I've given up the search. We will forget it all, as if it never happened, settle down again, even buy ourselves a new home, you'll see. We must let Ansel go. Let him go. Do you hear, dear?

Hurry, we're off, the store is going to close!

Do we have to do we have to do we have to?
The phone would not ring.

↻

Believe me, he is fishing in the dark, arrogantly sure that he is the poet who can land the big one. If I were you, though, I would let go his sweaty little hand. He is going nowhere with his bag of cheap tricks.

And being the sot he is, he glares for hours at even my few words, ready to throw them out before someone criticizes, finds fault and announces, You cannot do that! You cannot have a dead man talk!

Only now it is too late. There is no time to do it over. The one-month clock he has set for himself is ticking. And meanwhile he needs me, his crutch.

Yes, to do it all in one go, to spin a tale that would show that time has run out for spinning tales: This is the true, and maybe selfish, game. And we, you and I, are but the pieces of a desperate, fractured ego.

Remember breaking things as a child just to see if you could put them back together? Remember how you never could?

↻

Un autre, Papa?
  Pourquoi pas.
  So, I bought an old Ford, a clunker nonpareil, but enough to get around in. Beat the hell out of the local transport. I don't care what all the colorful guides say, those buses — with their drunk drivers, smelly peasants, farm animals and nose for cliffs — are ambulant coffins. I drove where I needed to go.

And even when she broke down (I named her Ruby on account of her outlandish red paint job), I knew exactly what to do, not having gone to engineering school for nothing. She had a working radio, but I sure didn't listen to that Mexican crap. In fact, I don't speak Mex. Don't want to, never will. Any language they can spit out that fast isn't worth learning.

50

I kept the little air conditioner on full blast, night or day. It was the only way to survive.

Now, as you might have guessed, Ansel was definitely nowhere to be found in Mazatlán, or for that matter in San Blas, a quiet village down the coast where, in another life, I would have happily passed a few weeks with a young lady in one of the blue-painted, red-tiled, high-ceiling hotels and literally abused her and myself until we were but pulp.

Yes, Ansel or no Ansel, San Blas was an utterly pleasant interlude. The kind that inspires you to dream again of unplugging yourself from the past and joining the slow dance of liberation. It became enticing to think of parking yourself on a big wicker chair in the courtyard of the hotel under the orange tree and sipping shot after shot of tequila and watching the brown maids in white dresses drift by until Hell froze over, until you rotted, until your flesh just fell away like paper and made a heap of gray dust on the floor to be swept away quietly in the earliest pale blue light of morning, your bones, your self, your memory dispersed into the flower bed with a flick of a young brown hand on a yellow corn broom, her bright black eyes flashing with the thought of the sweet lovemaking going on every night all night behind all the jalousies, in the blue dark under the high ceilings where the fans creaked slowly and the flies in the windows sat and sat as if time would never move again.

Enough. A few days off the trail was enough. I fired up Ruby and headed out.

🌿

Josiah Daniel, now that would be Ansel's granddaddy back in another century, would get the children out in the yard and have them run in a circle around him while he popped them on the legs with a bullwhip. That was in punishment for not believing in God as much as he believed in God. The children ran and ran, screeching. And he popped em good until they couldn't run no more. Until the yard was churned up good and the rain came down again on that Georgia land, driving them all inside. The little ones to lick their wounds. The old man to coil his whip and rock. Coil and rock in front of the fire and yell out, Now stop all that damn whining. His wife Sally fresh dead and seven kids to look after. What the hell did anyone *expect* him to do?

One of them brats was Ansel's daddy, Thomas. Who grew up to be a bogeyman, too, inheriting the bullwhip and using it on his own kids, especially on Ansel. And Ansel had had it passed on to him: strong and firm as it had ever been, ready to be raised, uncurled, drawn back and flung forward like a scorpion's tail.

Only Ansel never had used it. Had left it in the chest of drawers up in the attic. His daddy's chest of drawers with his old clothes in there, mud and grime and oil still on them. With the stink on them, burrs and spear grass, too. All neatly folded and stacked. With the bullwhip far in the bottom, under the soft gray long johns. Buried. All just so, as if Daddy would reappear any second, naked as the day he was born, to holler out, Mitzie Louise, where the hell are my clothes, woman! And she'd holler back, Look in the damn drawer, Thomas! Don't you be cursin me, woman! Oh, go to hell! And the children, Ansel, the eldest, egging them on, giggling at the breakfast table in the sun by the screen door as the cows moved in and out of the yard and pigs ran squealing this way and that and the red robins got worms out of the churned mud.

Why, here's my bullwhip! the old man'd yell out. Right here! Hell, I was wondering where I'd stuck that son of a bitch. Woman!

The kids would take one look at each other and get to school fast.

A few minutes later, the old man would come down, still tucking his shirt in and buttoning up and Ansel's mother would look at him and say, I never saw kids want to go to school so bad.

They'd laugh and sit down at the table and she'd slice biscuits for him and get lots of butter and honey on them the way he liked, and maybe he'd like them so much that when she passed over the third or fourth one he'd grab hold of her nice wrist and pull her hand up to his mouth and kiss it even though he hadn't shaved yet. She'd let him do it and then take her hand back and that'd be that.

You ought not use that bullwhip on our children. Throw it away.

Throw it away? Daddy gave it to me.

Your daddy was insane. Your whole family was insane. It's a

good thing you came to Texas to be rid of them.

He was a Methodist preacher, you know.

Let's talk about something else.

He used to make us run around —

In circles in the yard and beat us with the bullwhip until we had the fear of God in us and there ain't no way your own kids are going to grow up not having the fear of God in them, too, even if it means lashing them every day of their lives. I know, I know.

I think we should make love right now.

Whatever for?

Cause I want to.

Somehow, despite himself, he would have managed to say it in just that way that broke the ice and softened her face. He would take her wrist again and lead her upstairs into the dusty sunlit rooms and sit her down on the tall white bed and then lower her onto her back the way the preacher dipped you in the river when you were twelve. Far back, so far back that if you breathed wrong, you'd drown before he pulled you back up out of the green water.

Maybe the bullwhip'd be there on the dresser. Maybe it wouldn't. Anyway, when it was all said and done, when all the lovemaking was finished and the dishes were cleaned up and the chores done, when whole lives of chores were done and death carried them off, the whip was Ansel's to have.

But of course he didn't have the slightest idea what to do with it. Even when he became a parent himself, he never had any children who needed beating. He only had Frances. And Frances had never done anything that would inspire a man to take a bullwhip to her. Not Frances. Not Frances, who was half Violetta, half goddess, half holy flesh. No whip would ever touch her. And no whip ever had. It stayed in the drawer under Daddy's clothes like a snake in a cave. The kind you can't tell is dead or alive until you reach for it.

◖

Now some folks traipse around Mexico with a glovebox full of maps. Not me. Once I was certain I had lost his trail, I went wherever the road took me. The results were sometimes predictable, sometimes miraculous, always a test. A test on navigating in the world of anti-logic, anti-reason, anti-thought. The kind of world I like to believe exists alongside this sour swamp we tramp through at present. The kind of world dear to both the child and the old-timer. For you see, to be on Ansel's heels I had to think as he would.

There were a thousand and one dead ends. But instead of leaping out and, in typical foreigner fashion, kicking the car in front of the locals, I slipped Ruby into reverse and went my way. This newfound patience, I believe, represented step one of my transformation into a more savvy, more cunning creature.

There were a thousand and one intoxicating locales along the way where I would dally for days, drinking and thinking, or thinking I was thinking, walking around, doing whatever I pleased. I would do this again and again until something would go off in my head to remind me that I had a job to finish, that I couldn't just lie down in Eden.

It was not easy. There were downpours on mountain roads, gullywashers in deserts, daylong traffic jams in swollen cities, nights pulled over in jungles with no food, no drink and my middle-aged heart pounding in the heat.

Sometimes Ansel felt near enough to be in the back seat. Other times, a continent away.

Meanwhile, I was running out of money and credit. Meaning that something would have to give — and soon.

Yet I wandered on, sure that I was now as mad as my crazy lab partner in college who had a way of grinning enthusiastically at everything. Still sure that his grin was hiding some other message, some other game.

Was Ansel playing with me, too?

Everything seemed connected. But what was it all saying to me? What was all this foolishness about? Was not ever knowing what, if anything, was going on really the trick here? Was that it?

I began to believe it, and logically, or anti-logically, let the wheel do the steering. I sat back and waited. No need to press the pedal, or worry about braking or anything. It was all up to Ruby, Ansel and the tilt of the land. Perhaps, I dared to surmise, I *was* actually learning something in the bowels of Mexico.

❦

Violetta had dropped her black purse on the polished floor outside a store in the George West shopping center that sold cheap watches and jewelry.

No one had bumped her. It had slipped off her arm and landed with a soft thud. She had looked down, mildly surprised at seeing her own purse there. Yes, it was hers, although smaller now, far away.

She would have to pick it up, put it back on her arm and get to the car. There was supper to fix before Ansel returned from the fire station complaining that there was no challenge anymore to dominoes, that he was bored stiff, that he knew deep inside himself that he would never be totally well again, that the TV schedule was awful, that he carried an unbearable sadness for all that had happened, how he had wasted her life away, how he owed her more than any man could ever repay, how they ought to go to the Tastee Freez later and have a hot fudge sundae — would she like to do that? Of course she would, of course. To taste cold vanilla ice cream and the hot topping, to sit in red plastic booths and watch folks come and go, to talk to a neighbor about their grandchildren all grown up now, to be at peace as the sun expired behind the elms and the cement street turned smoky blue by the dark green lawns. Of course she would, again and again she would.

Violetta began her long journey to the black purse on the floor. It would all be over in ten seconds, and then she would never again be bending, stooping to pick up the fallen.

❦

It was possible, they say, that while he had failed to overcome many of his handicaps — bouts of nervousness and nausea, a tendency not to think before speaking, a longing for trash food, heavily blurred eyesight, muscle ticks and constipation, to name a few — he may have, unknown to his wife and others, developed a range of hearing that compensated, if only partly, for what had been burned away all those years of mornings ago. They say such a

55

thing is not the stuff of the supernatural, or even particularly un-usual, but a biological fact: Healthy parts of the body can be-come, as it were, superparts. So that it is entirely possible that he may have been concentrating deeply that afternoon at the fire sta-tion, counting to himself, calculating his next play and the ones after that, and then knew exactly what had happened to his Violetta. The old boys were perhaps talkative, especially since the Crawford place had caught fire that morning.

Andy Buford had been the first to spot it, driving back from fishing all night up Onion Creek. Already the flames were going good, and in their light he'd sighted the Crawfords, counting them, one, two, three, four, all there.

And so I stopped to help, he said. They was carrying on some-thing awful, especially the missus. I've seen people with plenty of troubles, but this mess, well I . . .

By the time somebody'd got the volunteers rounded up and out there, it was too late. By noon, it was a pile of smoking ruins.

Something better be done by damn, roared Dan Clinton.

What we need is a damn regular fire department, Tommy White shouted back.

I guess *you'll* pay the taxes, then!

And why not? I don't got nothing against taxes that saves people's homes!

Sure you don't, sure. I can see your hand shaking over the checkbook.

It'd been going back and forth like that since they'd all wan-dered in there after lunch after going over to see what was left. Shit, God sometimes is strange. I bet you Ricky done torched his own place. Been drinking lately, they says. Them people been drink-ing for generations nonstop. She ain't been looking that hot, ei-ther. Real tired, worn-out, you know. Probably some family trouble, then. Trouble is we never see it coming and then it goes off like a bomb.

Oh, hell, they were looking for it. I never liked a Crawford anyway. Did you know they supported the civil rights thing? Can you believe that? Haven't seen them in church since I don't know when, either. He was definitely lit, got drunk and got them all out there in the yard and then torched her. And then the flames were shooting out, like tails of the Devil Himself, while the smoke — man, it was green! — rolled up in big balls. Pitiful. Were you there? Well, no. I mean, that's what I imagined it was like. Why don't you just shut the hell up, then?

Ansel looked up at last, not really hearing them, but catching this thing from very far away, something, he was not sure, something like thunder before there is a cloud.

No, something else, far worse, and he thought he knew.

No, it is only the doorbell that rings: a tattered parcel from Mexico addressed to her. She tips the mailman, takes it into the kitchen, snips the twine and tears away the brown wrapping. An odor of mildew rises from wads of funny papers.

There is no note, just the horrible brown clay face with its evil eye-holes. Again and again she searches the papers — nothing.

A toy from Father! the older boy screeches. Give it, give it!

It is not a toy! Frances shouts, holding it high. You will not touch it. Is that clear?

It feels wet in her hands, and for days she passes the time moving it from one place to another in the apartment, hiding it, taking it out and setting it on the shelf, then storing it away again only to rise in the night and put its damp curve to her face and stare into the bathroom mirror and massage her sex.

After a long series of non-choices, non-decisions, non-thoughts, I found myself staring out the bug-spattered windshield at a blue-green sea. If my maps were right, I had fully crossed Mexico yet again and now found myself on the east coast of the Yucatán. Offshore here were pristine islands, apparently, with healthy coral reefs, big Creole women and good cheap food. My kind of place, I thought, ignoring my larger mission. But then what the hell, you have to live and let live a little, no? I rolled down all the windows and let the salty breeze blow through. It had been a long time.

They say that there are plenty of creatures on this planet that know where to go each season without any fancy gizmos to guide them, what we humans call following your nose. And the nose told me that maybe Ansel had taken a detour to these white sands and blue-green seas. To tan himself sick, go snorkeling, smoke hoochee and lounge in the shade thinking he'd tricked me good. That I'd never find him.

I shaded my eyes and tried to see the islands out there through the harsh glare.

*

I never saw such Swiss cheese in my life. Just like my daddy Thomas told me, Son, if you keep writing Swiss cheese into your school papers you won't amount to anything.

Upstairs, in the dresser drawer, you imagined heat lingering still in the bullwhip under the soft, cool clothes. Perhaps someone will need whipping again. That man running around the countryside these days calling himself the Man of Peace. Resurrecting the Jesus myth to hide from the destruction of the world? What crap! To hide from the indestructible crap that is the world?

*

Tu n'as pas un petit truc à manger, fiston?

Sea spray drifted among the palms behind the beach. High in one, I saw a monkey making what appeared to be obscene gestures at me, and, against all good judgment, decided to answer him with the same.

Soon, though, a rather fierce-looking black, who evidently had been named to the soporific job of guarding that stretch of coast, emerged from the misty grove. He wore a service pistol in a white leather holster high on his fat hip, jungle fatigues and a dingy sombrero. Don't get me wrong, but these Third World functionaries, with their splendid history of respect for humankind, can undo your bowels with a single glance.

I whispered a quick prayer, my first in untold years.

There was a considerable wait then, during which the functionary halted, peered up long and hard at the offending monkey in the tree, before returning it a *bras d'honneur*. Then he came near and mumbled some local gibberish as he bent down to inspect Ruby's chrome bumper. Convinced it was the right thing to do, he then worked his jaw and tongue into a muscular frenzy before launching a gob of spit thereupon and proceeding to give the spot a thorough shine with a pink handkerchief and to study his face and teeth at great length in the fresh brilliance.

Meantime, another beach guard burst forth from a thatched lean-to, smoking a big red cigar and rubbing his big yellow eyes.

Charles, come look at this Cadillac, the first said. The accent was British. How lost was I? Belize?

Charles frowned up at the monkey, which had turned its red backside to us all, then said, That ain't no Cadillac, J. B. Just be a damn Ford. Hey, Byron! he screamed at the monkey. Kiss off!

Man, I not tell you again, dear Charles, but this most assuredly is a bonafide Cad, J. B. said. I have seen one million Cadillacs and this is a Cadillac.

Byron began screeching, tearing out tufts of his hair, wadding them into balls and chucking them down.

What's wrong with that fool today? Charles demanded.

He's having his period.

Then they began to look me over. I kept my hands high on the steering wheel, in plain view. You never know. They conferred a few minutes, then J. B. approached and gave a sharp salute. He stank of insecticide.

Destination?

Just visiting, I improvised. Did I do something wrong?

Please step out of the Cadillac.

I did as told, careful not to make any false moves.

Now the other came over, dropped his half-finished cigar at my feet and mashed it into the sand.

I must've been a sight, my shirt and trousers stained with greasy road-food, my face unshaven and caked with dirt, my waxy hair mashed in various directions.

Indeed, as I stood there, my filthy appearance aroused the vulgar monkey, which broke into a falsetto giggle that pierced the air and spooked a hundred birds into flight.

Neither officer smiled or frowned. Neither allowed his eyes to stray. I tried my best to stand as erect as possible, but still they towered over me. My legs were half-numb from twelve straight days behind the wheel and shook as if carrying too much weight.

Passport, they said in unison.

In the car.

Where?

Under the floor mat, driver's side.

J. B. shook his head no at his partner.

Charles grunted and said, What's the matter with you?

Only people who want to be dead get in Cadillacs, Charles. I ain't getting in no Cadillac.

I'm telling you, it's *not* a Cadillac. Is this car a Cadillac, gringo?

No, a Ford.

See, J. B.?

He's lying.

Are you lying, gringo?

No, sir.

See, Jean-Baptiste? Get your makes straight, will you? Cad is Cad, Ford is Ford.

I'm still not getting in this car. I also would advise you, man, to have this stranger retrieve his own documents from the interior and present them to us properly.

And have him grab his weapon and shoot us both? Surely you learned better than that at the academy! No, I will retrieve the papers and simultaneously perform a cursory inspection of the Ford.

Be my guest, comrade. May this Cadillac put a whammy on you.

Charles studied the door a moment, then flung it open and took a skip back. Seeing no danger, he drew near again, slowly extended his arm inside, and using the tips of two fingers, carefully eased back the plastic square of floor covering. Then he abruptly let go.

No papers here.

J. B. bent near to verify. Show me.

Charles repeated the operation.

It was true. There was nothing there.

I swear I heard that monkey shout, Shoot the gringo!

Snaps popped on holsters.

Then there were several gunshots, several piercing screams.

The loudest of which was mine, which, thankfully, was enough to knock me awake again.

But, then, isn't there always a price to pay for everything?

For there I was, apparently where I'd been for days, sick as a dog, in a cruddy little hotel in some unknown little town, the air foul as a sewer, my bedding soiled beyond belief.

I cursed each and every cantina in the world and quaked with rage.

With the greatest efforts, I managed to roll clear of the mess, hit the floor and crawl to the lightless can. To sit and cringe in pain. To wish for death and the death of everything beyond death and beyond even that.

Contrary to everything I had been trying to achieve, contrary to all the faith I had built up inside myself, I was then quite sure that I would never find Ansel. The toothpick world I had made came clattering down and a purple fog of hate and despair filled the land.

It had all started to begin that afternoon when, quite by accident, Marc happened to observe a shirtless man taking a drink at a construction site. When he remembered his missing grandfather, presumed dead many years ago. Mother had gone to bed and stayed there. The world had continued to turn. But now the story had begun to begin again. A filling-in of the blanks, the holes in the Swiss cheese, a restoration of heat to the tip of the whip. For no reason, really, other than to do it. To defy the part of him that said he couldn't do it, would fail. To race the clock for the pleasure of racing the clock. To give a damn when no one else did. To assure that his grandfather's story, whatever it was, would finally be told.

The maid who came to clean my sty, a poor crippled girl, kindly informed me that where I lay as good as dying was in the town of Hoctúm, an inland crossroads of no note. This information, which

I took to be fact, served to deepen my exhaustion as I once again mentally retraced the steps that had taken me from one end of Mexico to the other. The revelation also convinced me that the battle with Ansel would be won only if I took drastic action to unlock what had become a pointless stalemate.

In a few days, I was able to take chicken broth and tortillas. With each bit of sustenance my thoughts cleared, as silt will sink and leave the waters clear.

Don't ask me how or why, but I resolved that I would no longer be needing the Ford. Perhaps this marked the beginning of my insanity, but such things can never be known with certainty. Again and again a voice in me had said that if you do get well you will not need the car, you will forget it, not go looking for it, you will give it no further thought. You will abandon it at this particular juncture and never look back. How else, I reasoned, or unreasoned, except via a radical departure from common sense, would I ever cross Ansel's invisible path again?

To seal my decision before any change of heart, I handed the keys to Ruby to the maid and described her color and make and her approximate whereabouts. For which she seemed extremely grateful, though she was gone before telling me so. I silently wished her well.

The hotel bill depleted my dough. But, oddly, for the first time in my life I felt liberated. Bravely, I took a bus back to the eastern coast and the Caribbean. This time, for real.

Ansel's domino landed hard, the double-five, which made 30 and gave him the game.

Jesus damn! they let out. The bastard was holding the gold all this time! I give up. Me, too! Hell with this shit.

Violetta, too, had landed hard, on her face. The purse knocked sideways, its contents spilled across the floor among the many passing feet — a change purse, a pink comb, a letter, a spool of red thread.

Someone help this lady up! a woman cried.

Men bent forward to recheck the final lay of the game. How

did you do that? Would you mind explaining how the hell you did that, Ansel?

A man crouched. I don't think you're supposed to move them when they fall. She might have broken something. We could get ourselves sued good. Call a doctor.

Ansel looked at them, his eyes gone red and blank.

Someone said, Hey bud, you don't look so hot for a guy who's just slammed us out of the park. You O.K.?

Violetta's eyes looked up at the ring of faces, but saw nothing.

That lady is dead. Deceased, someone corrected. Passed on, intoned another.

Come on, Ansel, maybe you've had enough for one day. Must be hot in here. We'll drive you home and you can get your old lady to fix you a nice tall glass of iced tea.

He did not seem to hear them. He still hadn't picked up the pen to make his three Xs on the score pad. He still hadn't said, Who has the guts for another round?

A red-haired man in the crowd around Violetta pushed through to the body, drew himself up straight and lifted his right hand high in the air. Lord Jesus! he hollered, I want you to save this woman, this holy child of God. I want you to look down *right here right now* into this shopping center in George West, Texas, and have mercy upon this woman who has slipped on the wax and tumbled down. Blessed Jesus have mercy, have mercy. Rise, my child, rise, rise! In the name of God —

Shutup, someone said.

Take me home now, boys.

5

I'LL TELL YOU ANOTHER THING: Living with this guy has got to be pure punishment. What does he do all day? Nothing but alternate — or spring, bounce, gyrate, you name it — from one mood to another. And when he's not doing that he's pretending he's writing a novel. Or, rather, many novels in one. Including even my novel? Now you tell me if that's not a picture of somebody with nothing better to do and maybe a screw or two loose. Down where I come from, when a critter gets wobbly like that, rotten with disease, we plug em and dump em in the Nueces in the night.

Try just being nice to folks. You know, one of those basic things folks have to do in life. This guy? He takes so much after his idiot father that it's got to be his genes. Old, broken genes you can't get rid of no matter how hard you try. (I guess that'd put me in a bad mood, too, come to think of it. But, hell, I'm missing a chunk of my brain, and I can still be nice to folks. It's second nature to some.)

Today was typical. There were angry words with his sweet wife Jeanne before lunch, over nothing, again. Each threw a newspaper at the other. The boy cried. The newborn baby cried. Yesterday, a jar of mayo. Today newspapers. I can't stand to think what will come of it all.

It is as if he were following in the footsteps of that scoundrel father of his. Doing what Henri used to do, making his better half always pay a price for any shred of good will on his part, and in

64

direct proportion to whatever effort he had made — to lift a box, clean a dish, pour a drink — until she bowed again to his foul will. Copying the worst dad in history.

I call that sick.

I stay in the shade with a cloud of black flies, feeling wide awake and impossibly drowsy at the same time, as if I were stuck on some ship floating through paradise and hell all at once. As if at any moment I would slip overboard — or be pushed by you know who — from this story in which love lies forgotten like a toy on the lawn.

❦

Marc dreams of the city nearly every night now. It starts on a spire of Notre-Dame with his secretary Samira, Vik the guide girl from the museum and brother Jean-Jean. The four of them up there in the orange evening light with the lights of the city coming on and blinking for as far as they could see, a breeze bucking them.

You go over, we all go over, right? asked Vik.

I'm less than in agreement, said Jean-Jean.

What're you talking about now? asked Marc.

Life and death, said Vik. What else is there to talk about?

There's also the beyond, Samira offered. Or, if you wish, the neither here nor there. An even better subject.

You would think so, said Vik, annoyed.

You bore me, Jean-Jean said, raising his arms, stretching up as if to grab hold of something.

Oh sit down, Marc told him. Who's got the corkscrew?

I do, I do, said Samira. Did you know that in Morocco, where my dear family, bless them, suffers still, what we're doing right now would land us all in jail for ages?

There's no churches in Morocco, fool, said Vik. Even I know that. Me, a second-generation immigrant prole from the Red Belt. So how could we be sitting on top of one down there!

Samira tried to continue. And did you know —

Do you always talk like it's Christmas morning? Vik asked.

Leave her alone, said Jean-Jean. We're friends here.

Samira nodded triumphantly, went on. And did you know that

if you ever mention politics down there, even among friends in tiny apartments where no one else can possibly hear you, that someday, sometime, somewhere, a man dressed in clothes like yours will suddenly come up to you at work, at the café, at home, and take you by the arm and lead you away to prison and that you will never be heard from again?

You're stretching the story, no, dear? asked Marc.

Exaggerating? Whatever for?

Why in Hades are we discussing totalitarianism up here at Jean-Jean's little get-together? Vik shouted. Where's our party spirit?

Right! cheered Jean-Jean. It's my party and I'll drink if I want to. Pass the bottle!

Round and round it went as the sky turned lavender, then purple. Clouds of pigeons circled, anxious to land, but they shooed them off. Below, a crowd gathered. To watch another street mime, suffer another street singer, laugh at a drunk, whatever. You drop a coin on the street in Paris and a pack of curiosity seekers immediately will form to see how it all turns out. Wouldn't want to miss a thing.

Vik began to spit, trying to hit them. But each shot merely sailed away.

Pfooey! she cried.

Grow up, Samira commanded. This is serious business.

No, no. Don't say that, said Jean-Jean. We're only up here for a round of drinks and goodbyes and then I'm jumping. That's all.

Hell, I'd jump, too, if I'd a daddy like yours, said Vik.

No one knew what to say, and they all looked at her. An imp from the cruddy communist wasteland. An idiot with a government job in a museum tending dead art. A fool girl who'd have fit much better in a Hugo novel as an urchin than as a smart-ass, gum-chomping illiterate trash child of the premature future. *Une petite conne, quoi.*

Jean-Jean took pity on her, though.

Precisely, he said.

Precisely what? asked Marc.

Precisely because of the father I have. I have no choice but to do a swan dive from the cathedral. Vik is right. Kiss me, Vik.

She leaned over and kissed him long and hard. It sounded like a plunger trying to unclog a john.

What a night, Marc said, smiling wildly at the blinking lights.

Perfect, said Jean-Jean, wiping his mouth. A little wind, but I should hit the river.

Why do I feel sad? said Samira.

Because nobody's banged you in the last hour, said Vik.

Samira pulled up her light summer dress and hung her bare bottom to the crowd below. There was a huge roar and the sound of firecrackers.

They're clapping, said Vik. I guess it's showtime. You ready, Jean-Jean?

Almost, almost . . .

❦

Since this narrative purports to be about me I will tell it like it really was.

When I was young, I lived in my dreams. Whatever around me was not part of the dream, I rejected. Or did my best to hold at bay. There were anxious, neurotic people to avoid, so-called friends and family alike. I wanted nothing to interfere with my travels through very private lands.

When I grew older, my father, Thomas, handed me a long wool sock full of hard-earned cash, saying, Ansel, take this and go see something of the rest of the world and then come back and tell me about it. I want to know what the rest of the world looks like, what the people do, what they say, everything. Will you do this for your old dad?

I was eighteen that day, and we were sitting on the porch of our rundown house in George West, Texas, where the land goes on forever with you stuck in the middle of it. I had no idea what there was to go see, but I did not reveal my fears. I said, Yes, I will, and thanked him for the money and went to pack.

He had freed me. I had the whole world at my feet. It had been his goal to send me forth ever since Mama dropped dead under the flowering plum trees so many hot mornings ago. Something about a promise he'd made to her way back.

67

Neither of us said a word as I left, even though both of us knew I might never return. I did not look back, either, even when I heard the glider creak as he got up and the screen door slap as he went in for his nap in the cool bedroom. I walked on.

In George West, I got a ride with an oil worker to Houston. Another lift got me over to New Orleans. Then there was the train up to Memphis, and from there all the way to New York City.

It was autumn and everywhere the land was spilling its harvest. I traveled with folks from all walks of life, old and young, with servicemen and drunks, old maids and crusty gents who thought they could remember the Civil War. There were Indians and blacks and Chinese. And there were rich people, couples who had maids to tend their children, who moved tons of baggage, spared no expense.

All the monied ones seemed headed for Europe. They spoke lustily of London and Paris and Athens, of southern Spain's golden coast, of the romantic Low Countries. The home of civilization, young man, the cradle of everything we are and ever will be, they told me. The Old World. Versailles. The Vienna Opera.

They might have been talking about Mars.

New York made me dizzy from holding back my head to try and see the sky.

I will never forget the very kind proprietress of my hotel who, one evening after supper, got out a map and showed me Europe. She had been there herself, she told me wistfully, years ago. She had most enjoyed Venice, its foggy Grand Canal, its old stone bridges and damp byways. I drank her fine coffee, leaned on the table with her by the gaslight, and dreamed the new dream.

That night, lying under the roof in a high feather bed, I spoke out loud to my father. I told him that I would take a ship across the Atlantic Ocean.

But, somehow, I knew that he was no longer of this world. I saw him in his bed, the spray from the lawn sprinkler hitting the window screen, making a rusty mud that ran down across the sill. His eyes open, seeing nothing, the moonlight bending into the room like fingers of yellow ice.

I grew stiff and could not sleep.

The beach at the end of the bus ride looked like the one in my wild dream except that this time there was no sign of Charles or J. B. or the vulgar monkey. In fact, there was no sign of anyone for as far as I could see north and south through the spray. I had found paradise.

For no particular reason my body moved south, along the beach, as into another country of dreams. Not sure as regards the search for Ansel of having accomplished a thing. At the same time, not really giving a damn. Going forward was all.

The air was cooler. I smoked and hummed a peaceful tune. Watched the soggy jungle to my right and laughed at the thought of any civilization hacking back all that to make its vain mark on the planet. All the bright-eyed journeys into the historical dark. The fanfare. *Bon voyage!*

Soon, however, I sensed someone was following, a presence like a hot breath on the neck. It soon became so intense that when I tried to turn and see what it was, I couldn't make myself do it.

And so, slowly, then much faster, I began to run, as if for my life.

There go his bad genes flaring again. Just now, right there in the middle of the evening peace of the yard, he finishes a fourth glass of wine and says to his wife, When I die drop my ashes over Popocatepetl.

Pardon? says Jeanne.

Over the volcano. A la Malcolm Lowry.

That was *under*, says Jeanne.

Peu importe. Just don't waste ground burying me.

You're drunk.

It will all be over someday and we ought to know how we are going to handle it.

I just don't think about it.

They stare at each other.

Then he gets up, pours a fifth one. I'm going for a walk.

Wonderful, she says.

Frowning, Marc starts away, glass out to one side, wavering. A few miraculous steps later, he swings open the gate in the wall along the river and disappears.

Jeanne waits at the white iron table under the blue cedar, thinking about the man who is adrift again, and the unfolding book. Her Marc caught in the twists and bends of maniacal construction, a teetering set of ideals and fantasy in which there is no room for her, where it would be unsafe to venture. Better not to peek over the old river wall and see him walking away alone through the grass. No, she'll not go after him, even though the dying light seems to call her to the gate, and the river-cooled air rolls along the ground like a wave over hot sand, beckoning her to move in it as along a shore at dusk.

She hears his steps thudding on the footbridge as he crosses to the island and the stands of poplars where the moonlight makes cages within cages to walk through until the grass becomes so deep and the poplars so tall that you begin to disappear.

Within the lightless house, the newborn cries.

Jeanne tenses, but she doesn't get up yet. She wonders, Could it be that Marc's love for the old man and his untold tale, for Mexico and death and ashes over volcanoes, for the tastes of words he will need to make it live is all that he can possibly feel, as when a river is full? Isn't this the only way he can go now, off with his grandfather into the dusty night, as if choice has been taken away by the dark power of place and time, usurped by old dry stones? But does a man ever return from there? She thinks yes, only it will be slow, as slow as the rest of the night and the month of nights, until it is done.

She goes inside to the child.

❧

The immediate family had been placed behind a thin lavender curtain in a special area on the side. Hundreds of folks had come, filling the air with every fragrance of toilet water and hairspray. With arctic wind spilling from the ceiling vents over the main seats, the women sat wrapped tight in shawls, while the men kept their heavy suit coats buttoned. Up front, dozens of chrysanthemums and gladiolas and irises formed a wall behind the light blue steel casket. A hymn was being piped in, the needle scratching along, sometimes sticking until an unseen hand set it free. The whole place buzzed softly, like a wasp nest.

Marc had been put next to Ansel, the widower, who held his grandson's hand on his wide knee. Nearby were Frances, weeping noisily, and the man she had chosen to marry, checking his watch. In rows behind them, in the purple dark, sat the rest of the family, faces that had not been seen in years, faces with little dry mouths that wouldn't say a word.

At some mysterious signal, the rabble began to file down the carpeted aisles to the front and peer upon Violetta's brightly powdered face a final time. This they did at a snail's pace, the women touching tiny handkerchiefs to melting mascara, the men knotting their big red hands behind their backs, the children skipping along and daring to reach in and touch her, only to get firmly, but soundlessly, slapped.

A preacher, one they all knew to be her favorite, a Methodist, mounted the tall pecan pulpit, eyes upcast, a plume of icy air fluttering the pages of his Bible as he laid it open on the lectern. After a slow survey of the attendees and the goings-on around the coffin, he folded his hands atop the Good Book and bowed his head in prayer.

Ansel leaned sideways and said to Marc, You want to see her?

I don't think so.

The preacher unclasped his hands, studied the ceiling with his mouth ajar as if he were about to say something, then sank back into silent prayer.

A husband and wife team, both in top-model wheelchairs, whirred up to the casket and parked. Both were long past even dreaming of pushing themselves up to have a glimpse of her, but made a big show of force by lifting their light little heads enough to have a look at the side of the receptacle. This done, each pushed a power lever and zoomed away.

The night I met her on the train to Venice . . .

To where? asked the boy.

In Italy. The night I met her she was wearing a dress the color of a ripe red plum. She was very beautiful in the dress. She's being buried in one just like it.

Yes sir.

There'll be a beautiful lady in a pretty dress for you someday, Marc.

Yes sir.

What say we don't go look at her a last time? When they call us, we'll stay put. That all right?

Of course, Grandfather.

You know what?

What?

This music is . . . what's that dirty word I told you never to use?

Grandpa!

It's O.K. What is it?

Sh . . . shi . . .

Yes, shit. This funeral music is shit.

The boy giggled and the old man squeezed his hand and smiled.

Some of Ansel's domino partners approached the curtain and stood there looking in, as if from another world.

Hi there, boys, said the old man, and waved.

None of them answered. After a few seconds, they nodded together.

Bye, boys, Ansel said, and waved.

Ansel, one said.

Then they returned to their chairs, which gave a single deep creak as they sat down in unison and crossed their arms.

This is kind of like a bad movie, Ansel said. You know, they ought to play some Country Western. Violetta liked that. I mean, after a while she did. Not at first, but then it sort of grew on her. I even got her going on the two-step, though she was awful. That's all right, though. She was so pretty she could've been terrible at everything there was to be terrible at and it wouldn't have made no difference to me. You understand?

The boy began to cry.

Whoa, there. Listen, I'm hungry. You?

No sir.

Sure you are. Let's go over to Dan's. What do you say?

I'm not —

Sure you are. We'll give this show a few more minutes and then go. Get us a big barbecue sandwich and some pickles and a cold cola. Sit outside under the elm where it's cool. I never liked a funeral.

Daddy, came the daughter's voice. How're you doing?

Fine. Why?

What do you keep talking about?

Sandwiches. Hot barbecue sandwiches. Right, boy?

The young one opened all the faucets.

The minister raised his arms toward the ceiling vent, let them slowly drop again, clicked on the microphone, and when the squeal had faded, said, Let us rise.

Hey, there's our cue, Ansel said. Head for that door there. We're gone.

🌿

By nightfall, I came to a little port where a river spilled yellow into the green Caribbean.

The brightly painted shops and houses were built on stilts, all taller than my head. At each, the ladder had been pulled up and stored away. Many of windows had been boarded up, and I would have thought the town abandoned if not for some faint rays of light escaping through cracks and murmurs of voices within.

Here and there I stopped to hail them, but no one answered. Lamps would be snuffed, a silence would reign.

Eventually I stood on a jetty in the moonlight, slapping at mosquitoes and counting.

I don't know how long I lingered there, half the night or all night long, watching the empty mouth of the port and imagining myself on some cheap film set, head high, hair tossing in the breeze, eyes on the horizon as if something, something dangerous from far away was upon us, and pretending I was the last one strong enough to be out to greet it, whatever it was.

It might have been myself. It might have been my own indifferent father. It might have been my vengeful sons. It might have been my frail wife. Then again, it might have been all of them together, hurtling down upon me as one. But to what end? What had I done to deserve this rendezvous with meaninglessness?

I wanted to sit and cry. I wanted to lie back and sleep. I wanted to sleep and never wake again.

Yet how did I know I was not dreaming even then, as before? Would I suddenly awake again in a bad hotel with diarrhea? Was I condemned to repeat the same sick cycles forever? Was this Hell?

Stop gawking and let's get a drink, someone said. Be happy hour soon. Wouldn't want to miss it.

I whirled around. Ansel?

Good question.

Ansel?

Is that my name?

It wasn't the same old man who'd left Paris behind all those months ago. No, it was someone else altogether. A big, healthy old man with a golden tan and a radiant smile. A giant of a man who looked like he'd never had a stressful day in his life. A tall man who looked like the daddy you'd always wished you'd had, one who'd been everywhere and done everything, and one who had no intention of slowing down now, not now, not so long as the whole wide world still breathed.

Without a second thought, I wished only to follow him.

I've finally found you, I said.

Found me? Maybe. But I let you.

Let me? Why?

Yes, there's that, too.

I started to reach out to hug him. Ansel! I'm so happy to —

Don't start, will you? he said, giving me a light push.

Start what?

The theatrics. Be a man for once. Now, how about that drink?

It's a miracle, I shouted.

Oh it is not. Shutup.

I could only obey.

Ansel lay in the bedroom for several days, Violetta buried in the George West cemetery, the funeral food getting moldy in the refrigerator. To mourn or grieve was not his style. He neither fretted nor cried but slept a good deal, and heavily, as if he had not rested in years. She was gone. He searched quietly for a way to turn. The phone rang several times. There were knocks, persistent and often, on the front door. He rolled over and dug into his dreams for an answer, any answer.

Again and again she would come, young as the day he first met her, and sit with him a while under the pecan trees and tell him not to be sad. Again and again, she would take off her beautiful burial dress and laugh and lead him down to the river to swim and hold him naked in the warm water and wash away some of the hurt.

It was Sam Adair who broke the door open after more than a week and stomped through the house and found Ansel pounding on a typewriter by his bed. There was a neat pile of pages going, maybe a hundred, maybe more. Ansel typing?

What the hell are you doing, Ansel?

Writing a little book, Sam.

You had us all scared to death.

Well, here I am.

Hell, Ansel.

What're you so mad about?

You've been holed up in here for days.

So?

Sam picked up a bright-colored book off the table. A travel book on the Yucatán? Now wait just one damn minute.

Leave me be, will you?

Who the hell wants to go to down there? Nothing there.

I might. What dif is it to you?

And what's this book-writing crap? You never wrote no books, Ansel. You can tell me if you're not feeling O.K., you know. I'm your friend. People can go and do weird things when death happens. But damn it, Ansel, you can't go changing like that into something you're not. You have to go on with your life. Even though she's gone. You've got to go on being Ansel.

Why don't you run along, Sam?

Now you listen to me, Ansel. You're not going to sit in here forever, you got that? I'm not going to allow it. The boys aren't going to allow it. Frances is not going to allow it.

Why? I want to write this book, and then we'll see what's next. I'm perfectly fine. Look.

Ansel stood up by the bed in his boxer shorts, raised his arms as if to wave to someone far away, lowered them, then sat down again and placed his hands on the typewriter keys.

Listen, Ansel. I want you to go up to Hot Springs, get to some horse races for a while. You can stay in me and Millie's condo up there. How's that sound? You can't stay here.

I have no desire to go to Arkansas.

Then New Orleans, maybe. See Pete Fountain. You know. Hit some bars, see a tit show, get you a Cajun girl.

Adair . . .

Something, anyway. Screw Mexico. Even the white-wingin has gone to hell down in there. You get robbed everywhere you turn. And writing a book? Who says you can even spell?

What's spelling got to do with it?

I've been over to see Frances, Ansel.

So? Has she given up on that fool she married?

She's going to move to Europe with him. Back to France, where he comes from.

Good for them.

That's all you have to say?

Hell, Sam, Frances hasn't been over here in months.

Maybe that's because you told her not to come over.

I don't like the Frog.

She wants you to go to Europe with them.

Like hell.

That's what she said. Said you were getting on and needed help. With Violetta gone, well, she said she wanted to start taking care of you. Said you couldn't stay here in this old house all by yourself now.

Figures.

She also said you'd been to Europe once. You never told me that.

A long time ago.

Well, I think she's got a point. And it sure beats going south of the border all by your lonesome like in some novel. Why not go on up to Hot Springs a while like I said, then come back and I'll help you pack for Europe. What the hell else are you going to do, anyway?

The hell else I'm going to do is write my book first. Now get out.

Sam leaned over and tried to read some of the words on the page in the typer, but Ansel shoved him away.

Get out of here.

Is it dirty?

Out!

＊

On the night of the new moon, the current Man of Peace gives a rare interview to admonish the people to lay down their evil souls once and for all, be as the lamb with the lion, the fly with the spider, the cat with the dog, the gazelle with the cheetah. His blah-blah putting to rest rumors of a putsch by the old men of war. Monkey see, monkey do, the world sighs with relief and the poised guns retract into the ground. Until next time, when He will have to wave his soothing fingers over humanity, as always, and forever.

Marc wads newspaper (stuffed with stories of Him and His Thoughts) for starting the barbecue fire under the old pine tree as his boy shoots his stick rifle at pigeons returning to roost in the crumbling *colombier*. Jeanne brings the dozen silvery sardines on a porcelain platter and sits cross-legged by the fire with her husband. How many days has it been since they had a moment together on this vacation? Why, it is worse than during the rest of the year! Each thinks of holding hands with the other, while the boy plays, while the baby sleeps deep in the house, but neither makes the move.

When I was a small boy and we were still living in Texas, he says, Mother kept boxes of batteries in the hall closet and the radio on all day and all night. If it happened the way they thought it might, the Big One, we had a plan to get in the station wagon and drive out to the lake. Somehow we'd be safer there, by the water. We even had a practice run, camped out one night. Daddy got drunk and played his trumpet, stayed up all night with the bottle of bourbon at his feet blasting out songs all wrong since we'd forgotten to bring his sheet music. We'll have to be sure and put the music in with the war supplies, he kept repeating, O.K., honey? Honey? We can't forget to bring the music for the final show! Boom! Ha HA HAAA!

In the end, though, nothing happened. Cooler heads prevailed. We moved to France. It would be safer there, he insisted. Frogs don't start wars. Something like that.

Jeanne pitches a pine cone onto the coals, shrugs. Can't we ever talk about something fun?

⚜

Ansel and I walked along the jetty, then and again stopping to watch the crabs among the rocks and the surging waves.

After a mile, maybe two, the wall ended and we stepped into a bright yellow sailboat and sat. I was anxious and wanted to know what we were doing. He let me squirm a while, then stood and hailed a man coming out with an ice chest on his head.

That's Otis, the owner. He'll take us out to Isla de la Luna and come fetch us in a couple of weeks. How's that sound? We need the break.

I could only hop on the bandwagon.

Roughly we go, Captain? asked Ansel.

You right there, man. No big shit, though. We make it right. We smooth in the way of the rough. No prob. *Nyet*. Who da fren?

This is Henri, my son-in-law. He's visiting from France.

Froggy!

I paid the insult no mind. Black clouds lined the eastern horizon. It was as if someone had turned on a giant fan and was slowly notching up the speed.

The boat rose and fell like an elevator, churning the contents of my sore stomach.

Weeeeee, cried the captain, whenever a wave popped him one, his thumb-size teeth flashing. Weeeeee!

Ansel hunkered at the bow, eyes on the flat little island ahead, unperturbed. I kept thinking he was going to fall out and be lost.

First time out, Frog? cried Otis. It make sick, all right. Hop, skip, jump you belly! Yes?

I puked in the boat.

Oh God. Nasty Frog! You going to clean that up now, hear me?

I nodded and puked some more.

No stinky in my skiff! No sir!

I dipped an oily bucket of the Caribbean and began to clean it as best I could.

Otis sang a dirty song.

Ansel fell asleep.

A hard hour later, after our clothes had dried and been soaked again by the violent spray, we reached the island, a long sliver of white. After Ansel paid Otis a handsome sum we watched him head back to the mainland. Whitecaps raced in all directions, and soon the little boat was lost among them.

Will he make it? I asked, wondering why I cared.

Look after yourself, son.

What's that supposed to mean?

You'll see.

The old man started down a path through the palms. In the grove, the wind fell sharply and the roar of the sea faded.

Sarah's place has 2-for-1 rum from 6 to 8, twice daily, he said. And if you're hungry, good food. Then there'll be some chores. I know you won't mind, though. She's alone now, after all.

So he'd become a bonafide drunk. The whole chase hissed at me like a leaking tire. I dreaded the thought of more wasted weeks on an infernal mission of mercy.

As if reading my mind, he said, Might as well relax, meanwhile. No sense making any plans until this is all over.

Until what's all over?

He halted, peered high overhead, sniffed the air.

Dno, baby!

In the tops of the tallest trees, I spied another of those little black monkeys crashing along with a coconut tucked under its arm.

Dno knows what's up, Ansel said, and redoubled the pace.

It felt like I had a cord on my neck.

79

6

THE THING FRANCES IMMEDIATELY missed the most was a yard which she could tend to, water and prune, toss the kids into, stand in on summer nights under the stars. Their new little apartment near a rail line coming out of Paris, however comfortable and immaculately decorated, could never replace a lawn, a big wooden house on a lawn, tomato patches, ticking water sprinklers, a dog, several beat-up toms and the occasional snake. No one in the building knew anyone else, and with Henri's long hours at the office, often seven days a week, their social life rotted and died. Gone was Gordon Tipton, the oldest man in Texas, who each day had come into their yard, rain or shine, out of breath from his blocklong walk, to say hello, maybe sit a while, maybe talk about France, how he'd gone over there and fought, how he was sure he'd left children there, so many years ago. Then there'd been another woman her age, Leigh Ann White, who babbled on about her fantastic sex life and the many men she picked up and dropped. And the kids, herds of kids all around, screaming and yelling yard to yard, kids of all colors making a music she had come to adore as she watched them all grow, her own, theirs, everyone's, as if she'd been the mother of that corner of earth.

Then they'd come to Europe just after Jean-Jean was born and Mama had died. Henri had become immersed in his work as never before. She and Marc saw him a minute each morning and were always asleep when he came in late. In the vacuum bloomed the obsessions, with cleaning, straightening, arranging and rearranging everything in the narrow rooms. Again and again she moved the furniture, shoving it around like the pieces of a puzzle, then sitting here and there for hours until her mind delivered another configuration.

Henri never seemed to notice anything, though, made no kind remark. Rather, he always appeared to be pacing, as if he did not, had not ever, belonged there in her arrangement, as if he desired nothing more than to break free.

The boy tried hard to relieve his mother's worries, and doing so only worried her more. For, lacking another guide, he would come now and then, to the cabinet and take out the dust rag and slowly go about the apartment wiping the furniture as she did each day and sometimes twice a day in the long-running battle against the fine, black dust. She would catch him dusting again and go to him and take away the rag and tell him to go play. He would smile, but instead of running along, he would sit and watch her continue dusting, slowly, carefully, as the polluted city sky fell in a heap.

Somewhere along the way came the irises. Back in George West, Texas, she had had thousands of irises, in every bed in the yard. Tufts of purple and rose and blue shooting from stiff green blades that resounded like rubber when you hosed them down in the evening. In Paris, two-hour irises were all that could be found anymore, the minutes always passing in a second before the final wilting brought a small cry from her lips.

The boy looking on, his stomach in knots, whispering, Should I practice my trumpet now, Mother?

Soon now he will come. The ultimate Man of Peace, who will kick sand in the eyes of every believer — Jew, Mohammedan, Christian, Buddhist, Animist, Environmentalist, Capitalist — any and all. None worth more than a drop of his energy. Without hitching his wagon to any star he will insist that true peace begin at home. And since to have peace at home, you must have a home, he will insist that we renounce our wanderlust, hang up our boots. *Chacun chez soi.*

He will make a home for himself, no more to wander the world. No more to make surprise visits among the poor and rich. No more to appear in leaders' bedrooms deep in the night to admonish, correct and instruct. No more to be found unscrewing warheads from rocket tops. With a cup of tea at his lips our lands will be flooded or drained according to his whims. Cities will be razed according to capricious techniques. People will starve or grow fat according to the mood he is in when they attract his attention. His neglect will cloak the earth in darkness, his concern will crash and crackle through the night, bringing warmth and light, dust and ashes, while he sits at home in his slippers, smoking his pipe, pointing and clicking with his cursor or watching the silent antics of his pen.

The long weeks of crisscrossing Mexico now over, a pleasant feeling of accomplishment came over me. Even as Ansel marched far ahead, sometimes almost disappearing from view again, I felt a strong urge to talk to him, to confirm that indeed he had gone from Patzquaro, where I'd first picked up his trail, to San Blas to swim, and from there to Guadalajara, thence to the capital and Chapultepec Castle to see the royal carriage and to the horrid zoo to see the newborn hippos, before zigzagging east via Puebla, Oaxaca, San Cristóbal de las Casas, a lake in the Yucatán jungle, to the coast in search of Caribbean sun. But I knew the answer was yes without asking, and quietly congratulated myself on a job well done.

After a considerable walk, during which he repeatedly paused and lifted his crabstick and made as if waiting for it to point the way, and during which I grew certain that, for some reason, we were circumnavigating our destination, we arrived at a green and pink house, a dovecote really, on tar-covered poles at the edge of the water. Its ample porch was set with pine picnic tables and benches. A hand-painted sign on the roof, much worse for the weather, read Sarah L.L.'s. Old fishing nets, faded buoys and plastic starfish adorned the walls.

Best food in the world here, said Ansel. Try the fried chicken plate.

Well, I am a little hungry, I conceded.

There you go. There's the spirit. We'll need your kind of spunk, son, to weather this through. Funny, I had you figured for a sissy at times like this.

He tested the bottom rung of the ladder with his frayed rope shoe, nodded approvingly and called up, Permission to come aboard!

I swatted a large red fly that had alighted on my neck and taken an ample bite. The crushed insect stained my fingers blue.

Ansel looked around. I forgot to warn you. Stings?

Not at all, I said. But have I got this ink all over me?

Yeah, all up and down your neck there. But that's the least of your worries. Stings?

I told you no.

It will. We better get you settled down. Old crap's going to flood you any minute now.

What?

Ho-oh! he cried. Bet you a dollar she's having a séance again. Always talking to her family up in Flada on the old psychic wire.

The house gave a shudder as if it had been bumped by a boat.

Yep, she *is* home, he surmised. By the way, Henri, don't let the fuzz get you staring.

What fuzz?

A shadow fell, cool and heavy.

Just smile a lot and don't say anything stupid.

We peered up at the huge, hamlike face, a wreath of short red hair appearing to bristle like dog's fur, but the tiny eyes glowing soft blue like morning flowers. A short, green cigar twitched and traveled from one side of the mouth to the other and back.

The voice hit like a sonic boom.

Rats acomin in gracias mucho it soon be real high tide y'all. We goin wash way our sorrers fo sure now. I love Miamey.

Sarah, it's me, Ansel. I brought family.

A bit of cigar ash came sprinkling down as she looked us over.

Ansel? Is that you, lovey? Lord, lord.

Yes ma'am.

Who is that with you down there?

Sarah, this is my son-in-law, Henri Du.

83

Family! I love family. But is he a communist?

No, ma'am, no commie. We came to help.

Well, fine. Y'all come on up. I gots to go finish yakking with Angelica. Some Palm Beach Jew knocked her up and she wants to change churches and all that crap. What is this world comin to? Come on up. I'm goin to kill her. Why nobody believe in Virgin Mary no mo? I'm goin to kill somebody. Grandbaby or not, somebody goin to pay. Come on up, boys.

I followed the old man up, taking several knocks on the head from his crabstick in the process. It was no great climb, but I nevertheless felt a slight dizziness upon reaching the deck.

Just check out this view, will you! Ansel cried. Now ain't that just worth ten thousand pictures, one million Kodaks? Jesus!

I steadied myself at the railing. It was true, the vista merited such praise. But my neck was beginning to itch, badly.

Really stings now, doesn't it?

Yes.

Stick to the railing. It's good business around here to hold on to anything solid you can. You never know when a plank's going to pop.

I did as he did, inching along, hand firmly on the rail.

We had gone halfway around the house when a small window suddenly filled with her face, beard, gold teeth, fresh cigar and all. Her lower jaw seemed to come unhooked as she shouted.

Now she's talkin abort the thing! I just won't have this insanity in my house, do you hear me? Am I goin to have to go all the way to Flada myself to straighten up these silly kids, Ansel? Am I goin to have to? I could do a little shoppin . . .

Take it easy, he said kindly. She was just trying to get your goat. Why do you let her succeed?

You sound like a philosopher or somethin.

Just don't worry. Don't we have enough problems *chez nous* without sticking our noses elsewhere?

I just love it when you speak Frainche to me, Ansel.

Sarah.

Yes, Ansel.

What time is it?

She thrust out her forearm, bent a tiny wristwatch near. Why, happy hour is what time it is! Y'all have a seat now while I get my order pad. *O gioia!*

Then she withdrew, belting an aria.

Violetta's last gasp, said Ansel. Oh joy! it was. Was it a final clinging to life, or a welcoming of death? Verdi does not tell us. Nor Dumas.

Lest he think me uninformed in this area, which I definitely was not, I said, No opera authority has ever asked that question nor felt the need to do so. Let's call a specious flap of the lips by its real name — hooey!

Ah, ah!

What?

That's the sort of wisdom that will land you in a deep pickle some day. To shun the unanswerable queries is to blind oneself intentionally. Don't you ever listen to the Man of Peace? *O mio dolor, O mio dolor.*

I knew that if I did not immediately find a perch I would collapse in a spineless heap. Can we sit down? I begged.

Why not? he said.

But no sooner had I made my first move to do so than I froze stiff, fixated on a nightmare I'd had as a child in which I played on a swing in a large park where everything — trees, grass, people — was violet. The swing seemed weightless, and easily rose higher and higher. I would always come to a point where I would push it even more, ever nearer the sky, and it would respond as if a living thing, saying yes, yes, higher, higher, so high that I could no longer see the earth below and found myself floating through the emptiness of space alone with nothing to hold to, no way to return, and knowing full well that this was forever and ever . . .

Finish sitting down, you fool, he ordered. She gets the idea you're a mime or something and you'll be out of here in no time. Sit!

Ansel had parked himself on a sway-backed bench and hooked his crabstick on the table.

I wanted to obey him, but the bug poison had unthrottled my heart, set it chugging at a rhythm that rang a thousand bells in my mind, all telling me, Keep floating.

Somehow, though, I sat.

No, no, he directed. Here. Next to me. That's her spot on that side. She's the boss, she gets the view.

I got up and came around and slipped in beside him on the bench facing the wall of the house. Exhausted, I forgot all manners and lay my head on the tabletop. A minute or two of blessed calm passed and then he poked my neck hard, right on the wound.

Boy, it sure gotcha. Long time since I've seen a *hole* like that from a fly bite. We'll get you on the rum, it's the only cure. But try not to talk, meantime. We'll just sit and be easy until she comes and takes our orders. Can't push things here, you know.

Ever get bit by one? I asked.

He rapped the table next to my head. Knock on wood, no. Maybe it's luck. But then maybe they're not attracted to me. They say insects can be that way — hungry for some, bored by others. In fact, I think these buggers have some way of knowing if you're worth nipping or not. Sort of a success-rate radar. You fit, obviously. But don't agitate. Couple of days it'll be over. In fact, you'll probably be glad the malediction came when it came.

I had a horrible urge to bawl my eyes out.

Sensing this, he turned to me. I know. You get a lot of guilt with this, too. It'll come up like old gas in mud. But let it come. Don't be afraid. You are among friends here. The only ones you've ever had.

I sputtered thanks, then let it flow. It had been years upon years.

❧

Jean-Jean, dear baby brother, why did you jump? whined Vik. That's what he'll say later on, I betcha.

I will *not*, said Marc. He's free to do as he pleases. I've always said that and I always will.

Oh listen to that crap, will you? Vik shouted. I'm strong, you're weak, go jump, see if I care. Well?

Please shut up, said Jean-Jean. I haven't jumped yet. You can argue over the retelling after I'm gone.

Anything you want, said Samira, as if in charge.

Vik snorted, popped another hock to the wind. Maybe we need a little sex to get us ready for this.

Sex? Samira tugged at her dress.

I mean mental sex, said Vik.

Oh, she said, and released her dress, as if caught stealing.

What the hell does that mean? said Marc.

Indeed. And will you be long about it? Jean-Jean asked.

Long? Short? Medium? Are you on a schedule?

What a wonderful crowd, said Samira. Just look at them.

What's wonderful about it? Vik asked.

Well, that they are so numerous. Back in my country, in Morocco, a crowd even one-tenth that size would get every single last one of them —

Landed in jail forever. We know, said Vik. As I was saying . . .

Somehow they all listened.

Mental sex is the coupling of your mind with the minds of others.

Oh, boy, said Marc, giving a sarcastic whistle. Breaking wild new ground here.

It involves all the elements of the dance, but without the contact. Today, imagine a union of minds between the current Man of Peace and me, Vik.

Slightly intriguing, said Samira. But likely illegal.

Stop it, Marc said. Go on, Vik. What're you saying?

What kind of union would we have? Just who is today's Man of Peace? Sure, we think we know him. How couldn't we? He's always popping up on the TV, in cyberspace, in your bathroom mirror, you name it. Sure, we know his face, we know his mug. But what makes him the peace guy? Is it because he's smarter than the rest of us? Is it because he holds the keys and codes to countless nuclear weapons? Is it because he brooks no dogma? We can only guess. In fact, is he even real? Isn't it possible he is created out of the clear blue sky just like they say the scientists and the Hollywoodians got together to stage the Moon landings? How do we know we've not been completely duped into thinking that this guy, this media clown who claims to spurn the media, is the answer to the planet's prayers? In fact, just what has he done for us? Name one thing!

This is seditious, Samira said.

Name one! Vik cried.

Didn't he push the annexation of Mexico by the United States, thus saving the lives of millions of impoverished Third World people and giving new hope to that tired land? Marc said.

That's right! said Jean-Jean. He did. He did do that. I remember.

Saving lives? Who are you kidding, Marc Du? He pushed the annexation of Mexico in order to secure a sizable chunk of land to build his dream boat. A base in the mountains for his pointless rantings. Who is this clown? And how many people has he fooled, led into yet another round of the endless copy-cat game? Why, we've got peace pretenders on every corner! Is there no place we can go to be free of him and his goofy acolytes?

Vik gasped, out of breath.

Perhaps you are making too much of this, said Jean-Jean.

Yes, said Samira. Just look at all those people down there, Vik. *They're* not worried.

They're French, Samira.

So?

Vik stood up, bent out over the edge. I'm wasting my breath. I'll say it again, why don't we *all* jump.

No, no, Marc insisted. The deal is Jean-Jean jumps. Don't go changing the rules of our little game here.

You know what I think? Vik said, gazing at the city.

We sort of know already, said Samira, giving a big yawn and scratching her armpits.

I think the Man of Peace is going to bring down the whole show. The way the Jesus figure overturned the world. Only this time, it'll be permanent. The seven seals will be broken. The seven angels will fly. The blood moon. All that.

Pas vrai! said Jean-Jean. They'll pull the plug on him and all his *sosies* way before that. Don't you worry. *Dis adieu.*

There wasn't even time to say it.

He missed the river by a long shot.

⚜

Marc, the man strapped to the thirty-one-day clock, dreams of being a vacationing boy in red bermuda shorts exploring a hotel garden in San Cristóbal de las Casas. Every tree and bush is sculpted into a bird — some fat and never meant to fly, some thin and light and poised to disappear into the night sky. Some boys grew up on ancient castle grounds, some in brick streets with row houses, some on the trash-swept slopes of great cities. Tonight, he is an American boy who'd never had to go and finish growing up in cold, nasty France. Tonight, he has Mexico and San Cristóbal twinkling beyond the gardens, and the swimming pool, like a jungle lagoon stretching away into the dark. All the way over to the new parts of the plush hotel, unfinished, windowless and black, where the girl with the mangoes walks with a red candle through the rooms after the workmen are gone. He never learns her name, never asks. On the balcony of the uppermost room they hold each other like lovers, but without any knowledge, and watch the red moon pull up. Always eating mangoes and putting their sticky hands together, slowly, twining them, laughing softly when they become stuck. His knees shaking as they squat, staring out like cats at the living night. The parents, everyone's parents, forgotten, far away in some violent rolling of aged flesh and sweat, the rum bottle tipped on the floor, the clear alcohol spreading, darkening the clay tiles. While the children's eyes, on fire, blink back in the cool gloom as the trees and bushes flap free into the sky over the lagoon, turn and dive to drink, turn and dive forever.

It is the summer they are shooting students in Mexico City. Over there in the foul bowl of carbon monoxide and coal dust and acid rain. Where whole districts explode into a billion pieces when a refinery blows, always just before dawn, just when the last worker has finished drinking and fucking himself to sleep and the last cigarette is still burning on the floor. Where Trotsky got it, and many a wife, in games. Where the blood poets know weeks in advance when earthquakes will hit and haunt the filthy back streets, madly staring as the young bodies are brought in from the *universidad* and the wailing begins.

It is the summer she opens her mango-colored legs, beckons him to lie there, and grips him with a force that stalks a man for the rest of his life. High up in the innocent mountains, in the sweet tourist gardens where the virgin maids leave lemon drops on your pillow when they come to turn down the sheets each night, where you lie naked flat on your back and gaze at the ceiling fan, your head bursting with the odor of ripe fruit, your skin tingling as if electrified. The soft drag of brown nipples across your chest. *Yo te quiero.* Unable to move. Clamped.

On the Fourth of July he finds a boy selling fat firecrackers made of newspaper. A lot of them are duds, but he gets a few to go off. Over the balcony while the parents are out to dinner. Terrorizing the old hotel cats. The boom so loud your ears ring as if someone had fired a gun by your head. Each bursting in a flash of white fire and ball of black smoke. Shreds of paper sprinkling down. The bitter stink on his fingers.

A soldier on the plaza jams a boot into a body. His partner has drifted away to smoke a cigarette with the others. So he bends, checks the billfold. *Nada. Chinga!* Then he checks the wound — a clean hole in the leg, another in the side, and sniffs. A burned smell, again.

He digs in for the coins anyway. Twelve pesos. Pockets them. Turns and looks at the sunrise over the university stadium, *muy bonita.* Later, before sleep, opens his wife's legs, stares there with a smile as she frowns up at him. The burning fuse touches the powder.

❦

Weeks passed in New York City before I mustered enough will and strength to pull myself away from the very nice lady who owned the hotel. Well-lettered, well-read, well-everything, she had taken a strong liking to me and would not part easily with my company. I admit I had no qualms about the free room and board she offered in exchange for my masculine services. And our long, late-night discussions about philosophy, geography, mathematics, chemistry, the Romance languages and so forth never bored. It was even a pleasure to listen to her speak at length of a man she'd met in Italy who had taken her heart away like never before. No, it will be hard for me ever to efface the memory of lying entwined with her in a deep sweat going over the main points of knowledge and love. I acquired countless facts, refined my language skills, broadened my Texas-empty mind. She, in turn, had her body turned inside-out and outside-in, so that by the time I bade her *arrivederci*, she had a splendid glow about her and a smile that said, Go forth and remember me.

The steamer ride to France was a nightmare. We weren't a mile out before I became viciously dizzy. I wheeled about the deck upbraiding well-heeled passengers, scolding children, admonishing the elderly. I stopped and spit on a man eating a hard-boiled egg, a big man, who immediately gave chase. This is all I remember of that foul departure, since while fleeing the gentleman I'd insulted, I slipped on the polished deck as on a bar of soap and delivered such a blow to my head that I can still feel the knot. To this day, I have no idea who rescued me from the mob, which surely would have chucked me overboard.

Not a peaceful passage for a young man on his first trip to the Old World. A kind lady doctor, again sent me by some mysterious benefactor, or so I imagined, gave me a variety of pills and powders and saw to it that I was brought consommé twice daily. Despite her intervention, her long waits bunkside, I remained in poor shape all two weeks on the high seas.

The only other visitor during the crossing was a young man with a cartload of books and magazines.

Try Tolstoy, he recommended, when I said I had no idea what to pick among his many offerings. Full of action, he said. Nice and long. Plenty of details. Characters, real ones, galore. Even some sex.

Yeah?

He thrust the heavy volume into my face. Bet you can't finish it before Calais. Bet you ten bucks.

I don't gamble, I said, piping Mother's line. Many a good man was ruined by gambling.

Bah, he replied. Forget I said anything.

My stomach heaved as he got onto the foot of my bunk. Rest my dogs a second, he said.

Normally, I would have objected to such forward behavior, as Mother had taught us, stranger or not. But I was too weak to care about protocol, and decided to try and enjoy some fellowship.

He was a good-looking kid, obviously well bred. He wore his short black hair greased and parted down the middle, leaving a sharp red line of scalp. His face was as pale as the moon, his eyes huge and light blue. His cologne smelled like violets.

He apparently had broken ranks with the rest of the staff by donning jodhpurs and a T-shirt, both black and immaculate.

Do you enjoy reading? he asked.

I felt like being honest for once. I said no.

Too bad. Tolstoy is pretty good. May I?

I handed him back the book. Anna Karenina, it was called.

The interesting thing, he said, is that you can dip in anywhere and find a pearl. Shall we?

I wanted to sleep, but said O.K. Besides, wasn't I on the vacation of a lifetime? Why doze through it?

What's your name anyway?

Ansel.

I'm Ted. Call me Teddy.

We shook hands. His grip was firm but cold.

You're on fire, he said. They give you aspirin?

That and everything else.

Hmm. Well, I'll dip straight in here and see what we find. I like doing this kind of thing. Besides, what the hell else is worth doing?

I almost answered, but then saw the hyperbole and relaxed back on my pillows as best I could for his little reading.

This has to be pure, he added. You read only where your eyes fall. Then we try to figure it out, set the scene, fill in the blanks. I think an eminent German quack saw a curative effect in this kind of activity.

Get on with it, I said.

Page 597, he said. *In the garden they came upon a man weeding a path, and without any longer considering that the man saw her tear-stained eyes and his excited face, or that they looked like people running away from some calamity, they went on with rapid feet, feeling that they must speak out and convince each other, must be alone together, and thereby both escape from the torment both were experiencing.*

One can't live like this! It is torture! I suffer and you suffer. Why? she asked, when they had at last reached a secluded seat at the corner of the lime-tree avenue.

Teddy shut the book, looked at the ceiling. Ah. Can't you just see them? Running along? The lime-tree avenue? Now, what do you think was up? Huh? What were they running away from? Whatever was tormenting them? Do you think they were —

Stop, I said.

What? he said.

This is not my idea of fun.

Oh yeah? Well, then, what does *monsieur* like to do?

Play dominoes.

Dominoes?

Yes, my father taught me. He is the greatest domino player ever. I mean was. He is dead.

I'm sorry.

I had a dream of him dead back in George West, Texas.

You did?

In New York City before we left.

I see. He reached over and pulled near his cart, shoved Anna Karenina back in her dark slot. Do you believe this dream was true? I mean, what makes you think it is true? I mean, did you check? Maybe —

He's dead. There is no doubt.

We were silent a while, unwilling to take the petty argument any further down its twisted path. Instead, we contemplated the ship's groans and clangs, thuds and squeaks. The book cart rolled gently across the cabin, returned, departed, returned.

The lime-tree avenue, he said again. Isn't that just beautiful? In our day and age writers just aren't capable of pristine simplicity!

Please, I said, tiring of it all.

He put a hand on my bare ankle, and looking dreamily around the premises, at the pile of my soiled poor boy's clothes, at the sea bursting gray against the porthole, at the sepia prints of Sirens on each wall, at the sooty lantern swaying on its ceiling hook, began slowly to massage my skin.

Don't do that, I said.

He peered at his hand, which was still working away, as if it were not his. Oh, he whispered, as if someone were listening. Sorry.

It's O.K., I said.

93

I thought —

No.

Well, no is no, isn't it.

Right.

He stood, arranged his person, started the cart out the door.

So, he shouted in a businesslike voice, no books today! Well, then, maybe tomorrow, sir! But who can know? I have a whole ship to service!

Don't be angry, I said.

Angry? Me? He shoved the cart into the hall with a huff. By the way, they're forecasting a pretty good gale. I advise you to secure yourself to the bunk with a belt or something. These White Star liners have their ways, you know. Good day.

The door shut with a boom.

For the better part of an hour, I lay listening to the thundering bowels of the ship, thinking of those unfortunate souls on the Titanic. I could almost hear Mr. Hartley's band playing ragtime as she listed and sank, switching to the hymn Autumn in the final moments, the strains pouring out across the icy waters. My home-town newspaper had even printed a photo of Commander Smith, with the caption, Be British: The Last Words of the Titanic's Captain. In a leap of thought, I imagined Teddy, my new acquaintance, would be like the one who, that horrible night in 1912, disguised himself as a woman to get a spot in a lifeboat. I, on the other hand, would have been deep in the doctor's quarters, filling myself with opiates and brandy, ready to accept my fate. There I would have remained until the black waters rushed in.

The next thing I knew I was sprawled on the floor. Immediately, the ship dipped, sending me crashing into my cardboard suitcases along the far wall. I couldn't see a thing, heard nothing but the roar of the storm, and reached desperately for something to hold to.

I seized a hand.

It's O.K., he said. Hold on tight. That's it, yes.

I gripped it hard.

You should've strapped yourself in like I told you!

What are you doing here?

I always come back, just in case. Hold on!

We broke into a steep roll, our bodies flying over each other again and again until we hit the door, frantically embracing.

We must have hit heads, for a shower of bright sparks, as from a flare, lit the cabin and in the light I saw the face. It was my dead father, grinning, toothless, bared gums shriveled and flapping. The lime-tree avenue! he hissed. Why don't we get out the old bullwhip and I'll chase you naked down the lime-tree avenue, you little pansy! What do you say to that, queer boy!

I screamed, bolting upright, the lady doctor seizing my hands.

It's O.K., it's O.K.! You've had a bad one. It's O.K. Shh . . .

Then she kissed me as a mother would, and I smelled violets again and tasted tears emerging from the deepest rock of my being.

It's torture! I whispered.

It's O.K., she whispered. Easy, easy. Shh . . .

I remember I had an erection, that she saw it and smiled.

It's O.K., it's O.K. Rest now. Rest easy. Tomorrow we'll be in France.

7

WHY, WAY BACK THEN, back when Ansel's Pa Thomas was still alive? Why, he'd moved all the way from red-mud Georgia to that black-dirt country in Texas where all you had to do was give the ground a good look and cotton plants would spurt out of it. Tom knew a good thing when he saw it and spent the greater part of his life moving the family from town to town building cotton gins. That didn't mean he got rich or anything. Only that the family survived. A lot of people were suffering way back then. Why, Ansel didn't even have shoes until he was growed. But that was then and this is now. And just because it's modern times now, it's not really a prettier picture. Why, that was exactly what Ansel was thinking that morning in George West after he'd done buried his wife and his reason for living and watched his only child pull up stakes and head off to the other side of the world with a fool and, worse, with a deal for him to come live with them. Along in there somewhere, Ansel figured he must have lost his mind.

It was auction day, and by the time it was over he'd been lightened of everything except a few special things, like his pa's dominoes. Everything had gone to the highest bidder, folks from all over the county, strangers who came in beat-up cars, mostly spooked-looking couples with packs of lean children. First to go was the furniture — the pecan beds, the divan he and Violetta'd had since the war, the maple dining table and chairs, and then all the junk, the rusted porch chairs, the rotten glider, 500 yards of leaky garden hose. Women went after the kitchen things — frying pans, measuring cups, mixing bowls, butcher knives, sifters, graters, Mason jars. Men snapped up the guns, picked through the tools, and somebody even bought the old red Ford. Ansel also kept the bullwhip and the family Bible. The rest? Dust to dust.

The house, sitting on a prime lot by the river and built of No. 1 pine, fetched a pretty penny. The buyer was an older man, a fellow nobody knew who'd showed up alone, out-of-county plates on his late-model Lincoln. As soon as he'd settled up the deal with the auctioneer, he was gone. North up the highway, slow as a funeral.

Ansel remembered how it rained that afternoon, too, and how it seemed like the whole thing would never end. Every time you started thinking there wasn't anything left anyone could possibly want to buy, here'd come another car full of white trash. They'd stay an hour, bug you wanting to talk, try to bargain on every last item and then bend your ear for the longest time about how poor they were, with no health insurance, no money for gas in the winter or clothes for all them kids or a roll of tarpaper for the roof. So what did you do? You started giving things away, the last of the last, even helped them stuff it into their rusted-out cars. You kissed the babies, acted worse than a politician, and stood waving goodbye to them as they sputtered off into the night, tailpipes dragging and sparking orange.

Sam Adair let Ansel sleep over at his house, then drove him to the Houston airport the next morning. They had a couple of Bloody Marys in the bar and said their goodbyes. Which didn't amount to much, except Adair repeating how it sure had seemed weird seeing him locked up in the house the whole last month like that and by the way had he finished writing that damn book? Ansel told him he had and that because it all hadn't really meant anything he'd gone and made a fire by the river and burned the thing and felt much better. That sort of confused Adair and he didn't ask anymore about it.

He did say, though, how he thought it was wiser for Ansel to be going to Paris where the daughter could take good care of him than to be running off to Mexico. Ansel listened to him with one ear.

Then Adair got him on the right plane. Said send us a card sometime and gave his friend a big hug. Teach them Frogs how to play dominoes, he said. And don't look back. So long.

You too, Sam.

The daughter had got her way. Ansel would come for a few months to start with, stay longer if he liked it, which she was sure he would.

He would have his own room and the run of the apartment. They would find him friends his age. They would teach him French if he wanted. It sounded reasonable and boring.

Ansel drank several glasses of orange juice during the flight, but turned down the food. The pretty stewardesses fussed over him, bringing him magazines and pillows and a blanket, some stopping to sit a while, take his old hands in theirs and chat. About Paris and Athens, Sicily and Casablanca, about his plans, their plans, romance and heartbreak. They kept him so busy that never once did the phantom steamer to Europe, that infernal ride so many years ago, rise from the black bottom.

No, Ansel felt as if he could keep flying forever, on and on around the earth, never landing, never arriving, staying in orbit, that would be fine.

During the spaghetti western, he dreamed that the mysterious man who'd bought the house came back in the night with a bunch of white trash kids, got them running in a circle in the yard in their ripped-up clothes and started popping them with a bullwhip. The kids were cheering him on as if it were some sport they practiced every night. Sickened by the screams, Ansel ran out on the porch and fired a shotgun into the air and shouted, Jump back, old Devil!

Satan ignored him, delivered sting after nasty sting. The yelps were awful and the kids looked like they might even come after Ansel. So he fired the gun again, this time right over their heads.

It only sent them into a higher frenzy.

Then, somehow, the house was on fire, the whole place all at once, every window billowing smoke. Satan blasted notes from a red trumpet and popped the whip as the children bent over and bared their bleeding bottoms to him and begged to be popped harder, harder! And pop them he did, on and on, as the house went straight up, the flames like a witch's hairdo in the black night.

Then he remembered Violetta was still in the house and ran back inside to try and save her. But his clothes caught fire and the flooring busted through and he was falling through empty space, the void they'd always said lay just under George West, Texas. And he fell and fell like a baby in darkness. Straining to see, seeing nothing. Unsure whether he'd found her or not. Unsure whether he was alive or dead. Unsure what mattered, if anything. Cracks of the bullwhip echoing in the cavernous vault and Satan crying like a carnival barker, Step right up, folks, and see the Jesus Lookalike! Hair like the Prophet Himself! In all His humble glory! He bleeds from real nail wounds! Come forward, come forward!

The next thing Ansel knew they were nudging him awake. Here's a warm towel for you, sir.

Still dazed, he took it and wiped his face. It smelled of violets.

Between the low clouds, Europe was appearing, flat and green.

See that port there? the stewardess said. That's Calais. Calais, France. We'll be in Paris in twenty minutes. Is it your first time?

Second.

Well, you enjoy yourself. And thanks for flying with us.

Father's story ran on, but Marc made no move to stop him. Whatever for? He'd never known him capable of such amusing clarity. Every detail rang true. It may have been the booze, but so what? He wanted it to go on and on. His concentration being only rippled now and then by a fear of Mother emerging from her stuffy lair to find them. Every creak of the floor turned Marc's head toward the hall door from which she would emerge. But hour after hour had gone by with no sign of her, and at last, Marc and his father went out into the cool garden at dark to finish their little talk on the bench under the blue cedar. Every star was out, and for the first time in his life, Marc somehow felt like he had a true father. If only this broken drunk man rambling on about an impossible voyage in impossible country chasing an impossible man. Father and son. For the first time there was a measure of complicity between them. Marc watched the stars pouring by as he spun the tale, thinking of Jean-Jean, listening.

Ansel turned around on the bench to face the view, then took hold of my shoulders and turned them so I would do like him, have a look at the span separating us from shore, the distant line of palms on the far side.

Try focusing on the view. You'll feel much better.

I tried hard to obey.

There were countless whitecaps now, churning the water gray. There were no boats in sight. The wind droned like a bomber.

Lots of fish get back in here, he said louder. We like to bait up with live shrimp, sit back, sip rum and play the Quiet Game. Then he folded his hands behind his head, tilted back sharply.

I felt irritated over the delays, sidetrips, dead ends, circles.

Look, I said sharply. I'm supposed to —

I stopped just short. What, take him back to Paris? Yes. That was my mission, and his every move was only an attempt to throw me off track again. Still, I firmly concluded, no sense being nasty about it. We were, after all, relaxed and calm, weren't we? It was time to lie.

I'm supposed to . . . *ask* you to come back home.

It didn't ring true, though, and he knew it.

So you've asked, he said. Now don't wreck the party. No one's going anywhere for a while, bud. So I say, *calmate*, take it easy, let go.

He put his hands flat to his ears and made as if taking off his head and releasing it skyward like a balloon. Above all, he said, don't underestimate your fly bite and its potential for —

Will you come back to Paris with me or not? I shouted. I need an answer now!

There you go. Relax, will you? Your ten-thousand-kilometer marathon is over. Ever been in a hurricane? The last thing you do is to get stressed up for it. Besides, you never really gave a damn if I came back with you. You only wanted me out of the house for good but were too afraid to say so to my daughter. And that's the only reason you are here right now.

I don't agree.

Fact is, you're only too happy to be on the road, gallivanting about, rubbernecking to your heart's desire. I'd wager you're having the time of your life. Am I right?

I chose not to rise to the bait.

I figure you regret ever marrying her, right?

I jumped up, paced. What's taking this woman so damn long? This is worse than Paris!

Shh. Don't get her dander up, will you?

A wooden shutter began to clap the side of the house, each blow a gunshot.

Damn it! came a cry from inside. Ansel, will you get that thang?

By all means, he answered, rising.

Relax, Henri. This is the safest spot on the island.

I watched him secure the shutter with a loop of twine.

Island? I asked. When did we leave the land?

He studied me from head to toe. Man, you *are* turned around. You don't remember taking the boat?

What boat?

The skiff from shore? The rough ride?

I sure don't remember taking a boat.

Well, forget it, but we did.

I'd had about enough. Of him, of the wind, the wait, the distances, lacunae, mirages, and blurted, Do you enjoy baiting people? Is that what gives you satisfaction in this life? And why can't we get a boat out of here?

Too late, he answered.

Sick of him, sick of the view, sick of it all, I turned back around. My knee caught the tablecloth and sent the hurricane lamp crashing at my feet.

What was *that*? she yelled.

Ansel's reaction was instantaneous. Nothing but this damn wind, dear.

Then he growled at me, Pitch it all overboard and get that other lamp off that other table and put it here like it was all the same. We don't want to blow it. She gets mad and tosses us out in the open, we can kiss ourselves goodbye in say — he checked his pocket watch — about thirteen hours, give or take.

I quickly did as told, finishing as she came through the shell curtain in the doorway.

Deciphering our rigid poses, she put her fists on her hips and took a long hard look at both of us.

I know you two done somethin.

I was showing my son-in-law this fine view you have, Sarah. Ain't they given you any of them restaurant awards yet? Them stars, one, two, three, they stick on your wall? Ain't you got any?

She smiled, said no.

I don't know what came over me, but I decided she was rather comely, despite her advanced middle age and bulk. Even with the beard, her face was kind and soft. And the arms were of the grandmother variety, the kind in which you wished to rest your tired head forever. She wore a man's attire — khaki trousers, a bloomy black blouse of which her bosom made a great tent, purple rubber boots, the ensemble splashed with flour. She had put her hair up in a net, and held her light green order pad limply at her side. Straight out of some perfect past, the image calmed me.

Then she asked, Where's my lamp?

There was a little accident, Ansel said.

You broke one of my lamps from Flada!

I'll get you a new one in no time, Sarah. Henri's sorry. I'm sorry. We're all sorry, so — he broke into song — Don't worry . . .

Be happy, she finished the long-since-unpopular lyric, atonally.

Sing it, Ansel urged. From the top! Don't worry . . .

Be happy, she said, refusing to sing. Hell, you guys broke one of my lamps from Flada. Do you know what kinda bad-ass luck that gonna bring on us?

But it happened at E minus thirteen, Ansel said.

I looked at him.

So? said Sarah. Make your point.

Break something precious in the thirteenth hour before a hurricane, and, well, you'll get a bit of anti-Joycean spin.

What? she yelled. Come again? The End?

Joyce hated thirteen. This fortunate accident just might save us. Do you follow?

Sarah looked around, trying to plumb his words.

You lost me, she admitted. You never told me about Joyce.

Ansel rushed to fill the fragile vacuum. Are those chicken wings cookin in there? They smell like ten million dollars!

She perked up at the compliment. Best wings around. Two orders?

You bet, Ansel said. And what about happy hour?

My, did I forget that again?

She raised the order pad to her tiny blue eyes and worked a stub of pencil, lip-synching as she went. Two wings, two rums . . .

Gonna blow? I asked, trying to make conversation.

Blow? she bellowed. Boy, you dunno what blow means! This place sure gonna go under. No mercy. Excuse my language, but da bitch is bad. Headed up here from Nickyragway. Gonna be very, very dark tonight.

We'll button things down, bring in the tables, stick the pig, Ansel offered.

She blushed. If you don't mind.

Mind, us? Hell, you need the company. We're not the kind to leave a woman stranded.

I think she said, Stop that talk, you're making me horny. Anyway, they exchanged a knowing smile.

Then she said to me, Henri Du? What a name. I like it, though.

She gave me a pat on the shoulder. It felt like I'd been hit with a board.

Du what? she asked.

I'm an engineer.

No, I mean your name. It don't just stop at Du, do it? That make no sense.

Her words were like commands. I could hear her pipes wheezing as she leaned over the table for an answer.

I said anything. Du Vent.

Of the wind, that means! she exulted. I do speak some Frainche you know.

I nodded nervously as she straightened up again and sighed.

Well here goes everything, she announced. *Bientôt, bientôt.*

Yes, I said, urgently adding, *Oui.*

She grinned broadly at both of us, apparently satisfied with our behavior for the moment.

But I'll run get your rum! You boys must be ready to throttle me!

We said of course not.

Well, I'll be right back! she screeched, withdrawing to her kitchen.

Ansel said, And another thing. Eat everything on your plate. Got it?

Got it.

Lifting a licked finger to the wind, he proclaimed, So far so good, but don't bet on survival, just get drunk. Agreed? I mean drunk.

His wish, my command. I scratched my bite.

ℰ

This morning he was clipping a hedge in the sun, his daily scrawlings all done in the early dawn, when I heard him mumble, Be a Mexican. He will sometimes do this, come up with a little phrase, try to live by it. He was thinking how he'd like nothing more than to abandon everything, go and be a humble gardener on an estate in Mexico, high in the mountains. To be an old man there, worry-free. Clipping his master's lime trees into great birds and dogs and bulls by the side of the pool. Wearing white cotton pants, no shirt, a straw hat. Living alone in a hut in a corner of the property with a kerosene stove to cook on and a gray wool blanket to wrap himself in on cold nights. Thinking nothing, owing nothing, existing until death in only the simplest terms. Be a Mexican: This is what he meant. By tomorrow, though, the picture will have faded, and the month of vacation shortened another day and night. It is almost necessary to feel sorry for him, no? There is nothing worse, more sniveling, than a struggling writer.

ℰ

It seemed that everyone had someone to greet them on the dock at Calais, despite the ungodly hour of the morning. There was noisy bustling at the bottom of the gangway as the wealthy families disembarked, maids and butlers and baggage in tow, into the open arms of long-lost relatives who crowed greetings in a dozen languages. The cream of America had landed. Sellers of pastries and fruit and wine cried their wares. A band stumbled through Yankee Doodle.

As things calmed, I came ashore, weak and unsure, among the stragglers. My legs, ruined from my having lain stateside all those grim days, were barely able to support my body, much less my two bags. Still, I was elated. Here was Europe. *Terre ferme* at last.

Don't ask me how, but I felt a surge of pride. I seemed to have accomplished so much in the way of instructing myself since leaving dingy old George West, Texas.

Taking the train? he asked.

It was Teddy, the book boy. I decided not to respond. The mission at hand was to get to the train station.

You'll be lost in Paris, I tell you this, he said.

Against all of my better judgment, I halted, set down my things. Look, I don't want any further association with you whatsoever. Am I clear?

Ain't we shined our vocabulary, *monsieur*! What, having a little surge of guilt? Asking yourself whether you might have liked it?

I waved for him to pipe down. This only provoked a burst of laughter. I quickly surmised that he'd gotten as drunk as a sailor and that I wasn't about to get off the hook without a struggle.

A couple of passersby, sooty older men who might have been working the engines all the way from New York, slowed to watch, pulling their pipes.

But you need me, Teddy insisted, narrowing the space between us.

Back off, I said. I can get the police.

Get them then, he whined. I want to hear your French.

Petit con, I said. I knew that at least. I said it twice.

He tried to slap me, but I raised my arm to block the blow. The contact hurt him much more than me, and he began to squeal foul.

Ho there, said one of the dirty men. What are you boys doing?

Nothing, sir, I said.

Teddy straightened and said, My brother has told me he intends to abandon me right here at the outset of our Continental voyage! And I have no money, nowhere to go! I don't speak a word of French, either.

Is that so? the sailor asked.

He's not my brother.

But you *do* sort of look alike, the other sailor said. You *could* be brothers. Nice brothers. Where you from?

George West, Texas, declared Teddy.

George West? Did you say George West? sang the first sailor. Why we're from George West, too! Now ain't that something! Jesus, the world is getting downright tiny, ain't it? I'll be damned.

I started away, disgusted with the lot of them.

You boys going to Paris, then?

Sure are, said Teddy. You guys?

We were thinking about a little cancan, said the second.

Hey, where are you going, Ansel? Teddy shouted. Look, guys, he's getting away!

Ho there! one of the sailors hollered. You can't drop your brother like this!

I stopped, having no choice, and let them catch up.

The first seaman threw a branch of an arm over my shoulder. Gonna have us some fun in Paree, yes sir. The city of ladies. Ain't had me a Paree lady in five long years. They all know me, though. I can hear them moaning in exp — expect —

Anticipation, I corrected, relieved to hear his preferences.

That's the word. I knew it. Anyway, they love my stuff. Big-time.

He smelled like garbage.

The other seaman had looped his arm around Teddy's waist and begun whooping and stumbling along with his find. And if the women don't bite, he sang out, well, then, we'll just have . . . chicken!

The remark tickled them greatly, and I confess that it took me several minutes to understand, the laughter redoubling when they saw me get it.

Admittedly, here everything touched bottom.

The air thus cleared, we moved into the heart of the town and soon entered the train station, a cavernous affair of scrolled iron and glass that had me aching for a camera. To my amazement, the main hall was deserted, the ticket windows shut tight and the quays empty. After a cursory tour of the area, the four of us dropped onto a bench to wait.

Now this is what you might call dead, my sailor said.

I'd prefer a lime-tree avenue anyday, said Teddy, leaning out to catch my reaction. Right, Ansel?

I ignored him. Further, I vowed that once the ticket window reopened I would reserve a first-class seat for myself, a luxury that I could not afford but that surely would spare me untold trouble. There our paths would part.

Presently, as if the Almighty were looking down, a tall old woman with a face the color of a beet appeared through a service door and began to mop a patch of floor. Her entry put hands back where they belonged.

When's the next train for Paree, Mom? asked Teddy's sailor.

She responded in French.

Speak American, honey.

She said ten-thirty, I told him.

Teddy let out a long whistle. *Monsieur parle Français comme un pro, n'est-ce pas vrai?* I knew you were cheating on the boat! Now I know why I couldn't get you into Tolstoy, you were learning French the whole time! *Quel faux jeton.*

Ta gueule, I spat back.

Ten-thirty, the sailor repeated. Why, that's four more hours!

I want some food, some real food, my man said. Pork sausage with mustard, biscuits and white gravy, grits and oatmeal and hominy, fried eggs and hot sauce, pancakes and maple syrup, regular bacon, then Canadian bacon, toast and honey and some apple pie and some peach pie and some blueberry pie and a cherry soda pop and an orange one, too.

The whole voyage backed up in my throat. Managing only to stumble a step or two away before it was too late, I remember seeing the cleaning woman give me a *bras d'honneur*, which I fully deserved.

Home sweet home seemed a dark universe away.

Jean-Jean gone, said Samira. Jean-Jean gone.

The bird has flown, said Vik.

See you, my brother, said Marc.

Stunned, they sniffled and stared at the scene below.

But the cops would be there any second and haul them all away, Marc thought. There would be an investigation. Perhaps murder charges.

Maybe we should go, he said.

The girls' crying redoubled.

Before the police arrive, he added.

Samira wailed on, but Vik straightened up, dried her eyes and said, They catch me and I'm in the slammer until menopause. Let's get down from here.

They had to drag Samira away. Having her arms pulled and her hair yanked got her going about Morocco again, about how they abused you when they arrested you, kicked you, fondled you, raped you. A scream punctuated each sentence as they hauled her along, so that finally Marc had to slap her a couple of times. Only to have her say, in the fiercest terms, Yes! That's it! That's their style! Go for it! Hit me!

Then Vik reached back and let her have it. Samira shut up and, making a light cooing sound, went along quietly to the bottom of the stairs.

Feigning a devout pace, they proceeded slowly through the church and out into the light. Marc then quickly steered them into a shady side street where a quiet bar beckoned.

Drink, anyone? he asked.

If you're buying, said Vik.

Samira smiled, as if she'd just left her *beau*'s loving arms.

They took a table in the back where it was steamy and secluded and began the long wait for a waiter.

Down the street, Jean-Jean was dead. Marc would have to call Father and Mother, now divorced, not speaking, both as distant as the moon from their surviving boy, who was getting dead drunk with a prole bitch from Iceland and an Arab whore, perhaps in bed with the two of them, humping their eyes out, rubbing away the image of Jean-Jean leaping out into the purple night with a whoop.

Marc looked over his two charges and decided, yes, they would both need it. If only to try and wipe up the mess a bit. If only to make it disappear a moment. Even if it was impossible, even if it made no sense. Jean-Jean was dead.

Vous commandez ou quoi?

A waiter, finally.

Qu'est-ce que vous avez? Vous êtes drogués, non?

Champagne, Marc said.

Ah bon! C'est cher, mon gars.

Marc flashed credit cards.

The waiter gave a nasty grin and shuffled off to fetch the bottle.

Champagne, huh, said Vik. Trying to get us drunk?

Yeah, trying to get our *clothes off*, Marc Du? said Samira.

That's the picture, Marc answered. And I see a hotel room with the three of us in it. Well?

Vik waited a moment, then gave a big smile. I'm in. What the hell. But it better be a *nice* hotel. Giant bed, giant bathtub, everything. Otherwise, no go.

Marc assured her it would be tops.

A few silent minutes passed, then Samira gave a tired nod to the proposition.

Hardly what we'd go do after a funeral in Morocco, she said. But then . . .

It'll be the funeral itself, let's say, Marc said. Jean-Jean would have loved it.

They looked at him as though he were the craziest person alive. Then they laughed and began to feel much better.

And this is your room, said Frances, easing Ansel in from the hall. And your bed.

It was a fine, high-built antique piece, a ship on thick blue carpet.

And that is the door to your very own toilet. We had it put in special. Handholds and all.

Frances, are you happy? he asked.

She went and opened the window shutter. Here is the best part, she said. Have you ever seen a view like this?

All Paris lay there, Eiffel's tower poking up grandly, buildings glowing pale yellow on the shore of the park. From the back of the picture came a helicopter that banked and puttered and settled onto an office tower. Colored kites rode over the trees.

Le bois, she said. You're going to be all right here, Daddy, I promise. We're going to take care of you. Tomorrow I'll take you to the Shakespeare Garden to see the flowers. They're wonderful. Do you want to do that? We have so much to do. You haven't seen anything yet!

You didn't answer my question.

What, Daddy?

My question.

He put a hand on her shoulder.

She pretended to be surprised, even flattered, and smiled. Of course I am happy.

She had cut her auburn hair, chopped it short and dyed it white. She had made herself thin, to please the man she had chosen to marry. She had made herself uglier the harder she tried to satisfy him.

Giving the view a last glance, she closed the shutter again.

You could leave it open, he said.

But it was as if she hadn't heard him, and she drew shut the curtains.

Soup tonight, she said. We eat only soup at night. Or maybe a salad. But that's all. I hope that's O.K.

Fine.

You know I hope we will be together from now on, Daddy. It is the right thing. Do you want to take a nap now?

I'll see.

You do like the room, don't you?

Yes, I do.

Frances, why in the hell are there no more ice cubes in these trays! Didn't I tell you to keep these damn trays filled up! What in hell's name are you doing back there? I'm hungry!

The master's soup, Ansel said.

Her face relaxed, softened to neutral. Yes, and later we will watch some TV. That's what we do sometimes. I mean, we don't often get out. But we'll translate for you. A little TV and then we'll go to bed. You don't have to, though. Isn't that funny, I don't even know if you like to go to bed early or not. Silly me.

Ansel stared at her, saw the casket plunging into the cut in the red earth, remembered turning his face and little Marc's face away, both of them spotted with barbecue sauce, so they would see something else at that instant, anything else, and it was a sun devil churning in a field miles away.

Writing his one-month book, in bits and pieces strung out all over creation, he resembles a man who fishes with several lines at the same time, straining to maximize the catch. All day long under the sun, his head in a green billcap, eyes darting from one dead cork to another, nothing biting. His wife, the newborn in her arms, and the older boy are parked nearby on lawn chairs. No one says a word. Until it is dusk, and then dark, hardly breathing, ears tensed to hear the bells jingle on the rods. Marc has drowned in the thought that nothing will strike, that the sun will take forever to rise again . . . Upon another day of silent waiting for one of the lines to sing out, for one of the rods to double over, for the vacation to end. For the other madness, the urban beat, to begin again. Fishing, writing . . . You bait a hook and drop it in. Maybe something will happen. Maybe nothing.

8

*L*OOK AT HIM TONIGHT. At his desk, stunned, thoughts twisted into hard knots. Another of the thirty-one days already gone forever. The desire to finish the book within the allotted time as I did all those years ago burning inside him so that he can think of nothing else but ugly green flames being born of fear. Now that he thinks the story is being taken away from him, being run into the ground by me. To be trundled off in some wild direction and left unfinished. Now that he thinks there is nothing he can do to make me stand aside, keep quiet. Me, in my lunar island paradise that he could no more knock out of the sky than he could make time roll backwards. For it's too late now, too late in the month to redo it all. The one-shot moon shot either hits its target or misses.

He wants to yell it out. One of his characters is stealing his book! But who would believe him? One of his characters cluttered up his book with his own junky tales of yore? And he let him get away with it? *You're working far too hard, dear.*

But it is worth the battle, he is sure! Worth it to try and make his book something bigger than its story. Once again out of the flames an answer rises brighter than the quetzalcoatl: Dive like the eagle, strike like the snake, and take back his damn book. Take Ansel's old hands off it. The plain workingman taking a drink out of a rubber hose. The man who happened to look like his Grandfather Ansel who disappeared in Mexico all those years ago. Write the book in words that are Marc's alone, Marc's to hold. Keep the old man's bones at bay.

But I, Ansel Gifford, seeing him smile at the thought that perhaps he has found a way to keep on, simply grin. I grin a wide crazy grin, for I have him right where I want him. Dropping through space, unattached, scared to death, reaching out for anything, anything at all. Only there is nothing there and never was. For how can he take back something that was never his?

What did he do today? Screamed at the paper that would only fill with my words, my thoughts, my wishes. High in the tiny room at the top of the stairs where he has now taken refuge to write. Or to think he is writing, dictation being the more accurate word. The big yell came midafternoon, and everyone in the house looked up at the ceiling. Whatever could it be? Was there a dangerous animal up there? Children were snatched up and held. Old people shook their heads, knowing better. And the mother of his children merely gasped, unable to fathom why she had ever married such a man, how she had ever made such a fantastically ignorant decision. And Mother, herself? She had merely groaned in bed, angry that she had been disturbed once again, and fallen back to sleep clutching the clay death mask to dream of Mexico and Daddy and how he disappeared down there . . .

On into the night he will sit undoing knots and knots within knots. I only wonder why he has not thought of hanging himself with his belt, or of doing a Jean-Jean. It's high enough. Up there, in the dead hours when the pages insult, when failure roars up from the dark below, a half-rotten thing that happens to look like me.

But no such luck. For ultimately he believes, deep down, that he can succeed at this business. Even though he has no more idea of what it requires of him than if he'd suddenly elected to trek to Mars. That will, this drive, lying deep in his disordered genes, is but a last, slim handhold, a hairline crack in the cliff. Yes, I grin wildly. Waiting for him to plunge.

The wait became tedious as the fly bite took hold. I remembered I had a wife and children back home whom I'd treated like trash all these years. I remembered I had a mission to fulfill here that, even if accomplished, would never quite redeem me in my family's eyes.

113

I remembered how I had so often proceeded with my manly instincts and drives despite my wife's strongest objections. I remembered kicking over a hundred barbecue pits because the charcoal had refused to obey me and remain warm enough long enough to cook the shish kebabs the way I liked them cooked. I remembered being constantly angry and slinging the dregs of countless toddies onto the little dead yard in front of the neighbors. I remembered how I had so often proceeded with my manly instincts and drives despite our young maid's strongest objections. I remembered sitting in church pews listening to the soft scratch of hose as women crossed and recrossed their legs and the pastor went on about burning forever in Hell if you didn't stop thinking about the flesh. I even remembered the first of many times my manly instincts drove me to place my hands, in the way a woman will, on another man.

The great mix of memories churned on, some of it genuinely mine, some of it belonging to some other man, an anonymous American I surmised, some white trash American, but not me, a simple Frenchman whose only real crime was having been in a bad mood all his life. Was all this some cosmic punishment, then? Desperate, I scratched my open bite.

Put that out! Ansel shouted. Trying to give me cancer?

To my surprise, I was smoking a cigarette. I didn't recall lighting up, but evidently the rush of nicotine had been tremendous, for my hands were jerking this way and that like fish out of water.

Ansel waved to clear the air, even though the cloud of smoke had long since been ripped away.

You'll die of that crap, Henri Du. Not of something dramatic, but of that.

I felt bold. I'll do what I want, I said.

Want to know how it's going to go?

Not really.

One morning you'll wake up and won't be able to catch your breath. They'll tell you its the Big E. Then you'll go on the oxygen bottle. Have to have it with you all the time. Even to go pee you'll have to take the damn bottle on its flimsy stand. How's that sound? Moreover, why do I sound like I care when I don't? Forget I said a word.

I steadied my hands enough to take another long drag, enjoying it immensely. Then I spewed it to the wind, took another.

You've got that bug-bite look in your eyes, he said.

So?

Pretty powerful, huh. You're trying to hide what it's telling you. Rough, huh?

Manageable.

It's because you have a buoy in the storm, this porch, this house, the food, the company. Otherwise you'd be spilling your guts like bad clam soup.

I doubt that.

No you don't. You know I'm right. And you also know that even if you do have a buoy for the moment, maybe later on you won't. And the bug bite won't be over then, no sir. It lasts days. So you'll spill your ugly guts, I know it. Beg forgiveness, say you're sorry, gush about how you should have loved everybody, whatever. Sooner or later.

I didn't want to hear it. Same old Ansel, I said.

Come to think of it, maybe I'd better go ahead and let you in on a little information and then we can just sit here and try to enjoy ourselves while we still can. What say?

I shrugged, indifferent.

He got up, went to the railing, lifted his crabstick and took aim at the storm with it, then spat, the wind firing the glob like a bullet.

They say I died during that brain operation, not once but several times, he began. I don't know, maybe it's true, anyway I don't remember anything special about it, other than the pain. But just knowing that — if it was true — had sort of dogged me. Did it mean I had some special deal? Did it mean I'd been rewired somehow to live on and on? And it dogged me right up to the day I saw a fortuneteller in Patzquaro who'd left her business card in my mailbox at the hotel. I might not have even seen the card had it not been for Little Ricky, the parrot. Well, there I was walking through the lobby minding my own business and getting ready to turn in after a hot afternoon at the bullfights. There'd been plenty of gore and I had got myself sunburned real bad in the cheap seats. I was about to attempt to put my foot on the first step up the stairs to my room when somebody said, plain as day and in real good English, Hey stupid. I halted, every cell of my being jarred by what clearly was the voice of my long-dead father. There was only one light on in the lobby, a 10-watt in a ripped paper lamp. The rest of the place was cold stone dead, safely lost in another, darker age, an ambience that I've always preferred as a means of catharsis.

You're drifting, I said.

No, Ansel corrected. I never drift. You stopped following.

We looked toward the kitchen window, whose curtains had blown free, giving a clear view inside. Her back to us, Sarah worked over a great iron stove, the right hand seizing a raw wing, throwing it over her head to the left hand, the left hand dipping it into milk and tossing it back to the right, the right rolling it in a mound of flour and then nestling it among the others in the frying pan. To one side a black and white TV with a loose horizontal hold showed a man giving a speech.

I recognized the soft, red mug, the evil lighting from beneath. It was a rerun of one of the very first men of peace giving another of his little speeches. He looked drunk and on the verge of falling asleep.

Not him again, I complained.

Watch your lip, Ansel hissed. She loves him.

Why?

Why not? Shut up about it.

The way the wind was blowing we couldn't hear a word the peace man was saying. Not that either of us cared. We knew what it was. His One Little Idea again. How, as regards human coupling, neither partner should ever again have the right to just say no to the other. No more, no less. He'd preached it for years. Spurring more arguments among human beings than at any time in their history, experts said.

Now and then, Sarah nodded yes at the screen, as if he were speaking directly to her, then gave a stomp that shook the house or stabbed her turning fork in the air in enthusiastic agreement with some point or other while the wings fried and the greasy steam billowed.

Going to be a bit, Ansel said. So we might as well relax and let her have her little daily fling with this joker. I wonder what she'll do when he's tossed off the air?

What do I care?

Shh. You looking for a backlash, son? So as I was saying, There in the good old gloom of the hotel lobby, the voice of my dad again said, Hey stupid. Only this time it added, Come here.

Get on with it, I said, trying to get a whiff of that fried chicken. I could eat anything, raw, cooked, whatever. So long as it could be chewed and swallowed.

Easy, boy, he said. So. So the voice said, Hey stupid, come here. And I said, Father? And it said, Pretty parrot, pretty parrot. I felt pretty dumb.

I can see that.

Someone had brought Little Ricky's cage in from the porch for the night. Little Ricky, you son of a bitch, I shouted, you had me going there, goddamn it. Pretty parrot, pretty parrot, he said. I went over and yanked off his cover. But he wasn't there. The cage door was shut tight, but he was gone. I looked around the lobby. But he wasn't in the dead plants, not under a chair, not behind the curtains, nowhere. Little Ricky! I called. *El maricón*, I added, knowing he would squawk. To no avail. No bird.

Y'all want white gravy, too? came the holler.

Sure thing! Bring it on! Ansel said. So there I was, thinking Ansel, Ansel baby, you are losing it. Probably all that afternoon sun I'd got. And all that bright blood. A drunk young gringo had gone out of his mind and climbed down into the ring and got himself gored. And it was the first bull of the afternoon, too, which meant you could kiss the rest of the *corrida* goodbye, quality-wise. The idiot got dragged around the ring I don't know how long while the women screamed and the men booed. Never seen anything quite like it, the boy, hooked clean through, being yanked around like that, on and on, guts flying this way and that like some sack of trash being spilled out, you know, when the dogs come at dawn and claw into it and drag it all out and all, you know.

Why didn't you leave?

I had sympathized with the bull, to tell you the truth. I also wanted to see how long the bastard would last after having killed a human being. Turns out it was nothing. Soon as they got the

American's carcass out of there, the matador walked up to that bull and jammed home the sword. The bull went to its knees, fell sideways and that was it. The crowd went crazy and howled every curse in the book. It was a bad afternoon all around.

For some reason, I had the strong sensation of remembering the story he was telling even before he told it. As if I were hearing it being played back on a tired tape recorder. I shook my head, but it only made me dizzy.

You with me? Ansel asked.

I think so.

So, my eye picked up a faint glow in my mailbox behind the check-in desk. It was a card. I took it out, rubbed a window in the dusty surface. I have piss-poor Mexican, but I could make out that it was *señora* so-and-so in the *calle* such-and-such and that she was a reader of the *estrellas*. Normally I would have tossed such a thing in the trash. But I was curious. None of the other boxes had a card. I'd been singled out, it seemed, or was simply the last person to pick up his mail. I wondered about it, and wondered all the way up the stairs, down the creaky hall and into my room. Still holding the thing, I went out on the balcony. Immediately, you came to mind, blasting your trumpet, drinking, slapping Frances around, her wailing, your children wailing, everyone wailing on account of your crap.

The wind rose a bit. Sarah turned the wings. The grease roared.

Thinking of you then, however, was providential. I had had of late my moments of weakness, times when I would work on a good bottle of tequila to drown the insane urge to return to you and your apartment in Paris. But now, now every thought of you steeled my nerves, bade me to plug ahead, all eyes forward, never look back. I knew with certainty that no matter how much I felt like a stranger in the world, any place was better than your Parisian flytrap. Any place at all. I thought of man's eternal dream of isolation in a paradise. I thought of long curving beaches, the din of the surf.

The wind seemed to redouble all at once, so that it became an exercise not only to keep the tablecloth in place but the table itself. With each gust, each hike in the speed of nature's gargantuan fan, the house gave a stomach-tightening cry like that of a lost child. Being well built, though, it responded by leaning back into the wind, defying it. Knee-high waves flowed across the straits carrying household garbage.

Does this storm have an official name? I asked.

Hell, who knows? Folks down here like to name storms themselves. You want us to call it Frances? Or something with more mystery, more allure . . . Ask Sarah about the '69 blow sometime.

The '69 blow?

Yeah, the one they called Two-Way Tina. A whopper! Everyone died except Sarah. We're talking about one of the most astounding feats since the travails of Gilgamesh!

She leaned out the window. Stop trying to flatter me, Ansel!

He waved at her and they exchanged a happy smile.

Food be ready soon, dears! Hold your hat if you've still got one!

Where's that rum? Ansel asked.

Oh yeah! How I keep forgetting! Comin right up!

So where was I?

You were saying anyplace was better than my Parisian flytrap, I said.

Right. So I said to myself, No, I will remain free of all of you. I can do anything. Go to the beach. Live with a diseased whore. Cut off my arm. Cart goods on my head in Nepal. Trim bushes into the forms of birds in Bogotá. Start a revolt in China. Or even see a fortuneteller. Why the hell not? I looked out across the *zocalo* and saw a man sitting out on a balcony of the hotel opposite. I said to myself, That could be Henri Du, ruminating, feeling sorry for himself, scratching his nuts and counting time.

I believe it was, I said.

Perhaps. Perhaps not. So, I put the card in my pocket, peered aloft for the hell of it to see if I could spy Canis Minor, could not, and went to bed. My upstairs neighbor, a youth by the name of Ché Ché, always seemed to know my needs and that night gently plucked Moon River. In no time I was sleeping the sleep they sleep in Diez Dormido, if you've been there. I dreamed of Violetta, of all the roads and lines that led me to her, the ones we later shared and traveled, the ones that tore us apart. I was not sad and there was no pain. My mind was whole again.

When I woke the room was full of light. Someone had left a bouquet of violets on the nightstand. I lay there, breathing their sweetness, having no idea who had sent them or why, and not caring, seeing no need to cut clear the veils. I lay there an hour until the room grew warm and the sheets began to stick to my skin. I wished the maid would open the door and come to me. I wished all the beautiful young maids would open the door and come in.

On that point, we were in utter agreement. It made me even dizzier, though, and I tried to banish the image of smooth brown hips and thighs.

Two-minute warning! Sarah called. They're drainin now and gravy's abubblin!

Whoa! Ansel grabbed the new hurricane lamp the instant it tried to sail away into the evening.

Good catch, I said.

He sat down again, across from me this time, abandoning his earlier caution about it being her rightful place, and set the lamp between us.

Get it if it starts to slide again, he said. Your turn.

I tried to concentrate on the lamp.

So the next day I was in the back room of the fortuneteller's house, a house sort of like this one, perched on a hill far out of town. There were maybe a dozen cats lying around on crates and barrels and hardly any light. We sat facing each other, like us here. She asked no questions, but motioned for me to put my hands on the table. Like this. Then she put her hands out on the table, too.

I went along with him, stuck my hands out.

You know, I don't think I ever looked her in the face, he went on. It didn't seem right to do so. I was edgy. You never know what might happen in a place like that. All I recall is that she smelled of violets. I thought of the bouquet I'd received that morning, and then, as if reading my mind, she said, in plain English, Yes, you can thank me. I thanked her and then she moved her hands until the tips of our fingers touched.

I moved my hands, he moved his, the tips touched.

It was like fire, he said. I went erect, I mean rock hard. But she sniffed the air and frowned and, just like that, my member sagged.

A cat brushed my leg, back and forth.

My powers are wide, she told me, for a price.

I said a hundred pesos.

Four.

Two-fifty.

Three-fifty.

Two-seventy-five.

Three-twenty-five and that's final.

I thought, What the hell is three hundred twenty-five pesos anyway? O.K.

No credit cards.

I got out my wad of bills, counted off the amount. She tucked them deep in the folds of her many robes.

The world is wide, she said, moving a hand in a circle over an unlighted lamp between us. The incantation begun, she bent her head toward its flue, her dark beads swinging out and tinkling against the glass and setting off a strange and pleasant music. I relaxed.

She asked, Is it not true that your mind is full of tiny clips?

From the surgery, yes. How did you know?

Shh, she ordered, putting her hands atop mine, sinking deeper into thought, leaving me hanging.

Ansel put his hands on mine. It was all I could do not to jerk free.

He said, No one had known that the surgeons had had to clip off hundreds of vessels up there to keep me from bleeding to death, that they had had to leave them there when they put my skull back together — no one, that is, except a couple of my domino buddies and Violetta. I felt I was smothering. I wanted nothing more than to run away as fast as my legs would carry me. I began to tremble.

Yes, she intoned, and you died several times, correct?

Thinking I understood her meaning, I nodded. It *had* felt that way. Exactly that way.

You think you have died more than once and thus have special powers, correct? she asked again.

Maybe, I said.

Don't lie to me.

I'm not lying. I mean I don't think I'm lying. Am I?

Ansel, you have never lied to me, so don't start now!

It was Violetta's voice.

Darling! I cried out. Is that you?

Don't look up! she yelled. Do not look at me and my dead face, Ansel.

I won't, I won't. Is it you?

It is me. And I have things to tell you. So many things.

What?

Change the wide foul world for me, Ansel. Change it for good.

What do you mean?

Change the whole wide world for me, Ansel. Be a Man of Peace. Take charge. Fix everything and I will be back. Will you do it for me? For your dear beloved?

Tell me how!

Will you do it for me?

I had no idea what she meant, but I promised I would.

Be easy now, Ansel Gifford. It was the fortuneteller's voice.

At that instant, the cat bit my leg, hard, and I shrieked. But the seer's hands pinned mine fast and I couldn't move.

Ansel pinned my hands.

The cat began to lick the wound, he said, wincing.

I swear I felt it licking my fly bite, too. Like sandpaper, tearing it. Opening it wider, going for the blood.

But too bad you will die first, gringo, and for good, the woman announced. Too bad you will croak—for real—before you can make her dream come true! Ha!

Then she let me go.

I pulled free. Ansel, you're spooking me, I said to him. Stop now.

Scared, are you? he said. Not half as scared as I was, fool. There I was, slumped on my chair, out of breath. I tried to check the bite but the cat refused to budge. What do you mean, too bad I will die first? I asked her.

My powers are wide, for a price.

She wouldn't budge from four hundred. Again we put our hands out.

This time I refused to play the part and crossed my arms. Get on with it, old man.

Ansel snorted at me, went on. No, she began, there is nothing special about you. You'll die but once like everybody else.

When? How?

I see a house, she said, breaking up in the sea. Consider yourself a goner this time around. No getting out of it. *Bientôt* is the magic word. No escape. You'll go under in a big storm one night soon. Nobody will remember you. Nobody will care. *Ciao. Sueña la trompeta.* It's worse than you think. For you will break your promise to your long dead love. Like a dry stick.

There was a great snap in the air.

I gave the cat a desperate kick, sending it into a pile of rags where it crouched and snarled at me like a dog, ready to pounce again.

So I saw, she said. You may go now.

Crazed, I bolted out the back door, slid down a trash chute into a ravine, and ran blindly until I could run no more and collapsed on a hard creek bed. After all the many years of impossible efforts I had made, it would come to this. A mere drowning, breaking all promises to my loved one. And I am a good swimmer!

Jesus, that's awful, I said, taken up by the whole thing.

Here come da wings! It sounded like the wedding jingle. Sarah was pounding toward us, three steaming plates lined up on one arm, a full bottle of brown rum and three glasses hooked on the fingers of the other hand. Anybody don't like these vittles be plain crazy!

Right! shouted Ansel, casting aside his tale, clearing out of her place at the table and taking up a spot next to me. Here we go!

Light the candle, Henri Du, Sarah ordered. I like a candle burning on the table when I eat.

It would take ten thousand matches, I thought, and looked hard at her.

What're you waitin on, son?

In this wind?

What wind? This breeze? You ain't seen nothing, boy. Now light that lamp so we can chow down.

Woozy, in need of a year's sleep, I dug for matches.

I was ill again several times that day, especially after I learned that all first-class seats on the Paris run had been reserved far in advance. Worse, a thousand images of home crowded my mind as the second-class car cut through the countryside past fields of sunflowers and alfalfa and beets where I'd known cotton and sugarcane and corn, lively villages at every turn in paved roads where I'd known only dead main streets, dead five-and-dimes, dead granite courthouses. Back there I would ride a squeaking bike in straight lines down dry red roads and dry black roads for miles and miles, hand high to block the sun. Here we hugged lush hills, limestone cliffs, shaded banks of deep brown rivers, squealed past gray farmhouses aproned with mud, hurtled through thick woods.

I said nothing to my unwanted companions, and they said nothing to me. They kept their distance, too, given my soiled attire and shaky state, preferring seats a few rows away with open windows to gulp for air. Hour after hour, I leaned against the pane, watching France, my head throbbing, wanting nothing more than a drink of cold water, for the train to slow to a crawl and then to a halt so that I could get off, be free of them, clean up and begin my journey anew. Despite the gorgeous scenery, with every bump and sway I grew more depressed.

I strained to turn my thoughts elsewhere but still found them being tugged to the old house. To Father alive and drinking coffee out of a thick mug at the breakfast table. In the light of dawn coming through the window, his handsomely unshaven red face looking smeared with blue mud. To Mother, alive and coming in from the orchard out back, setting a small basket of plums on the counter and smiling over how good they looked. In her cotton nightgown, her hair still pinned up in a black net for the night. Them saying something soft, sharing a thought only they could share. Ma taking up part of the newspaper and fanning with it, slowly, evenly, and having only a glance at it before lifting her head and looking out over the blue-checkered half-curtains at the hearse from Stedman's Funeral Home pulling up to Doc Shattuck's across the street. Already.

He sure didn't take long to check out, did he? she said. Why, it was only Thursday he was here eating supper with us as if the world would go right on forever. What do you think, are we going to the funeral?

Suppose.

I'll have to put a dress on.

Put a dress on. I like a dress.

They say his son is in Europe, can't be contacted, she said.

Could be, a shame.

Yes, a real shame. They're going to bury his daddy today and he don't even know.

Oh, I bet he does, he said.

You think so? she asked.

Night fell early and a conductor came through to light the gas lamps. My comrades were right across the aisle now, eating sandwiches and passing around a bottle of red. Teddy, squeezed from either side, giggled at the drop of a hat. While this appeared to amuse the seaman, now and again one or the other would clap a hand over the boy's mouth.

I dozed to the easy rock of the ride, to the sound of water boiling in the kettle on the big white stove back home, to Father saying to Mother we could go fish this evening after the funeral if you want, to the flare of Ma's face when she smiled, for it meant something between them, go fish, something soft only they could share.

The forecast is for more thunderstorms. Already, the sky has gone from blue to white as high clouds float over. Black ants file in through the doors, disappear under the flooring, resurface in the kitchen. A weak breeze sways the tops of the poplars. Dry thoughts spin in small circles around invisible points.

Flies. Everywhere.

In the night he said to himself, It can end anytime, with a period. But the day returns and everything beckons to live, to grow, as if there were all the time in the world. When there is so little left before it will have to die, done or not done.

While the train rolls on in the night, while the island wind begins to howl, while the old man paces in his new room in the

Paris apartment, while Jeanne rocks the newborn under the nut tree, while his younger, trashier self tries to get two trashy girls into bed, while he studies the sky, the patch he can see through the tiny window in the tower room.

Everything unfinished, unresolved, refusing to thicken and be something other than thin gruel.

Was that thunder? Again?

Birds go dead in the green.

Marc had chucked his dirty clothes into a corner, showered away some of the suicide smells, donned the thick white hotel bathrobe, found the room service number, and ordered Champagne. Vik and Samira took a long bath together, using all the bubble bath, shampoo and soap at hand, singing old Icelandic and Bedouin folk songs at such a professional clip that the young man who delivered the bubbly felt certain he'd stumbled into a room with one of those famous music groups that sometimes tips you a fortune. At last.

Marc quickly set the boy straight, however, giving him nothing and sending him on his way with a cold pat on the shoulder. Then, making sure the bottle and glasses were neatly arranged on the table, and scarfing a handful of the complimentary green olives, Marc lay back on the kingsize bed thinking that the day might not turn out to be so bad after all. There was still the round of phone calls to make, to give each parent the news, but it would have to wait. For the moment, it was still an unspoiled deal between brothers — Jean-Jean had jumped, Marc had not, Jean-Jean had died, Marc would not mourn. And a deal between brothers was sacred.

Marc listened to the girls being loud in the bathroom. A scene entered his mind in which he went ahead and charged in there to do what every man would have done, but he chased it away. This was not that kind of a party. It was simply friends who were going to make very slow love to each other until all the pain, everything, was buried.

Here we are, Vik said, emerging first, naked, doing her manly walk.

Samira came a step later, hands over *touffe*, smiling like a girl at her first dance.

Look, more Champagne! Vik cried. Now we're on the decadent side!

Marc poured for them, then served olives to both.

Boy is very polite when he wants something, Samira observed.

Don't be petty, Vik told her. Just say thanks and eat your olives.

Samira frowned, but then smiled upon seeing the not-so-little trouble that Marc was having keeping the bathrobe shut, the not-so-little problem trying to burst forth.

Snake about to strike, she said. She gave a long hiss.

Vik laughed, too, and Marc sat and crossed his legs and pretended to be in awful pain, and then they all laughed together.

A toast! he shouted. To Jean-Jean, dear brother!

To Jean-Jean! the ladies joined in, both relaxing, their legs opening, their fires beginning to burn.

Marc's heart pounded hard. For it was one of those moments that comes but maybe once in a lifetime. To have before him all the pleasure he could possibly handle for as long as he chose to handle it. Right there, right there before him, begging to be led the one step it would take to get to the very large, very white bed. One step. One step to take with one beautiful woman on one hand and another beautiful woman on the other hand. To the foot of the bed, to the precipice. Then to leap.

The door boomed.

What the hell? Who is it! No maids. *Non, merci*! Marc yelled.

Hotel security, sir.

Probably been too loud for these idiots, Vik said. Just what you'd expect from a *bourgeois* place. These people make me sick.

The pounding grew louder. Open up!

Samira covered her *touffe* again. It's the police. We'll all end up in prison forever.

Shutup, Marc said. Let's ignore them.

What? said Samira. Resist arrest? Why, in Morocco they'd —

Shut the hell up, Vik commanded.

Into the bed! Marc said.

They jumped in. Pulled the sheet up to their chins and waited.

Blows shook the door again, again.

Open up immediately!

This won't work, said Vik.

Let them break the door down first, Marc said, climbing onto Samira, then reaching out and pulling Vik near. Jean-Jean is dead and it's not the cops that're going to —

Get off me! Samira said, shoving him.

Yeah, are you crazy? Vik yelled, giving him a poke where it counted. Go answer the damn door!

There went the day. There went everything.

He crawled to the end of the bed, stood up, went over, and after giving the door a good pounding on the inside, opened up.

What the hell is it!

It was the boy who'd delivered the Champagne. Alone. His face red and tight, about to burst.

What do *you* want?

I thought you might want to know, sir.

Know what? What *is* it?

That I've always hated idiots like you and your punk band floozies. Maybe you'll tip a struggling student next time, O.K.? Long live ancient Basque music! Kiss my ass!

He drew forth a small black pistol, shot Marc point-blank and fled.

The women screamed on the big white bed as Marc fell back into the room, blood splattering the white carpet.

Marc felt no pain, kept thinking, Something has finally happened to me, something completely strange has finally happened. If only a bullet hole in the arm by a music ethnology student.

Then he remembered and turned his head to try and see the ladies, the goddesses on the bed waiting for him, the gorgeous angels. Oh, but they wouldn't get to do it now. The long ugly day was over. The rest of the night was gone.

Hey, Vik, give me a drink.

What did you do to that guy? she demanded. What did you say to him? Look at the mess we're in now!

Something about the tip, love. Oh, but it's all over now.

Guards arrived with revolvers drawn, and the shouting began.

9

SARAH HAD US SHIFT the table near the kitchen window so she could look in and watch TV and where a small harbor from the wind allowed me to get the candle going. When we settled down again, they both said a prayer, likely to different gods, then waited for me to take my turn.

Proudly I said I had no god.

Not yet you don't, Ansel said. How long you think before he sees the light, honey?

Could be five minutes, could be five hours, she replied. But who cares whether he sees the light or not. We have bigger problems on our hands than Henri Du's salvation.

We do, Ansel said. But, first, I propose a toast.

Good idea, I said, filling the glasses with rum. The thought of alcohol was cheering, and the sight of the fried wings, mashed potatoes, white gravy and white bread was intoxicating. I recalled a hundred Sunday spreads back in Texas when I was courting your mother during my university days. I recalled all the watermelon we had for dessert on her back porch. And the clouds of lightning bugs after dark. The summer moon and how it shone on my love's hair. All that and more came racing back.

Ansel lifted his glass. Sarah and I did the same.

Wherever you're going, I'm going your way, he announced. Cheers. *Salut.* Chin chin!

What kind of a toast is that? I asked.

He ignored me, leaned over the table toward Sarah. They kissed

129

four times, in the French provincial style.

I decided to try not to think, just drink. Instantly, a flush of good feeling warmed my cold bones. To everyone's astonishment, I, too, leaned over the table and, grinning broadly, kissed Sarah on the mouth, in the enthusiastic Russian style. Then I turned and kissed Ansel the same way. Despite their curses, we shared a hearty laugh, refilled our glasses and tore into the hot wings.

There are meals and then there are meals. From the outset, this get-together had the feel of a Last Supper. Maybe it was their praying that set off such a useless thought in my head, but as I shoveled down the groceries, as I worked gobs of manna into my long-neglected *ventre*, I began to split at the psychic seams. Fearing the end was near, all the ugly dikes I had built over the years sprang a thousand leaks. Every lie I had ever told, every tale I'd exaggerated to my own ends, every twist I'd made in reality to hurt someone else came howling back into the vacuum of my mind. I thought my head would explode, the dumdum package of the past striking the muskmelon right there at the table.

I was about to start raving when Sarah set her fork in her half-finished plate, downed her rum in one go, then lowered her face and covered her eyes. Where is my Stann? Where is my man Stann?

Now, now, Sarah, said Ansel. Don't start beating yourself up again.

I want my Stann. What year is it, Ansel dear?

Any year you want, baby.

Not '69, O.K.?

She peeked at him to see if it was O.K.

He nodded. It's not '69, honey.

But I can remember it! she shouted, straightening up and wiping her face. Like it was a minute ago, huh. Like a second ago! My man Stann standin right there on the beach with his long-ass hippy hair flyin like a mop in that bad-ass wind and laughin that crazy laugh of his and screamin out how it wasn't nothing, how it was just a little ole wind and no big deal, let's drink, let's make love, hell with the storm! I remember. I remember how he dragged me down to the Moon Bar over there and got me drunker than a whore and dragged me back here and made love with me against my will. I remember my wild man Stann. I remember what a no-good he was, too, how all he did all day was take hippy kids from Flada and Germany and Fraince out in his skiff to the reef and get them all snorkelin all day while he sat and watched. Them kids really liked that crap, too, seeing all that coral and all those fish. And they'd drink rum and smoke up their dope in the boat and then get back in the water and snorkel some more. Maybe the girlies would take their tops off. The boys would stare. And all the while they'd be burnin their white asses to a crisp. While Stann sat there smiling. Once in a while something would get them all spooked there in the water and one of the kids'd scream out how he'd seen a big mother white shark and so Stann would nod and say very calmly now why don't y'all get back in the boat until the shark decides to leave? And then there'd be a tad of panic and in no time everybody'd be in the boat drying off, rolling joints, looking at the water. That's what he did all day. My man Stann.

I yawned and said, Yeah?

That's right! she shouted. And you want to know what else?

I told her I had no idea.

I remember wakin up late that night still drunk from our little outing and peekin through the jalousies and shinin the flashlight and seein waves coming *over* the island. The house was shakin bad, but Stann was gone to this world. I kept tryin to wake him, pulled his hair, hit him, kicked him, nothing worked. It made me *mad*! Here was my house, my pretty little house I done built with my own hands, about to be smashed into tiny bits on account of this sorry hippy rapist. So I dragged him right out here and chucked him overboard. Kerplop, goodbye.

You did what? I said, appalled.

That's right, she said. Over the board. Bye, bye. Swim if you know how. You got a problem with that, Henri Du?

Ansel frowned at me, a caution to steer clear or be hooked in a fight Sarah was sure to win.

No problem at all, ma'am, I told her.

So there we were, the storm apilin in like maybe it was my time to pilot Noah's Ark or somethin, and my flashlight batteries was goin fast, and the jalousies was screechin somethin awful and . . .

Ansel said to me, Don't mind her. She'll be on this tangent a while. Long as we talk quietly, though, it won't bother her. She's

131

really talking to herself, you know. And it can drag on, so . . .

Talk about what?

Well, I was finishing *my* story.

Oh yeah, I said, preferring his. So, there you were on the creek bed below the seer's house, if I recall . . .

I'd passed out from all that fright.

By the way, is this the storm the fortuneteller foresaw? Is this the one?

What do you think? Anyway, when I came to I was in Acapulco.

Huh?

I mean, I didn't right away know I was in Acapulco, but I found out soon enough.

How'd you get there?

I suspect the power-mad seer had something to do with it. But will you just listen?

I had some more rum.

So, what had awakened me was the cool cloth that a young lady was using to soothe the swelling of my cat bite. I'll tell you this, Henri, frankly she was the most beautiful woman in the world after Violetta. They say the *mestizos* will never lose their inferiority complex, but once you have lain in their arms it is as if you have never been held before in your life. When I shook, she stilled me. When the sweat poured forth, she toweled me dry. When my eyes thirsted to see all of her, she disrobed and sat nearby. When the sun hurt my eyes, she gently closed the curtains. When I told her the story of how I had learned that I was going to drown in a storm, she cried silent tears and crossed herself and lighted white candles on the nightstand. When I called out for love in the night, she moved from her pallet and stretched out atop me and cooled my fires with her own. What man has ever known such joy? *Para servirle, para servirle.*

Despite my strongest efforts, something inside me went ahead and gave, and everything crashed through. I never loved anyone! I shouted.

Ansel and Sarah both stopped their stories and looked at me.

I didn't know what else to say and stared back at them.

They waited a few seconds, then took up where they'd left off like it was nothing, a glass crashing in another house, of no concern really.

But I was on autopilot, determined to be noticed, heard.

So, Sarah! Do you have any weights! I feel like working out!

She stopped again and looked at Ansel, Ansel looked at her, and then they both looked at me again.

Stann didn't do weights, she said.

You sure?

Ever seen a hippy exercise?

Pardon? Look, I remember dining with a doctor many years ago who told me that weights were the best thing that ever happened to him. And here with this dangerous storm coming and all, I thought maybe some weightlifting might help.

I was talking fast, like a broker.

How exactly? she asked.

I don't know. Isn't there something you've got I can lift? I'll lift anything. You just point it out. I'll lift it. One, two, one, two. O.K.?

Sounds like some kinda X-rated deal. We ain't into that here.

No, ma'am. But I'd like to try weights. Look at my weak constitution.

She went over me, agreeing. You *are* a sight. Well, go to it. There's iron skillets all up and down in there. Don't bust nothin, though, you hear?

I hear, I hear.

I ran in, got a couple of big ones, brought them out and started a routine beside the table. Rotating them clockwise and counterclockwise like a crewman on an aircraft carrier guiding in jets. It felt good to have my sockets yanked.

They watched.

Don't mind me, I said. Go on with your stories. Really.

They looked from me to the horizon and back.

Are you trying to signal somebody out there? Sarah demanded.

Nobody, nothing. Don't worry.

Don't you be signaling people out there, she said. I won't have any more customers tonight, you hear? You're signaling friends, right? That's it, isn't it? Trying to save the world?

No, he's not, said Ansel. He's on random, is all. He got the bite and is skipping along on anything that happens to happen. You know.

133

The bite. Poor thing.

I'm fine, I said, giving the pans another big swoop. Really.

Now, where was I? Sarah asked. Oh yes. Stann had crawled back up the ladder and there he was drippin all over the carpet and I said, What the hell are you doing drippin on my carpet, fool! He didn't say anything, though, just stood there gawkin at me. I said, Stann, what are you doin dripping on my brand new carpet from Flada? But he didn't say anything and I went closer to see what was up with him and he said, Sarah, I'm going back to the Moon Bar and I'm going to drink some more whether you like it or not! I thought about punching him out, but off he went. I let him go, the good-for-nothin, and sat myself down and cried the longest time, on and on . . .

Listen here, Ansel said to me. Don't go off the deep end with her. Put the pans down and come listen to *me*.

Already? I asked.

Yes, already.

I took them back into the kitchen, hung them up, returned.

Where were we? I asked him. But before he could answer, I blurted, You know, Ansel, I never loved anyone except myself.

True enough. Anyway.

The words want to come out, you know. I can't stop them.

That's the Du curse. Stuff coming out like there's a reel going in your mouth you can't stop. Anyway.

I never loved anyone except myself, I insisted. Not my children, not my wife, not my parents or their parents, not my siblings or their spouses or their children, not my in-laws, not my friends, not my acquaintances, and never a stranger. Who am I forgetting?

Ansel pushed back his plate, which he'd shined with his bread crust, the chicken bones having been tossed to the wind.

Can't imagine who, he said. Give it a rest. Give everything a rest, Henri.

Somehow, I obeyed straight away, and quickly cleaned my plate as he had done. My wrists throbbed from the workout.

Excellent groceries, he shouted.

Yes, quite delicious! I added.

Sarah had only picked at her plate. *La Traviata* was now on the TV, and while she pursued her *récit*, she also concentrated on the goings-on on stage. It was a cheap production, a shaky video shot in someone's island hut, the lusty libretto overlain with a reggae score.

In the end, though, there was only one thing I could do, she said. Go down to that bar and fetch him once again. This time, though, you were takin your little life in your hands. It was dark and nasty and every gust billowed your bloomers and nearly sent you to Neptune's bosom. I waded and waded, fought a thousand waves, a thousand flying coconuts, and by the grace of Our Lord Jesus made it over there. But the Moon Bar was all dark, and waist-high waves was pilin in the door. My heart sank like lead. He was gone. Washed away. This time for good.

That's awful, I said, genuinely sorry for her.

My man Stann, she blubbered.

I reached over to try and pat her on the shoulder, only to have her seize my hand and clamp it to her breast.

My man Stann was lost! Everybody was lost! And I myself, me, Sarah Lee Lee, was fixing to be lost, too, if I didn't take care of business. So what's I do? I begins to run and run through them ugly nasty waves. I begins to curse and yell at them salty bastards tryin to suck me under. I fights and fights and then I sees him.

Who?

Stann.

Stann? Alive?

And sober as a preacher, right there on the porch of this house. Right there! She pointed to the head of the ladder. And do you know what he said?

No, ma'am, I don't.

She kissed my hand, then released it as you would a butterfly. I put it back on my lap.

He said to me, Sarah Lee Lee, what the hell are you doin out there in the storm? This is bad karma! You're going to mess up my yin and yang, crash my astroplaning self, you know. Oh my, what a pity.

Bad karma, smarma, I told the son of a bitch. I've been lookin all over creation for your ass, fool! Where were you? I almost got myself kilt!

Where was I?

Yes!

I was here and there. It is important where anyone really is? Where are *you* really at, Sarah Lee Lee? What exactly do they mean by *really* and whatever can *at* mean, too? These questions are profound. Do a doobie with me, lady?

I could have kilt him, but —

But you didn't and that's that, Ansel said.

That's right, she said. I didn't and that's that. I'm tired of talking now.

But whatever happened to Stann? I asked.

Him? she said, gathering the plates. Oh, he ran off with a new pair of tits that very winter. German bitch. *Auf wiedersehen*, I said. Dog gone.

I scratched my bite.

My man Stann, my man Stann.

You seem to still miss him, though, I said.

Nah, she said, not really. I just got in the habit of saying, My man Stann.

You say it all the time, Ansel reminded.

That's right, sweets. Habit. What's the one thing that's worse than anything else on this planet, Henri Du?

I had no idea.

Habits, she said. Stann told me that. He was smart that way.

We nodded and nodded.

So what do you do with habits? she asked.

We didn't know what to say.

Break em. Break em all. So I'll break mine now and vow to stop saying, My man Stann. And stop telling the story the way it happened. I'll tell it another way now. What y'all think? How do we even know what happened or didn't happen or whatever?

Go for it, Ansel said. No rules here.

I gave a little cheer, as if it were a game.

She clapped her hands like a little girl and said, O.K., so say I *did* find him in the Moon Bar with a bunch of white girls . . . And saw how he had them all drunk and dancing, and how one gal had her top off and her big German-mama dugs flopping in the air when I came in . . . O horrible night . . . With the wind ablowin and the cocos flyin like bombs and the radio out and all the rest of the black night to come . . . Think I kilt the girl with the big dugs with a fist to the jaw? Anyway it doesn't matter if I did murder or not, everybody be dead . . . Dead and washed away to the bottom of the ocean forever, goodbye . . . Anyway after I kilt the German girl I slapped him so hard you coulda heard it up there in Miamey Flada Youessay . . . Knocked him right out, kerwhop . . . All the rest of them scurried off like rats into the storm . . . Then I was thinking for a minute do I carry this goof-off slob back home where it's safe or do I leave him lying right here on this sandy floor to meet his maker when the waves comes crashing through? And I was thinking some more and even takin a hit off the rum bottle and askin the forgiveness of the Lord Our Maker for what I was about to do to this Good Man . . . And thinking how I needed even another hit off that bottle before I could fully make up my mind . . . And the German girl was lying there in the corner dead as a doornail . . . And then, as if God Hisself was lookin down, Stann was wakin now and rubbin his eyes and sayin, Honey whyever did you do that I was just here having a last little ole drink and then I was coming right home? And then sockin him another one for good measure, this time gettin a little blood for the show and picking him up and heading out the door with the carcass over my shoulder. I took about ten steps just like on the road to some sort of Calvary before I said to myself, I am not my brother's keeper or my lover's keeper or anything else, and I dropped his sorry ass right there and got on home. O night of horra and woe! Turning that last bend and seeing that the house, this very house, was gone . . . Gone in waves so tall you couldn't see the tops breaking! O night everybody drowned! O night my man Stann drowned because I abandoned his ass! O night my soul drowned!

Oh my, I said, overcome.

Shh, Ansel warned. Let her finish or pay the price.

What price?

Shh.

O wind! O tree trunk! *O gioia.*

Her head fell back against the wall of the house with a clunk. She snored.

So what happened? I demanded. Which story was the true one?

She lashed herself to a tree trunk, rode it out, and everyone else died, Ansel said.

Violetta lay dead on the little stage on TV.

I'm confused, I said. Is she ill?

She'll be all right in a while. The memories of her many Odysseys have left her prone to a mild form of narcolepsy. But when she has returned to us, she won't give a hoot what happened.

I poured us another, generous round. These quickly dispatched, I repeated the operation.

Taking note, as I myself was, of some newfound ease in my various movements, Ansel said: You're getting toward the back half of the bite cycle now. How do you feel upstairs?

Cogent, I said. Did it occur to you, however, that my saying earlier that I never loved anyone but myself was merely another way of not quite facing the facts?

You *are* recovering. Now that's my kind of question. Takes a common statement of guilt but and adds a lemon twist.

No, I corrected. It's taking a phrase that purports to be laden with meaning, and in this case, with pure admission, but that means nothing and is thus a mask, yet another mask. I grow depressed.

Easy on the bottle, son.

So is there an answer? I asked.

He smiled. Well, what was I doing in Acapulco?

I sat up straighter, enlivened, grateful he had changed the subject, as from dry to wet. *Para servirle*, I reminded.

Mamacita . . . I stayed there alone in her room a month, he said. And when the month was over, she opened the steamy sliding door and said get out, and I did as told. It was over. Love's last gasp. But as I stared at her closed door, I felt a million feet tall, as if I could go anywhere, do anything, be anything. All was possible. All was ahead of me. Then I turned. I was in a dump behind a nice hotel. Dogs and children stared. Scrounging mothers and virgin daughters held up their ugly finds, the used napkins of rich *gringas*, bloodied panties, slimy condoms, wads of toilet paper. Smoky-eyed drunk fathers and rapist sons hissed, *Para servirle, para servirle*. I ran and ran. Wrenched open a rear door to the hotel, plunged into the cool lobby. A sweet-faced boy in white pants and shirt handed me a Tequila Collins with a single maraschino cherry. I dropped onto a fine leather couch and read a bit of the Herald Tribune. There were food riots in Caracas, a report said. I called the boy, ordered a hamburger, cut the *jalapeños*, and cottage fries with just a touch of paprika. Of course in no time one of the *jefes* appeared and, remaining very polite, said he would escort me to the front door. I went along, slowly, checking out a pack of American girls coming in wet and burned from the beach. There is nothing quite like a sunburned, wet-haired American blonde. Anyway, I got no winks, looks, nothing. Curious, I halted at a mirror, despite my escort's objections, to study myself. I immediately understood everything. Soiled jogging shorts. Bare feet. No shirt. Heavily matted hair grown long in all directions. Teeth either missing or coated with something like the tar you pick up on the beach. Skin yellow as lemon, rough as crabapple rind. Tell me, I implored the hotel dick, do I really look that bad? *Señor*, he said, your bag is kindly awaiting you at the front door, please. I said, Did I check in here? He looked around, concerned that I not raise my voice. *Sí señor*, four weeks ago, but now it is time to go. *No más crédito*. I shook my head, perplexed. Nothing made any sense. Why in the hell would I even go to Acapulco, long a rathole nonpareil! What had I been doing in a shack *behind* the hotel instead of *in* the hotel? And who the hell was the second most beautiful woman I had ever met? Had a cat bite done all that?

Sarah laughed in her sleep. Spittle the color of mercury dripped down her cheek. I averted my eyes.

Then, whoof! I was out through those electric doors and into the ovenlike streets. Taxi? a guy said. I said, Fuck, yes. Where you want to go, meester? *Aeropuerto*! I had no idea where I'd go, but as luck and synchronicity would have it, my driver pointed the way. I said to him, If you had the choice to go anywhere in the world you wanted, where would you go? Oh, he said, Los Angeles.

You went to L.A.? I shouted at Ansel.

Of course not. I said, to hell with that I'm going to the Yucatán. Catch a skiff to the islands. Get my tan back.

Answer me a question, will you, Ansel? I begged.

Shoot, kid.

Did you not go to San Blas from Patzquaro?

No.

And from there to Guadalajara?

No.

And then to the capital and Chapultepec Castle to see the royal carriage and to the horrid zoo to see the newborn hippos, before zigzagging east via Puebla, Oaxaca, San Cristóbal de las Casas, a lake in the Yucatán jungle and finally the Caribbean coast?

The coast, right. But as for the rest, you're way off.

So who was I following all that time?

Did he look like me?

I thought back. I remembered sighting him, hailing him, having him wave to me, only to disappear again. Or so I thought.

Hmm, he said. Don't pester yourself about it, Henri. These things happen. Birds fly from point to point, but do they ask how?

Sarah awoke shouting, Damn it to hell the TV's out!

We hadn't noticed, but it had gone black.

No TV means bad wind, she announced. Bad wind means get ready. Pass me the plates, children. We has work to do now. Who'll stick my Hambone for me? Don't be shy.

❧

The air is molten, as if they'd been sealed in a hothouse. Nothing can move except the eyes, slowly, from the red tree to the blue tree, from the yellow one to the black one, each drooping, fading like a flower. The days are numbered in dry stone.

Beyond the garden wall in the next house a child plays Chopin in fits and starts. Marc listens, can't help but listen, his mind ticking like a metronome at slow speed. For a moment things are more or less the way he wants them, but nothing more.

Today, in every room of the old house, lies a tired body, freshly arrived family friends from the city come down for another weekend. Who *are* all these people, he wonders. Who invites them? Why are they here as if it were their house, their dreamland?

He sips thick coffee, keeping a tense vigil on a deck chair under the tulip tree. Sweat burns as it drips. There is a tar stink in the air.

Again the advertised rain fails to come.

In the steam appears his son, holding something, a doll, a doll by its feet, the head bumping the ground.

Look me!

The doll is screaming and twitching. The head is twisting. It is the newborn. He has taken the newborn from her crib and is dragging her around the yard.

Marc cannot move.

And the boy knows it and runs away, dragging her mercilessly, laughing.

Alarmed at the sounds, a body, then another and another pokes its head out of a window of the manse and looks down at him, immobilized on the broad lawn, on the manicured sea of green, staring after his son and the screaming doll. Why doesn't he do something? Why does he sit there all day? Oh, but don't you know? He's looking for the rest of his mind, if indeed there is any left to find. He writes half the night and then plays the zombie the rest of the time. It's so annoying.

Marc looks up at them. Without intending to, without thinking, he gives them a little wave.

The bodies freeze, then drop out of sight.

What is he doing, trying to signal us? one asks another.

Mon dieu. Il semble qu'il veut être gentil!

Mais non, mais non.

141

10

S TOP. TO HELL WITH the long storm tale, Henri and his miserable fly bite, Sarah and her iron-skillet rule. To make a long story short, I, Ansel Nobody from Nowhere, Texas, am blown away that dark night on the island. Blown far away, blown free. Then lifted to safety on a wing. To my surprise, cloaked in the garb of the current Man of Peace. As in a Bible School dream, only this time . . .

My white linen suit nicely accenting my deep tan, I stand in a new house up in the Sierra Madre looking over wallpaper samples with a salesgirl, a highlands Indian struggling with her first day on the job. Evening is approaching and we go toward the bay windows and look out over the mountains at the Mexican moon, a soft yellow orb low in the purple haze.

They say there's a dead man in the moon if you look at it right, I say.

Man in the moon, I've heard of, she says, but never a dead man. Anyway, what was it you said about papering the bedroom ceiling?

With stars! I shout. And a big fat yellow moon!

Whatever pleases you, she tells me.

I, the Man of Peace, seize her and kiss her all over the head.

Sample books clap shut, slam to the floor.

Perhaps this is always part of the job, she thinks. The moon rises and she imagines the dead man therein watching them, the jealousy of the ages boiling the silver dust in his heart, feeling less

142

dead than he'd felt in years. Over my shoulder, she is sure she can see him up there, gawking. The dead man, leering. Ah, but it is an odd world this world of the Man of Peace. Just who is he really and what's this big house he's got all of the sudden and why is he trying to tear my panties off when I'll just take them off if he'll let me. Is this part of getting to Know Him? If so what exactly will it mean for me in the long run, an escape from these poor, crude hills? She feels like swooning.

I issue a quiet command to bring her back. Immediately, she concentrates anew. It is, after all, quite peaceful that night high in the mountains in a great white mansion on a dry yellow peak with not so much as a streetlight for as far as the eye can see.

The samples girl puts her hips into it now, thinking, you never know where this might lead.

And it is very peaceful indeed.

~

It was still dark when I woke. I was sure I had slept an entire day. I had a strong urge to urinate, I was erect, my thirst raged, my stomach growled, my head hurt, the gunk in the corners of my eyes had dried hard as rock. It was several minutes before I could unlimber my body, several more before I recovered my balance after sitting up.

To my great surprise and happiness, my traveling companions had flown the coop. Indeed, I now enjoyed the privilege of having the railcar to myself. At both ends of my rolling palace burned a gaslight. I began to wonder where they had all got off, what they would do. Would they remain as three? Would they split up, and if so would one or the other claim the boy? But then I thought, Banish them now. And did.

After which, and for a good while, I remained immobile, obsessed with many questions, as I am prone to be.

Had I switched benches in my sleep, or had someone moved me, and why?

I begged the cosmos for a reference point.

I begged the cosmos to turn off the questions.

Nature screamed.

143

As I made my way down the aisle, I teetered and tried to hold firmly to each seat along the way, using this opportunity to be sure that none of their belongings remained and confirming that, yes, I was *tout seul*. Short of breath, I reached the WC.

Locked. I pulled and shoved, using a not immodest amount of force, but to no avail. Then I knocked, but there was no answer. I concluded that the person within was either dead or unconscious. Yet no sooner had I begun to apply this result like Tiger Balm to my aching temples did my bladder cry out.

I burst out onto the rear platform into a cool, silky breeze.

My heart chugged as I did my duty. I watched the full moon overhead, gigantic and violet. To this day I swear I have never felt the moon that near. Who is to say? Had there been no moon that night, to throw off my compass needle, to scramble the magnetic lines, reverse the vortex of self-love, had all that not happened, who is to say I might not have slept on and on and completely missed my rendezvous? Clearly, I owe all the brief happiness of my life to that one summer moon, that inelegant, garish, lumpy bitch with the sleepy slit-eyes who rules all men from head to toe. I love her. I loved her then, and I love her now.

All was still to come, however, and I admit that I dwelled only briefly on the size and color of the moon that night. I was tired. I decided, for the sake of sanity, to believe that I had missed Paris altogether, that the train had arrived there hours upon hours earlier and that my companions, however unwelcome they had been, had simply elected to abandon me.

No, we were long past Paris. Long past the City of Light and heading . . . southeast. Yes, southeast. I struggled to remember what nations lay that way. I longed for a map.

Passport!

I would have gone straight overboard had his strong arm not latched onto mine in time.

Jesus Christ! I shouted.

My apologies, he said. Are you all right, sir?

You make it your job to go around scaring people?

Sir, I'm afraid only train personnel are allowed out here. If you would please step back inside? I will need to check your papers. There are lots of vagabonds and part-time spies in these parts who leap onto trains and then blend in with the general crowd so that many an international security structure is compromised.

I gave him a look and fished for my documents. He turned up a lamp, sharpening the jet until it cast a strong white light. Oddly, he had the same sweet features of the book boy, only older, more mature, the lean gone fat, the smooth crisscrossed with wrinkles. He stank of garlic and wine, but did not appear bilious or inebriated. His kind eyes fixed on my hands as I shuffled some papers.

What time is it? I asked.

No idea.

That's impossible!

Sir, have you lost your passport? Is that it?

He could see that it was not among the brochures, guides, postcards, envelopes and receipts clumped in my hands.

I had it, I said. Those sonsabitches took it. What the hell for?

Pardon?

A batch of papers slipped free and popped out into the night. Damn it to hell!

It's O.K., sir. Remain calm. They must have got you while you were asleep. I was afraid they would and hung around as much as possible while you slept. But they got you anyway. Do you mind if I ask what a nice man like yourself was doing with those guys?

Beg your pardon?

No offense, sir. It's just that you look like someone with a better background.

I come from the dust of nowhere in the middle of nowhere.

Oh?

And I don't owe anyone anything, except Mama and Daddy and that lady in New York City.

See, the conductor said, I knew you were an upstanding person. You're not offended, are you?

I guess not.

Good. Oh, look, I guess I better tell you.

What?

I gave you a powder back there. Must've been four or five hours ago. You were boiling. Hope you don't mind.

Thank you.

You swallowed it right off as if you had been doing it all your life. Some people can't take a powder, have to have a pill. But not you. You're from the Old South, ain't you? We prefer powders.

If you want, I said, tired of the discussion, eager to return to my seat.

He sensed my impatience and waved me away.

I went and sat down.

But I had only begun to think that perhaps I might be lucky enough to be left alone a while when he came and sat across from me and mopped his face with a red handkerchief the size of a bath towel.

Well, we'll have to see the authorities about your passport. Leave it to me, Danny Corn. I'll do the talking.

My heart began to race again. Danny Corn? I asked.

Yep.

Where are you from, Danny Corn?

Middle Water, Texas.

The Middle Water that's south of Dalhart?

That's the one. You know it?

I got kinfolk out there. Giffords. I'm Ansel Gifford. I'm from George West, though. Which is a fur piece from Middle Water.

Pleased to met you, Ansel. Never been down to George West.

You didn't miss nothing. So, tell me. How'd you end up a conductor on a train in Europe? Or am I dreaming this?

Who the hell knows! How'd *you* end up here?

Following my nose, I guess.

Well, then, me too. And so here we are. I can't tell you if we're dreaming or not. All I can tell you is here we are. Or think we are. Whatever.

Whatever, I said back. Middle Water's an awful place. Hated it the time we went up there for one of my uncle's funerals. We just planted him and came home.

What'd he do?

Ran a furniture store or something.

That'd be Don. Don Gifford.

That's right! I shouted. I'll be damned!

Yep, Don ran a furniture store right there in downtown Middle Water. Fine fella. You hear about how he died, though?

They said heart attack, I said.

146

Well, it happened right in the middle of a twister one Sunday morning. That sonabitch, I mean the twister, was coming right in off Chuck Riley's sorghum field and into town and there we all were in the church listening to Rev Barker's sermon that'd been dragging on and on like always and cutting into our football programs. Well, it didn't take a whole lot of sense to figure out that we was all fixin to go meet our Maker if we didn't get our butts to the storm cellar, and so up right in the middle of the commotion, Don Gifford yells out from the back of the church, The white man wasn't supposed to come out here in this God-forsaken land in the first place and kill all the Comanches who were really just people like us and so here comes His Wrath! I know for sure no one gave a shit about the Comanches or anything else, it was more like every man for himself with people bolting every whichaway. But I swear it wasn't two seconds later the roof was sucked right off that old church and there we all was staring *up into* that twister hovering there and spinning like the drainhole of Hell. Everything was silent. I mean dead-in-your-casket-down-in-the-ground quiet. And there we were staring up at our Maker. Waiting to die. Then Don Gifford yells out, Us white people were never meant to come out here on this damn plain and kill all the people who lived here before us and take their land, so go ahead and punish us and punish us good for killing so many of our fellow men in cold blood, raping their wives and daughters, stealing everything they had and herding the last of them off to sure-fire death in some hellhole. For this, he concluded, we are truly sorry and beg you to go right ahead and punish us right here, right now. We deserve every last bit of the mighty punishment you could throw down. Go ahead!

My God, I said.

You can bet your ass people were hoping he'd shut the hell up fast, and his wife Betty Helen was poking him something bad with her elbow. Even I was about to jump over there and let him have it. Then someone said shutup, real loud, and then some others said it, too, and then everybody was crowding around him ready to send him to the other world.

What about the tornado?

It went away.

147

Yeah?

But not before it took him for a little ride in the sky.

Don?

Well, you went to his funeral, didn't you?

I sat there, stunned. Deep memories seeping up of my home town, my parents, my kin. I could smell bacon in the old frying pan, taste the sweet in a honeysuckle bloom. My stomach went into knots the way it used to do before a storm.

Danny Corn smiled at me.

I smiled back. Then it occurred to that maybe . . .

You make that up?

What do you think?

Goddamn it! I hollered. I get caught every time!

I'm real good at it, huh?

Sure are!

Well, sir, we'll be in Milan in about an hour, Venice by dawn.

Milan?

Yep.

Then I did miss Paris.

Paris? Why, that was yesterday. You're headed to Venice now.

How's that?

When you didn't wake up in Paris, I pulled your ticket out of your pocket. It said Venice on it, so I got you to the right train. It just so happened it was my train, too. But then you and I are no strangers to coincidence, are we?

Had there been some ridiculous mistake? Had the agent in Calais sold me the wrong ticket? I rummaged for it. No luck.

I never bought a ticket for Venice. What's going on here?

A beaut of a spot. What's the problem? You did come to look around, didn't you? Paris stinks and it's too expensive. You'll love the Italians.

My patience with this whole unexplained affair came to an abrupt end.

Thank you for all your help, I told him. Meaning go away now.

He sensed this and fired back, Look who's flighty.

I gazed at him as you might a sick animal. Still here?

What's the problem?

I held my tongue, hoping he'd give up.

Oh, I get it, he said. You're one of those types who's friendly one minute, ready to give you his mother and sister, and meaner than a prairie mule the next, ready to kick your ass from here to El Paso. Flighty.

Spare me.

And uppity is the other word we use for people like you. By God, it still applies. Nope, some words never lose their true meaning. Folks gets an itty bit of education, and what do they do? Go off and forget their past, their roots, their people. So that the next time they run across folks from back home, folks who for all practical purposes could be their kin, their very own flesh and blood, what happens? Why, Mister gets uppity. Acts like he ain't got no more time for us regular people. Your kind chaps my *derrière*, if you know what I mean — and I'm sure you do.

I'd had enough, and chose to let him have it, for his own good, for once and for all. After that, I'd straighten out this whole mess about being on the wrong train in the wrong country in the middle of the night with the moon shining way too big and violet.

I did enjoy our little chat, friend, and especially your tale, but there is, believe me, nothing at all, nothing whatsoever endearing about West Texas.

My interlocutor screwed his face up and said, Who you talkin to?

I went on, saying, I am willing, if such a thing is possible, to commend you on your verbal prowess in the hopes that this will, as it were, let me off the hook as regards further discussion. Yes, I will say, and without the slightest equivocation, that your tale of the funnel cloud and the prairie justice did indeed spellbind, and bring to mind those tales recounted long ago by that infamous daughter of the vizier, Scheherazade.

Corn gave a sound like a pig in mud. You know what?

What!

You're still a kid. Don't care how old you are.

I'm nineteen and a half! I yelled out.

A punk.

Spell Scheherazade then.

He cleared his throat and shook his head. You see, little buddy, it's like this. I don't *have* to be able to spell Shezawhatever to

149

know that being *kind* to people is *all* that counts and *will ever* count on this planet. Do you read me?

Oh, I sighed, that old Baptist moralism.

Son, that ain't Baptist nothing. Just plain common sense. And you know I'm right as rain.

No, I don't.

You know what, then?

What's that, Corn?

You are a little *shitass*. Hell with you. Them Eye-Talians? Why, they gonna eat you up like pizza. One bite and you gone. *Ciao*.

Shaking his head in disgust, my erstwhile friend smoothed his trousers, rebuttoned his official coat and donned his official cap. And with a crisp salute he marched out of the car on his ten-thousandth trek to the front of the train.

Good riddance, I said aloud.

I did not like the way my voice sounded, or the thoughts I was having, or the way my youthful trip was turning out, or a lot of things and held my head in such a way that an outsider might have thought me ashamed.

But, things being as they are, and trains being trains, we rolled on. Soon taking a sharp curve and picking up some speed. The strange moonlight filled the car. I was hungry and paced the gloomy aisle.

Thinking of Italy, of Daddy dead on the bed, of the book boy in the bowels of the steamer, of the foul funnel cloud.

Italy, whispered my distant New York City lover, her head turning to the window, to the snow burying the streets, I feel as if I died there, in peace. Go all the way to Italy if you can. Yes, I had forgotten her suggestion, but it seemed that chance had been at my side the whole time. Now I *was* in Italy, coming down out of the mountains, into the only place she said she had ever felt any joy.

To honor her, to thank her if I could, I asked forgiveness for everything, only to hear someone laughing in the distance, her perhaps, or Daddy, or Corn, or the world at large.

The train speeded up even more, as if angry. The snow on the Alps was purple.

Tonight Marc brought me back from my new mountaintop dream palace in Mexico, sucking me to his side as you will a young lover, and made me walk with him along the river under the poplars deep in the French countryside. The water was rising steadily, pushed up by the sea many miles away. He had wanted to bathe naked, but the tide had covered the surface with patches of weeds and algae. Here and there a muskrat drew a black V across the surface and disappeared into the shadows of the far bank.

That afternoon he had sat in the house of an ailing family friend, the fat *paysanne* housekeeper, and told stories about nothing in particular that made her laugh, perhaps helped her forget her many afflictions. The girl's near-deaf mother, slumped in the carcass of an old chair, yelled each time she thought she'd missed something and fanned herself with a piece of cardboard. The doctor was hours late, once again. One minute they spoke of his cures as miracles, the next as catastrophes.

After a while, the old mother offered Marc a *pastis*, and put out a small plastic bowl of peanuts. The daughter lay straining to breathe on a foldaway bed along the wall, her rosy face lighting up whenever his eyes met hers. Her back was out again, strained from holding aloft her huge body. There would be bedsores, she whispered, and oh how she hated bedsores.

The television blared in the corner, and the old woman wrung her hard white hands. It was a children's program, about a group of kids getting lost in a cave and the ceiling of the cave falling in and trapping them. Would they get out? How? We'll run out of air! one of the little girls screeched. All the children were crying. The old woman crossed her legs, twitched a foot. The poor things, she said, the poor little things. Who let them go in there in the first place?

Mama! the daughter shouted, the voice grave and manlike. It's only a TV show, Mama. Your blood pressure now.

It was like this all around the world now, Marc thought. TV sets showing crap, sick folks in hot little rooms mesmerized until cataleptic, waiting for doctors to show up at dark and be tired and condescending and take all their money and leave them for dead with orders for batches of pills and suppositories, creams

151

and drops. Until the next time . . .

He had a second *pastis*. Thinking how he had never told either of them that he wrote the questions for the most popular quiz show ever broadcast. Thinking that somehow he had failed to do a damn thing with his whole life. Thinking and thinking, while the children in the cave found a blade of light in the broken ceiling and began to cheer at the top of their lungs and dance in a circle.

I must go.

So soon? rasped the ill one.

I'm afraid so.

Good of you to come by, the mother yelled. You come again next year. We love to see you. Give us a kiss.

Marc leaned toward her chair and kissed her cold cheeks four times. Then he kissed the daughter, her oily cheeks buoyant as blisters.

Until next time. Thank you very much.

Goodbye. And look out for yourself!

I will.

The alcohol had him back to the house in no time, where a few sedentary guests (who *were* these people?) were serving whisky and white wine and pistachios at a white table under the blue cedar. An empty glass was thrust into his hand, a question was barked, a liquid was poured, the pistachio bowl neared but departed as he reached for it.

Didn't this all mean something? Marc asked himself. The stupid simplicity of the question instantly sparking a surge of regret, a wish to withdraw it. What did he mean by all? What had he meant by something? Just exactly what was he asking?

Another question was barked, more liquid poured, only more sloppily this time, by a young man in nice clothes from an expensive store.

Thank you, Marc said, unable to remember this one's name. A new *Jules,* somebody, it didn't matter. They all looked the same, talked the same.

Until next summer. Until they would all be back again, more numerous than ever, all copies.

Ah, houseguests. And the quaint way these reunions quickly decayed into arguments over nothing. As bottles emptied. As voices

152

grew louder and louder until no one heard anything. The whole circus carrying over to the dinner table, the fine meal soon being ruined, abandoned in a storm of shouts and tears and slamming doors.

Indeed, what did all this mean? Why couldn't he be like everyone else and stop thinking? After all, hadn't he almost finished the book? Wasn't it clear that it would be done on time after all? That his battle with the calendar would end in victory? Yes, but how would it turn out? How would everything turn out?

A little more than a week to go, no more. Then it will be done, one way or another.

And so it was long after dark that I followed him away from the riverbank and across the fields until we came to a dead cherry tree on a ridge overlooking the valley. A place to which he always returned, to squat, back to its crumbling bark, and look down the slope at the gigantic rolls of hay waiting like the pieces of some unfinished game. It was always here that he rested a while, once a year, thinking already of the drive back north to Paris.

He waited until he saw the hawk circling, the hawk that never failed to appear, and then rose to go, his shoes crushing the hay stubble.

Heat lightning flashed in the great open night.

For once, I saw a man within. But it was like a glimpse through a dirty window, no more.

The air smelled of dust and rust and rain.

Ansel most missed the lawn, the shade of the fruitless mulberry trees bulging out of the sandy loam, the cement goldfish pond where he and Violetta sat evenings in silence shelling pecans for pies. The banging of freight cars being shunted to and fro at the edge of town, the popcorn smell of the oats factory, the cotton fluff sailing in off the road and catching in the grass. The tap of the screen door. The horned toads in the petunias and cannas. The slow tick of the sprinkler.

Frances had set him up a card table in his Paris bedroom.

When he got tired of cheating to win at solitaire, he opened the nightstand drawer and got out the dominoes. Turned them all over, put his hands out flat on their cool backs and stirred them around. Dealt seven to each of the three others, then seven to himself. Set them up on their sides in neat walls. Saw what he had, began counting, figuring. Tossed one down, for five, maybe ten. Started the scoresheet with / or X.

Around and around the table he went, playing each hand as skillfully as he could. Knowing full well it was impossible to play the game that way, but doing it anyway, using every twist he could think of to pass the time.

One day adding some voices, those of Adair, and Arnold Thornton and Virgil Groesbeck. That'll teach you. Like hell it will. Hell, I know ten-year-old girls can play better than that. Nice funeral, Ansel, far as funerals go. How much you pay for that casket? Now don't y'all be meddlin in his business. I don't even know how much she cost, my brother took care of it. I like your brother. Well, thank you. A strange profession, though. Wonder how many he's buried. I wouldn't want to clean up the body and all that, can you imagine? Are we playing or yakking — your turn! Hold your damn horses, hold your damn horses. That'll be twenty-five, gentlemen. Damn! Who's going to get us all another damn beer here? Hell, I got some last night, boys, and I mean ummm. What's that? Yes, sir, it was like we was twenty all over again!

So what, I've died several times already, said Ansel.

What? Adair said.

You heard me.

What the hell's that supposed to mean?

What I said.

O.K., so . . .

So anybody else here died several times like me?

They didn't say anything back.

Then Adair said, Maybe you'd better backtrack and explain to us.

I said what I had to say.

You did?

I did. Y'all can just go think on it.

Wait just a minute, said Thornton. I get it. He's talking about that operation he had all them years ago. Y'all remember. When his head swelled up like a watermelon that time. I tell you what, boys. I'd like to kill every doctor in the whole damn state of Texas! Snap ever one of their goddamn necks like chickens! Look what they done to him!

They all looked at Ansel.

Ansel looked back, then seemed to wake from a dream, and shook his head.

Sorry boys, he said. I didn't know what I was saying. Forget it.

Don't worry about it, Adair told him. Let it go. We're just going to sit here and play dominoes and be real cool and easy and if things don't feel right you can just say it to me and I'll fly you on back to Texas, you hear? I wasn't a bomber pilot for nothing, you know. You just say the word, O.K.?

Right. I will, Ansel said. And did you know that with all those clips they stuck up there in my brain back then I can pick up voices?

They all looked at him again.

Voices? Groesbeck said. My God.

Yes, voices. Especially this one voice. A voice of peace.

You mean like Jesus?

Sort of.

The Messiah? asked Adair.

Maybe.

What's he saying to you, Ansel?

He's saying, Whip those boys at dominoes, then go be the next Man of Peace.

The next Man of Peace? Thornton said. What're you talkin about?

I don't know. That's all the voice said.

You don't know?

That's all it said.

And you picked this up on your brain clips?

Just like a jillion-watt radio station.

Radio station? shouted Adair. That's downright weird, Ansel. Are you O.K.?

Sure I am. Long as I know you're all fools enough to believe me!

There was a long pause, then they all laughed. All four of

155

them. There in Ansel's room in Paris. And it was a happy laugh, but then it went on and on until it wasn't happy anymore.

What's so funny?

It was Frances, bringing in a tray, setting it on the table. There was a teapot, a cup and saucer, a slice of lemon, a sugar cube.

Nothing.

Thought I heard you laughing.

You mean like a looney?

She peered at him. Well, I didn't mean it *that* way.

I know you didn't, Ansel said. He began raking in the dominoes, lining them up in the box. I know you didn't.

You should teach me how to play, she said.

I could. It's not hard. Long as you can count by fives.

Oh. Look, Daddy, we're going out tonight. The kids are fed and in bed already, so if you can keep an ear open. You don't mind, do you?

Of course not.

She poured tea through the silver strainer into the pink China cup.

I can't remember the last time we went out.

The tea was for her. He never had any. But every evening like that, she would come in to see him and bring her tea. The habit went way back, too, to a screen porch and the Depression and a barefoot girl in mismatched clothes. It went way back, to sitting with Violetta and the child staring out at the yard, like the floor of a furnace in the late afternoon. The girl and her mama having hot tea, and no one saying anything, everyone waiting for a miracle, for something to make the windmill creak, if only for a minute.

I made you a salad, Daddy. Now don't let it waste.

Where in the hell is my blue shirt!

Here came Henri.

Ansel pushed up out of his chair and, anxious to avoid it all, shuffled to the window.

Don't tell me it isn't even ironed yet! Jesus it's been a whole damn week since I put that shirt in the goddamn wash!

It's coming, she said. You could wear another one anyway.

I don't *want* to wear another one, Frances. I *want* the one I asked for!

It's coming. Go finish shaving. I'll have it ready.

But Henri the Bear wasn't done. He came a step closer to her, his pale blue boxer shorts pulled high, black chest hairs puffed up, the slopes of lather on his face starting to slip.

What did you say? he demanded.

But Frances was used to it, knew better than to give him the satisfaction. She slammed down her teacup, then saw that the handle had snapped off in her hand and frowned.

Daddy's going to watch the kids. So just get ready, Henri.

What do you think I'm trying to do! Listen here, Ansel, if those kids get up while we're gone you throw them right back in bed, clear? They know better, they know the rules. Don't let them take advantage of you. Understood?

Daddy likes kids. Don't you, Daddy?

Did you hear what I said, Ansel?

Ansel turned toward the man his daughter had chosen to marry, the man who thought himself master of his house, and crossed his skinny old man's arms. He wasn't about to answer.

It was dark outside.

Did you hear what I said or did you not hear what I said, damn it!

Leave him alone, he heard you, Frances said. Now, look, Daddy, if you don't want salad, there's fresh ham and cheese. You decide, O.K.?

Just keep those kids in bed!

I've got a story I can tell them, Ansel offered.

No stories! bellowed Henri. We *don't* tell our children stories. Tell them one story and the next thing you know they'll be having temper tantrums until we tell stories every night for the rest of our lives! In my house, no stories. Clear?

Ansel and Frances looked at him.

Maybe a short little tiny story if you have to, Frances said, ducking sideways in jest as if Henri would strike her, then giving her father a daughter's grin.

But Ansel had ceased watching them. He was heading for the bed now, to park himself there until they finished their nonsense.

Not even a breath of a story, Henri repeated. Now, come on, honey, get me my shirt!

Honey, she sang out. Honey honey honey! If only you meant it!

What's that supposed to mean?

Lather avalanched off his left check, plopped on the carpet.

The new carpet! Go get a towel, quick!

He ran away. Damn it, damn it, damn it.

The old man watched his daughter studying the foam on the floor.

Sure enough, though, the peace, my vision of a moment of peace here on the mountain begins to break up under the world's gaze. For someone has been advertising me to the seeker tribes. By the hundreds the fevered masses come, parking their campers up and down the hills around my abode. Their generators hum all night. I've been buried in a hive of idiots.

The Indian decorator girl, Chulmetic, seems irritated by it all, too. When she is not lying in my arms or sitting on my lap she stays at the bay windows, staring at the comings and goings. She seems at times like a forest child who has never seen people and all their modern baggage, like the innocent one discovering the world with all the intensity of a youthful lover. I watch her go naked from our bed to see the latest arrivals rolling into the highlands, motorized caravans of old men and their young women that flow like lava day and night. She stands there, a living statue, and the people draw near, shyly at first, then more boldly, climbing right up into the yard. Flashbulbs pop. The old geezers grab their maidens the way you cling to a cliff to keep from falling — only these cliffs cling back and there is muttering up and down the countryside. Chulmetic, I finally call, and then she comes back to me in the bed and settles atop me and slips her legs, closed and narrow, between mine and waits. Waits as I peer into the low green fire in the back of her eyes.

Outside all is voices, endless discussion. A hundred questions ringing out all at once. The agitation in annoying, and I grow weary of it. Even appeals to the *Federales* to clear out all this riffraff come to naught. Everyone waits, thinking I will finally give in to them and step outside on the porch and preach some stuff. Preach peace.

Why should I? Why should I do anything? There's no one giving orders here. I can do what I want, can't I?

Following that line, I may start taking potshots anytime now. Look at them. Crouched around their little electric stoves, rubbing their hands against the winter wind, glancing every few seconds at my house, praying I, wise old Ansel, will appear, say something smart, deliver them from themselves.

How dare the world at large show up when all I wanted to do was settle down here? How dare it be presumed that I have any message at all, much less one more important than any of my predecessors in this role?

Bah!

⚜

The strong old doctor with soft white hair to his shoulders who spent long summer afternoons gliding on the river in his dark green canoe with his old terrier came stomping down the hall shortly before dawn and plunged into Frances's room. As if it were his own room to come home to after a long night's work, as if it were his own house he was barging through in his green rubber boots and slicker, as if it had been raining that night when a million stars in the clear vault cast a glow in the yard you could see by.

Everyone heard the doctor arrive, go to her room, then his deep voice resonating through the floors and walls. Everyone but Marc, who lay in his bed in the room above, dreaming of demons and shades of the future, like underage drunks, having a last round for the road in an all-night bar, ignoring all, their host, the emergency going on downstairs, the creeping dawn, the coming storm.

It doesn't matter what you say, James said, Grandfather Marc suffered from classic schizophrenia. *Comme Schumann, comme tous.*

Oh how theatrical, hissed his twin sister.

Shutup, Rosha, said James. You're here to sit and listen. If you can't sit and listen, then go make a quarter on the sidewalk . . .

I don't have to obey you, brother.

But you like to eat. So shut up.

What is your point! boomed an older child.

Indeed, another chimed.

Do you not see the peculiar sadness? James asked his friends. Suffering thus, Marc could bring nothing to a mature end — was destined, in the determinist fashion, to fail for want of resolution. Resolution, friends.

Revolution? Rosha rasped.

Did I not tell you to shut up?

What're you going to do, give me a taste of the family bullwhip? Try to make me see the Light of the Ages? Talk Jesus to me?

I might.

Not in here, you don't, said the midget bartender on a nail keg. No whippings in here. Out in the street for that shit.

Ah! James said. Closing time. And so there lies the story, which, as I was plainly trying to say, has always been half-alive, half-dead. Why, just last night I had a dream . . .

Oh no, said Rosha.

Yes, a good dream, too.

Make it quick, said Mick, giving the bar a pop with a red towel. I got all the flies to kill before I can crawl into the sack and plug my jelly hole.

So in this dream I was lost along a road.

Who isn't? said Rosha, glancing out at the storm.

A road that followed a beach. I didn't know the name of the place I was going to, but I did know that I absolutely had to go there. Someone, evidently someone I loved, needed me there, and soon. So I had gone out on the road and begun hitchhiking. I waited and waited and then out of the blue came a bright yellow bus. Like those school buses they had all those years ago?

What school buses? What's school? they all asked.

It stopped and the door flapped open and I looked up the stairwell at the driver. My age, he looked friendly enough.

Where're you headed, pard? he hollered.

Next town. Sick loved one.

Climb in.

I got in and shook his hand. James Du.

William Corn. Have a seat right there behind me. That way we can talk. Gonna be a while. Five, six hours down there.

Sure, I said, and took my place.

Wanna sandwich? Ham?

I declined, and he didn't press it, and then we both smoked cigs and looked out the windshield. Beach grass poked through the broken-up asphalt and sand snaked this way and that across the rubble. To one side you could see the long stretch of white sand with black breakers as big as houses crashing down and kicking up a fog. On the other side lay the flat land with nothing on it.

Getting hot, he said, wiping his brow.

It was actually quite cold, a few degrees above freezing.

Hey, what say we pull off at my place and have a beer? Mama'll be happy to see us and we'll sit and have a slurp, what say?

Your place?

Yeah, it's right here.

With that he gave the wheel a sharp jerk and tore down a side road.

We raced along at top speed now, the whole contraption rattling and clanging as if it would split and spill us out. I wanted to cry out but held back, gripping the seat to keep from slamming my head into the ceiling. Talc-like gray dust swirled through the bus and I began to fear for our lives as the driver hurtled blindly along laughing at the top of his lungs. The radio kicked on and the current Man of Peace began preaching in that falsetto voice of his about how the end of the world in a nuclear puff or two had really been the best thing for the world and weren't we all much better off, we the few of us left, we the chosen ones, we the cool, we the made-its? What, he asked, was a little atomic snow on the land compared with the greater good of having rubbed out our surfeit? Think of it, he implored. A group began to rap Good Night, Irene . . .

Here we are! shouted the driver, slamming us to a halt.

I saw him dive out the door and quickly followed, choking and coughing.

Look what I brought home, Mama! he called.

A live one! she called.

Yeah, Mama! We're going to have a little beer and cool off and then head on down the road to town. He's going to see sick

161

kinfolk. Is there cold beer, Mama?

In the box, son. Bring us all one. You know how you can forget.

Yes, ma'am.

You, come sit, she commanded.

I swiped at my dirty clothes, spat.

Don't you worry about appearances around here, she said, sweetly. You want, you can take a shower out back. It's all hooked up. Now come sit next to me, honey.

She was parked on a flimsy lawn chair in front of a red salt-box with a sagging roof. Every window was busted out, the TV antenna lay crumpled like a dead insect in the side yard, and trash lay all round — hundreds of rat-chewed Reader's Digests, thousands of rusted tin cans, deformed plastic doll parts, every size of worn-out tire, a million colored shotgun shells and critter droppings of all kinds.

What's your name, son?

James Du. Jimmy.

Jimmy Du. You from Paris, Jimmy?

Maybe.

Maybe?

It seemed to make her mad.

I mean, Yes, ma'am, I'm from Paris all right.

Thought so. Dus are thick up in there. I went to Paris once. Pretty place, but I wouldn't want to live there. That was way back *Before*.

Before, yes.

I've seen a lot, you know.

Yes, ma'am.

Billy's gettin us a beer. You goin to have a seat or not?

I took a milk crate, flipped it, sat down.

That's the spirit, she said. Have to make do out here. I ain't got no time to be messing with real furniture. Yep, back Before it was different.

Yes ma'am.

Before, you had a whole world of things that needed doing. Now you don't. I like it better this way.

Now is better?

You darn right it is. Billy's dead daddy was Billy, too, and boy if I had it to do over again I sure would think twice before marrying a Corn.

Oh.

Sick folks, the Corns. Why I got hooked up with that bunch, I'll never —

Oh, Mama, leave the invite alone.

Here came her Billy with the beers, three cans, no labels.

Have to be generic, I'm afraid, he said.

What're you talking like that for, son? she asked.

Like what, Mama?

Saying *I'm afraid* and *generic*. You don't talk that way.

Billy laughed, popped his top. We joined him.

A toast, he proposed, lifting his can.

Hell with that, said his mother, raising hers up high and downing it in one go.

Mama!

She belched.

Now who wants to take a shower?

Easy, Mama. Slow down.

Like hell! Look at your friend. He needs a shower! I'll go get it ready back there. Then y'all come around. I can't stand lookin at such filthiness.

I don't need to shower, really, I said.

Did I ask your opinion? she said.

Billy gave me a look that said don't answer. I didn't answer.

Whistling Dixie, she went off around back.

Look, Billy, if it's O.K., I don't really need a shower . . .

Mama won't hear of that. You got to take a shower. Then we can go. After.

But —

No buts. Let's go.

We got up and, threading our way through the refuse, our shoes crunching along the salt-caked path, the sea breeze popping our shirts, went around back. Mama wasn't to be seen. Billy stopped a moment, looked around for her.

Well, she's done it again.

Done what?

I didn't see any shower facilities, no water tank, nothing except a small mudhole a few yards out on the flats.

Jumped in before us. She just can't wait.

I looked out at the mudhole. The surface was smooth. No Mama.

In there?

That's her thing. Mama and that mudhole is kind of like two sisters.

I think I'd better go, I said.

Yes, get the hell out of there! Rosha shouted. Go!

Shutup, girl! everybody told her.

But Billy said, Nah, let's go see what she's doing for a couple of minutes and then we'll tell her hell no about taking a mudbath, I mean a shower, and then we'll go on down the road. Come on.

I followed him out to the edge of a steaming mudhole. Deep black mud, smooth, no movement. We waited.

She's *in* there?

Yep.

I stared at the mud. Then I began to see the outline of the woman. Face-down, rising up and down in it. Lithely, the way a young woman might do atop her lover. The hips moved down and up, in and out, and you could hear a moaning.

What the hell, I said.

Shh. It's her moment. Let her have it.

Her body, and then the body she was atop of, both rose higher and higher in the mud and then I could see that the second body, face up, the lover, was another woman, a young woman, dead in a torn dress. Then one eye opened, like a black pearl in egg white, and looked me up and down.

Rosha swooned and the others grabbed her and held her.

Go on! they shouted. Go on! Even Mick was pounding the bar to hear more.

It was Mama, *my* mama in that mud looking at me with one eye. It was my mama already dead — yet not dead, I didn't know which. I opened my mouth for some reason, but nothing came out. And I couldn't move.

Looks like we don't need to get on down the road after all, Billy said. Seeing your mama's already here. Well, you better get in there, too, son.

What?

Get on *in* there!

And he gave me a shove and I was falling and falling toward the old lady and Mama making love in the mudhole.

Here he comes, Mama! Yee haaa!

Wake up! Marc, wake up! The doctor's down there with your mother again. Something bad is wrong. Wake up!

Marc jerked upright, looked at Jeanne and fell back on the sheets.

Get up! she shouted.

11

A T DARK SARAH STUCK Hambone, the hog she kept under the house. I can safely say that I'm glad neither Ansel or I agreed to take the family knife and do the job for her, as chivalry normally would have required. Although unspoken, it was clear from our point of view that the swine could go right ahead and drown as the sea swelled. There was no way we were going to tackle the beast and do the dirty deed.

Seeing instantly through our pretense of great fatigue, Sarah commanded us instead to do the dishes. Come hurricane, Great Flood or Armageddon, Sarah Lee Lee's place was going to be shipshape. For, as she said while she sharpened the bowie knife, grinding it so hard on the whetstone that sparks flew, you never know when She, Our Lady Upstairs, might decide to drop in. Nodding vigorously in agreement, as did Ansel, I rose to execute our chore and said, just to please her, I really like doing dishes. Me, too, said Ansel. Moments later I'd donned a red-checkered apron that two men could have worn at the same time, found the soap, got a tub of water going on the stove, stacked the dirty pots and pans and plates just so, and begun to sing a cheerful French song about lovers kissing on a park bench in the rain. You'll dry, I ordered Ansel. He somehow did not resist.

Sarah kept a dream of a kitchen. Firstly, there was more than ample room in which to work, there being nothing more maddening than a cooking area in which a person cannot turn around without running into himself. Secondly, there was a view out over

166

the sink that took your breath away for its sheer spiritual grandeur and took your mind pleasantly off the task at hand. Thirdly, there was every imaginable utensil, spice, cookbook, and spirits a chef could ever need. And although Ansel paced about during the long wait for the water to grow hot, I found this mild inconvenience rather calming, the delay allowing me the time to make a mental map of her culinary setup for some future use. If I had one secret that I kept all my life, it is that I wished to be a good, rich and famous chef. It didn't matter where, only that I be the best and that everyone know it.

I was just squirting in the soap when the blood-freezing squeal pierced the air, quickly followed by a child's scream, the two sounds racing parallel higher and higher, then falling sharply, then rising again as if each were giving chase to the other in some aria of Hell's darkest repertory. My reverie shattered, a million soap bubbles cascaded from the tub. I stumbled back from the mess, overcome again by fear.

Get hold of yourself! Ansel yelled. We've got a major home accident on our hands!

I looked around as the bubbles flowed, aghast, unable to act.

Ansel pushed me aside, wrenched the bottle of soap from my hands. *Imbécile!* Don't you know how powerful that stuff is?

Hambone's and Sarah's screams had me hypnotized, yes, like a kid at a horror film, but also like a romantic who hears poetry in tragedy. Is it possible that this woman actually loved that hog? I saw the bitter truth of loneliness. I undid the apron and dropped it on the floor.

Where the hell are you going? Ansel asked. I'm damn sure not doing all these dishes by myself! Come back here, you *branleur!*

I rushed down below in time to see her catching the blood in Mason jars.

The various effluents of the house emerged in bursts from a many-elbowed tin pipe straight into Hambone's voluminous pen. The contraption seemed alive, giving deep growls and high-pitched blasts, every tube shuddering and threatening to unhook from its neighbor.

But Sarah was paying it no mind. There she squatted, her wide bottom firmly planted deep in a soup of violet algae, soap suds and hog blood.

Not a pretty sight, she shouted. But somebody's got to be the Executioner. Come closer.

The struggle with the Poland China clearly had been just that. The myriad wounds she had inflicted upon it ran like faucets. Sarah, a lady of many talents, seemed to play it like some musical instrument, her arms reaching gracefully, the jar in each hand catching the flow now here, now there, all up and down the creature. She sweated heavily, but smiled over her labors. I kept a safe distance, if only to stay clear of the foul mixture, which appeared to be moving, as if someone were slowly pulling a quilt away.

He fought me, she said. He always fought me, Hambone. And he's fighting me now bleedin too dang fast!

I then spied the bowie, hilt-deep in the tough neck. I thought of colorful *banderillas* thrust into a bull, then the long, lovely sword, the creature going to its knees, the crowd coming to its feet, blood pooling in the dust, quickly darkening, roses showering down.

Help me here.

I hesitated at the little fence of tarpaper, hubcaps, pallets and fronds.

She was holding out full jars, anxiously glancing back at the precious fluid being lost.

Take these damn things! she shouted.

I tried to leg it over the fence, but halfway through the attempt saw that, first, I could not estimate the depth of the muck and, second, given the height of the makeshift barrier and my crotch, the twain were sure to meet. Thinking perhaps more quickly than ever before, I kicked a hole in the fence and touched bottom inside with a much-gnawed mop handle. It was only a couple of inches deep. Satisfied, I ventured in.

You is the slowest thing on earth! Get yourself over here!

It is pitiful, I said to myself, how death and disaster, and especially the two together, completely blow most folks' circuits. I used to think it was the simple people who could weather adversity the best, emerge the least wounded of all, ready to do it all over again. But no more. I now know that the simple are simple because they are. And if you look hard, and carefully, you will see the cracks in the humble veneer, the terror quaking deep down in their fat-clogged hearts.

I got over to her, slipping buttwise after my first step brought me down, and took the jars, hot as teapots. This done, she reached into a nearby milk crate and retrieved more gallon containers, yanked the dead hog closer, planted their lips.

Hell if I'd known . . .

Known?

I liked Hambone, she said. Liked him a lot. I mean Hambone was all I had. It was just me and Hambone, know what I mean?

I said yes.

She said, No, you don't. I should've see this coming and sent him to Flada for the summa. He liked to do that. I'd pack him up some goodies, have some boys come over and haul him to the airport and get him on the flight to Miamey. My daughter's got a fine place with a big yard and a swimming pool and all and they just loved having Hambone. I mean that had to be hog heaven. I missed him, though. I miss him now.

She stared at me a moment, for I must have been quite the picture. Sitting crosslegged in the gurgling waste holding two gallon jugs of hot hog blood, my face contorting in the wind as though being worked over by some sadistic masseuse.

I returned the favor, even pitied her a bit. Her eyes had puffed up round and hard like lemons. She had either splashed her chin with blood, bit her lip, or had a nip of the stuff.

Something caught my eye and I turned to see a chicken fly by upside-down. Stunned, dead or asleep, I couldn't tell, but *peu importe*. The signs were clear — *Ne plus ultra*.

She spluttered, Hambone is dead because of my selfishness! Hambone is dead because I was only thinkin of myself. Hambone is dead because of me. Hambone is dead . . . dead.

She lay her cheek on his and, letting her jars drop into the muck, sobbed for the ages.

At last I lost patience.

He's bacon now, woman. Pull yourself together and let's get the house battened down. It's a hurricane!

Even as I admonished her, the wind was getting so strong that words, once spoken, were torn away. One could no longer be sure of having been heard at all.

So I was not surprised when my bacon remark failed to rouse her. She simply had not heard.

I set down my jars in the shallowest spot I could find, went and shook her shoulder.

We must go inside. Come now, we must go.

Something like the squawk of a mynah issued from her, and I withdrew. That is one bird not worth talking back to.

Stuck, I sat and dreaded the thought of shouldering that bacon, since it was now clear that the carving would have to be done topside. I made plans to inquire about plastic sheeting and old towels, anything and everything to minimize the mess to come.

At my buried feet, an ancient slice of watermelon smiled up at me.

She cried and cried. Hambone quivered, gave a final poot like a popgun being fired at his own funeral.

Marc's gunshot wound had been superficial, a mere breaking of the skin on the wrist. It hardly hurt anymore, and ample insurance washed away any other pain. Samira and Vik never showed up to visit him as he convalesced, but he was not sad about it. Life was that way. Best to stay out of hotels.

Jean-Jean's suicide had made the papers, but there was no mention of any speculation concerning anybody who might have been up there on Notre-Dame with him. He'd been a hardworking government employee who'd climbed up there on a Saturday and leaped. For no apparent reason, so case closed. It happened a couple of times a year.

Marc's parents, the poor creatures, had come to see Marc in his hospital bed, but it had gone very badly. Father quickly ran out of things to say, fidgeted with the TV set, messed with the colors. Mother, as ever, straightened the sagging flowers in the ugly vase, and babbled on, saying nothing, sure she could set things right but her face showing an agitated sea, boats foundering, crews drowning, all going under into the unknown. The youngest child destroyed in a foolish flash. The incomprehensible older boy showing no remorse. Jean-Jean was dead. Marc lived on. Henri and Frances were neither dead nor alive. Yes, the little hospital scene went badly, and then they made off separately into the yellow evening as the nurse came to slowly change the tiny bandage on Marc's wound a final time. You're out of here tomorrow, friend. Marc wanted to kiss all two hundred pounds of her.

Come morning, his first morning out, he decided to walk home to his apartment. But it was not the streets he remembered. Not the streets the way they'd been before Jean-Jean flew down. Not the streets a young man can walk in with his head high, thinking about the future. Not the streets for any man to be in, dangerous streets, full of falling objects, flower pots, vases, bodies. Tumbling from the lips of tall canyons, cascading down, trash and body parts and gallons of foul fluids. Spilling down and flying this way and that in a screaming wind. Where there was nothing he could do but run, duck and run as hard as he could. As everyone else was doing, hard, toward the river, leaping over corpses and the half-dead with stiffening arms upraised, tearing away hands that groped, careening on and on to reach the yellow Seine and climb atop a balustrade on a bridge. Thinking he could fly better than Jean-Jean, convinced he could succeed where his little brother had failed. Raising his arms and getting ready to fly out over the river like a gull and follow it to the open sea.

What do you think you're doing?

It was a policeman.

Marc saw himself climb down from that perch and walk away without a word. As if something had been settled, some great forces had shifted. Now, suddenly, the streets were as calm as any other May evening. Gone were the flying objects, gone were the flying people. Couples lingered and embraced, solo artists whistled in narrow *ruelles*, pretty women let their shoes ring out. Travelers pitched tents in front of museums, making campfires and roasting pigeons.

As ever, as it always will be.

A place so stable, so intimate that you could expect your own brother to come walking down the street toward you any time. To put his arm over your shoulder and lead you into the nearest bar and keep you there for hours. To go over everything, through everything, past, present, future. Leaving nothing untouched. If only because it is a special power, if only because few brothers could ever do such a thing, see straight through each other and through everyone else and the world at large as if it were peopled with shades, as if nothing else was real but them, the brothers, one alive, one dead, opposite charges spinning one around the other forever.

I'm telling you, Jean-Jean said, it will all come down to a final confrontation.

Not that again.

Yes, that again. The armies of the Catholics will have spent dozens of years drawing up a massive defense perimeter across southern Europe, loading it with division after division of conscripts and stocking more armaments in that arc than ever assembled before in one place on earth —

Marc had heard it many times, read it in a dozen books, heard it in a hundred bars, but let him go on. If only because everybody now had swallowed this particular theory. A whole Mediterranean Confrontation genre flourished.

And opposite this, Jean-Jean would say, will lie the Mohammedans, a ragtag sea of the lesser-armed but greater-spirited, a million means of transport at the ready for the final assault on the north. All through the summer of, say, 2042, they will pound the European wall, suffer horrific casualties but only pour more men and women into the battle, the smoke of which will circle the planet and cast a pall unlike any pall ever known to man, as long ago predicted.

Who gets the *frites*?

It was the sloppy waiter. It was also 3 A.M. It looked as if the cook had dumped the whole vat of oil in the plate.

No one, I said.

You guys *ordered* these *frites*! Pay now.

Who is this idiot? Jean-Jean asked.

A waiter, a mere waiter in Paris.

Oh, well, then ignore him. After all, they've been ignoring *us* for years.

What did you say, son?

He didn't say anything, sir. How much do we owe you?

Yes, he did. He called me something!

Nothing. Nothing at all. *Vous pouvez disposer, merci.*

What's that? I can kick both your asses, you know. So don't get wise. We close in one minute, so eat, drink and get out. Clear?

Hell with this, said Jean-Jean.

Marc couldn't have agreed more.

They made a run for it, setting off a round of shouts and missiles of all kinds. Brothers in the night, with the war of 2042 raging off the southern coast. Two mythologies battling it out in one final showdown in the stinking, algae-choked bathtub. Sickly, like children. No, worse, like adults. Thinking they could settle things once and for all. Christ wins! No, Mohammed wins! No, both win! Both lose! Whatever.

And they say, Jean-Jean said, that you will see the lights of the show all the way up here in Paris. If you get up in a high place and try you will see the colored flashes down south. If you get up high. Say on Notre-Dame.

Not up there, said Marc.

We could call Vik, and Samira! Make it a party!

Please, haven't you shown off enough? We're not getting up on Notre-Dame again. *Compris?*

Then we'll just walk around then the rest of the night. Have no fun.

Anything's better than going back up there again. I won't do it.

You have to let go, not care. That's the only way. Once you do that, you're free. You can jump. You can go up there a second time and jump, too.

I know.

It never takes you long to hear me.

That's brothers.

They walked along the Rue des Mauvais Garçons.

So how does it turn out, this war? Marc asked, even though he knew the answer very well.

Turn out? How does it turn out?

Yes, how did it turn out?

Simple. The Buddhists hold back in Asia and wait until the slaughter is done. Then they drive here in their little cars and take over. Just like in olden times. Hordes out of the east. This time,

173

quietly, though. They simply take over empty cities, move the furniture around, change the wallpaper, settle down, have babies. That kind of thing.

Rather boring in the end, Marc said.

Yeah, a little.

The Third-Eye guys get the goods. And the world is saved.

Well, part of it, anyway. However, one mustn't ever think that the root quarrels of society will ever —

You there! Time to come down now! Everyone here wants you to come down! That's an order!

It was the policeman again.

Marc saw himself still on the balustrade. As if he'd never climbed down for drinks and talk with Jean-Jean. As if he'd been standing there, ready to go ahead and jump, to be done with it, for hours. A crowd had formed, jazz musicians played in the back, the roasted chestnut guys had set up here and there, a thousand tourists milled and chatted.

Marc looked down at the yellow river. He had no desire whatsoever now to jump. However, he also had no desire whatsoever to climb down off the balustrade, either.

Comme c'est mélo, a woman cried out. *Descendez, connard!*

Vik?

Of course it was.

Once upon a time, Grandfather Ansel began that night in Paris, there were two very happy people who lived in a nice house with a big yard in a small town.

He paused, looked his two story-starved grandsons over, saw that he had their full attention.

So down below the house was a big river and the two happy people who lived in the house would sit on a dock there in the evening talking and waiting for the moon to come up. Every night they went to the river when it was cool after the long hot day, and sometimes they would take off their shoes and put their feet in the water.

A giggle sounded from the younger grandson.

We've never done that, said the older.

Well, one night, far down the river they saw a little green light coming their way. Look, a boat, the man said, I wonder who it could be. I don't know, said the woman. So they waited. And the light grew brighter and brighter, and then they could hear the motor going putt-putt, putt-putt. Here it comes now, said the man. And so soon the boat pulled up to the dock and stopped. Hello there! the woman called to the boat. But there was no answer. Is there anyone there? the man called. Again there was no answer. So they walked over and looked into the little boat. It's empty, she said, no one at all! How strange, he said. How very strange, she said. How can a boat come here by itself? he asked her. I don't know, she replied. But there it was, the little boat with its green light on and its motor still going putt-putt, putt-putt. They looked at it some more, then looked at each other, but did not know what to say. Just then, very slowly, the boat began to move away. Look, she cried, it's leaving! Hurry, he shouted, we must get on! Are you sure? Where will it take us? I don't know, he said, I don't know, but hurry, hurry before it gets away! And so the two very happy people ran and leaped into the little boat and off they went back down the river straight for the big violet moon that looked like it was coming right up out of the water. Are you thinking what I'm thinking? she asked. Yes, I am, he said. The little boat is going to take us to the moon! But it is so far away, she sighed. No, he told her, look, you can almost touch it already, see? And there, right there in front of them, was the moon, big as a whole house, and the little boat with the green light went putt-putt, putt-putt and came up to a dock right on the moon. Here we are, he shouted, here we are! And out they jumped onto the moon dock. It's beautiful, she cried, so beautiful! It was early morning on the moon and a plain of violet dust stretched away as far as they could see. Can we stay here? she asked. Yes, he said, yes we can, and forever, which is a very long time. And so the two very happy people looked back at the little boat with its little green light gliding back into the night. Goodbye, little boat, and thank you for bringing us to the moon, she said. Goodbye, he said, goodbye. And then the little boat was gone.

Ansel stopped, unhappy with it. What would become of them?

Why was everything violet? It somehow seemed sinister, too, as if the lovers were walking into a deadly trap.

Had he scared the kids?

He leaned forward to check. The younger one was out.

The older one, wide awake, hands clasped behind his head, said, Grandfather?

Yes?

I don't like the moon like that. And why did the little boat leave them?

It's only a story. They wanted to go, so they went. A lot of people have dreamed of that. Now I think it's time to go to sleep, don't you?

Are they going to die up there?

Shh now.

I don't like the moon violet like that.

Shh.

All right. Good night, Grandfather.

Goodnight, son.

Ansel waited a while longer, stroking the boy's hair and cheeks. Was there not someplace beautiful for old men to go and die? He put a violet moon in the sky over Mexico. He put himself in a little boat at night on a lake surrounded by jungle. The moon in the black water. The boat passing into the moon as through a web, tearing it, the light shredding, scattering, sinking. The boat lifting out of the water. A woman in a long violet dress waving from the dock on the moon, beckoning. The boat driver, a brilliant poet named Neruda, saying, *Señor, He aquí violetas, golondrinas, todo cuanto nos gusta.* Here are violets, swallows — all the things that delight us.

What did you say, Grandfather?

Nothing. Now go to sleep.

I'm not sleepy.

Yes you are. It's late.

Frances and Henri came home early.

When the man who thought he ruled his kingdom found his older boy still wide awake, he burst into Ansel's room and demanded an explanation.

Have you been telling them stories? Is this why Marc's awake and looking like he's seen a ghost? Well?

Ansel ignored him.

I'm talking to you, Ansel Gifford!

Ansel stirred his dominoes, yawned.

No more children's stories! Do you hear me!

Oh, leave Daddy alone!

Don't start, woman! Don't start!

Doors slammed. Things were broken. Lights flickered. The world seemed stuck in a cheap play.

Later, Henri played the trumpet on the balcony. It was Moon River, and it was very bad. Again the neighbors yelled and the police came. Again Frances locked herself in the bathroom and cried. Again the old man and the child sat on the stairs, listening, holding hands and hearing it all. And again Grandfather kissed the grandson's face and told him that all would pass.

I, the current Man of Peace, plant a bean and tomato and okra garden in the side yard of my sprawling mansion high in the Sierra Madre. Even though winter is here. Each inserted seed brings a roar from the crowd as they bend to mimic My Work, poking their fingers among the broken rock and cacti again and again.

They will do anything I do.

For the Man of Peace is all. A mere Christ would never do, no mere Messiah. No, only a true Man of Peace born in a spontaneous wrinkle of circumstance, with no religious, political or medical affiliation can be their guide. And if I want to plant a little garden in the wrong season, then it is because that is the right thing to do. Dig, dig! they shout at each other. The young women ram steel pikes into the rock hour after hour while old men sprinkle in the seeds.

In those quiet moments, a measure of hope reigns down in the valley of the shadow of the Man of Peace. Old men around fires say, Come a good thunderhead up in here and we's goin to have the biggest damn veggie garden on earth. Goin to feed ourselves! Goin to get mighty fat! That's the secret, ain't it now?

All through the night the I, Ansel, the Man of Peace, lie with my moon goddess waiting for the crackle of applause in the distance as the people, here and there, think they understand something, anything.

So when are you going to preach to them? Chulmetic sometimes asks me. When are you going to spell it all out?

I don't know, I answer. Perhaps never. Is there a rush?

Never say never. Say soon, she says, and be done with this mystery play before boredom sets in. Besides, I wouldn't mind getting out of here for a few days.

Out of here?

Isn't this getting a bit macho? Keeping me pinned in here like this? Watch out, or I'll start making decisions on my own, Señor El Pacificador. I'm not your rag doll. Now how about my massage?

Already?

Already.

I rub the moon goddess in front of the bay windows in the winter moonlight while hundreds of pairs of binoculars focus in and a hush falls over the multitude.

They're watching us again, I say.

I like that part, she says. It gives them hope.

Mere lewdness?

No, pulsing jealousy. It drives all, or didn't you know?

I don't answer. I work the heels of my old palms down her alabaster spine. She undulates and moans.

Preach to them? Whatever would I say?

Something bright, something simple, Ansel.

Bright and simple, eh?

Something. Anything. Soon.

I seize the goddess's buttocks and the crowd goes wild.

12

*F*RANCES AND HER DOCTOR, the two old lovers no one ever knew about, sat on the bed and stared at each other in the dawn. This time it was more like she was holding his hand, comforting him, instead of the other way around. The way it had been for untold weeks as she began her descent. Now there was nothing more he or anyone else could do for her, the woman he had taken for a night ride in his canoe and kissed like a young man when they were both past sixty. One midnight, one kiss, and all the two-hour flowers, all the years of Henri's foul mouth, all of that blew like dust off an empty road. One kiss from a new man already an old man but the best she had ever had, maybe the only one she had ever had. Cruelly perfect, now that life was almost over.

Now Marc barged into her room. Did you call? Is something wrong?

Come near, son. And say hello to the doctor.

But the doctor was already putting his green rain slicker back on. There was nothing more he could do.

❦

Father stopped his story of the storm and stiffened in his chair as if he'd seen a ghost. Frances?

Marc, too, looked toward the dark, sunken house, at the thick limestone steps stretching up to the open door. There was no one there, it seemed, only the black mouth of the manse, and the river

179

mist sailing slowly by. Perhaps she had been there for a long time, just out of sight, straining to hear the story. Maybe she was still there, seeing them looking toward her.

But she would not come out. There being nothing to say to the man who had ruled her for so many years. So many long, hateful years.

No, Father. She never leaves her bed anymore.

Worse and worse, isn't it.

But his pity was fake, and Marc didn't know what to answer.

❧

Ansel had found a hatchet and begun busting up the tables and chairs on the deck to use for boarding up the windows. My first view of the destruction he had wreaked upon Sarah's porch furniture got me to scratching my fly bite as I hunkered nearby, out of breath, having somehow got up the ladder with a good two hundred pounds of hog on my back. I could only stare in terror at what the old man had done, sure that as soon as she saw it we'd be out on our asses. With night coming and the waves building.

Then I realized that Ansel's mouth was moving, that he was saying something to me that the wind was stealing away. I reshouldered my load and took a step toward him, the better to hear. But the weight of Hambone propelled me mercilessly, buckling my knees, and I collapsed forward.

Do you need some help?

Now I heard him. But before I could answer, events abandoned me.

There she comes! he yelled, as if seeing a ship on the horizon.

I managed to turn and watch Sarah get up the ladder with a dozen jars of blood, a feat that amazed but disturbed one's convictions about the laws of physics. Smiling, she appeared to have put her malaise over the *bête* behind her, and taking stock of the demolition work done in her absence, she launched into a long, and clearly audible, tribute to the old man.

Ansel thanked her with a gentlemanly bow.

I'll put this blood away till sausage-making weather and fetch

180

the nails, his admirer announced. I do even have a hammer you know, *ja*! Couldn't be nailing the windows shut with a shoe, could we?

I got the hog off me and sat up, quite the picture, one pitiful *Homo sapiens* among the jillions. I wondered if she had a bathtub, but quickly chided myself for entertaining the thought.

Ansel kept shaking his head as if I'd passed away.

What's it with you? I asked.

I seen better-looking orphans in the *favelas* of Rio, he said.

In the what?

Slum cities. In my next life I want to be the father of all the fatherless children. I want to lead them back into the forest, to the deep green forest. I want to sit with them under the trees and read to them from The Children of the Forest. Just like Mrs. Miller did, the sweet words flowing from her lips and touching us like a breeze in that horrible little oven of a classroom in the middle of hell-knows-where Texas.

Ansel stopped, apparently moved by his own tale.

I hadn't remembered that in years, he gasped. They say you do, though, at major transitions like this.

No time for chitchat, I said.

Not when it comes to saving your own hide, I guess not, Henri Du, he replied.

I ignored the bait, dragged Hambone inside and, at Sarah's behest, parked him by the couch on an old throw rug.

He looked like a bloated pet whiling away the hours.

He'll be all right there for a while, she said.

Don't you want to cover him up?

He was still percolating, and giving off a bit of steam.

Oh what's a little blood. You is Frainche, all right.

Madame, si vous voulez que je vous explique ce que je pense de votre putain de cochon —

O.K., shutup, you win. Wouldn't want to be scarin y'all to death. I've got Waverley's old dog blanket somewhere. We can use that. Poor Waverley. Crabs got him.

So sorry.

Hell, he had cancer of the balls. Don't make me no mind and I'm sure not him either. Crabs just about had him picked clean when I went down with his canfood one mawnin last summa. Awful sight. I bashed me a few of them crabs with Daddy's ole baseball bat . . .

Eventually, we tucked in Hambone with an ancient Red Cross rag that harbored so many fleas I swear I saw it move.

A couple of hours later we had the windows boarded up, the back door, too. We got down the TV antenna. We put cinder blocks on the roof to hold the iron sheeting. But from the looks of the black clouds racing in, only a fool would have believed the place would hold up.

The lady of the house rewarded our hard work with more rum, which we imbibed out on the now-cleared deck. The wind blasted us bad.

What's it up to now? I inquired.

Fifty-seven, said Ansel.

You could put your hand up to it and walk your fingers as though along a wall. You could use it to massage any part of your body.

Part of me was thrilled, like a child in an amusement park. But another part of me, socked by the alcohol, begged to get inside, to safety, dryness, windlessness.

Anyone for a stroll before we close up this popstand? Sarah called out. Who'll take the lady to go see the big beach waves yonder?

I couldn't hold back any longer and said, I'm no meteorologist or oceanologist, but it seems highly inappropriate at this time to —

I'm revising my estimate, Ansel said.

He was struggling to hold his index finger high and straight.

What you get now? Sarah asked.

East-southeast, sixty-nine.

I'll just stay here and guard things, I offered.

Do what? Sarah demanded.

Be sure nobody breaks in, you know.

Honey, there ain't nobody *out* here but you, me, Ansel, Felix the Nazi and the wind. You come on the final hike with us. We gonna see the beach before it's washed away. What's your problem anyway?

I tossed reason to the wind, raised my hand and, in French fashion, wagged it at her, the gesture indicating clearly that I strongly wished to have it come into firm contact with her flabby jowl.

What foul logic is this? I screamed out. And who's Felix?

Ansel spoke into my ear. That won't get us anywhere. Just do as the lady says and maybe you'll survive. Maybe. She's been through this before. She knows what she's doing. Listen to me on this.

Caught by my temper, I continued to wag my hand in her face.

She only smiled back, though, the tiny wheels of her mind spinning to the conclusion that I was trying to be funny. After which she slapped both hands over her mouth and blushed.

Seeing an opening, Ansel locked his hand on my arm and forced it down, firmly and slowly.

Now, he ordered, say you'd *love* to go for a stroll. Say it.

I'd *love* to go for a stroll, I said.

Her knees thwocked together in an awkward curtsy.

Her father was a British tourist, Ansel explained. So keep it clean about the Queen. Then louder, Well, now, let's get going! *A la plage!*

Oh do let me fetch my hat, Sarah sang out. And, oh, oh I have just the *perfect* outfit!

With that, she bounded like a puppy into the house.

Ansel and I stood together at the railing and surveyed the frothing whitecaps.

House seem like it's shaking to you?

I looked at my feet, but I don't know why. Then I looked at the side of the *baraque*, and up at the ridgepole. Still couldn't tell. I tried reading her against the background, but the trees were thrashing, making judgment doubtful. There was the light shudder in my cowardly legs, but that was usual for me.

Don't think so, I said.

Still concerned, he bent far over the railing, his faded swimsuit slipping low. Hit by a fear that he might yank me overboard with him, I backed away.

Algae's all *over* the place now, he said. What a scene!

You're going to fall, Ansel! Pull up!

He righted himself, rubbed his chin a moment, and then announced, We have ourselves a fourteen-degree list to the west-northwest.

What does that mean?

That the house will fall over.

When?

I'd say she's got about fifteen or sixteen degrees to go. That's assuming a more or less classic distribution of weight. Of course we are at . . . seventy-eight mph now and the wind speed has been increasing at a rate of thirteen point thirteen per hour. How many vectors is that? Will simple algebra work his out, or do I need trig? He produced a small pencil, the eraserless stub one gets at a golf course, and began to figure on his tattered sleeve.

I ignored him, listened to the waves pounding the beach on the ocean side of the island, watched the bands of clouds climbing higher and higher like sheets of lead.

It had to happen, though, and then it did. My heart jumped, got off beat. I was officially scared to death.

Boys! Sarah bawled. Ain't I the prettiest thang you ever did see?

Good Lord, Miss Sarah, said Ansel, swinging his head in mock amazement. I can't believe my eyes. How about you, H.D.?

I dared to look at her. It was beyond my worst nightmare.

She wore a hot pink sundress over a farthingale as big as a kingsize bed and a bright yellow sombrero as big as a dining table. This combination flopped crazily in the wind, keeping her off balance. Not to be showed up by a mere hurricane, however, she made as if she were dancing a little jig and grinned. I have seen many an act in his life . . . Somehow I held my tongue.

On y va, Ansel finally said, bisecting the way forward with a cleaverlike chop of his hand. You've never seen waves like these, H.D. Five, six stories tall. Hey, Puddin! I wonder if that ole crazy Felix'll be out there surfin!

My name ain't Puddin, she said.

I won't explain how, but we all got down the ladder, impeded only momentarily by the predictable arguments about the protocol of order, the macho view being one thing, the feminist view another and the bi perspective yet another. But such was mere ostentatiousness beside the necessity of not damaging the ancestral farthingale.

We only had to wade a half-dozen yards to be free of the now sea-borne algae, which had grown quite warm since the hog sticking. I'm no biologist, but the stuff appeared to be consciously trying to save itself. For when I looked back upon the shack a final time, I saw it massing around the supports and climbing in threads.

Stick together, I said, as if in charge.

This is a stroll, not a parade, Ansel said. *Du calme.*

Sarah skipped ahead toward the beach, flapping her stubby arms.

Caught in their web, I had no choice but to try for once to be brave. Yet it took only a moment's reflection there in nature's tumult to know it would be impossible. There were tremendous creaking sounds followed by tremendous splitting sounds. There were distant screams and close-up cries. There were booms and bangs and blasts as if a war were on. I scratched my bite, dug my nails into it.

Ansel drew near. Easy. Give in and you'll sink like a stone at midnight. Understand? Don't you want to see ole Felix surf? Sarah's brought rum in her hoop, too. Live and let live.

Unable to find any words, I watched as he scanned the treetops until he had done a full circle.

What're you doing now?

Got to be on the lookout.

Can't we just go? Get this over with?

That's the spirit! Off we go now! I knew you'd get with the program!

Again, he cleaved the air.

Then one day Frances gave Ansel a crabstick and the old man came back to life. At first, venturing only a few steps out the front door, down the hall, to the landing. Then, the next day, down the stairs to the street and the sidewalk, where he stood and watched the passersby. After a week of this, he went even farther, to the corner, to the store, and then he began to take the bus, to ride

185

along wherever it went and come back around with it. Frances watched his comings and goings, but hardly noticed the pattern, the gradual unwinding of the leash. So that it was more or less a complete surprise the day he failed to return, as usual, by dark — the day she got a phone call from him saying that he'd taken the train to Chartres to see the cathedral and then some of the countryside and that he'd be back when he got back, not to worry. Of course, Frances worried. Henri questioned. The grandkids wondered. But it wasn't the end of the earth. It was only an old man spreading his ancient wings a bit. So be it, his keepers decided. He was, after all, a grown man, was he not? Your grandfather can take care of himself — came here before, you know, as a young man. He'll be home soon. Now everybody off to bed!

Chartres, then Poitiers, then La Rochelle, the leash tugged and stretched until the old man's pocket money ran out and he called for help. Frances would beg and Henri would bring Ansel back. Then it was Nîmes and Nice. Frances begged and Henri reeled. Then it was across the border into Italy. How far could he go? Was he looking for something? She begged her man in a way a woman shouldn't have to beg. Loving and hating it all, Henri reeled.

Which made for one of the most exhausting summers in family history. Which made for quarrels and slammed doors and drinking bouts. Which made for angry love and sweet hate. Leaving the children confused as the old man struggled to break free for good.

The going was rough. Ansel and I soon abandoned all efforts to follow the old path, now strewn with debris, wads of driftnet in which deep-sea creatures lay dying, hundreds of bald whitewalls, two or three Japanese TV sets, a wide range of '50s jazz records, a case of '69 Entre-Deux-Mers, several large window panes, a Timex watch and the fender of a lime-green 2CV. I suspected a French cargo vessel had capsized nearby, although its flag, admittedly, could very well have been Cameroonian.

To keep a correct heading for the beach, we followed the bursts of hot pink in the distance, the flash of her enormous sundress being as powerful as the beam of a lighthouse. But sea spray at times blinded us, and we would crouch down behind a crate, a fallen trunk, a barrel of Cognac, to dry our tears and argue.

You hate me, I said.

Not that crap, please.

You *do* hate me. You've always hated me. From the first day I met you in George West, Texas, you've hated me.

Ignoring my taunts, again Ansel started a scan of the treetops, this time creasing his brow with concern.

What *is* it? I demanded, staring up at the thrashing fronds.

I thought I saw . . . Dno baby! Ho, Dno!

There it was again, high overhead, the little black monkey we'd seen earlier, practically flying along. It was carrying a single coconut and appeared to be coming our way.

Ansel was elated. If Dno is out, then it's still safe, he said. Dno knows everything. I bet you anything this means the eye won't be over us until midnight at the soonest. Bet you a hundred dollars.

I wondered why he trusted a monkey.

Ho, Dno! Down here!

Does he bite?

Dno bite? Nah. He just gets jealous. You know, when someone else is around me. You see, I saved him the other night. This businessman from Hong Kong was down at the Moon Bar demanding monkey for dinner and Felix — he runs the joint — was about to trade the life of his pet, Olga, for a wad of American dollars. It was pure luck that I walked in just as Felix was tying down Olga on a cutting board right there on the bar . . .

Dno had come into the palm under which we were crouching and, hanging from the trunk, swung like a flag directly over us. It cocked its head as if listening, then and again screeching at the wind as if to tell it to pipe down.

These Hong Kong operators, they like their monkey fresh, Ansel said. So with Olga strapped on that board screaming her little monkey head off, Felix carts her over to the businessman's table and says, Will this do, sir?

Bei pijiu, he said.

Felix looked at me. What'd he say?

He wants a beer with it.

Olga exploded into a death howl, annoying our Asian guest, who produced a yellow silk handkerchief, reached over and, with consummate skill, popped it into her vicious little mouth.

Ansel lifted his head, gave Dno a big wink.

Now custom says, he went on, you cleave the monkey's head open and then show its brain to the customer before the *cuisson*.

Rum and chicken wings rose in my throat.

I liked that monkey, Ansel said. I'd spent many an evening getting drunk with her and singing old German songs with Felix and trying to get her to sing along, too. Once or twice she almost did! It was like a scratched record on 78, but we loved it all the same.

The monkey above us chattered.

They *can* understand what we're saying, you know. Anyway, I said to the famished customer from the East, *Wo xuexi Zhongwen*. Or, I'm learning Chinese. But he didn't even look up, so I said, in plain American, Hey, bud, that critter you've ordered for dinner is my friend. This drew his attention away from a large red fly crawling across the back of his hand.

Well, then, he began, how much is a friend worth?

I thought a second and retorted, All the money in the world, by God.

That was silly, Ansel, I interjected.

Quiet! Meanwhile, Felix was getting impatient. What am I supposed to do with this monkey? It's gonna suffocate and spoil while y'all is dicking around. I knew that time was quickly running out, that I would have to improvise, even though that concept is a *trompe-l'œil*, and fast. But nothing came to me. Nothing at all to save the life of a monkey.

I swear it, a flurry of gnawed coco-shell splinters defied the winds and sprinkled our hair. Believe me, I did not look up.

So I cried like a baby, Ansel confessed. I'm no Latin, but I pulled out the stops. Dr. No, or whatever his name was, watched the fly on his hand take a big, long bite, then swatted it, swept it aside and stood. Men don't cry, he said. I bawled. I sobbed and moaned and bawled. Men don't cry! he repeated. I dropped to my knees, seized his overstarched bermuda shorts and begged for the monkey's life. Even Felix got misty-eyed, and Olga, she had twisted her poor little head around to see how things were working out. She is my best friend! I exclaimed. I let him spit at me in disgust and shout, Who could eat in here with all this garbage! This done, I signaled to Felix to show the gentleman the door. But Dr. No stormed out on his own, issuing threats about how he would return one day and, using the investment vehicle of his slave-based conglomerate, buy out not only the Moon Bar but the whole island, which, in turn, he vowed to transform into a breeding ground for monkeys for mainland restaurants back home.

We let him go. The fly bite would do the rest.

Felix untied Olga, who tore the handkerchief from her mouth, tossed it aside with a theatrical flip, and leaped into my arms.

She's yours now, said the Nazi.

I was taken aback. I couldn't, really.

Yes, you could. No man's ever cried for her like that. No man. How could you live without her?

Olga is yours now, he insisted. I'll even give you the brand-new collar I got her in Argentina. What do you say to that?

That won't be necessary. No collars. No bridles for this wild one.

Whoa, said Felix. You have to keep her reined in. You've seen her drunk. You know what I mean.

I wouldn't hear of it, and dropped my bombshell. I intend to see her free!

Free? Olga?

That's correct. Right here on the island. Who knows but that there may dangle out there somewhere the *beau* of her monkey dreams. She could have a regular family and not end up an aged barmaid bitch. For that, I got a nip on the neck, which to this day has yet to heal.

Ansel pulled down his collar and showed me the spot, about the diameter of a thumbtack. It was capped with a shiny white scab.

My mind wandered as it dawned on me that we'd been under that tree talking about that damn monkey long enough that we could've hit the beach, had our little fun and gone back and settled in for the night back at the shack.

So, I said, are you bringing Dno in from this storm, or what?

Dno knows what Dno wants, he said. Now Olga and I were about to bid Felix good day when he said, I have a little something I need to tell you, Ansel. What's that? I asked. Well, you see, Olga's a she, but she thinks she's a he. She thinks what? She's convinced she's of the male species. Male is not a species, I corrected. Wanna bet, Ansel?

Let's get out of here, Ansel.

He ignored me, went on. So I peered at the creature, which was looking me right in the eye and smiling as if it knew something wonderful. I was about to say something about this turn of events, and it was probably not going to be very kind, when the critter cuddled right on up in there and gave me a big kiss on the mouth like this!

My father-in-law kissed me.

I shoved him back. You slimy ole son of a bitch! Get off me!

In retrospect, the subsequent blow to my head was surprisingly soft to have had such an effect. And as I held the coconut that had inflicted it, which had bounced into my hands, again I heard Hambone's death squeal. Again, it sounded like a child being murdered. It was only when the old man jammed shut my mouth that I knew it'd been me.

After that, I saw a moth, a very large moth, twirling toward me. You're not supposed to watch it, they say, or risk it seeing that you are in any way interested in its presence. I remembered this from the only college course I even remember, the one on the relationship between the habits of the io moth, or *Automeris io*, and occultism among white investment bankers.

Again I saw hot blood in Mason jars.

I slurred my words. Whoo nee aw tha blaad, Ansaal —

Didn't you notice Sarah's sudden good mood when she came back from the sticking? he answered. She had a big shot of that blood down there. Man, it's got enough iron in it to bridge your consciousness from here to Timbuktu, that is if you're into that kind of travel. Now can I finish my monkey tale?

I was fading fast from the coco blow, doubtless launched by the critter above. The light was going.

Well, I said to Olga, Olga why did you kiss me? And do you know what she, I mean he, did? He *shrugged*. Well, I said to Felix, he'll sure as hell need a new name, now won't he! A guy can't go around trying to meet pretty young girl monkeys saying, Hi, my name is Olga, now can he?

I don't know, Felix said, looking sad.

You don't know what?

I've always called her Olga. Nothing else would fit.

I don't know either, I said.

Felix and I and Olga stood there in the Moon Bar, thinking.

I wanted Ansel to be done with it. I also wanted to go ahead and die, finish whatever it was that was happening to me.

I hissed, Cah eem, ah dno —

Right, Henri Du! Ansel shouted. We did.

The light went out.

This time Vik does not look good, but thin, addict-like. Her voice rings forth as tough as ever, though, as she tears into Marc like a mother dog into a wanderlust pup.

Thought maybe you'd go the Jean-Jean route, eh? What self-centered garbage! Just like the *petit bourgeois* you'll always be! Thinking you're better than the rest of us. Sure that you'll die with more flair, more color, more everything. As if we didn't exist. I spit on your kind. Truly.

Dear Vik, Marc says, putting his arm around her as they stroll away from the death bridge over the Seine.

It seems that a lifetime has passed since Jean-Jean's suicide day, since the hotel room, since the gunshot wound, even since he himself had been preparing to leap into the yellow river, into the yellow afterlife where weak light falls through old curtains, the place Jean-Jean had gone to await his brother.

Dear dear Vik.

Stop saying that. I'm not dear anything.

Her bones jut out as if she has some unspeakable disease and her dusty skin is gray and grainy. All manner of things are caught in her tangled hair, as in an old mop head, and she smells of urine.

How long has it been, dear?

How can you say that! You think all is forgiven just like that?

191

I never heard another word from you after the hotel. Or don't you remember?

Yes.

Say it louder! I remember it well, friend. How your face turned to pale marble when the boy came to the door with the message that Jean-Jean had jumped from Notre-Dame. How you turned to me and Samira and insisted it wasn't true, that your dear brother would never—

Please stop.

Never have done *that*. Then you said that we needed to keep on drinking, that Jean-Jean would be along any minute, as soon as he got off work and found the note to meet us there for our little party. That all we had to do was keep waiting and he would come.

We waited a long time, Marc says.

Yes, we did. And got very drunk. And then, damn it, you wanted to make love to us. Which you and Jean-Jean must have been planning all along. Then it began to seem possible that Jean-Jean was dead, because you didn't want to go out of that room and see that it was true. Instead you tried to climb on us. Only it wouldn't work for you. You'd already become an old man. So we did nothing.

Sat there.

Not long, though. Samira dressed and left. Then I did. But not without telling you to go to your brother. You just stared at me. Then I never heard a word from you and now you're calling me dear? You're as sick as all the rest.

I'm sorry.

Don't start *that*.

Why can't we try again. Do it right this time, grab onto our lives.

Are you crazy? You're nothing now.

And Samira?

Who knows? The anti-everybody people have probably shipped her home.

To prison.

Hell, Samira wanted prison. That's all she ever talked about. Being locked up and forgotten. With guards to come in and bang her everyday. But the things we fear most are the things we really want, *n'est-ce pas*? So you're headed for the museum?

Pardon me?

To the Dead Art. It's a whole new show now. Where've you been?

I'd rather you take a bath and then get in a giant bed with me and do it for a couple of weeks. Like old times.

How can you *say* that? Look at me! *Un sac de merde!*

People stop and laugh. A tourist takes a picture.

Marc leads her by the arm into another street. What have you done to yourself?

So do you want to go to the Dead Art with me or not? I work there, so you'll get in free.

I really had better —

What, finish your errands? What's the wife got you doing today? Flowers, maybe?

Cut it out.

Drop your duty, Marc. Come to the show. Change your path, deviate. You'll be an old fuck any day now. When are you going to start living?

She begins to seem crazy. Why suddenly does she want him to come along to the museum? Doesn't she hate him, despise everything about him past and present? It's like meeting a whore you've known well, Marc thinks, only she's ancient now long before her time. You regret ever having touched her. Perhaps it is best they go their separate ways again. Whatever is there left to say or do together?

I don't think so, said Marc. Some other time.

In Iceland, we dump your kind in a geyser just to perk up the bubbles. Pfooey on you.

She turns to go.

Wait, Marc calls, not sure why he has.

No waiting. You want me, I'm at the Dead Art.

Wait!

He wants her back. But she is gone, quick as a sheet of paper in a storm.

Marc waits there a long time, wondering if he might write another book, another of his one-month tales, just to do it, just

193

because the head was forever swallowing the tail and the spinning refused to stop.

A car horn sounds. He is standing in the street.

Get out of the way, goddamn fool!

Marc gets out of the way, but not before the kid in the car fires a large gun.

The Dead Art, he thinks, as a crowd gathers to see if he has been hit. He has forgotten where it is.

Are you O.K.? someone asks.

An old man, an old man who looks like his grandfather. A simple workingman who'd seen it all, the flash of the gun, the speeding car, everything, and come running across the street from a construction site to see about the victim.

Tell me, Grandfather, where is the Dead Art?

Are you hurt?

Marc spreads open his coat to show he is all right.

The Dead Art Museum. Where is it?

You sure you're not hurt? Those bastards! I was sure you were a goner. You ought to sit down for a while. I'd love to plug every last one of them. Ship them all back to Morocco where they came from.

Grandfather?

Sit down a minute. Have a drink. You don't go walking around after you've been shot at like that.

You look like my grandfather who disappeared down in Mexico all those years ago. About whom I once wrote a book in thirty-one days.

Better go sit down.

Sir, you look exactly like my grandfather, Ansel Gifford. Quickly, tell me your name.

The old man spits on the ground and walks back across the street to work on the row of tourist toilets.

Your name? Marc calls.

The old man stops and takes a drink of water from a hose running into a barrel. A young man carrying blueprints steps out of a yellow shed and shouts an order. The old man nods, takes up his shovel and bends to mix a pile of black cement.

Grandfather?

He's in shock, someone says. Thinks he's found his grandpa!

Several jerks are standing there laughing. Marc stares at them a moment, or for a long time, it doesn't matter which, then goes his way feeling older than the earth.

13

As THE SUMMER MONTHS ran into the fall months, Ansel didn't settle for Italy, he kept going. To Greece and Turkey. Telephoning when the cash ran out. Being rescued by Henri and hauled back to Paris once again. The silly cycle repeating itself again and again until one night late in August new orders came down. Like the granite lid on a tomb.

No more travels, Henri commanded. No more anything. You will stay home.

The man who thought he ruled his kingdom still had spoken, Frances had fallen back like a tree before the wind, and the children had scattered. His will was done.

Fearing something bad, Ansel did as told, accepted his sentence.

The apartment walls seemed to crush him.

Ansel, looks like you're going to have to make yourself some decisions here, his buddy Adair, always near, soon said. I mean you can't be hanging on with these people. They ain't worth your breath, they ain't worth being with. Why don't you just go on home?

Home? Come on, Adair. No, I was thinking Mexico. Old Mexico.

That again? You know what I read?

What'd you read?

How all down in there now it's gangs of criminals running around. Long time ago it used to be banditos and crap like that and people was afraid to set foot down there. Now it's high-powered gangs of killer kids who'll plug you if you so much as look at them the wrong way or the right way or any way. What's wrong with Vegas? I can give you some tips.

You can't live in Vegas.

That depends. Now, go straight to the dice —

I've got my heart set on Mexico, Adair.

I won't come fetch you when you're bummed out down there. Don't count on me.

I don't count on anybody.

Yeah, you do. You know people like me can't let people like you just run around crazy. It's dangerous. For everybody.

Bullshit. I wish we had a beer.

All you have to do is go in there and say, Damn it, Henri, where's the beer?

He's liable to punch me.

So? Be a man. Weren't you on the George West football team?

The bedroom door opened slowly. It was little Marc.

Brought you a beer, Grandfather.

How about that!

Here you go. Father didn't see me.

Ansel took the can of beer. Want to sit down with me a while?

O.K. Why is Father so mean to you?

Oh, he means well, I guess. You'll have troubles, too, someday, so we have to try to understand what makes people do what they do.

He's mean.

I don't think so. Just irritated.

Are you going to run away again?

What makes you say that?

I had a dream you did. For good.

You did?

You went to Mexico. And you did what you wanted to do.

Which was?

You were walking in the jungle for a while and then on a beach and then you were sitting in a bar drinking cold beer and watching the ocean out the front door. That's all you were doing. You were very happy.

Hmm.

Can I go with you?

Who said I was going?

I know you will.

What's going on in here!

It was Henri.

Ansel set the beer can on the nightstand. Marc stood up.

You're giving the boy *alcohol*, Ansel?

Of course not.

Out of here, Marc. Out!

Marc ran out.

Just what do you think you're doing, Ansel! Can't you just leave the kids alone? What were you doing, giving him beer and telling him scary stories?

Ansel stood up. That'll be enough, Henri Du.

Oh yeah? Enough of what?

Enough of your lip.

And with that, Ansel Gifford reached far back into the strength of his youth, reached back with his high school passing arm, took aim and let fly the greatest bomb of his entire career, a ninety-nine-yarder with one second left on the clock, the state championship on the line . . . There it went . . . floating, spiraling, sinking now. Connecting. Touchdown!

Henri Du hit the floor with a boom and Ansel stood over him.

The boy ran back in.

Grandfather, what have you done!

And the little boy gave his old grandfather a big hug around the legs.

Now, son. Help your father up.

Marc bent down to his dad.

Giving the boy a pat on the head, Ansel walked out of the room, went into the kitchen and kissed his daughter. Without a word he took his crabstick from the umbrella stand, opened the front door of the apartment and disappeared from the world.

That night, Frances heard the front door slam a thousand times.

Henri . . .

My nose hurts. Leave me alone.

You'll have to find him.

Like hell. *Plus jamais*.
If you don't find him —
What?
I don't know, but I'll think of something.
Oh yeah?
Frances lay there wide awake in the steamy night. But it was as if a battery of projectors were shining down on her. Making her invisible in a flood of light. So that when, right on time, Henri rolled near to do his business, to say he loved her and then reach for her, she was no longer there.

But then there *is* something nice, though I damn that word, about having all the world at my feet, as it were. Just waiting for whatever it is I am going to say. Who gets such an opportunity in a lifetime?

As in another special act men are driven through a mixture of pride and fear to perform with their particular goddesses, I hold back, slow, let it last as long as possible. After all, what is the use in shooing off the crowds just when they have arrived? When more are arriving each day. The Popes of yore could only pray for such attendance.

Sometimes it makes me sad at heart to see them all out there quaking with fervor, bursting into applause when I merely walk in front of a window or upon flushing the toilet, the other end of which dumps in their midst. It is then I recall seeing Catholic faithful crawling on their bloody knees up to church doors all over Mexico the one time my father took us on a trip. I was only twelve years old, but the stripes of pilgrims' blood leading to the brown sunken church doors are still fresh in my mind. That and the fat women in blue shawls sitting in the shadows nearby, their pyramids of mangoes stacked high. Their black mouths chewing the yellow meat in the halflight, smiling as the bloody ones made their way inside the church to pray to the Virgen de Guadalupe. It gave you nightmares about whole populations being made to perform the same act. To crawl from city to city, popped by the whip of faith. To bleed here and there, everywhere you can, until you have bled your life away for Her. For Her and Her Son and His Father, all of them.To wake feeling ill knowing it was your blood they were after, your life they wanted.

But now it is my time to dispense with the rules, isn't it? My time to say No to crawling on knees from city to city to pray to a plastic doll virgin in a glass box lighted by a flickering fluorescent bulb. The baby doll virgin with cracked plastic skin and cobwebs across her breast. If anything, when I make my big speech, say my big thing, such pilgrimages will be outlawed, their practitioners banished. The Christians will surrender. And if I get my way, the Mohammedans will, too. And all the others. Or so I tell Chulmetic.

Fat chance, she says.

I listen with one ear.

My other ear listens for the thunder of applause. Sometimes I get a thirst for it, especially in the wee hours of morning, and go out on the patio to smoke. I have no more gotten my rear end onto my deck chair, my legs crossed and my cigarette lighted, than the sky rips open and spills fireworks and ordnance. Night becomes day. A bittersweet stink chokes the air. And, should anyone of the faithful have been sleeping through it all, street drummers from the four corners of the globe produce their plastic buckets and begin to pound in unison. It is the beat of the old black-and-white movies of African tribesmen surrounding the big kettle in which the white man squats about to be boiled alive as the flames lick higher and higher. That's me. The man in the pot, but at least there's a moment of glory in this life. If this is glory. I think of the witches of Salem and of Jeanne D'Arc.

When the time comes, I will speak my mind and bow out. Then Chulmetic and I will make love day and night, tend to the little vegetable garden, maybe see about starting a lawn. So long as we all have our little jobs to do, Pa used to say, peace is ours. And Pa knew his stuff.

❦

A crowd awaited the train in Milan. We had not even come to a stop before dozens of people began clambering aboard. Fathers shouted directions to wives and children, young men swung bottles of wine and laughed and stumbled, old people elbowed their way through, couples stopped in the flow and hugged. Soon not a seat was left untaken and the aisle was jammed. Still more were surging in off the platform, where vendors at wooden carts waved sandwiches as long as your arm and a sea of friends and relatives sang goodbye as a forgotten toy or book or bunch of wildflowers was handed up. It seemed a choir was singing the ancient song of a great family setting out on a grand adventure, and the voices swelled chaotically until the train gave a jerk and began to pull out and a single cheer rose. Last kisses were blown and caught, hands reached and touched, handkerchiefs fluttered, the engine rumbled, the whistle screamed. Venice, we were on the way, we would arrive at dawn, we would see the canals, visit the palaces, ride the gondolas, walk the romantic byways and kiss and hold hands and make love or dream of making love and eat and drink and kiss again and hold hands and make love or dream of making love and dream and dream and dream. Look! The moon has almost set!

The shout came from afar, a powerful yodel that silenced half the passengers. It was my conductor friend, at the other end of the car. He was wagging something in the air.

I stood up to see. He cupped his big red hands around his mouth and shouted, Found your passport in the WC! It's your lucky day, boy!

Grateful, I thrust aloft a clenched fist, in victory. He answered with a solemn Boy Scout salute.

Little did I know how, but evidently my little spat with Danny Corn, conductor, was over. The rest of the trip would be smooth. There would be no run-ins with the authorities. Maybe it was the moon, the full moon, that had reconciled us. In fact, just when he had appeared with the passport, an elderly lady nearby had been telling me in passable English that it was the month of the blue moon, the month during which the moon is full not once but twice. We had been marveling over how violet it appeared in the sooty train window.

Now the passport was being passed hand-to-hand through the car. Then I was holding it, unbelieving. I thought, I must thank Corn and apologize for being short with him back down the line.

But, as fate would have it, when I looked up after giving my passport a quick thumbing, he was already gone. I said a silent see-ya, and tucked my precious passport away and let go the twitching sadness, a freed butterfly.

Humanity bubbled around me, and a new breath of life was blown into my dry lungs. My fear of crowds evaporated. I was shown a thousand smiles, given a thousand pats on the head to congratulate me on my *buona fortuna*, and asked a thousand questions I could not understand. They even fought over the seats near mine and passed me bottles and cigarettes and morsels of exquisite home-cooked food, insisting, lustily clapping their hands whenever I accepted, took a drink, an amateurish puff, a bite. The rigors of my voyage and all the petty complaints that had floored me through the weeks washed away, and I felt I could hug them all, ride and follow them forever, wherever they were going.

Then I found myself holding a newborn. I mean, a naked baby girl, all brown and fat, was pushed into my arms, I'm not sure by whom. Suddenly she was there. Of course I understood such things often happen on public transport. But this wasn't a sack of potatoes, a rooster or a four-year-old. I tried to pass her on to the old woman who'd told me about the blue moon. But she raised a long bony finger and wagged it no. Meanwhile, the girl began to bawl, screaming so hard she was turning persimmon.

The congregation fell silent and stared at me and the baby, their olive faces glistening with sweat. Then the throng parted, and a young woman in a violet dress came through, whispered something to an old man sitting across from me and sat down on his knees. As she made herself comfortable there, he began to smile and look around proudly until the old woman next to me gave him a boot on the shin.

I thought I would die from the way the young woman stared back at me. I ached to put myself in her arms, to gush and let go.

Murmurs broke out in the throng. And you could hear them all smiling.

She only had to touch the child to make it quiet. Are you the American?

The accent was sweet and mysterious. Yes. Ansel Gifford. Yes, American.

Everyone held their breath. The only sound now was the quickening click-click of the car as we gathered speed. Or maybe it was our collective heartbeat, for everyone in the car was as One.

I looked down at the baby, then at her, and knew all.

I am Violetta. And this is your child. I am the one you have dreamed of always. I have always loved you and will love you forever. For years and years this moment has waited for you to arrive.

She slid her hand across my cheek. If it was fire, then I was incinerated. If it was ice, then I was frozen solid. I have been numb ever since.

I tried to speak. But her fingers softly closed my lips.

Venezia! A parrot squawking. Venezia!

I felt as if I were falling.

Venezia!

I felt as if I were falling and had dropped our child. As if we were all falling and the baby and the gorgeous young woman were just out of reach.

Then, abruptly, we all caught each other.

Sir!

We were no longer falling. I forced open my eyes.

It was her. Sitting right there across the aisle.

You've had a nightmare, she said.

There was no one else on the train. No moon, no child — only her.

I wiped my face with a handkerchief.

Very sorry, I said.

She had shut her eyes. I looked at her a long time.

Was this the way things happened in life? Coincidence and longing banging together like old freight cars in the night? I had not been looking for love. I had not been looking for anything but as many miles as I could put between me and George West, Texas, and my dead father moldering in his grave. For there would always be the homeward voyage to face someday, the last part of any story. I barely understood how, but already it was clear to me that this woman, whoever she was, would return with me as my beloved, my wife, the mother of my children, my companion for as many years as chance would allow. There was no question any-

203

more. All one had to do was take the hand and lead.

It was a very strange dream.

Everyone dreams. Just don't think about it.

You were in it.

Her eyes came open.

Impossible.

I swear to you.

Impossible. You were asleep when I sat down here. And you don't know me! The idea!

She shut her eyes again.

I sat and stared. Perhaps I had deluded myself again. What reason was there to think this meeting something special? Wasn't that another element in the great game, that some encounters are destined to create great branchings of chance while others remain sterile, give nothing? Didn't one have to accept this, too? It had been weeks since I had touched the opposite sex, and so wasn't that, too, a factor here? I chided myself for romantic notions and vowed to get back on track, which involved no more than completing my voyage across Europe and then returning home to do as my forebears had done. Whatever had given me the idea that I was somehow different?

Still, there was a half-smile on her face. As if she wanted to laugh.

What is it? I asked.

Nothing, nothing.

I plunged forward, seizing her hands. I know it was you in the dream.

She pulled free. You are mistaken. Now please leave me alone.

Where did you get on the train?

Milan. You were asleep.

You were with your family.

She lifted a guide to Venice and began to read.

With your mother and father and everyone, I said. There were dozens of people and we were all going to Venezia!

No family, the woman said.

Why were you smiling a moment ago?

I wasn't smiling.

Yes, you were!

Look, please stop. You're going to force me to call the conductor. Stop now.

Your name is Violetta, isn't it?

She flipped the pages of her guide.

Violetta . . .

What?

She clapped a hand over her mouth.

I must tell you the dream.

I don't want to hear it.

I began anyway. From the moment the crowd got on in Milan bringing her to me. From the moment I stepped out of the yard in George West, Texas, bringing me to her. And I went on and on until we were rolling through the brightening fog into Venice. With so much left to say. Where, as the train came to a halt with a jolt, we found ourselves standing in the aisle, alone, face to face. The story about to end when it had only begun. I couldn't speak another word for fear that it would be the wrong one, or the last one. That it would be the one that set her on her way away from me.

It was a nice love story, she said.

It's not finished.

Who would believe it?

Can't we?

It's also a little too . . . good? Is that the word?

As in sweet?

Yes, that's it. I prefer a little sour taste, too. You know?

I knew, and nodded, smiling.

But we have time for that, don't we? she said with resolve. All the time in the world. And so where are we now?

I knew she knew perfectly well.

In Venice. In the fog.

Then show me Venice in the fog, Ansel Gifford.

And we went down from the train, the thick white cloud swallowing our dark forms, arm-in-arm, everything starting to begin. As in a miracle.

14

I AM DRIVING A GOLD CAD into George West, Texas, at sunset.
Pardon, Père?

I know, I know. But the coco knocked me out there on the
island and this is what happened next. Or didn't happen next since
maybe I dreamed it. Whatever. We don't want to get into *that*
discussion, do we?

Of course not. Please go on.

Well, let's say I think I am driving a gold Cad into George
West, two days of black beard on my sun-parched face. The air
conditioner has given out and I've burned the hell out of my arm
hanging it out the window. Ansel is half-awake on the back seat in
a sea of beer bottles.

I am thinking, why are we going back to George West? Weren't
we just in the middle of a hurricane down off Mexico? I am thinking this as we head into town, not knowing the whys and
wherefores of anything, just going with the wind.

So I check us in at a downtown hotel, leave Ansel sunk in
some bubbles that smell like violets, fix a strong drink and go out
on the balcony to see what there is to see.

To tell you the truth, son, sitting there in the shade staring out
over the rooftops of George West, a perfectly free man, free to go
or stay, run or not run, I feel like one million dollars. No attach-
ments, no bills, no worries, no hassles. So complete is the sense of
freedom, that even my principal mission — getting your grandfather back to Paris — seems senseless. The old man has no desire

206

whatsoever to return to crowded, sour Europe. Nor do I.

So I drink my drink, make another. There's the whole evening ahead there in George West. I hope to share my little epiphany with Ansel, if he is in the mood. But for now I hold back, let the moments come one by one.

Have you ever seen George West at sunset? I tell you, it has got to be one of the oddest sights upon this earth. All burnt orange and spooky, hell, I don't know, creepy. But the creepy that doesn't scare you, the one that turns on everything in your head and heart all at once. I'm not very good with words. But there we are.

Ansel has come out in his towel to sit with me.

I say, Well, what're we up to here in George West?

Want to see the old house a last time, that's all, he said. Then we'll get back to the island.

Want a drink, Ansel?

Hell, no. Slow down.

I ignore him, throw back some more of my poison.

We let a few minutes of silence build up, with the dead little town sitting there in the dusty air, the glow of the sunset fading to purple and a few bluish stars coming out. It doesn't look like a bad night, just a long one. No cars pass, no one is out walking, there's hardly a sound.

This is real dead, I say.

Sort of. Look, I want to get on over to the house now.

Don't you think we ought to wait until tomorrow? I mean we can't barge in on folks at this hour.

Don't worry, I only want to look at it a minute, walk around in the yard. I won't even ring the doorbell. Nice and simple. All right?

I don't say anything.

Put your damn drink down and let's go before curfew.

There's a curfew?

Just kidding.

We get ready. Put on the baby-blue leisure suits someone's left in the dresser there, and the pink rubber thongs. We're the picture of insanity.

It's only a few blocks to the house, but we take the Cad. Get my new Willie Nelson tape going full-blast. I'm thinking about all the kids that ever grew up in George West and how cruising town with the music up loud was all they had ever or would ever do in their lives before they got married and had a pack of babies and had to stay home nights and look at them and the wife in her curlers and the bills piling up and the mother-in-law calling to say she was going to send the police over there to help her sweet daughter get all her stuff out of the house and the kids and all and leave and never come back, never again live with a foul stupid hick drunk idiot like him. It was over! And the local kid taking a Smith & Wesson shotgun and wasting himself there in the empty little saltbox, blasting his brains all over the old yellow wallpaper on which someone a long time ago had taken a pencil and written, I love you, Irene, real small, down by the floor, where you had to bend down to see it, one of those little jokes he'd played on her way back when they were still lovers and when picking up pecans with her along the river on those windy fall Sundays was pure heaven, especially when she wore that white dress that made her look like the sweetest angel that had ever lived, way back when they'd kiss under those old creaking trees, pecan crumbs in one mouth moving to the other mouth, back and forth, as they fell into the cool, thick grass . . .

The neighborhood has changed a lot since my Frances-courting days. All the houses have shrunk and become jammed together. Every tree and bush, every bit of greenery has been sculpted into perfect form, as if with tiny scissors, as in one of those impeccable West Coast cemeteries. Gone are the huge St. Augustine lawns, now reduced to patches the size of doormats. Gone are the playgrounds where children ran until midnight catching lightning bugs. Gone are the white picket fences and yellow streetlights. Not one window glows.

Is *that* it? I ask.

No way.

Are you sure?

I know my own house, Henri. No.

What's the number say?

It says 1492.

Ain't that your number?

We didn't have numbers when I lived here.

Sure you did. 1492. I remember. This is it!

It isn't it, I'm telling you.

Sure it is, Ansel. Look, there's your little ceramic black boy by the door.

Ansel looked. Oh my. That.

Yep, your little racist statue. Right there.

But what have they done to the house?

House? You mean complex.

It's as if someone had come along and cut the house up into little room-sized boxes, chucked them all up in the air and let them fall down in a jumble. Then quickly nailed them together any way they would go so long as the assembly made close contact with its sister constructions to either side and did its part in being another block in the wall that stretched one way and the other for as far as you'd care to see.

Where's the river? Ansel asks.

Behind these apartments, I guess.

We have to get to the river.

I thought you just wanted to see the house. You've had your view.

I have to see the river, too.

I bet you want to get some good ole home cooking, don't you? We've seen the house. Let's go chow down at the café. What say?

Nope.

He gets out and starts toward the wall of apartments like a man willing to walk to the other end of the earth.

Ansel! Wait up!

Shutup, fool, he snarls. Help me find a crack in this damn wall and get to the river. For once in your life, help someone. Come on.

Then I find myself creeping along in the cold dark. You can hear people talking in bedrooms, hear lovemaking — the sounds young women make like puppies crying in the night, the low roar of young men trying to hang on and on. You can hear all manner of machines humming: hottub equipment, air conditioners, freezers, videocassette recorders, handheld vibrators. Everything harmonized and sanctified, as if time will go on forever and there will be no end to living in tiny apartments.

I hear no babies, no children, though. That isn't part of the picture. For an extraordinary moment I miss Paris and the family scene. But the thought melts as soon as it is formed.

Just look what they've done, Ansel hisses. Everything smells of glue. What kind of living is this? What's happened here?

It's called the future, Ansel. Look, there's no way through to the river. Let's go.

Like hell there isn't. Stand back!

He gives an apartment wall a kick, and lo, his foot flies through. Easily. Right inside.

Goddamn it, Ansel! What do you think you're doing?

Going to the river, son.

He tears open a wider hole. The stuff rips like newspaper.

Come on, son.

He steps inside. Like a dog, I follow.

It's a bedroom with a very high, fluffy white bed sitting on thick white shag carpet. A James Dean poster adorns the wall.

Just like Frances's room, he says. In fact, this may *be* Frances's room.

Shh. Someone's going to hear us.

No one home, Henri.

How do you know?

There's no one at home in *any* of these apartments, son. Don't you understand yet?

I can hear people talking in the other rooms. I can hear beds creaking, water running, feet pounding, doors slamming, you name it. Not only is everyone home, they're all awake!

Ansel stops at an intercom panel by the bedroom door, stares at it a moment, then punches a series of buttons. The residents' din halts. All is silent.

I know a recording when I hear one. Now, let's get to the river.

We go out of the bedroom, me tiptoeing, him stomping. Then down a hall, across a sunken den to sliding doors giving onto a cedar deck.

Here we go, he says, going out. We can see the river from here. Hit the lights.

I fumble around and find a switch behind the silk curtains. It illuminates a hundred green spotlights in a grove of pecans all the way down to the river.

There, down in the hollow there. See it?

I see a cement drainage ditch with trickle of black water in it.

That's the Nueces?

Yep. That's my river.

Ansel, what have they done?

What do you mean?

Just look at it, Ansel. That's no river.

Oh hell, what's the difference now?

I know he's lying and stare down there with him from the ersatz paradise. I try to think of something to say, but nothing comes. All is blank.

Here's their barbecue pit, he says. Hit the gas. We'll warm up by it, watch the river a while, then go.

The sea-green spotlights waver as an icy breeze rushes through the trees.

He says, I used to have me a dinner bell on a pole down where it drops off to the river there. We didn't need the bell for anything but it gave the clearest, cleanest sound you can imagine. Ringing hard out over the water. We put a white tree swing right next to it where you could sit and listen to the bell clanging and imagine you were seeing the sound floating blue through the evening. You pulled the chain once, sharp, and it'd ring forever, slowly, the metal tone filling your ear. It would last so long you had the feeling that a bell like that never quite stopped ringing, never quite stopped humming deep inside itself, inside you. Way back when. When you couldn't see one light on the other bank, when it was just pasture and the sound of cows moving around over there. We'd stay so late we'd fall asleep and wake up with dew all over us and the blue light starting to creep into the sky. Big red spiders would've made some new webs in the bell and maybe you'd see somebody going crappie fishing, heading upriver. Violetta'd take my hand and lead me into the house and we'd sleep in each other's arms some more, the sound of the bell still all around us, an invisible shield to keep out evil, pain.

We stand there a good ten minutes warming our hands and gawking at the drainage ditch as the sudden Norther blows in. Then we cut back through the apartment, exit via the hole in the wall, get in the Cad and head out.

A block or two later, he says, well, I saw my river.

You mean your sewer pipe.

Don't you understand anything, Henri?

The Willie Nelson tape breaks after the fifth note of South of the Border.

Damn it! I shout. That tape's not two days old!

Who cares? Ansel says quietly. Patsy Cline did it so much better. Take us back down to Mexico now, will you? We've got a storm to ride out. Sarah'll be worried. Thanks for bringing me here.

He pats me on the arm. I hate it when he does that.

By the way, he says, you can't cement them over.

We speed off into the night for Mexico. By some miracle, some strange twist in the fabric of causality, South of the Border cranks up again, from the start. Only this time it's Patsy, the real thing, and it rolls on and on. Sweet as candy, smoky as a leaf fire, everything you always wanted a song to be. Then we are singing it. Loud as we can, with all the windows down and snow starting to fall.

The road snaps this way and that like a cat's tail.

The doctor was putting on his battered panama, too, and taking up his bag. There was no time for niceties. None of that. It was simply goodbye. It was six o'clock in the morning and Frances was dying and there was nothing anyone could do. Except wait for it to finish. Like a wall of water that crashes down, a black, boiling monster, one bright summer day, years upon years after everyone had quit thinking about that old river that used to flow through there long ago, a deep, broad river you could swim and fish in way back then. And the wildwater would flush out all the trash of everyone's lives, the detritus of memory, the ashes of words and thoughts and longings as it broke over the flimsy buildings and swept everything away — lives, bodies, coffins, gravestones, all.

Death was coming for Frances. And soon. She knew it, the

doctor knew it, Marc knew it, Jean-Jean, wherever he was, knew it. And when it was done the survivors would emerge and try to pick up where they'd left off. All would have to be rebuilt. All would have to be done again. And it would be very hard, there in the bottoms with the sun blasting them again and every insect in creation flying in great clouds, where already, only an hour after the disaster hit, the mud was starting to dry, to harden, stolen bodies half-hidden in it, here an arm upraised, there a child twisted like rope, over there someone's dog stranded on a plank barking its head off. Why did it sound like a hungry baby?

That's old Mr. Death, son. Shut your ears from it. Shut your eyes from it. Don't let ole Mr. Daithe getcha. Why, your Great Grandpa Thomas wouldn't have been scared of a little ole Texas flood. Dang if it didn't wash the town away, though. Everybody but him and his wife and their little children. They was the only ones saved. Why? They had God. Ole Tom whipped them kids and sometimes his wife, too, with his pa's long ole black bullwhip. He whipped em before the flood and even more after the flood. Sure that all that whipping was saving their lives, keeping them straight with the Big Man Upstairs, just like Papaw Josiah had said. Are you listening to me, Marc Du? This is what death is like, son. Are you listening?

I'm listening, Mama.

You will get hints of it all along the line.

Hints?

Things that happen that seem like death's flood. But it's not death's flood yet. Just a rumble in the hills. But a warning nevertheless. To keep your eyes open. To watch and live your little life vigorously while you can. Do you follow me?

I follow you, Mama.

I had just about had it with the two-hour flowers and you screeching kids and your daddy off in Mexico looking for your granddaddy. It got so bad waiting those long months with your daddy off down in there that I wanted to go up to the top floor of our three-story building and jump. This was long before Jean-Jean even had the idea. And I almost did it, too, went up there and stood at the spot where you'd jump if you were going to jump. Looked down and saw it wasn't high enough. Maybe I'd break a

213

leg or my back or something. But I wouldn't die. I'd be a cripple for you kids to take care of. So instead of killing myself I did the next best thing.

Which was?

I left your father.

Marc knew the story. But it was only a little after six o'clock in the morning and the doctor had said a final goodbye and left and Mother was dying and there wasn't anything anyone could do about it now. It was going to have to run its course, like the black river bursting out of dry hills when there wasn't a cloud in the sky for a hundred miles.

Nine months in Mexico without a word from him, just that Mayan clay mask. The dog had shacked up with some Mexican bitch, I figured. Gotten himself too drunk and too stoned to move. While I sat in Paris. While you kids wondered where your daddy was. While helicopters buzzed back and forth over the park and we all sat on the balcony watching for hours to pass the days and weeks and months.

Then, like those cut flowers I was addicted to all those years, something died in me. Said it was over. That there was no more sense in waiting. He wasn't coming back and I didn't care.

Suddenly it was one of the easiest times of my life. I saw everything with clarity. Brought you kids to the country house, got you enrolled in nice clean schools and planted a flower garden. Sure that we would be at peace here deep in the French greenery where you can disappear for the rest of your life. Or at least until your father called drunk from wherever last night to ask, Is there anything I could do to fix it all back like it's supposed to be? I told him I was dying. Of some unspeakably unfair disease that had dried me up. That I was a husk now. About to be crushed into a handful of dust. Your dad said nothing at first, as if unable to absorb anything anymore, drowned in his own sour fluids. Then, as if out of guilt, he spoke a few minutes about that old Mexico mess. But haphazardly, the details escaping him. Saying nothing, really, trying to taunt me by holding back again. Then he hung up and the question remains unanswered. Your dad and my dad got caught in one of the worst storms of the century down there. I like to think your dad died in it, though. But no such luck.

And Grandfather?

I'm still waiting to know. Won't you tell me? Before you go back to Paris? Couldn't you do that for me?

How? I don't know what happened down there.

Sure you do. You've heard enough that you could finish it. You just begin and tell me and I will listen. To the words like water running over round rocks in the sun. Like that. Like it's supposed to be.

But —

You go ahead. Tell me what happened to my father lost down there in Mexico all those years ago. You're very close to the answer, aren't you?

It was only a few moments after six o'clock in the morning and you could smell the rain coming.

So there he is, his mama dying, his one-month book jammed up in time warps, his newborn squawking, his wife wondering where it will all end and the rest of the world not giving a damn. They call this life. Is he *enjoying* it?

I will grant Marc this: He has given me ample space, a whole empty range of white space in which to say my say. For now I ride high atop my mountain in peace, with only the little problems that always accompany semi-sainthood, none of which I can't manage. In fact, I'm having the time of my . . . what is this? Afterlife? Part Two?

No matter. With a little old-fashioned luck, Marc will be wise enough to leave me alone up here on my peak. Not come barging in. Let me have my little fling in the power chair for as long as it lasts. The people — tired old men, anxious young ladies, cripples of all ages, even doe-eyed children, all of them — thirst for it like never before, so why not give it to them? Yes, soon, I will start my series of speeches. They won't be long, or tedious, but to the point, like spears to the breast. And after each pronouncement, each toss of the truth, I will retire to the sack with Chulmetic for further inspiration. Into the arms of my moon goddess and float with her through the milky night for the duration of whatever all this is.

Ad infinitum. This is the winning formula.

Everything before seems fake. Only now do I stand on the precipice, my long hair flying back like a thousand snakes, with hundreds of people from many countries camped out for as far as the eye can see awaiting my every move.

Chulmetic keeps grinning, pacing at the window, the happiest woman on earth.

❦

It smelled like I'd been buried in a field of violets. Patsy, I said. Patsy!

No, Sarah's the name. Sarah.

My eyes opened. It wasn't a field of flowers I was in, and that stink wasn't violets. I was stretched out with my head on the fat island lady's lap.

Ah, sighed the old man. He's back. How do you feel? Did you know you can sing very well? You could've done something with that, son.

How long was I out?

How long was he out, Sarah?

She lowered her face to mine. It looked as if I were seeing her through magnifying lenses, distorted and menacing. I tried to wiggle away.

Where you think you're going?

How long was I out! I demanded.

Awful pale, maybe, she observed.

Oh he's fine, said Ansel. Always was a little whitey. Had to have *all kinds* of creams every time we went to the beach, that is, when Frances and I could coax him into taking us. Always having to wear a T-shirt to keep from burning, even on the Norman coast, and a hat, a dumb floppy white hat, you know, the kind old English women will wear in the tropics. What a sight!

Sarah cleared her throat and spat. Well, I happen to have great admiration for English women of any age. You meant old English *men.*

Excuse me, of course I did. Anyway, don't get worked up about him looking like a sheet. That's his natural state.

I wanted to protest.

Besides, the coco wasn't that heavy, Ansel said. He poked a finger like a nail at the wound on the crown of my head. Damn it, Sarah, ole Dno is gettin real crotchety. He could've *killed* somebody.

I let them have their little laugh.

Then I opened my mouth to cry *Morbleu!* But nothing came out. So I shut my mouth, tried it again. This time, something emerged like the sound of a bottle being emptied.

Think he's thirsty, Ansel said. Jesus, though, isn't this view just wonderful?

That do be a fact, she singsonged. I'll get the rum.

Lest it somehow be forgotten, Miss Sarah had set out from her bungalow for the beach in a farthingale that extended her effective width to a world record for a human being and then some. At present I lay, as best I could judge, somewhere upon this bed of springs and wire and straps and chiffon and wool and nylon. And given the relative ease with which her short arms reached my face as needed, I surmised I had been parked near the center of the universe of her attire. The pleasant addendum to this quick calculation was seeing that Ansel, too, lay on the bright field, seemingly oblivious to any possibility of danger. I myself might simply have taken advantage of the relative comfort had I not unexpectedly been caught by a wave. Not a wave of the sea, no, not yet, but of the great lady's accoutrements. Then I was under and rolling, hitting bottom, bouncing up, only to discover that up had not been up and bottom not bottom. Again I rolled, hearing her voice in the middle distance crying, Here it is, here it is! Whatever it was. I called for Ansel. I heard that laughter again. Then I went ahead and did what a man must do. I cried, Help!

Instantly, I was pulled topside by the nape of my neck. A bottle was plunged into my mouth and fire ran down my throat. I choked and spat.

Damn it, you's gettin my dress *all dirty now*, you fool Frainchy! Stop that there spittin up, you hear me?

I obeyed, lay back, and still gagging, forced a neutral look.

She removed a section of her red wig, leaving a sizable hole in the rear of her coiffure, used this to dab up the mess I'd made, then chucked it aloft where the wind fired it away like an artillery shell.

I awaited my punishment.

There, there, honey, she said, pulling me up until I lay more or less as a baby would in her arms. Mama gonna fix you up.

I could now profit from my newfound elevation to see that we were perched atop a dune on the ocean side of the island. Enough of the rum had hit home that I let slip a thrilled smile, for I have always loved the sea. Great black waves burst into clouds of white as they battered the reef a mile out. The spillover rebuilt into walls, raced our way, collapsed on the beach with a boom like cannon fire and surged violently up the sand toward us, stopping just short.

The wind seemed to bypass us as if we were in an air pocket.

Again the mouth of the bottle was jammed twixt my lips. Just a little this time, she coached. Just a little.

I obliged her, swallowed some, then jerked my head free. We'll die out here, I blurted.

The shove she gave me sent me rolling a couple of turns. From there I managed to crawl to the edge of the contraption and onto the sand. Here the wind fought me. But back on the edge of her skirt, I was safe from the storm. Back and forth I crawled, testing and retesting this finding, concluding that it was, in fact, true. Seeing this, they both grinned their goofy grins.

I think, however, that it was precisely at this point that I gave up trying to understand how all this was possible. Sure, I was to battle with doubt some more, but for the most part, that was it. Hence I would go *with the flow*.

Feeling better, I stretched my limbs on the edge of the farthingale. This act half done, I collapsed.

People *do* die from coco knocks, Sarah said.

She had a point. I lay very still.

Good kite weather, Ansel said.

As if on cue, Sarah untied her sombrero and cocked her arm. Watch me, everybody!

It was a feeble toss, but high enough that the wind ripped it away, the brim a perfect wing, and carried it off over the bowing palms. Then it was gone.

My hat, she said. Mother's hat. Oh my.

The next wave crabbed across her skirt, wetted our feet. The water was quite warm, steamed.

Time to get back home now, Ansel said. You still have that rain barrel, honey? I sure would like to take me a last bath. Wouldn't you? We'll get out that ole back scratcher.

Her eyes searched the heavens. Mother's favorite hat. It was from Flada.

Let's go, doll. Another little smart-aleck wave and we be swimmin.

I want Mother's hat back.

Do you recall what I told you? he asked, softly.

Speak up!

Remember what I said?

No, what?

I said, Sarah, don't be a slave to —

She flapped a hand to make him stop, then finished it.

— to objects. I know, I know. But that was Mama's!

Mama won't know, she's —

Don't you say it! I am going to find that hat!

With a tiny leap she was up, the farthingale inflated, and skimming inland. We could only grab a handful of skirt and hold on for dear life.

I looked back once.

A wave had gobbled the dune and the sea was crashing through the breach. Riding it was a very tall man in a black wetsuit. He gave me the infamous Nazi salute. Without thinking, I returned it.

The sky broke in the middle of the morning and the rain hummed in the gutters. Thunder shook the heavy rock walls. In every room a houseguest awoke and opened the shutters to see it spilling, the trees thrashing, the flashes over the flooding lawn. Each poked out a dry hand to catch a few warm drops before withdrawing as though stung.

Marc went out, lifted his face and let it pour. Far out on the middle of the wide lawn, he tried to remember when he had last felt the rain. Many storms ago, in another body, with another mind. Climbing down a mountain in the Alps, alone, with heavy green clouds spilling all around, the birch forest a tangle of white limbs, the soft moss beneath his feet swelling like a sponge. His body growing light and each step a leap, a bound, as if he were on the moon. Heading down and down into the dark valley that opened onto the plain and its cities like light pools. Years and years of mountains ago . . .

What are you doing?

It was Jeanne, hands on her hips, calling from the door, white cotton nightgown billowing.

Standing in the rain, he said.

Why?

It feels wonderful.

Somewhere once he was sure he had seen his grandfather looking up at the clouds with a blank look in his eyes and the rain running down his red old neck like oil.

Come out, he called. Come stand in rain with me! She considered it a moment, then shut the door. A baby was crying and it had to be fed. The man in the yard was losing his mind. She wanted no part of that road now.

Marc stood in the rain. He wanted to hold the newborn in his bare arms in the hot rain. He wanted to turn and turn in small circles on the lawn with the naked newborn girl in his arms.

※

We were gliding along through the coconut grove when all at once Sarah gave a high scream and tumbled like a boulder.

I panicked. What the hell do we do now?

Shutup! Ansel commanded, scrambling to her side with the rum. Hold her skirt down! Be useful!

I did as told.

Ansel planted the bottle in her mouth, where she nursed it, eyes screwed tight, arms out straight. When she had had her fill, she began to snore, muffling the hurricane.

Why was he only deepening our predicament?

What have you done? I shouted.

Put her out of her misery. Her back's out. It was the only thing to do.

I looked at her a long time, then at him, having no idea what to say.

How strong are you? Ansel asked.

Not that strong. *No one* is that strong.

Do you always have to insult people? he asked. Has it never occurred to you that there *are* obese human beings who are actually easier to port than the skinny kind? You of all people should know this, Mr. Civil Engineer, Mr. Urban Nightmare Builder.

This woman is not my responsibility, I said.

Would you prefer I punch you again, Henri Du? Is that what you're looking for?

A vos ordres, I said instantly.

Run to the house and fetch my crabstick then.

Right away.

A coconut rebounded off her great bosom and crashed into the underbrush. We covered our heads, scanned the heights for Dno.

See him? I asked.

Nah, Ansel concluded. Dno's surely on his high chair down at the Moon Bar getting drunk while Felix surfs. He'll get likkered up, then go out and tie himself up high in a tree. Now get going. And if you see her mama's hat, for heaven's sake pick it up. Move out!

No one could have guessed it, but we were only forty strides from sanctuary. I wanted to march right back and give him this good news, but stopped myself.

The bay waters roiled knee-deep under the house and dozens of blue and yellow crabs clicked and clattered on the sprawling trash pile, a million pincers waving and snapping.

I got up the ladder quickly.

On deck, the whole extent of which now harbored her entire colony of storm-shy algae, I stopped and observed the boiling sky. Why should I do these people's bidding like this? I thought. Why should I save them when I should be saving myself? Who were they, after all? Indeed, how did I know I was not dreaming some insane dream from which I would never wake to know whether I'd been asleep or dreaming?

Crabs raked the deck, and a few had even gotten up on the roof. Another mass of them was climbing out over the kitchen

221

windowsill, having, I supposed, come up through the drainpipes.

The crabstick. Get the crabstick, I ordered myself.

I slipslid on the algae, dove through the seashell curtain, peered left in the gloom. There it was, as he had said. I whispered thanks.

As my hand touched, then clasped, the varnished rod, I became aware that I was being watched. Then, as my eyes adjusted to the halflight, I saw ranks of the large, colorful crabs frozen in place, pincers high, all staring at me.

I won't bother to draw a picture of poor Hambone's ultimate fate.

I came forward with the crabstick. Out! All of you!

In a minute there wasn't a single crab left in the house.

I examined Ansel's stick. Had it done that? Was it empowered somehow? It would not divulge its secret.

I then thought it best to remove any reminders of Hambone's demise and had set about this when, kneeling by the console, I noticed Sarah's radio was on. I had to press my ear to its speaker to hear.

A pleasant female voice was saying, With light southwesterly winds turning westerly and pressure rising in the following regions . . . It was maybe a half-hour before she concluded with, The next forecast will be broadcast in one hour's time. This is London.

Bells chimed.

I spun the dial, caught nothing at all, and clicked it off.

The house swayed and creaked, dishes and lamps rattled, the cheap pictures on the walls dipped left, then right, the throw pillows, much abused by the crabs, spewed wads of nylon hosiery that sailed weightlessly on the air.

Was the world coming to an end? Or had it ended already?

The crabstick gave a tug toward the deck, and before I could think again I was already across the slick porch, down the ladder and rushing back along the path. Again and again the stick wrenched my arm.

What the hell took you so long? Ansel demanded.

I didn't answer. I didn't say it would be beautiful tomorrow in Yorkshire. I didn't say I'd always dreamed of seeing Yorkshire under the sun.

Somehow he had gotten her out of her farthingale and was walking barefoot up and down her back. She cooed and groaned loudly, her face half-buried in the sand, happy enough, in my opinion, to call the game of life quits right then and there.

You've done wonders, I said.

He hopped off. She recited something that had to be a voodoo curse.

Help me help her up, damn it, he said, jerking the crabstick out of my hand.

What do I do?

Kneel right there.

I did.

Put your hand under her neck and hold her chin up so she won't choke.

I wanted so much for all of this to be over. I shut my eyes, dug into the sand, found her flesh. Ready, I announced.

Ansel backed away, lifted the crabstick. Up, I say. Up!

The ground seemed to shake, or perhaps it was me, and the body began to buckle as though she would get on all-fours.

Come on, I said. Do it, baby!

Ansel jabbed and thrust and poked and swung and waved that stick like a pro, spicing the theatrics with incantations that would have raised the dead.

Then, abruptly, she sagged. The eyes rolled up. Her massive behind gave a sound like a car door being slammed.

Now we're cooked, he said. You can let go.

I pulled free my hand, which had gone to sleep.

Ansel was bitter.

I don't understand it, he whined. My stick never failed me before. And to think it was certified as a prop on the Moses set! I have the certificate right here!

He rummaged his pockets.

I let him play out his scene, leaned back against Sarah.

Then he shook the offending staff skyward. It always worked before!

The howl of the wind didn't waver.

He looked at me and shouted, You saw it! It almost worked! It almost worked, didn't it?

Almost, I said.

It's got to be some magnetic interference because of this damn storm. Or some bad-ass alignment in the heavens. Damned if I know!

I nodded.

There's only one thing to do now, he concluded.

From the waistband of his trousers, he produced the bowie knife she'd used on Hambone.

Move aside, Henri.

15

OF COURSE IT WAS very probable that Grandfather, once upon a time, would yet again take up the telling of the story, to anyone who wanted to hear, of the two very happy people stranded on a violet moon one night. Where they waited and waited looking back at the earth and began wondering to themselves why they had ever been so foolish as to climb into the little boat that brought them there. Why they had left behind everything they had known and loved. Why they were waiting there on a dock on the moon gazing homeward, unable to find the words to say that it was becoming more obvious by the minute that the boat was not coming back. Why they were not frightened out of their wits and carrying on like two normal Americans would in a similar situation. Why they were behaving with complete aplomb.

Perhaps it was the quiet. The dust absorbing all. The thick violet dust like your mother's talc just beyond the edge of the funny dock made of moon rock. Giving off a sweet smell, like violets, of course. And stretching away to the horizon, empty and inviting. Fueling a strong temptation, a longing to step off into it and go wherever one had to go, hand in hand, over the rise. To see what was there.

They waited on the moon rock dock, each trying to decide whether to say to the other that it was somehow impossible to make up one's mind about whether or not to climb down off there into the talc. Might one sink up to one's neck? Would one drown? Or sneeze to death after a single step? Clearly, there was no way to

225

know how to proceed, if at all.

They say there's a dead man on the moon, he said.

Pardon?

Did you not sit in the yard with your father or mother on a summer's night and gaze upon this heavenly body? Did you not try to see the dead man in the moon?

Man, yes. Dead man, no.

Didn't you think he was dead the first time you saw his dark, empty eyes, and that mouth twisted as if calling from some deep Hell?

You are being very strange.

Well, we are on the moon now. And I am thinking of him.

I want to go home.

Back to all that squabbling? Are you insane?

You've become very forward with your language, my husband.

But what's back there for us? You know how it's going to turn out. You'll die or I'll die and then the other will be left alone. To go live with our child in Paris? The hell with that.

Ansel! You're upsetting me.

Better to go disappear from the earth altogether. Don't you see?

She looked back toward the earth, a soft blue ball in the black. See what?

The little boat that came and took us, it was our godsend. Our way out. And here we are. No cancers, no brain surgery, no strokes, no pain. We can do whatever we want.

Which is?

I'm thinking we ought to test this talc.

Get in it? To what end?

To see. Then we'll go from there.

Hmm.

They held hands. They smiled at each other a long time and gripped tight. Then they jumped and the violet powder held firm, letting them sink only an inch or two.

Done! he shouted.

Off we go! she cried.

But where? Where would they go on the desolate moon? There were no houses, no yards, no lakes, no streams, no clouds. Only emptiness and dust. So, thinking better, Ansel climbed back onto the dock and pulled her up.

The dead man could've got us, by God!

You don't know how you frighten me!

Don't I? Don't I, dear? Why, what if I were the dead man?

Ansel Gifford!

And if the dead man in moon wanted to kiss you right now right here? With his huge twisted mouth opened in a death scream?

She fainted.

But he did not bend to help her. He stood on the dock and laughed his dead man's laugh at the woman who would never again be standing, never again be asking impertinent questions or making him watch his language or finish his plate or stop burping or any of the thousands of tiny things she demanded. Frightened her, then? Not just any woman could survive up there on the moon with the dead man! He had to have more than a youthful lover who flowered and then had a stroke at the shopping mall and died before you could bat an eye. He glared down at her, a little ashamed of his rage, a little sad, too, and unsure what next to think.

But here she was, coming to now.

What happened? Where are we?

On a dock on the moon, dear.

We haven't been rescued?

There is no rescue, dear.

Then took her warm hand in his cold hand and led her off into the dust. This time it came up to their knees, and with each step away it grew deeper. Until they went under. Without a word. Without a trace.

The museum seems to come to him, like a light that will chase you in the dark, so that before he knows it, he is caught, exposed, shoved ahead like a prisoner.

Through another turnstile, to your left please, now right, watch your step. Guards in the darkened corners wait with their baby machine-guns. Packs of tourists from around the world surge this way and that, hands flying, mouths snapping, barking a dozen languages.

A skinny guide tries in vain to shout them down, then gives up and the crowd spills over her.

Mark goes to her. Vik? Are you all right?

Weak, emaciated, like the mother of the Holy One, she raises her eyes to him and, in a faraway voice, replies, You must be in love with me or something. Go away! Go away or I'll summon the guard!

But you asked me to come, didn't you? Vik?

Can't you see I'm busy here? Go away! We're going in circles is all, you and I. Go away and grow up. Wake up from this circular circus of yours!

I *am* in love with you, Marc says.

Oh no, you're not. No, no. You just came to see if the old man who looks like your grandfather who disappeared down in Mexico all those years ago is still on display. So go have your cheap view of him. Give him a hundred francs and he'll even chat with you. That's the Dead Art! Get of my hair forever, Marc Du!

Didn't you hear me? I'm in love with you Vik.

Pfoo! You're in love with yourself and your silly story.

With that she tears away again, fast as a light turned off in the dark.

Marc eases forward to a garish display. This time, instead of swaying in a red-lighted window frame like a stripper, the old man stands neck-deep in the barrel of filthy water. A cobalt blue light shines down on his bald head, casting his eyes into deep shadow. A small pump hums nearby, turning the drink in the barrel just enough to keep a dozen tourist apple cores bobbing in orbit.

So you're back, he says. How time flies when you're bored off your rear with existence, so to speak.

Marc takes a step back. The mouth hasn't moved and the voice seems to have come from somewhere behind the works. But it is dark back there and he doesn't dare go see.

So . . . the old man begins again. What is it you wanted?

I'm not sure.

Even after all your perambulations, you're not sure? How is that? How old are you? Have you not raked up anything among the old coals of your past? Nothing at all?

Yes, I feel I have. But, then again, I'm not sure. You look so much like my grandfather who —

Disappeared down in Mexico all those years ago. I know the lines. Have you got some kind of problem, some fixation thing going here? Are you perhaps so glued to the deep past that you can't see your way forward for yourself in the here and now? Might I also surmise that you've been in this particular predicament your entire adult life?

I'd have to think —

How long has it been since you were in here on the last day before that splendid summer vacation? Since you were standing right here gawking at me just moments after you'd seen one of my real-world *sosies* out on the street? Has it happened yet again?

Apparently so.

And are you not once again thinking that you don't know quite what to think, quite what to believe, whether I'm live art or dead art or who's who, what's what and all that?

I think so, yes.

You *think* so? And are you not once again *thinking* how the time line has gotten completely out of control? What in fact are you really up to? Quick!

I am —

Bah! What you are really doing in here is trying to get it on with the Iceland girl, you old dog!

Not true!

No? And what makes you think you're the only one who comes in here saying, My, doesn't this chap look like my long-lost grandfather? He does, he does! You think I believe all this crap? You're all after the girl!

Others coming in here?

Can I help it if I look like everybody's grandfather?

But you don't. You look like *my* —

Silence! For once and for all, the girl is mine. Vik and me are going to be married. There! Wake up from your reverie, son. Pinch yourself. The girl doesn't want you. And I didn't want to talk to you the first time you were in here and I sure don't want to talk to you now. Move along!

Why this hostility?

229

Why this *hostility?* the old man singsonged. Because I'm me and you are you and that's that! What is this, another of those quiz shows? Answer ten thousand psychological twisters in one hour and win a free ticket to the freak show at the Dead Art?

He dips under the surface.

Marc waits a long time, but nothing happens. He waits long enough for a person to drown, then goes to peer at the oily surface.

Ansel?

A guard releases the safety on a machine-gun. Please step back from the display.

Marc wheels around. Vik?

Keep ten meters from the display.

Marc steps toward the voice in the dark. Vik?

Keep ten meters from the guard.

Vik, that's you, isn't it! You were watching us all along.

Do not speak to the guard. Stay ten meters back. Repeat, ten meters. Repeat —

The old man pops through the surface.

So! Caught you two at it again, have I? Can't leave you a moment, Vik, before you spy another. Whatever happened to good old fidelity?

Crapola, says Vik.

It *is* you, Marc shouts. Come out of the dark!

Merde, she groans, and comes forward, dangling the gun by its strap like a girl with schoolbooks. *Merdouille.*

Hello, Vik, says Marc, lunging toward her.

She lifts the gun to stop him. Stay back, damn it.

But Vik, it's me, Marc Du! You told me to come here and meet you, remember? It was only moments ago, out on the street, remember?

Shh —

What's going on here! bellows the man in the barrel. Clandestine meetings, eh?

Oh shutup, you old fuck, Vik says. Everybody shut the fuck up. O.K., Marc, so maybe once upon a time I did say you could find me here. But this ain't no tryst. It's your party, kid, you can cry if you want to.

My party?

To celebrate the day you break the circle. Get out of this mental mess.

What mess?

Look, you're supposed to come and have your view of him a last time and go away for good realizing how silly the whole affair has been. So why can't you just do that and leave me alone?

Indeed, why can't you, Marc? says the man in the barrel.

I don't know, he tells them.

Don't know? cries the old man. What is this, a therapy session?

I love you both.

Oh-la-la, says Vik. Now it's getting strange . . .

Honey, get away from that kook, you hear? Or shoot the son of a bitch. Blow him out of our lives. This is our love story, babe. You and me and the wide wide world.

Vik looks at the dirty old man in his barrel, then at Marc, dear Marc, still so stupid. Where is the choice? Who are they kidding? Who needs them?

She drops the gun to the floor.

Mais non! says the old man.

The hell with both of you, she announces. You only used me to get you where you are in this story, which is nowhere, really. I'm going back to the suburbs and live off unemployment for the duration with all the rest of the happy immigrants. At least the state truly cares about me. You guys can finish this *petit bourgeois* slide show without me. Don't say I didn't warn you that it all doesn't add up to a hill of beans! Image has vanquished meaning. Pictures have taken over the world. The eye rules, the mind dies. *Adieu!*

But Vik!

But Vik! mimics the old man. *Flûte! Elle est partie.*

I don't understand.

Who thought you would? Now it's your turn to go. *Au revoir.*

Wait a damn minute, Marc says. Tell me your name!

Ansel Gifford. *Voilà.*

Grandfather Ansel?

Yes, yes. You've found me. You've unmasked me. At last.

Grandfather, is that *really* you?

Shh! I can hear a Japanese tour group coming. Do you know how much money they'll chuck you? I can get a thousand, easy. Now move along. You've had your view. Guard!

But Grandfather!

Grandfather, nothing! I'm a workingman now. Now move along and let me work!

Japanese tourists fly into the room, each in a yellow slicker and crotch-high boots, all flicking small plastic flashlights this way and that in the mist.

The old man dips and hides. Marc stumbles away.

A recording starts up, telling visitors where to toss their cash. Soon little wadded bills are flying like snow.

But Grandfather refuses to surface.

The group waits a long time and then one of the men goes up and knocks softly on the side of the barrel. It is answered by a sharp knock on the inside, and the man jumps back laughing. Then the whole group is chattering and begins to move along.

Son of a bitch, Marc hears one of them say in English. That cost us a fortune.

Oh, we can afford it, says his friend. But not much life here . . .

Somehow feeling younger than in countless years, Marc goes back to the barrel and waits for Grandfather to reappear. He will help dry him off and get him into a cab and take him home. Where the two of them will try to restart their lives again, if they can. Grandfather and grandson, just like old times. They'll drink beer and play dominoes and smoke cigarettes and sit around making up their minds about what to do next, if anything. They'll talk about Mexico and all the strange things that happened down there. Hell, they might even decide to write a book about it together. The whole wild story. Make a nickel, make a mint, it doesn't matter.

Grandfather? Come on up and we'll be on our way.

The surface is as smooth as oil.

Leaving Marc to think it over a last time, as before a fatal plunge. Wasn't Mexico the place to be? Down on the island? Why drag around in dirty old Europe? Why not take control of one's own story?

And so Marc, feeling quite young again indeed, decides that the surface will not break again. That this old man is not his grand-father at all, but rather a professional *artiste* trying to make a buck telling you what you want to hear. No, whoever he is, he will stay down for good. Dead, alive, in-between, whatever. So that the story can go another way, as the month in the country hurtles toward its end, as time runs out on this twist in the big tale, as the blue light over the display goes out.

You're right. Break free, boy, Marc hears. Turn the page.

Merci, monsieur.

Pas de quoi.

◆

I'll get some bandages, said Ansel. Henri, you start tacking down the jalousies. Now where'd that hammer get to?

Sarah had dropped onto her favorite chair, a beat-up black recliner, cranked it all the way back, and was blowing lightly on the tip of the index finger of her right hand. At the spot where Ansel had pricked her with the knife stood a single drop of blood, refusing to fall. Studying it closely, she said, *La lune devint tout entière comme du sang*, to quote the Good Book. And sometimes like Philadelphia cream cheese! God, I want a snack!

With that she sucked away the blood drop and smacked her lips.

I still hadn't begun my chore and lingered there by her chair to see what might happen next.

What you waitin on, boy? Didn't Ansel tell you to get after them jalousies? Get to tackin!

Yes ma'am, I said.

One of my more admirable skills is knowing where to find things, especially things I've never seen before. I might add that I've applied this gift successfully all my life, the better to get what I want when I want it. Whether we're talking about mere objects or people, there has never been any stopping me for long.

Where was I? Oh, yes. I went straight to the coffee table and retrieved the claw hammer from under the August issue of National Geographic, which featured the latest research on the many

233

relationships between global warming and the recent increase of large, ocean-bred storms. Then I went straight to the right back-hand pocket of a nicely faded pair of jeans hanging on a peg on the back of the door to the WC and pulled out a box of copper tacks.

This feat drew a half-alarmed smile from Sarah. I smiled back, content to see her wondering, squeezing her tiny brain to know how I'd done that, perplexed as the fool who stands before the pantry wondering where the coffee is when it's right there before her eyes.

I worked as quickly as possible, securing louver after louver. Curious about the goings-on of the storm, several times I broke my rhythm to have a peek through the rough boarding job we'd done on the outside. A burned caramel light reigned over dark forms that appeared, then stopped, then moved on. I thought I saw many things, including an iron bed and a child sitting on it, an angry mother standing by the bed unaware, as ever they are, that she was the prisoner of a bigger debacle. I heard her shout. And the boy on the bed begin to bang his forehead against a post and cry, I hate you I hate you I hate you. I saw and heard these things out there. And I saw Dno in a nurse's bright white dress glide by on the discarded farthingale, as on a magic carpet, squealing.

I hammered and hammered.

After a while, Ansel came and asked me to help him find Sarah's box of bandages, his lengthy search having failed to turn up a clue, and the lady of the house having no idea where she'd hid it. I obliged, went to a nearby bookshelf, reached up high for a hard-back entitled *La Pharmacie du Bon Dieu*, pulled it down, handed it to Ansel, then got on my tiptoes, peered into the dark crack the book had left, stuck my hand in and pulled out a rusted tin of bandages.

Here you are, I said, flipping him the container.

He smirked and wrenched it open.

I went back to my louvers. I had hundreds to go before I would sleep.

One tiny bandage and one outburst of pain later, the wounded hand gently cradled in the other, Sarah said loudly, like a lawyer summing up her case, And the last thing Grandma said to me was, I never spanked you, child.

I stopped hammering, it seeming wrong to go on.

Ansel got on a red recliner next to hers, kicked back and clasped his hands behind his head. Although it surely was Stann's old chair, Sarah accepted Ansel's presumption with a booming, Kick on back now, baby, as he got comfy and pulled an afghan over his legs.

How old did she live to be? Ansel asked cheerfully.

What's that supposed to mean? For your information, she is alive and well in Miamey at 123.

I'm sorry. Yes, good for her. So why'd she say she never spanked you?

Why? She thought I was her daughter. Me and Mama do look a lot alike.

Did.

Do.

But didn't you say your mama's —

Ansel! She popped upright and wagged the bandaged finger at him. You know what I am now beginning to understand about you, Ansel Gifford?

Tell me!

That you've got something against Mama, my mama who is alive and well and 93 years old and living in Flada. You simply cannot stand the very idea of her being on this precious earth, ain't that right?

She had turned red in the face and was tapping her thongs on the floor as if playing the pedals of an organ.

Ansel looked ready to choke. Now, darling, I never said . . .

I subdued the impulse to join in and returned to my task. The best way to save myself, thought I, was to pick a tune and whistle it. Not so loudly as to draw a protest, but with enough volume to drown out the chatter. I selected *Der Mondfleck* from Schönberg's *Pierrot Lunaire*, for I, too, have had many a rage. And as their verbal fencing continued over who was or who wasn't dead and why or why not, I was able to move on through *Serenade*, *Heimfahrt* and *O alter Duft*, that world that never was. I hammered and whistled and sang.

Somehow, after a good hour on the job, I still had thousands

235

of louvers to go, as if they were multiplying even as I worked. Worse, when I looked back at the windows I'd supposedly completed, I could see the wind starting its nasty disassembly, setting the slats to winking. Clearly, the moment I was done, if ever, I'd have to begin again. I began to lose hope.

What *is* that garbage you're whistling? Sarah asked.

I pretended not to hear, held the hammer loosely and waited.

Ansel said, How is your back, then?

Fine, Sarah said. Why wouldn't my back be fine?

Don't you remember?

I remember that you haven't found Mama's sombrero. I remember that you took off my Sunday farthingale and abandoned it. I remember how you pulled out that knife and, all the while pretendin you weren't going to hurt a hair on my head, made my finger bleed! I remember running away from you, running as fast as these fatty legs of mine would take me right back to the only place on this earth I can trust, home. I done been abused.

Ansel stood up. Nonsense, woman. Did you want to drown out there?

She ignored him. I'm really ready for a snack. What we got?

Ansel thought a moment. Might be some ham left on that bone in the icebox.

She gave a short, soft cry. Where is he? Oh my!

Ansel went around the room. Well, now that you mention it, it seems we *did* leave him in here. Hambone! Hambone!

He's *dead*, she shouted, throwing her wounded hand over her mouth. I mean, I mean he's —

Let's have some pistachios, Ansel said. That'll hold you until we cook up the storm food. We could boil some crabs later.

There was a great clattering on the roof.

I have to open pistachios, though, Sarah whined. I can't with my finger.

Oh, I'll help you, Ansel said. Poor thing.

It look him the longest time to find the nuts, but when he did a victory cry louder than Pancho Villa's whole cheering army went up. He beamed as he came back in from the kitchen, sat down again and opened a handful.

Ahhh, he called.

She gave him her dentist's face. The pistachios flew, hit their mark.

There you go, honey.

Why does everything seem to mean everything? Sarah mused, chewing.

We're talking about a confluence, Ansel told her. A point when anything goes because everything fits, the envelope of chance having been steamed open by this weather.

I *like* it when you talk like that. Makes me feel so much better. Give us a kiss.

He leaned over and did as told. This time they traded six.

Now leave me alone, boys, will you? Sarah said, going horizontal again. I want to sleep this baby through. Y'all be sure and shut the door on your way out. If I'm lucky, I won't wake up before the sky is clear again. *Adios.*

Ansel whispered, Sarah? Sarah Lee? What did you mean, On your way out?

On your way out, she said. That's plain enough.

You mean you want us to leave?

What did you think? That you were going to spend the night here with a single woman on a tropical island? Get out.

But Sarah.

She closed her eyes.

I put the hammer down. Do you think she means it?

Hell, yes, I mean it, she answered. Now good night!

Ansel took a deep breath and was about to begin reasoning with her again when snores as deep as the ocean arose from her chair.

We thought of staying even against her wishes and discussed this together for some time while she slept, only to have the debate ended when she raised her head and announced, Your very presence here will continue to wake me every ten minutes until you leave. This is the first time. There ain't goin be no second.

We thought of conking her on the head with a heavy object. However, my recent experience outdoors notwithstanding, we turned away from such a scenario, fearing the blow would produce only half the desired effect and simply enrage the beast.

We thought of planting the bowie knife where it would be one hundred percent effective. This ugly temptation must have hit us both simultaneously, for it served as the catalyst toward the ultimate conclusion, which was that there was no answer.

Cowards both, we went out.

☙

Being the current Man of Peace, even if only briefly, like the summer meteor, is at once beautiful and sad. Beautiful for the leisure, sad for the fakery involved. Great for the sex, awful for the mental anguish. Today was no exception.

Chulmetic decided that we certainly must go to Mexico City to see the newborn hippos, a first in this fleabag of a nation. I had no intention of doing any such thing and told her we wouldn't be setting one sandal off the property. As to be expected, many a door was slammed and silence reigned throughout my abode all afternoon.

In the middle of the long, simmering wait for a resolution of this particular issue, I went to the window for perhaps the twentieth time that day to check the crowds. The thick smoke from their fires clouded the valley, their bright-colored trash lay spilled this way and that. A forest of satellite dishes pointed to every point in the heavens.

And Chulmetic wanted me to drive out through them to Mexico City to see some baby hippos? I scratched my head. Once again rapping myself for forgetting that women are women and men are men. I mulled and mulled, unable to resolve it.

When darkness came, I found myself still standing at my bay window looking out at the people. Camp fires glowed, turning the night's underbelly a pale orange. Despite the swelling sea of humanity, despite the clank of pots and pans, I felt a strange, if not exalted, desire to fling open the sliding doors, go out onto the patio and preach to them. But better than the TV evangelists ever did. Better even than the man on the shore of the Sea of Galilee. Better even than the blue-glowing Buddha . . .

But no sooner had I resolved to do this did fate step in and stop me.

I'm sorry, Chulmetic whispered. I have been crying and crying all afternoon and then I looked at myself in the mirror and said, Why are you crying about not getting to go see some silly hippos in the Mexico City zoo? Stop it this instant. And so I did. Go apologize to your man! And so here I am. I am sorry. I am yours.

She dropped her cotton robe and her long brown arms reached out for me in the evening light.

I forgot about preaching.

Chulmetic, my little moon goddess, did a long, slow dance at the window — for me, for them, for the world — then took my heart in a dream that night, my old heart like a wad of gristle, and carried it out through the sea of acolytes and on higher into the mountains. Up there where the peaks are hollow and home to the dead. To a slit in the rock in the clouds. Where the wind tore past screaming. And set my heart on a ledge as an offering.

When I awoke, her hand lay softly on my chest.

Four-thirty in the morning. Time to preach. Say it all. Let them have it. Time to make the break. Let the world have it right on the kisser.

16

TWO DAYS OF HEAVY RAIN had left a fog in the house as Mother called in her loved ones to alternately scold or praise, solemnly kiss them or wave them off, give her final blessing or withhold it. She was like an ancient child now, with melted candy clenched in her fist that she either gave up or did not, her head, an empty paper sack, tilted to one side, the eyes fading to white, there being nothing left worth seeing, really. Some discussions grew loud, others remained soundless, while the mildew-stained Virgin and her fat child in their cobwebbed frame above the bed stared down on the departing lady, while nervous eyes darted from one to the other of the black crucifixes that clung to the white walls like scorpions. Frances's scorpions. The better to keep away evil and thoughts of the devil and bubbling, boiling Hell, where they said you'd go if you danced, if you played a musical instrument in God's House, if you touched yourself, if you fornicated, if you ended your marriage, if you harbored any hate, if you didn't harbor enough love, if you ceased to believe, if you didn't believe enough, if you abandoned your father or mother or husband or child, if you abandoned yourself. Frances peered at the drooping canopy slung over her bed like a circus tent as she thought of God up there waiting to take her in his arms.

Mother?

Marc. Just in time, she told him. I was becoming delirious. I even thought I had a huge family here in this God-forsaken country and that each and every relative came and said goodbye. I also

240

was dreaming of Heaven.

That's wonderful, Mother.

It is? Anyway, now that you're here . . .

The black, insect-like legs emerged from the sheets, the arms seemed to move in slow-motion in all directions at once, the head tilted wildly, as if on a spring. She huffed and gasped to her feet, a skeleton in a pink silk nightgown, and crept across the bedroom to a dresser, where she latched onto the top drawer.

Blow, you bastard, blow! she hissed at the nearby window.

There was nothing there but the fog.

Mother?

Everything is as wet as a sponge, Marc. Rotting. Nothing will ever be dry again.

It didn't seem possible that she'd be able to get the drawer open, but she gave a high shout and wrenched the fat, swollen thing out and plunged her bony hands into the mounds of silky things inside, as into colorful, bobbing clouds. Deeper and deeper the search went until she was in up to her elbows in finery and sweetness, her fingernails scratching the wood bottom, searching.

I know they're here.

What?

Things. You're the only one I have to give things to.

What things, Mother?

Ah!

The hands flew up, each with a goody. Here we are!

She quickly raised her nightgown in an unwomanly way to try and hide them from view, to prolong the suspense, and grinning for the first time in months, began to make her way back to her tattered circus tent. Again the bones clacked and the flooring popped and the arms flailed, and again, somehow, she made it, with a gasp and a fart, the objects spilling from her hands onto the soiled sheets.

It was the old bullwhip and a narrow box of dominoes, like a miniature coffin. Family icons being passed on. Because we can't do without the ritual, the made-up rites, the little somethings to help us complete the voyage.

She spoke like a child now. You do want them, don't you?

He could only say yes. But it was like a shot being fired, as in

241

his dream the night before of her coming to his bed with a pistol and demanding that he help her. She had sat on the bed the longest time imploring him to take the pistol and shoot her. He had kept trying to ignore her, to go back to sleep within sleep, but every time he shut his eyes she reached over and opened them again with her bony fingers. Wake up! Finally, then, in the deepest hour of the night, he had sat up and listened to her pleading. And he had no more begun to listen than her hands, like steel traps, latched onto one of his hands, jammed home the gun and lifted it to her face. Forcing him to put the barrel of the gun into her dry mouth. Pointing it sharply up, toward the brain. Her voice somehow coming through, Fire it, Marc. Fire the damn thing! And he had.

No, he could only say yes. And fly with the mementoes over the river into the stand of young poplars like soldiers in the fog awaiting orders to plunge into battle.

What you got there, boy? All the soldiers take a step forward, somehow, and laugh.

And what's that, dominoes? That a box of dominoes? Why, I can whip your ass at dominoes any ole time, son. Set em up! Draw seven, make a boneyard, my down! Double-five, kick your ass, yes sir!

The battle horn sounds and the soldiers fly forward, cheering, young branches in a gale. Only there still isn't breath of wind. And not an enemy in sight, only a white bank of nothingness, the unseen.

Marc waits until the whole army is gone and then crosses the empty, torn-up field, all too conscious of never having done anything valiant or courageous in his life. Of never having done anything to be honored for, or taken any risk, or put his flesh and blood on the line for something. Hadn't he guzzled Champagne with two bitches while Jean-Jean's broken body still lay in the street after having fallen out of the sky? Hadn't he thought how wrong it was to be sitting there drinking and hoping to make love to the two of them while his brother's warm body still bled? Hadn't he thought how he would someday be thinking back to that moment and saying to himself that it had been one of the wrongest moments of his life? Hadn't he refused to listen to himself and pretended that such a thought would never return, and certainly not in a foggy field on Mother's death day as he stumbled along, family relics clutched to his chest like booty?

Sergeant Death slogs along a black mud bank, his red silk uniform torn and dragging, his hair choked with brambles and burrs, mumbling, Who's got my whip? Who stole my dominoes? I'm going to rip somebody open like a hare in a dog's mouth and spit steaming entrails into the fire!

Marc chucks his inheritance down a muskrat hole and flees into the white bank, into the unknown. Back to his dying mother's bed, to her side, to wait with her as long as waiting was needed. Having never left, really, still holding the mementoes in his lap, the leathery old whip, the baby coffin. Watching and waiting, daylight hard against the face, for a long time.

The door flew shut behind us with a loud report, leaving the seashell curtain to whip in the air. We backed away with great difficulty, rears to the wind, slipping this way and that on the algae, until we reached the edge of the deck and seized the splintered railing. Taking quick stock of the situation, we began to trade some of the foulest insults imaginable.

Darkness soon fell, yet on and on we raged. I cursed Sarah and her evil selfishness and heartlessness. I cursed Ansel, the man of a thousand deaths. I cursed my wife for dispatching me on this death trek. And, yes, I assailed myself for feeling the thrill of at last being part of a true adventure. For good measure, I cursed Montezuma's Revenge, all Fords, all Cadillacs, Third World civil servants, weather forecasters, my fear of handling crabs, yes, even dead ones, my reptilian brain. I cursed my tears and cowardice, and my longing to reach out and hold the old man's hand there in the dark. I cursed it all as loudly as I could.

But then it hit me, as if someone had switched off all other sound, leaving only the sickening squeal of my voice in the void — and then nothing.

I was sure it was the heavy hush of death.

Ansel?

It's the eye, boy. I figure we'll have five minutes to relax.

All stood still. The moon, full as a baby's face, shone in the vault above. You could see the dead man in the baby's face, his malformed mouth ready to suck you in like a spicy tidbit. It gave me goosebumps and I vowed not to look aloft again for the duration.

I sat down on the deck and shivered from the wet. Ansel joined me, Indian-style, apparently not much worse for the weather, a light smile playing on his tired face.

Son, looks like tonight's going to be our last hurrah.

I hated that use of the first person plural.

I'm going inside this house and take shelter, I said. She can't keep us out.

What makes you think she can't?

It would be tantamount to murder.

And you think she cares? You've made a presumption that —

Silence, Ansel!

For once, he dropped it, shrugging.

Seeing my first opportunity in ages, and maybe my last, to tell him a thing or two, I decided to strike like a coconut and let him have it. I scratched my festering fly bite, but the words would not come.

He sensed my embarrassment and gave me a friendly pat on the shoulder. It'll all work out the way it's supposed to, son.

Why do you say things like that?

Because you look like you need me to say them. I don't give a flip, though, how you feel.

I say we kill her.

I will admit that I want to also. But now, with this big survival test staring us right in the eye, I finally get it. She is trying to see which of us is worthy of her love, don't you see?

No.

She's making up her mind, get it? Which man is stronger, that kind of thing.

Frankly, if asked, I'd have conceded —

Of course you would have. That's you, Henri Du. Always thinking of Number One. But why can't you just go along with the games people play? What's wrong with the flow?

I'm not interested.

Well, then, I *will* be her boy after this is all over, then. If I make it. Take up Stann's old role, only in the platonic sense, mind you, for she'll never have another true love, that much is sure. I'll get out the box of flippers, masks and snorkeling tubes and start ripping off the tourists again. Have Sarah cook for me and all. Eat chicken wings and mashed taters the rest of my life. Watch my skin get tanned and tough. Watch my hair grow longer than the Lord's. Enjoy the fading of you and all your kind from my memory once and for all. Enjoy the emptiness that follows, the dead nothingness, the boom of the sea at night on my own damn island. Just me and the lady I've always wanted for a mama and the sunshine in the music, you know?

All yours, I said.

What are *you* going to do with yourself when this is all over? Go back and torture my daughter some more?

I chose to ignore that. How much time do we have now, anyway?

One minute.

We're going inside.

You go ahead. I'm going through my rite of passage come hell or high water. Hell or high water! Ha!

I crawled boldly toward the door, feeling sorry for him. Sure that I had taken charge of life, and that salvation was at hand.

But no sooner had a smile started to build on my face, a smile like a baby's when it tastes something sweet, than the wind suddenly returned out of nowhere like a giant open hand and slapped me away into the dark, into the unknown, and I went tumbling head over heels.

Hold on! I heard Ansel yell.

He caught me by a leg.

Damn fool!

Let me go!

He refused, dragged me close, poked me a couple of times on the chest with the crabstick.

What're you doing, trying to kill yourself?

Let go!

Trying to steal the show, is that it? I *ought* to let you go. Let you fly to the wind like a bad thought, be done with you, Henri Du!

Do!

Again he jabbed my chest with the stick. It had a calming effect, there in the roaring dark.

I reached out and held on to him, too. As the storm rolled over us. As the end of the world flew by far over our heads. As all time and meaning came to an end. As the unseen moon rained its final blood into the skies of earth, far below, where mere men sat clinging to each other on the final night, having a last chat as if nothing else existed.

Seems to me the lesson here is pretty clear, Ansel said. Don't ever mistreat a woman. For mistreat her we must have, though I'm not sure exactly when and where. But we must have, to deserve this punishment.

I guess, though, he went on, that if I had to look back and try to figure out where things definitely started to go downhill, I'd say it was the moment I found you wandering all by your lonesome and invited you to come along. What possessed me to do such a thing, I'll never know. Then again, maybe it was the moment I didn't have the instinct to shoot you when you came courting my daughter back in George West, Texas. Then again . . .

I wanted it done. I wanted to stitch up the rip in the fabric of things and get back to Paris. I wanted to be free of the whole damn story. But no, there I was clinging to a crazy old man in the storm to end all storms. Why me?

Nope, looks like we're not going to make it, son. Jig's up.

What?

You know, he said, even on this side of the line, here in the not-quite-gone and not-quite-arrived, you are utterly . . .

He shook his head as if to pity me.

What? I demanded.

Pathetic. I can see you're not at all ready for the suite.

What suite?

The Final Swim.

Speak plainly.

You think dying is just dying? A quick little skitter? There's a lot more to it than that!

I shrugged.

The sea bottom was churning up clouds of mud. Buoys clanged a dirge.

Look, I said, if you'll turn me loose I'm going to swim for the tallest tree. This part didn't even happen, O.K.?

Didn't happen? Who are you kidding? You're just afraid.

That's right, Ansel. I'm afraid. And now I'm going.

By the way . . .

What?

Swimming will get you nowhere, believe me. Sorry.

I stayed put, unable to speak. What had I ever done to deserve such a demise? Why couldn't things be simple and easy? Why all these layers of complication? I began to have a headache.

Ansel?

He was snapping his fingers in my face.

Come around! he commanded. Come around!

It was like being hit with a cold towel and we were back in the middle of the storm.

The hurricane had thrown a massive whammy. Rearranged the doors of perception, opening some, sealing others, changing still others into colorful entrances to Heaven or Hell as the sea heaved in great arcs and dropped onto our heads. The wind was starting to mash Sarah's flimsy deck like cardboard.

It's the end! I shouted.

Not for me, I'm going inside! he cried back, his will to survive suddenly healthy. Hell with this! The fat lady ain't sung yet!

As if she'd heard him, every light in the little house came on. Every louver blinked wildly, as if sending some final, cosmic message.

Could it be, Come back in? Or, I love you both, come home?

With no discussion, we decided that had to be it. An appeal. A cry of distress. She wanted her boys back.

The crabstick! I screamed at Ansel. It'll get us to the door!

The cane sucked us up onto our wobbly legs, like two fools in a minstrel show, and dragged us across the deck on a thick mat of algae. One wanted to wave bye-bye to the night. One wanted to smile and wave one's hands high overhead and say, nighty-night to the blasting rain. One wanted to laugh for joy and hug one's buddy and order a trucker's breakfast and . . .

The door swung open, and there stood Sarah, Mother in the night, Mama waitin on her chillens, half-jar of blood in one hand, shotgun in the other.

Sarah! I called. Sarah!

Ansel called, too, and began to make homeboy hand signals.

She waved, but it was not the wave you wanted to see. It was the other kind. The kind that says, Go away, get out of here, one step closer and I'll unload my Smith & Wesson where it counts!

Only the crabstick didn't know it. Kept drawing us closer and closer.

Whoever said there was no divine intervention in this world was wrong. For in that instant, a special gust of wind knocked Ansel and me into a bone-splitting embrace and the crabstick snapped between us with a crack and a boom and a burst of yellow and blue sparks.

Let go of me, fool! he cried.

We slid toward the sea. We could hear Sarah squealing with laughter. I could hear Patsy Cline cranking up South of the Border. A roof full of strumming, grinning mariachis sailed by.

As we tumbled off the deck, each vainly gripping half of the accursed crabstick, the broken halves writhing in our hands like snakes, I gave a big whoop — and let go of the old son of a bitch.

It was every man for himself.

❧

Why, one time this hurricane came busting through northern Georgia, up there in them red hills, in God's country where we'd always minded our businesses, which was farming and having big families and ministering to the heathens. It tore up everything there was to tear up, drowned the animals, flooded the old gold mine, split all the trees, knocked over the churches, the white houses of God where I, Josiah Daniel Gifford, preached many a Sunday to the ignorant, where many a Sunday I spoke of the wrath of the Almighty and how it can strike at any time. It only has to please Him for Him to want to strike out at us. But it is not ours to question why, it is not ours to be like Job and doubt Him. It is ours to hunker down and hope the roof doesn't fall on our head in the night when the storm breaks over the land like a fifty-foot wave of mud and trees and rock and houses. That was the night I put my bullwhip to those children extra hard on account of their screaming and carrying on as if God did not have some plan for them, as if they had the right to resist His Will. That was the night the wind blew and blew as though it would blow everything there was off the earth, mountains, everything, leaving nothing but a naked plain of mud for as far as the eye could see. That was the night my wife tried to stay my hand as I whipped those children again and again, and that was the night I had to strike her, knock her away, in His Name. For why did we come to this virgin land if it was to curse God and curse His Will and His Way? For why did my granddaddy come here and die in the glorious battles against the Tory element? To sink shallow roots that would make a weak tree? To leave behind descendants who, hit by a mere storm, would cower in the mud and cry out that God had forsaken them? I knew better and put the soft old black leather to their white bottoms until they bled. There was no other way. The house was coming down. The world was ending. One had to be ready to meet one's Maker when the Maker called.

All through the night, I whipped and whipped, and the children collapsed and my wife Sally collapsed, but I, I grew more and more powerful, like the God Himself, surged taller and taller until I was thousands of feet tall and nothing could hide from me, nothing. I cracked my whip like lightning in the howling night and its light flashed in all directions. I sent my wrath down upon my neighbors' heads, upon their fat farms, upon their fat children and wives and cows and fertile fields. I sent my wrath down upon the last of the stinking Indians who dared linger on our land up there. I sent down my wrath upon any fool I could find, sure that I was the one and only true Man of Peace, my peace, peace the way I wanted it, with no people to bother me, no haggard wives, no foul-tongued sons, no cold daughters, no fondling preachers, no other gods. None of that. Just the wide mud plain with nothing on it but me, towering there, whip in hand, daring the future to defy me in the west, daring the past to awake in the east, one wild eye north, the other south, saliva flying, hair alive with snakes, and black storm after black storm rolling in with thousand-foot waves but barely brushing my feet, far far below, down on the scummy earth, where nothing dared to crawl on one of the worst nights in the history of man, when all spilled off the continent and into the sea as I popped the whip and tore holes in time and crawled through, as through the warm valves of a beating heart, and came out onto the fresh, green grass at a picnic with my Sally late that last summer before she up and miscarried bad and died and left me with them seven snot-noses to raise.

Josiah? she said. You're all red in the face. Are you feeling well?

Going to come a storm, I said. I dreamed it.

Praise be, then, she answered. If He wills it.

Sally, I mean the storm of all storms.

Lord, yes, she said.

Sally?

Yes?

Where are the children?

They've run up to play Indians in the gold mine. Why?

I think we'd better all get in the house.

Sally stopped eating her apple and looked at me. Then she put down the apple and raised her soft white hand to my forehead. Are you unwell, dear?

I seized her arm and pulled it down like a lever. She relaxed, went with it, lay back and smiled up at me.

I think you are quite well, she said.

It's going to come the storm of all storms, woman.

I can see that, she said, giving a giggle.

The air was clear and her bright young face drew me near, until I was touching it again. Only my fingers, each of them, had become the soft black leather tips of tiny whips. But I did not hurt her. No, I never hurt her. Simply brushed the little whips across her plump cheeks and smiled down at her. As she closed her eyes and smiled, too.

Don't be afraid, dear. They're way down in the mine.

To steel myself, I looked up at the sky and saw God, in a nice suit, new shoes, legs crossed, watching us from His Throne.

The Lord is with us, I said to Sally.

Again?

The Lord is always with us. Always.

She sat up, adjusted her shirt collar, frowned at the sky. Maybe you are right, husband.

Right about what, wife?

The storm of storms. I can feel it coming. There's a taste of rust in the air. Can't you taste it?

She spat like a man.

Then she rose and began to walk down the red road toward the gold mine in the cliff over the river. To go see about the children. To dally along the way and recite poetry in fields of flowers and then go on down to the mine and call her little ones. Their voices would echo up out of the red ground as they came rushing up to her like angels freed from the deep. The smallest ones would hug her and show their handfuls of fool's gold. The middle-sized ones would tell her about the tribe of Indians living down in there, yes, it was true! The older ones would come around behind her and spook her with loud whoops.

Sally would seize her bosom and faint in a heap.

Mother, Mother! they'd cry, bunching around.

Mother! Are you all right? Mother, Mother, wake up!

Then she'd pop up and scatter them with a laugh.

Mother!

We must get home now. Father says it's gonna come a big one. The biggest of all the big ones, too. We have chores to do.

No chores! the boys cried. No more chores!

Is he goin whip us agin, Mama? the girls asked. Is he goin whip us?

Of course not! Wherever did you get such an idea?

Well, Mama, last time, you remember . . .

I, Josiah Daniel, deacon of the Mossy Creek church, humble keeper of the faith, sat on the pretty picnic blanket in the sun, waiting for them to come home and thinking my thoughts of God. Thinking of Him and the mission he has for me and the mission he has for all the seed that I can spill on this land, until we have peopled the continent from shore to shore with our likenesses. Of course I would give Sally the seed in the night when all were sleeping. When the storm would be beginning, when the tin roof gave

251

its first light rattlings, when the animals awoke in the barn, their big wide eyes shining red in the dark.

Already, up high, streaks of black crossed the chalky vault of heaven. Here below, red dust sailed out of the trees and into your mouth. It was coming. The kingdom of heaven was blowing in. I clasped my old hands, lifted them up and gave thanks.

17

As I dropped into the fury of the storm, I heard Floria Tosca sing O *Scarpia, avanti al Dio* before leaping to her death and I heard my mother come into my bedroom, felt her lift me up and hold me safe and let me pick the flowers printed on her summer dress until I was sure I had gotten every one. I lay in her loving arms until I grew to be a tall young man who could play Chopin like no one who had ever played him. I became a virtuoso with a coterie of believers who trailed me everywhere. Applause burst out each time I was sighted in public. It was impossible not to love the adulation, the countless favors, beachfront homes, insatiable mistresses. No one disputed my primacy. No one dragged me down. Not in that reverie of reveries, no one.

There was a loud cracking sound and then I was detached, clear to go anywhere, forward or backward, into past or future. I took my mother's warm hand in mine again as we sat on the riverbank in the evening to watch the moon rise. I held my own head in my own hands as an ancient man on the verge of death in a bad Guadalajara hotel. I held my newborn children and loved my wife again in Gay Paree. I played Scriabin and Brahms better than any other had ever imagined. Banks everywhere called and begged me to deposit my cash with them. I started a fad of carrying gold coins for pocket change. I let my white hair grow to my waist.

Then I imagined I was sailing along in a brightly colored dirigible over an old ocean of time, countless devotees trailing me in

paper skiffs, holding up offerings of milk and grapes and fine li-
queurs as my airborne palace bobbed above, just out of reach.
The skies were eternally clear and the breezes blew the way one
pleased as I sat in my vessel and played for my maddened follow-
ers. Frances joined me on the piano bench, blue irises draped in
her arms, and smiled down at my wonderful hands moving effort-
lessly up and down the pristine keys. You, my children, Jean-Jean
and Marc, stood on either side, dressed in fine uniforms, ready to
plunge into battle for a national cause, ready to join the air force
academy, like young men everywhere. And you were proud of me,
and I of you. There would be no wrong choices. No one would
become a mediocre civil engineer with two brats, a deranged spouse,
and the worst trumpet technique in the world. No one would be
declaring despair and jumping from Notre-Dame. No one would
be stooping so low as to scrawl questions for TV trivia shows.
No, no one would be doing any of that! Rather, you all would be
standing there nearby, at the ready, adoring me, your father, as I
played my fine grand piano, the best money could buy, riding in a
great old dirigible over the Seven Seas. Where no bombs flew, no
jet fighters buzzed, no storms roamed. Where men of peace, television inventions all, were never heard from again. Where we were
free to be what we wanted to be. Where even God dared not interfere.

So long as we stayed out of the ocean. So long as we did not
touch the forbidden sea. Touch the water, even brush it, and you
were a goner. The dirigible would dip, causing the concert grand
to spill to one end of the vessel and out through the skin like a
bullet, carrying us all with it into the drink. No, everything had to
remain in balance. The slightest deviation and . . .

But we would have none of that! I played Rachmaninoff better than he played himself. Same with Liszt and Schubert. With all
of them. My sleek hands seizing their flimsy notes. Ripping them
up like soft wildflowers and jamming them home into the heart of
hearts. Nothing to it. You only had to wish and all was yours.
Everyone loved it. A million-and-one trailing torches became ten-
million-and-one, until the lights plying the ocean below looked as
thick as a metropolis, as if *terre ferme* had surfaced again from the
sorry deep, a muddy pedestal for the voracious faithful ever strain-

ing to reach up, to touch the vessel of harmony.

Not so fast! I barked at them, laughing, and with only a thought, took us ever higher, up where the real galaxies sail, out among the stars. Goodbye, sad sea; goodbye, crushed humanity. Far below, the world looked on fire. I began to play Moon River and you boys sang along. Frances dozed. But it was O.K. She could doze all she wanted, for she was my lovely wife again, and there would be no separating us, ever. I played and played and the galaxies whirled.

⚜

The final apparition that night had me in the middle of a school of fish I somehow knew well, as if I had spent a lifetime around them. They were as thick as cats and dogs at a full trash can, squabbling over who would get the choicest morsel, me. Round and round they circled as I thrashed my arms to try and scare them off. But they were not impressed, and tightened their circle again and again until they were right on me, their fins cutting my face, their eyes in my eyes, until we were one.

El náufrago is coming to, J. B.! But he needs a bath, whew!

It was one of the fierce-looking functionaries I'd crossed so long ago.

Byron? I said.

Byron? Why, no, mister. I'm Charles. Ain't I seen you before? You be a sight for sore eyes, though. My Lord!

I lay on the ground roped to a short section of coconut palm trunk. Evidently some benefactor of mine, some guardian angel, had tied me thus and the storm had driven me to the continent. How much time had passed between the one and other I was unable to guess. All I knew was that every bone ached, every joint cried out, every muscle twitched, and I was deeply thirsty and hungry. For all I knew I'd been lying there for days, scrap for crabs.

Untold numbers of rattletrap buses and junky cars roared past. The other officer, decked out in a fine red uniform and resplendent white gloves, was directing traffic as best he could, but it was an unruly exodus. Things appeared to have been out of hand for

255

quite some time when they had stumbled upon me in the ditch.

The one called J. B., who, if I recall correctly, saw a death-trap Cad in every car, approached and stood over me.

So you're awake? he demanded.

Alive, I said.

You got voodoo on you!

Still delirious from my voyage in the psychic ether, I looked for a spot on my shirt, then shook my head hard at my silliness.

You got voodoo all over you. Smells like catfood!

Do we dare untie him? Charles asked.

Yes, I answered. Untie me.

Good question, J. B. said. I think I'd rather get a bottle of rum, sit here on the gravel and watch Byron tickle him to death. What say? That sure get rid of the voodoo, no?

Wait, I said.

No, J. B., said Charles. You want to get voodoo on our pretty baby Byron? I say leave well enough alone.

I demanded to see my ambassador, I appealed for international justice, I recalled the Geneva Convention on the treatment of prisoners of war, I cited the Ten Commandments, I said a voodoo curse in my own fashion.

Oh Mama Big One cut your thing right off. Oh Mama Big One flash the knife in the night. All little boys go screamin home cut, and the rooster don't crow no mo. All your blood gonna run real free and all your old lovers go hee hee hee.

They frowned, checked their zippers, scanned the skies a moment . . . untied me.

They drove me in their old Ford to the nearest town, Chetumal, and dropped me at the French Consulate.

They apologized a hundred times for anything they'd said or might have said, had thought or might have thought. They even tried to give me Byron.

I declined, disturbing them to no end. I assured them it was all right if I didn't take the beast, that I had no malice in my heart toward them, that if they would back off and keep their damn monkey I might forget about the whole matter.

This said, Byron was tossed into the trunk and the lid was slammed.

Done, said Charles. *Bon voyage, monsieur.*

Oui, bon voyage, monsieur, said J. B. *Et pardonnez-nous encore une fois . . .*

I shook their hands, there on the steps of the consulate, there in the sunshine, with the storm of storms long gone, with the world picking itself up by its bootstraps and going on. Workers scurried this way and that, businessmen called out orders, mothers dried their tears and the little ones went back to play. Life would go on. Good, clean life would go on forever, it seemed, there on the steps of salvation that morning with the sky as blue as turquoise and the air as fresh as a mountain vale. Gone were the nasty nightmares of the deep and ugly death awaiting all.

I heard the monkey moan in the trunk.

Why not let him go, gentlemen.

Charles went and popped the lid. The monkey stood up and stared at the three of us.

Byron, said J. B., you are a free monkey. Be gone, chile!

The monkey looked at us.

Be gone, chile, I tell you! Lift this curse off our heads!

Charles hissed at the creature the way you try to scare a cat.

Byron sprang out and into the crowd and disappeared into the chaos.

Curse lifted, I said. Now *ciao.*

I think they wanted to kiss me, but I shoved them back. The gates of the consulate were opening and a soldier was signaling me to come inside. There would be drink and food, clean sheets, a bed, a toilet. There would be nurses and doctors and all the medicine you pleased. There would be videocassettes to watch, newspapers to read, cheeses to eat, wines to savor.

Bienvenue en France, monsieur, the soldier said.

Merci, merci.

Where are you coming from?

The islands.

How?

Tied to a palm, blown to shore.

Pas croyable. Were you alone?

It was only then that Ansel crossed my mind. It was only then I realized that it could only have been Ansel who'd tied me to the tree after the fall from Sarah's porch, thus saving my life. It was only then that I looked down and saw I was still clutching my half of the crabstick, that there wasn't the slightest doubt that I had gotten the long end of it, and that good fortune had been mine.

There were others, I told the soldier. My father-in-law, some locals.

He shook his head. Too late for them.

Too late?

It was the biggest blow in a century, *monsieur*! Those sand-bars were flattened, swept clean. No one could have survived. Even you weren't supposed to survive.

I wasn't?

C'était un miracle, c'est tout. Les autres sont sûrement morts.

I nodded gravely.

Now please move along, he said. You'll find fresh coffee and croissants in the main foyer. Ask at the desk about accommodations. We'll repatriate you if you wish.

And leave them out there to die?

Mais pour qui vous prenez-vous? Il n'y a plus rien à faire! Move along. You've had your little jaunt through paradise. We have *work* to do here. There's been a disaster, you know. Now let me do my job! *Allez, dégagez!*

I gave up, did as told, went in and stuffed my face. Ate and drank everything I could get my hands on, then went to my room and lay on the white sheets, wide awake, trying not to think. Trying not to imagine what had become of Ansel. Of Sarah and Felix and Dno. Trying not to care.

The next morning, they put me on a bus for Mérida and a flight for Mexico City and Paris. It was over. I was going home. Alone.

At first, the immediate past dogged me like a foul street person, the stench never letting me rest, the low, sick voice hurling insults with every breath.

Soon, however, a few drinks down the hatch, I began to raise my head and look forward. To cast off the shackles of the past, the missteps, the errors. After all, I was only a middle-aged man and a good portion of the future lay before me. No longer would I take that road that had gotten me into so much trouble. No longer would I berate my wife, scold my children without pity, be rude to the rest of the planet. I would change my ways, live, grow again. The word resurrection repeated itself in my mind as if sung by a church choir as we touched down at Charles de Gaulle airport early Monday morning and I took a cab into the City of Light.

ɤ

A bluegray mist moved through the air as I rammed home the key of my apartment door. How was it possible that I had not lost it or anything else I'd had in my right-hand pants pocket upon leaving Paris so long ago? No, there it all was, my keys on their Mickey Mouse chain, my handful of change, four lead slugs for practice balls at the driving range, a ticket stub to Emmanuel VIII, matches from the Tour d'Argent. These things seemed mine — and not mine — at the same time. Or was this another time trick?

My hand shook turning the key.

I'm home! I let out.

Of course Frances didn't hear me. She had a mixer going in the kitchen. Something was baking, too. Or, rather, burning. I couldn't stop a sneer.

Nor did the children surface. They'd always failed to surface before when I arrived home, so why would things be different now? Clearly, I had my work cut out for me after an aeon of bad fathering.

I left my bags by the plastic palm and headed for the liquor cabinet at the far end of the *salon*. Ah, but didn't that thick carpet feel fantastic even through my boots? I let my hands brush the edges of the expensive furniture. How long had I been deprived of home's comforts? There were blue silk irises in that indigo vase I bought Frances all those years ago in the Rhineland, the one she'd snatched up in anger one night and thrown at me, the one that had sailed past my head and out the window while she screamed. I gave it a closer look. A poor replacement, it appeared. But didn't it mean she had regretted breaking the original, had wanted to set things right, wanted me back? I sniffed the cloth flowers and smiled. She'd sprayed them with something sweet. But why all this effort?

259

Had she somehow been expecting me?

I'm home, honey! Honey?

No answer. Just the whirring of the mixer in the kitchen, and the smell of whatever was burning growing stronger.

Hey, something's on fire in there! I called. Are you O.K.?

But why worry, I told myself. Surely she had things under control. Just as she had all the months I'd been gone. There'd been no choice. She'd had to fend for herself, make the decisions, be the guiding hand. Now I was back. Now I would be guiding things. No, rather, I would be taking her hand in mine and *we* would be guiding things together. Keeping you boys on the straight and narrow until you could fend for yourselves in the great wide world. Keeping house, saving for retirement, preparing for the future. Together. I felt like celebrating and made a strong drink.

Against my will, I looked at myself in the mirror behind the bottles on the bar. It was not pleasant.

I downed my drink.

Already, the old man ceased to matter. Soon, I would forget him altogether. There was no undoing all that. What was done was done.

Then Frances too ceased to matter. She was no more in the kitchen cooking and burning things than I was on the moon. Who was I kidding? That was no mixer whirring in there, there was nothing at all.

And already, you children ceased to matter. You were no longer cowering in your rooms. Already one of you was on the road to suicide and the other unreachable.

No, I'd been wrong. The apartment had emptied of my family the moment I arrived. As if my coming had made you all disappear in the middle of whatever you were doing. Disappear from me forever.

I made another strong drink and, as I used to do, sat on the long leather couch and drank until I was drunk enough. Then I went out on the balcony.

Ready to jump, ready to get on the damn railing and dive.

Where were you all? Where had you gone? Why had you left no word at all? Had I been that bad?

I knew I had, but then, it seemed too easy, too cheap to fling oneself from a mediocre height in broad daylight. For others to see? So others would deduce that you hadn't been able to take it anymore? What good would that do anyone?

Then I saw it. Sitting there in the corner, grimy and mildewed, its seams split from exposure to the elements. My trumpet case.

I broke it open, lifted out the tarnished instrument.

No, I wouldn't jump. Take the romantic hack's way out. Besides, I didn't have enough nerve.

I'd found my trumpet.

I went back inside, leaving the sliding door open and the sour wind blowing through, then down the hall and into the dead bedroom. Then I played it — it was Moon River, you remember — and I played it right.

❦

So what ever happened to Grandfather?

I'm afraid I've told you everything I know, son. My, but time has gotten away from me tonight. I must be going.

You never heard anything?

I would tell you. But, alas, no, nothing. One shouldn't assume the worst, however. Or the best. It's like life. It's a bit of both. Understand?

I'm not a child.

Why do you take offense? Did I teach you that? I do not know what exactly happened to your grandfather in Mexico. I'm sorry. But I have something for you. Will you walk me to the car?

Certainly, Father.

They moved across the yard, both smoking their last cigarettes, no better than strangers. It was that odd moment before dawn when the evening's whisky lies low in the gut and a ghostly glow hangs from the wet edges of things. Mother lay in the house, surely long since asleep.

Unseen cows thudded through the pasture by the driveway.

Henri opened the trunk of his Peugeot. The light shone feebly on a mound of maps, cans, bottles, boxes, golf clubs, old clothes.

I'm sort of living on the road now. Replacement chef. I go where they need me. Engineering is dead.

261

Pardon?

He coughed hard, spat into the dark. I always wanted to cook for a living. I also wanted to be a professional pianist, but —

I'd never known that either until tonight.

Henri stopped his rummaging and sat on the edge of the trunk.

Marc, do we really want to fill the gap?

I'm not sure.

It would be very long, very hard.

Maybe it would be better to leave it to our imaginations, say. The way Grandfather wanted.

His is a far better story, son.

Then Henri saw what he was looking for, stuck a hand into the mess and withdrew a longish piece of a broken crabstick. The part with the curved handle.

I want you to have this. Then I want us to shake hands like gentlemen.

Grandfather's?

If he's alive, he surely has the other half. You can have it now. I must go before I'm late. This week I'm filling in for the chef at a two-forks place just down the road. If you want to come I'd be —

I don't think so, Father.

It's for the best. You're right.

They shook hands.

Then Henri shut the trunk and, coughing hard again, went around to get in.

Ah, but being a chef in this country has got to be the most nerve-wracking profession there is! You wouldn't believe the tangle of red tape. The hours I spend writing figures on government forms! How much tax I pay! I lay awake at night trying to catch my breath and thinking how one day the artisans will rise up and start their own revolution, you know?

It was definitely getting light now.

Good day, Father.

What, you don't agree?

Of course I agree. But —

Fine, then. Sure you won't bring your mother to taste my cooking?

I don't think so.

262

You're right. Foolish idea. Well . . .

Goodbye.

Goodbye, son.

Henri drove to the gate, turned down the road and was gone.

Marc lifted the crabstick and swung it slowly in the air, as if to draw a circle. It was true, the thing did tingle in the hand. Like a wire with a tiny charge. It was enough to set his heart pounding even harder as he went down to the river and thought about walking straight out across it, crabstick pointing the way, as though such a feat were nothing.

He stood there imagining such things until sunup, the cows now and then lifting their dark heads to look at him, wasted mouthfuls of river water gushing out into the light.

☙

I died several more deaths that final night on my mountain, in my well-stocked citadel where time was screwed down so tight my whole stay up there would later seem to have all occurred from the moment I, too, went headfirst off Sarah's porch into the sea and the moment I found myself awake on my tropical Cross. But first tales first.

So, I am going out to the patio at 4:30 in the morning to let the world know what I think it needs to know. More exactly, I go outside hoping I know how best to say what the world needs to know. Which is to say, I am not sure exactly what I am going to say.

I do not feel the least bit confused, however.

The air is fresh, pleasant. It is the hour I prefer.

And in that calm space between the need to know what one is going to say and the actual saying of it from the pulpit, I feel perhaps the purest sensation of peace I have ever felt. Little does it matter whether an arrow strikes home or misses. Little does it matter whether I aim or not. If A and B are meant to connect, then so be it. And if not, so be it, too.

Yes, a measure of peace fills the Man of Peace.

If only for a moment.

A million-and-one projectors are turned on me all at once. I can no more see than the blind. I cannot move. I cannot speak. I cannot do anything. Chulmetic, I think. Where are you? Save me now!

But she does not come. She is asleep inside on the king-size bed, the projectors shining through the windows onto her naked form. Flashbulbs are going off everywhere, making silver stars that swirl around me. Will I pass out from the fright? Our Man of Peace? The man who has kept them camping on these barren slopes for months in the hope of a single word? The man with the final say who hasn't said it yet, whatever it is?

Speak, I hear them say as one.

The word lands like a storm in the face.

What is peace? I ask.

What? they say as one, as if they can't hear me.

Work is peace! I answer. Unemployment is sin. Find a job, any job, and keep it. Even a little, insignificant job. Get it, keep it. There is no other way. For in sloth we sin. In sloth we fail. So says the Man of Peace. Child, man, woman, all must work. No job is too silly. Pick up sticks, comb your sick neighbor's dirty hair, pack lightbulbs in cardboard boxes, write a book in a month, scoop turds off city sidewalks, wipe baby bottoms, transplant a heart, sew on an ear, fly to the moon, fish for mackerel, stalk a pretty lady in high heels, deliver dry ice to a high school, pick up every single rock around here and chuck them all in the next valley, lay out a huge sprinkler system, ship in a thousand acres of thick St. Augustine and roll it out, mow it to a height of exactly two inches, then watch me and my lady lounge upon the prettiest lawn in the Sierra Madre till kingdom come. *Voilà*, today's Help Wanted. Go to it. Tomorrow is another day. Amen.

Cries of disbelief resound through the valley. What? What's that you say? What we want to know is how you satisfy the señorita! the old men shout. How do you do it? *Oui, comment fait-il, le diable!* Is it the water up here? The air? The lack of air? *Mais non, mais non, c'est son truc.* Is it like Mr. Longfellow said, That which the fountain sends forth returns again to the fountain? Maybe it's that old antique song we heard last night! *Misterioso* of the ages. I say it's a drug thing. *Ou une crème, une crème spéciale.* Chantilly? Indeed, fellow seeker, one must also consider the possibility of cold fusion, no? *O mein Papa!* I say, The end is where we start from! Hear, hear! Could it be love? Of course it could, for it was a lover and his lass, with a hey, and a ho, and a hey nonino, That o'er the green corn-field did pass . . . *Ça suffit! Plus de spéculation! On veut savoir!* Have pity on us gippers! Whatever happened to sharing with your fellow man? Tell us your secret! We sure as hell didn't come fer nothin, now did we? Wait, everybody, it's the moon! This old Mexican moonlight! He's been bottlin and drinkin it or somethin! Tell us! *Accouchez, enfin.* End our moonstruck madness!

A long minute passes while the crowd waits to see if I'm going to oblige, then the lights, as if on a timer, go off.

I still can't see a thing.

There is a sound like a bomb falling, and it grows louder and louder until all the bombs in the world are falling straight down on the very place I am standing. In an instant, I will be vaporized, my atoms mixed with the stars, the stars mixed with the universe, the universe mixed with another until there is no trace of any knowable thing.

But then the squealing stops, and after a moment of silence, I hear a thousand car doors slam, ignitions going off, tires grinding in the dirt, a unified honking of horns that wails on and on for a good two hours until at last everyone is gone.

What did you say to them?

It is Chulmetic.

Did the exodus awake you, love? I ask.

Of course it did! So what did you say?

I said work is peace.

You said *what*?

But I didn't know I was going to say it —

Before you said it! What foolishness!

But baby . . .

No baby, not anymore. You've blown our whole setup. It's all over!

But, wait. I can —

What? Whistle them back? You've broken the faith!

But it's true. What I said, I mean.

True? What's true, old man? You think the people want the

truth? What planet are you from?

I stand there mesmerized as she seems to tower higher and higher over me, her smooth nakedness becoming a menacing armor, every part of her body challenging me.

Do you think anyone would ever have come to you if I hadn't told one of my girlfriends how good you were in bed? That started the whole thing! All you had to do was remain mysterious to them, speak in riddles. Instead your message is: Find a job! Stick to it! I'm too digusted. I'm leaving. No, get out. You owe me the house at least.

I feel lost in a bad opera with the special effects out of control, the wind machine winding up and tossing me aside. Blowing me off the patio into the half-finished yard, and away into the brush. Through scrub and cactus, over cliffs and down rocky valleys until I tumble into the sea to be washed on and on by the pitiless tide. Cast aside by my Indian moon goddess, now in charge on the heights.

There goes my everything, I want to cry out. There goes it all. I die. I die again and again, each time the blade striking deeper. Through the red and white bone and into the heart.

🌿

It was Felix who found me the next day, roped a good twenty feet off the ground to a palm that had been sheared just above my head. He might not have seen me up there at all had it not been for Dno, perched upon my shoulder, picking trash out of my hair and humming a reggae tune.

Well, now, look what the cat drug in. Ansel Gifford!

Cut me down, I demanded.

Ja ja. In due time. What is this, anyway, some kind of Passion Play? Hungover a tad, are we?

Cut me down!

Couple of questions first, man. Where were you all night?

Felix, if you don't cut me down from this palm this instant —

Answer da question!

Riding out the storm!

So did you see my new black-and-red surfboard from California? I lost it. It saved my life and now I've lost it!

No, I did not see your surfboard. I was blown off Sarah's porch with my son-in-law and —

I don't see no son-in-law here.

How would I know where he is!

Very convenient for you and your little story.

Cut me down, damn you!

Felix whistled for Dno, flipped him a pocket knife. Cut down our lordship, will you, dear?

Dno obeyed. Clambered up to me, sawed through the old boat ropes, rode my shoulder and tried to kiss me as I slid down the sloping trunk to the ground.

I immediately collapsed, exhausted from the night's travels and travails.

Now speak! Felix commanded. Where is my new black-and-red surfboard from California?

I waved him off with my busted cane.

You will answer my question!

Again, I waved him away. The world could go to hell, Nazis, monkeys, fat ladies, hurricanes, men of peace, goddesses, all. All I wanted to do was sleep.

Wake up! Answer my question!

He was kicking me in the side with his big toe. But was this really a time of vengeance or retribution? I thought not. I thought not, and let him rail on, poke me to his heart's content. For I was, it appeared, quite alive. No, I had not *really* been blown to the top of the mountain to be the world's Man of Peace only to flub it. All that had been a mirage high atop the palm on the island as the waves crashed through all night long. The predictable insanity of a terrified man, no more, no less. For here I was, mostly intact, after all. Wasn't I?

Surfboard? I said.

Yes! cried Felix. Where?

Where's Sarah, Felix? Have you seen Sarah?

She's home, like always.

The house held?

Of course, fool. It's got safety voodoo all *over* it, man. Now what about my *board*!

Speek! Dno said.

We looked at the monkey.

Dno? I said.

Dno me ees dno me, it said.

When did he start talking?

Just *now*, Felix said proudly, giving the critter a knuckle rub on the head. Must've been the storm.

Dno said, Oba dewe! Atta way!

He pointed toward the beach.

Has he ever lied to us? Felix asked excitedly.

He couldn't even talk until now, fool! Have you been drinking?

Not enough! Happy hour all day today! We'll have a board party!

You mean your bar didn't wash away?

Voodoo, man . . . But first I'm off to catch some more of these great waves. You should have seen me last night! Man, the girls would've gone *wild*!

I looked at him the way one does at the very dim.

Insulted, and with a dull thud of his bare heels, he spun about on the sand and charged off to retrieve his favorite board at the very spot where, only a short while before, he'd stepped off it after a whole night's acrobatics and, for the thousandth time, immediately forgotten its whereabouts and come begging anybody who'd listen. I could only hope one of those giant curls would suck him under for good someday.

Only then did I have enough strength to properly raise my head and have a view of the end of the world. For it was no less than that. The tidal wave had broken everything in its path and washed it into the sea, which had turned the color of milk. Every tree (except my palm Cross), bush, picket fence, car part, trash can, chicken, tomato plant, toilet, sink, book, record, poem . . . gone. The only standing structures were, Sarah's place far north, and the Moon Bar, far south. The sun shone down with a strange white light that seemed to come from all directions at once so that you couldn't tell if it was morning or afternoon.

But first there was Sarah to check on. I stood up, slapped the salty crust on my rags. Dno came and helped. Then we headed out across the muddy battlefield. Two survivors, two old soldiers.

I was in no hurry. Dreaming away in her shack Sarah probably wasn't even out of bed yet. I'd have to wake her, tell her what happened, about Henri's apparent demise, about my Dno-orchestrated crucifixion on a palm and instant resurrection. She'd make me fix her breakfast (that was one meal she had always refused to make) and bring it in to her. She'd complain about my poor cooking, just like old times. So long as the voodoo of life kept working, so long as the spell lingered a while longer with us trapped in it like kids in a play gone out of control. With no end in sight, the beginning long ago lost and the meaning abandoned between. With nowhere to go but forward through the malodorous muck.

I stepped high.

18

*A*GAIN I SEE HIM, the rigid young man, frowning as he walks down the sidewalk a month ago, watching everything as if the world would disappear a second later in blazing flash. Again, as he sees a shirtless man taking a drink from a hose running into a steel drum, I hear him recalling that no one knew what happened to Grandfather who disappeared in Mexico all those years ago. And thinking, Couldn't the story now be told?

Tomorrow, he will take the road home, open the door to the apartment and lead his family within. He will make a strong drink, unpack and set out the clothes he will wear to work, beginning the cycle all over again.

For work is peace.

And his Jeanne will come and ask him to make a light drink and they will sit at the ends of the long leather couch with every lamp in the room on and feel at ease again after so long, their legs stretching out toward each other until their feet touch. There will be nothing to say, only the moment of peace to savor now that he has returned from all those places, those islands where you flee to try to shed your skin, your old thoughts, to be reborn in sunlight and salt. There will be nothing to say now that she is emerging from the spiral of pain and fear and all-night vigils over the wailing newborn, from the spinning pit of doubt and questions and bitter remorse where week after week she lay pinned against the black, turning walls, retracing each fateful step, seeing so many wrong turns and bad decisions that somehow brought her to this moment. The moment of a semblance of salvation, of escape from the thrashing grass, the walls of dark water, the unbearable light of the violet moon that shrouded her in its poisonous cloak, so that she can now stand to keep living, to give and be given to, in balance again, if only for a while.

And yet . . . there will be no end of things to say, now that they have come back from over there. They'll unite against the deluge of quiz shows and instant death specialists, the TV preachers and twenty-four-hour talk show hosts, presidents and paupers, fools and savants, credit card companies and back taxes, dirty old men and dead art and the sleepwalking fatty masses. One against the muck as the cup of life overflows and oozes forth. One against the final gasp and shriek in the face of the irrevocable mess, in the foul addled finale of life as we've ruined it. One against the end so near, so near you can taste it. Rust. Rust on the tongue, burning in the eyes. As the sky dips down like the brim of a great black hat in one last bow to the stunned seekers . . .

And I? I will live on the island, where everyone secretly wishes to be, until the sand swallows my bones, as into talc, as on the moon.

In only hours now they will head north into winter.

*

Mother wanted to die on the last day of the vacation. To be done with it. Because death was very near, like a boy who wanders into the yard and stays. He had come several times that day to her window and stood looking in, his white moon face flashing then and again, nervous and shy, only to disappear again when she climbed off her bed and started toward him. A day that seemed to go on and on, refusing to end.

But darkness did come, and Marc decided to burn the mound of brush down on the riverbank, all the summer garden clippings, as he did every year, a final act on the last night. Not so long ago, it had been a gay affair attended by everyone and all their cousins, but people were scattered now, isolated in hatred and suspicion, cold to the old joys. Why, it seemed only moments ago that dear old Grandfather had come along when the flames were as high as

271

the house bringing the gramophone and a stack of records and had waltzed with Frances as the low fog crept upriver from the sea. While everyone else ate the elaborate midnight dinner and drank heavy wines from crystal glasses and lay back in the tall grass to stare at the glow of the flames. Remember that year they'd burned the rotten rowboat and how the thick tar on the planks sent the flames into a frenzy and everyone backed away in fright, silverware rattling on plates, wines spilling on summer dresses, the *tilleul* nearly catching fire? Remember watching the smoke rise into the black night, and the clouds of red sparks bursting aloft to die among the stars? Remember the hunting dogs howling late in the night like it was the end of the earth, of everything? It seemed only a moment ago, the thick, heavy needle scraping along and the music being thrown one way and then another by the swirling heat. It was a very hot fire that should have died quickly but somehow always lasted until dawn. When the clouds of night lay white on the ground and on the sleeping faces of the very young ones and the very old ones, buried in the grass, as the diehards sat crosslegged by the coals, arms crossed, looking within, all words having been said, all dances having been danced, the summer extinguished and the cold just ahead. An early fisherman would always catch them in the dying moments of their fete, stop and set down his poles and tackle and have a glass of something. Some liqueur or other, a clear fire in the gut, and the men would slap him on the back and send him on his way with all manner of advice on where and how to fish the best fish. Every man knew the bottom of the river as well as his own children. And then the parents would begin a silent count of heads, to see who might be missing. But no one ever was, and the littlest ones would be carried off to bed to sleep the day away while their older brothers and sisters lingered in grumpy distress at the thought of having to face schoolwork, while the mothers and the mothers of mothers sighed and went around plucking wine glasses and silverware from the grass, while the fathers and the fathers of fathers lighted last smokes and watched the fisherman, just upriver, whipping his line in the morning light over the slow current.

Only a moment ago Marc had stooped to light the fire and sit and eye the smoke rising in balls, and be bathed in its red light with the whole night yet to come and the glow through the trees dancing darkly on the face of the house. Where Mother, dying behind her closed shutters, suddenly became aware of a strange light coming through a knothole and crept from her damp bed to watch the devil at play. To watch the summer bonfire and imagine the both of them, the two inseparables, standing in it with their arms upraised, tall crystal glasses full of heavy red wine lifted high in a toast, their eyes filled with blue flames. Her daddy and Marc taking one final bow in the cleansing fire.

She dressed and went out.

Finding the boy, her middle-aged boy, alone. Lying back in the weeds looking at the stars.

Sitting beside him and saying nothing. As the burning branches popped and hissed and collapsed.

Later on, there would be the moon, and maybe a glass of schnapps. Just when the damp started to climb your back and you needed it most, as the fire shrank and you scooted closer, arms around your knees, dreams thickening and making your eyes heavy.

Remember burning the rowboat? Marc asked.

It's a shame we never got another one, she said. There was something about rowing on this river, something fantastic. When the moon was up you felt like you could rise to it. You felt the current and the moonlight in the current carrying you toward it. You thought it was possible. Everything.

She laughed.

And then you'd feel a stiff bump and find the front of the bow square in the mud bank. With the cows looking down at you in the dark. You started to shake a little and wish you'd brought a sweater. Then you rowed back to the house, hoping the children wouldn't catch you coming in so late. For what would I have said to you? That I was out rowing in the middle of the night like a madwoman? That I believed the moon tugged my rowboat? That I believed life to be more wonderful even than that? What would you have thought of me? What would you have said? No, I went silently to my empty bed and lay awake, drifting and drifting, the boat never stopping, the moon a little nearer each night.

It was a weak fire, really, and soon it went dark.

I don't know, Marc said. Not a good fire this time. Too green.

No, it was perfect. Just enough.

You think so?

It was a very good fire, son.

In a little while he would help her back to her room. Where she will try to die now that she is sure she is ready. There were still the coals to watch a moment. And the stars straining against the showy moon. Like other times before, when they were both likely to linger and look around at the world. So that now, this time, Marc could ask her without fearing the answer would bring some unbearable weight or twist in the chain of things so carefully laid out this long month.

Did you ever discover what Grandfather's book was about?

She seemed to have been waiting for the question.

I like to think, she began, poking a poplar branch into the embers, that it's the story of Daddy and Mama living out their old age together in a white beach cottage full of sunlight and wild-flowers on a long clean shore. I like to think it's about them living out their old age there in young, strong bodies so that they make love together all day all over the house and laugh for hours at nothing and then lie entwined and look out the big open windows at the surf, long-running and wild, and the spray billowing up in bright clouds. I like to think it's a slow love story that goes on and on with no quarrels and no pain, all the old times of falling and choking and dying banished forever, the new times beginning for them in a place of countless days and nights with nothing more to do than live and breathe and stare at the changing sea, their eyes, of course, soon learning to see far away, far over the horizon. And what they see is good and full of light and smooth as driftwood and there is no ending.

❧

Much later but still before dawn Marc sits at the table with his manuscript, vain as ever, unable to move, unable to conclude. A sort of clear flame seems to be rising off the pages, making them waver.

His Jeanne comes slowly into the room with the newborn in her arms. That morning they will go far north again. Already, it is out of their hands. Already, the story is ending.

But first, she tells him, there is the last of the night.

She turns off the lamp. The room is white.

Look, she says. The moon's in the yard.

Without a word, they go out. Quickly, like children, to where the light, bright as day, takes them.

And then it's as if the night is not coming to an end but racing on, the moon so near it seems to be flying below the thin clouds, just out of reach. They go to the wall by the river, through the door and down the old steps into the grass. It is cooler here, damp, and they move closer together and look out at the moonlight on the water. The way they did all those years ago when it was just beginning between them, back before the obsessions (or obsessions about obsessions) when there was still patience.

It seems the time to say to her that this month of dreaming dreams on paper had brought him out on the other side and back to her and her eyes catching the milky light streaming through the poplars. Because it is simpler now. To look slowly back up the river and see your life's fires glowing here and there on the bank, some still flaming high, others low and dim, and then to look down the river, see it widening, slowing, easing to the ocean with deeper purpose, carrying all. But Marc doesn't have to say anything there in the heavy grass as they watch the flow.

It was the tale of the two very happy people on a dock on the violet moon. This time, say that they hadn't yet leaped into the dust. No, they were still discussing their little predicament of being stuck there. Was there a future on the moon? If so, why had they been singled out to be pioneers? And what of the dead man there, that dandy, that ladies' man? The two happy people sat on the dock and dangled their legs over the side so that their shoes just brushed the surface of the violet powder. They talked as lovers will, with abandon, forgetting the time. Pushing the story ahead to keep it moving, to keep it alive and warm like the feeling between them that night up there on the moon. Despite the mess they were in.

Shutup with that monologue, will you? Felix commanded.

It was a slow night in the Moon Bar. Just Ansel and Felix and Dno, drinking the night away.

Confess, Ansel said.

Confess what?

You do want to know what will happen next!

Da dno! cried Dno.

That's Bottoms up! in Russian, Felix exclaimed, giving his rickety bamboo bar a pop with his fist and reaching around for a new bottle of rum on the sagging shelf.

No, it's not, Ansel corrected. It's *Do dna!* Or you could say, *S Otyezdom!* which means, Happy Journey!

Whatever, said Felix. Just cut it out with the kiddie story, O.K.? Change stations. Did it ever occur to you that you're stuck in the past? Do you think *I'd* think of such things? No, you'll never meet a Nazi with regrets. Do you think they gave us these hateful eyes to look back with? No, sir. Down the road. I've been working on some sketches for a Moon Palace. Want to see them?

Ansel, atilt on his favorite barstool, its legs aslant in the sand, wondered. Yes, it did seem he'd told this story a hundred ways with a hundred endings. But, if so, which one was the right one? Or did he dare believe that there was no right or wrong in this world, so that it didn't matter which one he picked? Yet . . .

The thought fizzled. The sea lapped the shore. The moon rose over the reef. Dno snored. Felix rattled on, waving his cocktail napkin drawings in Ansel's face.

You've got to imagine the full picture here, Ansel. We're talking size. Forty-five stories tall, all white marble. Covering the whole island. The World's Largest Bar on the roof. The World's Largest Hotel below. A beach going all the way around with perfect waves, about knee-high, say. And lined with every German beauty that ever lived! What'll we call her? *Mein . . . Mein* something. I can't think!

He downed another shot of rum.

Ansel slumped. Next time, he thought, maybe he'd have the boat come back and get the two very happy people and take them back to dear old Earth. Where they would be caught in a hurricane the night they arrived. A storm so fierce it would blow a whole night and a whole day, destroying all. The two very happy people would not be sad, though. All would happen as it was supposed to happen, and they would simply begin their lives again there on the island. As if nothing too awful had happened. As if this were the best of all possible worlds. As if they'd never been to the moon like that and faced those hard decisions. As if time had stopped for them and them alone. Down there where no one knew if you were dead or alive or what. Down there were no one cared, where no one, near or far, ever thought of you again. Or had he already told it that way?

He looked as his partners in paradise. Neither looked alive. Maybe he *had* told it that way. There were a thousand and one possibilities. And a thousand and one nights to make each of them up. So long as the rum flowed. So long as the moon rose and the fat old dead man looked down from above.

He finished his rum, said good night, got a couple of grunts in return, and strolled out into the moonlight, his stub of crabstick pointing the way.

Off we go, one last time! he said to himself.

Off we go! he heard Violetta say. That night, back from the moon, if only for a moment. If only to hear her say it didn't matter that he hadn't changed the world, he'd been a Man of Peace all down the line anyway. If only to say that she was the only moon goddess worth knowing. If only to say that she would wait for him until he came, and that they would hold each other in the purple talc, in the warm, smooth powder, and make dead people's special love.

The soft sand gave and Ansel sank deep, but it was no worry. There was no rush. Not anymore. That part of his long life, at least, was over.

He passed among the palm stumps toward Sarah's and the rent room she'd had built for him underneath her house. Hearing him rattling around, she'd come down and see about him, of course, and get mad about his drinking again, of course, and squawk about him not being able to get up on time to take the tourists snorkeling. And he'd assure her again that of course he'd be up at dawn ready to hit the beach, drag forth the boat and buzz out to the reef. The way he'd done every day since they'd picked up the pieces after the hurricane and started their little business, the two of them, after thinking it all out, having agreed that the mother-son relationship was the way to go. She would stay on his tail and he would shake his, period. No discussion, no fights.

Every night she'd tuck her old boy in tight. Just like Mama used to do. And he would sleep the sleep of ages. The one you wake up in walking around a pretty little moon yard outside a pretty little moon house by a moon river with your moon lover and thinking you've found paradise at last.

※

That night, Frances puts the clay death mask to her face, tries to die and fails, as if something is holding her back.

While dreaming of rowing.

Of the thick, green current.

Of the violet moon.

On and on, staring through the damp slit-eyes, for as long as she can.

※

The boy is playing with the dominoes on the back seat. There seemed to be no harm in going ahead and giving them to him. They only would have sat on a shelf, absurdly off-limits, a family treasure not to be touched.

The bullwhip, though, was different. Marc would keep it hidden. In a bottom drawer under old clothes, in a place where no one rummaged. Someday he'd pass it along, too, with all its stories, but not yet. Not the old bullwhip.

They had said their goodbyes to Mother and started the long drive home. The summer seemed to fade instantly, as if it had never happened. What, ladies and gentlemen, is the meaning of winter? You have five seconds! Already, it is starting again, the sick routine. Already, it is out of the quiz-meister's hands. What did you do on your summer vacation? You have two seconds! Why did you do what you did on your vacation? You have one second! You're out of time! I'm sorry, but you're out of time!

Thanks for playing! The applause light comes on. Like the red brake lights ahead as the traffic jams up in a sudden downpour.

Marc slows to a halt. There being no choice. Where are the choices anymore?

His boy, annoyed, begins to chuck dominoes into the basket carrying his baby sister. Setting her to shrieking.

What choices? Couldn't he not go back to Paris to write quiz show questions and fret over how he had wasted his summer over a frivolous tome? Couldn't he exit and drive off into the countryside? Find a big house to live in surrounded by empty fields to walk in? End up wherever he ended up, no questions asked?

Not a car was moving.

Choice? There is no choice.

As the dominoes fly and Marc starts to think of the bullwhip again. Of the power of the bullwhip. Looking in the mirror at his son. Thinking it through. Now there's a choice. There for the taking, a family tradition, no?

Stop.

What about Mexico? Why didn't they drop everything and go to Mexico? Take the children, find the old man on the island and join up with him, put the pieces together, see what happened. Wouldn't Miss Sarah welcome them with big open arms? Wouldn't there be fried chicken and mashed potatoes and gravy for all? And endless hours of diving off the reefs with the old man, each time going deeper, parting the long, streaming weeds, until they got down to where the light went faint and cold and the big fish moved around you like shadows? Down there where you were either a man or you were not. Then even deeper to where the light died and nothing moved, down where the truth of all matters appeared in the gloom like a fine electric net, enveloping them in the sweetness of youth and wonder, warmly now, all things becoming clear in its light as if one had simply blinked and found oneself back above again in the boat under the pounding sun watching the old man's snorkeling students splashing around as if time would never end for anybody.

Oh, look, says Jeanne. We're moving again. Good.

It is quickly getting dark.

The lava oozes ahead, a red tongue burning into the blackness. Once again, left and right, grim faces stare over at you, the sickening despair of *le retour* twisting their mouths into black knots from which cigarettes droop, embers flaring as they ponder you, fellow traveler in the migratory fire. Some move their black lips as if to speak to you in some silent language, to ask if you too believe that Paradise awaits the jammed masses at the end of this burning path, this Via Dolorosa curving and plunging through the night. That when you reach that steepsided bowl of light, there will be safety in numbers, with wives and husbands in every bed, un-troubled children sleeping quietly and docile ancestors floating above and nodding with a goofy joy in their angelic hearts that everything is well. Smoke swirls and clouds of sparks burst like fireworks. Marc catches his own, drawn face looking back at him from the windshield and dares to hope he might be different some-how from the imprisoned people who are about to mock freedom by launching a last hurrah, honking their horns in an end-of-sum-mer symphony, a wild summons to the ultimate vacationland. Let it come! Let it blow!

Now Marc sees Jeanne's face in the curved glass, somehow afire and afloat, blue flames wavering in her mouth. Is she, too, praying in the heart of her heart for it all to be over, to end with a boom and a giant red puff? For the black ashes to float down and the air to bring the stink of burning tar while she drifts, at once terrorized and at peace, just out of reach. As if she were letting go of everything she had known, slowly setting out for some place far away. It doesn't matter exactly where, only that he go with her and not let the past swallow the future. Not miss the chance to catch this beginning before it is gone.

Yes, they are simply returning to the city after a month in the country like everyone else, after a monthlong burn. But he will keep going with her and watch her white eyes, big as moons, with her and touch her skin lying open, infinite fields once entered never left, with her and taste the orange and cedar in all that trailing dark red hair. They are setting out, he and she, and with a hurried sigh Jeanne reaches into the back seat to take the newborn from its basket and quiet her in her arms, the pale thing with wide black eyes that see you and don't see you, a writhing mass of life and possibilities. Jeanne rocks the baby nervously, as if she would shake her back into slumber, and yet she relaxes, falls silent, takes up staring into space again, her puffy hands moving slowly this way and that as if she were reaching for the swirling ash above this river of fire.

The voyage is all this time. Every detail, every movement another open field, another river, another island covered with a forest of her hair under the violet moon, the yellow dust of Mexico like chalk on her lips as Marc stares into the glass at her and through her into the night of fires and fire within fires for as far as you dare to go in this world of worlds within worlds where unsleeping eyes bear down until the smallest thing in the molten flow rises to you, comes to you like a boat and you step into it and she steps into it and you go the way it goes.

Now something gives, the smoke parts, and there is a huge release of worldly metal boxes up out of the valley to the top of the hill from which they can see the capital. Cars fly ahead, caught anew in the smacking flow, and the fingers of fire curl east and west and then join the pool of light. The baby sleeps face down on Jeanne's lap and the mother rests her hands, so much bigger and softer than he'd remembered them, on her daughter's tiny back, leaning slightly forward, eyes on the spectacle ahead, the race beginning again, the little dream of freedom quickly dying.

Back home soon, she says.

Back among our things. Back behind curtains. Back in the fine black dust.

She stiffens, sits up straight again. The better to see? Or to brace herself for the collision? Sensing danger, Marc finds himself doing the same, his spine turning to iron. Then the boy, rising from his nap in the back, puts his small hands on their shoulders, easing away their fears, and stares with sleepy eyes at all the lights, saying nothing, the mystery ahead filling the mind and leaving words lost in fog.

Together they are setting out, but it does not so much matter where they go, only that they push off from the bank and out of the shadows into the open where anything can happen in the glow of the thousands upon thousands of humming lights. And Jeanne can still frown and pinch her big eyes if she wants to, let loose a sigh for everything, for all the mounds of crap ahead and behind them, Marc's goddess of the tall heavy grasses with the black streaks under her eyes from the weeks of strain and worry, still the impossible beauty with the dense red salty bush at the top of her white thighs and the long cold feet that search between his legs at night, Our Lady of the River who will burn on and on until she hits the sea in a cloud of steam. And Jeanne can give the city, the bowl of light and dreamlessness, a long look of disgust, her lips stretched thin and white, her nostrils flared, and slump back with a huff and decide that it is now long past time to close her eyes, pull within, shut it all off.

The traffic tightens again, more horns sound, motors groan and pop, and then the boy lies down again. Papa will get us home, somehow, Papa will take care of everything. Another hill, another turn and Marc's family is sleeping and the country is now the city and the city is all light and fire, a huge cauldron bubbling with random sounds and movements, full of new meanings.

The highway narrows to a road and the road narrows to a street and another and another between walls like canyons. There are no shadows. All is light, and he drives slowly from corner to corner, hesitant, as if he's never been here before.

🦋

Come to my island? Him and his wife and those kids? To try and get in on my snorkeling business? Rock my boat? I don't think so.

But then I know he won't do it. He'll forget the whole idea within a week. Once the city gets hold of him again, squeezes him like an anaconda.

Which, thankfully, leaves me in peace down here in the only part of the story he seemed to get right.

Oh, there are days when even I get tired of this place and think of the razzle-dazzle of Paris and feel a need to visit. Hit a museum or two, see some dead art. Shop and eat out. Go to a titty show. Eat some couscous and ride the Métro.

But then one of my pretty young snorkeling students walks by and I feel that old yellow glow firing up inside. Of course she pauses to look at me — Buddha with his back to a coco trunk in the shade — and smile that smile that lifts you out of your tired body, out of all the sour trash of the past.

Is tonight our midnight class, Ansel, just you and me?

She sounds so much like Violetta, and I look closely at her.

Well, Ansel, what's it going to be?

I nod yes and she laughs and heads on down the beach, her smooth high hips moving just so. I let free a sigh, unsure whether I'm sad or not (it doesn't matter), and then, with the lightest of efforts, scoot my toes into the cool sand, shade my eyes and watch for the next one.